"A triumphant celebration of life and love."
—*ForeWord Reviews*

"A compelling novel that through the storyline addresses the deeper issues of both love and marriages, which do not of course always travel together."
—*NB Magazine*

"An appealing indulgence in nature, food and drink, and, above all, friendships."
—*The Guardian*

"Here it is, the most beautiful novel in the world."
—*Corriere della Sera*

"Thundering applause for *Fresh Water for Flowers*."
—*La Marseillaise*

"The balance between laughter and tears is spot on."
—*Lire*

"A bad, bad, bad case of love at first read. This is a splendid, moving book, my favourite of the year."
—*C'est au programme*

Valérie Perrin

FRESH WATER
FOR FLOWERS

*Translated from the French
by Hildegarde Serle*

Europa
editions

Europa Editions
8 Blackstock Mews
London N4 2BT
www.europaeditions.co.uk

Translation by Hildegarde Serle
Original title: *Changer l'eau des fleurs*
Translation copyright © 2020 by Europa Editions

A catalogue record for this title is available from the British Library
ISBN 978-1-78770-311-7

Perrin, Valérie
Fresh Water for Flowers

Book design by Emanuele Ragnisco
instagram.com/emanueleragnisco

Cover photo by Galya Ivanova / Arcangel

Prepress by Grafica Punto Print – Rome

Printed and bound in Great Britain by Clays Ltd, Elcograf S.p.A.

To my parents, Francine and Yvan Perrin.

For Patricia Lopez "Paquita" and Sophie Daull.

FRESH WATER
FOR FLOWERS

1.

When we miss one person,
everywhere becomes deserted.

My closest neighbors don't quake in their boots. They have no worries, don't fall in love, don't bite their nails, don't believe in chance, make no promises, or noise, don't have social security, don't cry, don't search for their keys, their glasses, the remote control, their children, happiness.

They don't read, don't pay taxes, don't go on diets, don't have preferences, don't change their minds, don't make their beds, don't smoke, don't write lists, don't count to ten before speaking. They have no one to stand in for them.

They're not ass-kissers, ambitious, grudge-bearers, dandies, petty, generous, jealous, scruffy, clean, awesome, funny, addicted, stingy, cheerful, crafty, violent, lovers, whiners, hypocrites, gentle, tough, feeble, nasty, liars, thieves, gamblers, strivers, idlers, believers, perverts, optimists.

They're dead.

The only difference between them is in the wood of their coffins: oak, pine, or mahogany.

2.

What do you expect will become of me
if I no longer hear your step, is it your life
or mine that's going, I don't know.

My name is Violette Toussaint. I was a level-crossing keeper, now I'm a cemetery keeper.

I savor life, I sip at it, like jasmine tea sweetened with honey. And when evening comes, and the gates to my cemetery are closed, and the key is hanging on my bathroom door, I'm in heaven.

Not the heaven of my closest neighbors. No.

The heaven of the living: a mouthful of the port—1983 vintage—that José-Luis Fernandez brings back for me every September 1st. A remnant of the holidays poured into a small crystal glass, a kind of Indian summer that I uncork at around 7 P.M., come rain, or snow, or gale.

Two thimblefuls of ruby liquid. Blood of the vines of Porto. I close my eyes. And enjoy. A single mouthful is enough to brighten my evening. Two thimblefuls because I like the intoxication, but not the alcohol.

José-Luis Fernandez brings flowers to the grave of Maria Pinto, married name Fernandez (1956–2007), once a week, except in July—that's when I take over. Hence, the port to thank me.

My present life is a present from heaven. As I say to myself every morning, when I open my eyes.

I have been very unhappy, destroyed even. Nonexistent. Drained. I was like my closest neighbors, but worse. My vital functions were functioning, but without me inside them. Without the weight of my soul, which, apparently, whether you're fat or thin, tall or short, young or old, weighs twenty-one grams.

But since I've never had a taste for unhappiness, I decided it wouldn't last. Unhappiness has to stop someday.

I got off to a bad start. I was given up at birth, in the Ardennes, the north of the *département*, that corner that consorts with Belgium, where the climate is designated "transitional continental" (heavy rainfall in autumn, frequent frosts in winter), and where I imagine Jacques Brel's canal, in his song *"Le Plat Pays,"* hanged itself.

When I was born, I didn't even cry. So I was put aside, like a 2.67kg parcel with no stamp, no addressee, while the administrative forms were filled in, declaring my departure prior to my arrival.

Stillborn. A child without life and without a surname.

The midwife quickly had to come up with a first name for me, to fill in the boxes; she chose Violette.

That's probably the color I was from head to toe.

When I changed color, when my skin turned pink and she had to fill in a birth certificate, she didn't change my name.

They'd put me on a radiator. My skin had warmed up. The belly of my mother who didn't want me must have chilled me. The warmth brought me back to life. That's probably why I love summer so much, never missing a chance to bask in the first ray of sunshine, like a sunflower.

My maiden name is Trenet, like the great singer Charles. It's probably the same midwife who, after Violette, gave me my surname. She must have liked Charles. And I ended up liking him, too. I've long thought of him as a distant cousin, a kind of rich uncle I'd never met. When you like a singer, forever singing their songs means you do end up sort of related to them anyhow.

Toussaint came later. When I married Philippe Toussaint.

With a name like that—the day for visiting the cemetery—I should have been wary. But there are men called Summers who batter their wives. A charming name never stopped anyone from being a bastard.

I never missed my mother. Except when I was feverish. When I was healthy, I shot up. I grew very straight, as if having no parents had inserted a stake along my spine. I stand straight. It's a distinguishing feature of mine. I've never slouched. Not even on sad days. People often ask if I did ballet. I tell them I didn't. That it's daily life that disciplined me, made me do barre and pointe work every day.

Let them take me or let them take my loved ones
since all cemeteries one day end up as parks.

In 1997, when our level-crossing was automated, my husband and I lost our jobs. We were in the newspaper. We were seen as the last collateral victims of progress, the employees who worked the last manual level-crossing in France. To illustrate the article, the journalist took a photograph of us. Philippe Toussaint even slipped an arm around my waist as he posed. I'm smiling, but God how sad my eyes look in that photo.

The day the article appeared, Philippe Toussaint returned from the employment agency with a sense of dread: it had just dawned on him that he was going to have to do some work. He'd got used to me doing everything for him. When it came to laziness, I'd won the lottery with him. The correct numbers and the jackpot to boot.

To cheer him up, I handed him a piece of paper: "Cemetery keeper, a job with a future." He looked at me as if I'd lost my mind. In 1997, he looked at me as if I'd lost my mind every day. Does a man who no longer loves a woman look at her as if she's lost her mind?

I explained to him that I'd come across the ad by chance. That Brancion-en-Chalon's council was looking for a couple of keepers to look after the cemetery. And that the dead had fixed schedules and would make less noise than the trains. That I'd spoken to the mayor and he was ready to hire us immediately.

My husband didn't believe me. He told me that chance wasn't something he believed in. That he'd rather die than go "over there" and do the work of a vulture.

He switched on the TV and played *Mario 64*. The aim of the game was to find all the stars in every world. As for me, there was just one star I wanted to find: the lucky one. That's what I thought when I saw Mario running around to save Princess Peach, abducted by Bowser.

So, I persevered. I told him that by becoming cemetery keepers, we'd each have a salary, and a much better one than at the level-crossing, and that the dead were more profitable than trains. That we'd have very nice on-site accommodation and no expenses. That it would make a nice change from the house we'd been living in for years, a place that let in water like an old boat in winter, and was as warm as the North Pole in summer. That it would be a new start, and we needed one, that we'd hang pretty curtains at the windows so we couldn't see the neighbors, the crucifixes, the widows, and what have you. That those curtains would be the boundary between our life and others' grief. I could have told him the truth, told him that those curtains would be the boundary between my grief and everyone else's. But no way. Say nothing. Make believe. Pretend. So that he gives in.

To convince him once and for all, I promised him he'd have NOTHING to do. That three gravediggers already took care of maintenance—of the graves and the upkeep of the cemetery. That this job was just a matter of opening and closing gates. Of being present. With working hours that aren't demanding. With holidays and weekends as long as the Valserine viaduct. And that me, I'd do the rest. All the rest.

Super Mario stopped running. The princess tumbled down.

Before going to bed, Philippe Toussaint reread the ad: "Cemetery keeper, a job with a future."

Our level-crossing was at Malgrange-sur-Nancy. During that period of my life, I wasn't really living. "During that period of my death" would be more accurate. I got up, got dressed, worked, did the shopping, slept. With a sleeping pill.

Or two. Or more. And I looked at my husband looking at me as if I'd lost my mind.

My working hours were horrendously demanding. I lowered and raised the barrier almost 15 times a day during the week. The first train went through at 4:50 A.M., and the last at 11:04 P.M. I had that automatic barrier bell ringing in my head. I heard it even before it went off. We should have been sharing that hellish routine, taking turns. But all Philippe Toussaint took turns at was his motorbike and the bodies of his mistresses.

Oh, how the passengers I saw travelling by made me dream. And yet the trains were only small, local ones linking Nancy to Epinal, stopping a dozen times on every journey at godforsaken villages, as a favor to the natives. And yet I envied those men and women. I imagined they were going to appointments, appointments that I would've liked to have, just like the travelers I saw shooting past.

* * *

We set off for Burgundy three weeks after the article appeared in the paper. We went from grayness to greenness. From asphalt to pasture, from the smell of railroad tar to that of the countryside.

We arrived at the Brancion-en-Chalon cemetery on August 15th, 1997. France was on holiday. All the locals had taken off. The birds that fly from grave to grave weren't flying anymore. The cats that stretch out between the potted plants had disappeared. It was even too warm for the ants and lizards; all the marble was burning hot. The gravediggers had the day off, as did the newly deceased. I wandered alone around the paths, reading the names of people I would never know. And yet I immediately felt good there. Where I belonged.

4.

Being is eternal, existence a passage,
eternal memory will be its message.

When teenagers haven't stuck chewing gum in the keyhole, I'm the one who opens and shuts the heavy gates of the cemetery.

The hours vary according to the seasons.

8 A.M. to 7 P.M. from March 1st to October 31st.

9 A.M. to 5 P.M. from November 2nd to February 28th.

The jury's still out on February 29th.

7 A.M. to 8 P.M. on November 1st.

I took on my husband's work after his departure—or, more accurately, his disappearance. Philippe Toussaint comes under the heading "disappearance of concern" in the police's national file.

I still have several men around me. The three gravediggers, Nono, Gaston, and Elvis. The three undertakers, the Lucchini brothers, named Pierre, Paul, and Jacques. And Father Cédric Duras. All these men stop at my place several times a day. They come for a drink or a snack. They also help me in the vegetable garden, if I have sacks of compost to carry or leaks to fix. I regard them as friends, not colleagues. Even if I'm not in, they can come into my kitchen, pour themselves a coffee, rinse their cup, and set off again.

Gravediggers do a job that prompts repulsion, disgust. And yet those in my cemetery are the gentlest, most agreeable men I know.

Nono is the person I trust the most. He's an upstanding man who has *joie de vivre* in his blood. Everything amuses him and he never says no. Apart from when there's a child's burial to attend to. He leaves "*that*" to the others. "To those who can bear it," as he says. Nono looks like the singer Georges Brassens, and it makes him laugh because I'm the only person in the world who tells him he looks like Georges Brassens.

As for Gaston, he invented clumsiness. His movements are uncoordinated. He always seems drunk, despite only ever drinking water. During funerals, he positions himself between Nono and Elvis just in case he loses his balance. Beneath Gaston's feet there's a permanent earthquake. He drops, he falls, he knocks over, he crushes. When he comes into my place, I'm always afraid he'll break something or injure himself. And since fear doesn't avert danger, he invariably does break a glass or injure himself.

Elvis is known as Elvis because of Elvis Presley. He can't read or write, but he knows all his idol's songs by heart. His pronunciation of the lyrics is terrible—you can't tell whether he's singing in English or French—but his heart is in it. "*Love mi tendeur, love mi trou . . .*"

There's barely a year between each of the Lucchini brothers: thirty-eight, thirty-nine, and forty. They've been in undertaking for generations, from father to son. They're also the fortunate owners of the Brancion morgue, which adjoins their funeral parlor. Nono told me that only a partition separates the parlor from the morgue. It's Pierre, the eldest, who receives the grieving families. Paul is an embalmer. He works in the basement. And Jacques drives the hearses. The final journey, that's him. Nono calls them "the apostles."

And then there's our priest, Cédric Duras. God has taste, even if he's not always just. Since Father Cédric's arrival, many women around here seem to have been struck by a divine revelation. There are ever more female believers in the pews on Sunday morning.

As for me, I never go to church. It would be like sleeping

with a colleague. And yet, I think I'm more confided in by those who pass through than Father Cédric is in his confessional. It's in my modest home and along my cemetery's avenues that families let their words pour out. As they arrive, as they leave, sometimes both. A bit like the dead. With them, it's the silences, the gravestone inscriptions, the visits, the flowers, the photographs, the way visitors behave beside their graves, that tell me about their former lives. About when they were living. Moving.

My job consists of being discreet, liking human contact, not feeling compassion. For a woman like me, not feeling compassion would be like being an astronaut, a surgeon, a volcanologist, or a geneticist. Not part of my planet, or my skill set. But I never cry in front of a visitor. That can happen to me before or after a burial, never during. My cemetery is three centuries old. The first dead person it received was a woman. Diane de Vigneron (1756–1773), who died in childbirth at the age of seventeen. If you stroke the plaque on her tomb with your fingertips, you can still make out her name carved into the dove-colored stone. She hasn't been exhumed, even though my cemetery is short of space. None of the successive mayors dared to make the decision to disturb the first to be interred. Particularly since there's an old legend surrounding Diane. According to the inhabitants of Brancion, she's supposed to have appeared in her "raiment of light" on several occasions, in front of shopwindows in the town center and in the cemetery. When I do the garage sales around here, I sometimes find Diane depicted as a ghost on antique engravings dating from the eighteenth century, or on postcards. A false, staged Diane, disguised as a common phantom.

There are many legends surrounding tombs. The living frequently reinvent the lives of the dead.

Brancion has a second legend, much younger than Diane de Vigneron. She's called Reine Ducha (1961–1982), and she's buried in my cemetery, avenue 15, in the Cedars section. A pretty young woman, dark-haired and smiling in the photo that hangs on her headstone. She was killed in a car accident at the edge of town. Some youngsters apparently saw her, dressed all in white, at the side of the road where the accident took place.

The myth of the "white ladies" spread far and wide. These specters of women who died accidentally are supposed to haunt the world of the living, dragging their troubled souls through castles and cemeteries.

And just to reinforce Reine's legend, her tomb shifted. According to Nono and the Lucchini brothers, it was due to a landslide. That often happens when too much water accumulates in a vault.

Over twenty years, I reckon I've seen plenty in my cemetery. On some nights, I've even caught shadows making love on or between tombs, but those weren't ghosts.

Legends aside, nothing is eternal, not even burial plots held in perpetuity. You can purchase a concession for fifteen years, thirty years, fifty years, or eternity. Except that with eternity, you have to beware: if, after a period of thirty years, a perpetual concession has ceased to be maintained (unkempt and dilapidated appearance), and no interment has taken place for a long while, the council can reclaim it. The remains are then placed in an ossuary at the back of the cemetery.

Since I've been here, I've seen several expired plots being dismantled and cleaned, and the bones of the deceased placed in the ossuary. And no one said a thing. Because those dead people were seen as lost property with no one left to reclaim it.

It's always like that with death. The further back it goes, the less hold it has on the living. Time does for life. Time does for death.

Me and my three gravediggers, we do our utmost never to leave a grave neglected. We can't bear to see that municipal label: "This grave is subject to retrieval proceedings. Please contact the town hall urgently." When the name of the deceased person resting there is still visible.

That's doubtless why cemeteries are covered in epitaphs. To ward off the passage of time. Cling on to memories. The one I like best is: "Death begins when no one can dream of you any longer." It's on the grave of a young nurse, Marie Deschamps, who died in 1917. Apparently, it was a soldier who put up this plaque in 1919. Every time I go past it, I wonder whether he dreamt of her for a long time.

Jean-Jacques Goldman's "Whatever I do, wherever you are, nothing fades you, I think of you," and Francis Cabrel's "Among themselves, the stars speak only of you" are the lyrics most quoted on funerary plaques.

My cemetery is very beautiful. The avenues are lined with centenarian linden trees. A good many of the tombs have flowers. In front of my little keeper's house, I sell a few potted plants. And when they're no longer worth selling, I give them to the abandoned graves.

I planted some pine trees, too. For the scent they produce in the summer months. It's my favorite smell.

I planted them in 1997, the year we arrived. They've grown a lot and make my cemetery look splendid. Maintaining it is all about caring for the dead who lie within it. It's about respecting them. And if they weren't respected in life, at least they are in death.

I'm sure plenty of bastards lie here. But death doesn't differentiate between the good and the wicked. And anyhow, who hasn't been a bastard at least once in their life?

Unlike me, Philippe Toussaint instantly detested this cemetery, this little town, Burgundy, the countryside, the old stones, the white cows, the folk around here.

I hadn't even finished unpacking the removal boxes and he

was off on his motorbike, morning till night. And as the months went by, he sometimes left for weeks at a time. Until the day he no longer returned. The policemen couldn't understand why I hadn't reported him missing sooner. I never told them that he had disappeared years before, even when he was still dining at my table. And yet, after a month, when I realized he wouldn't return, I felt just as abandoned as the tombs I regularly clean. Just as gray, drab, and dilapidated. Ready to be dismantled and my remains thrown into an ossuary.

5.

The book of life is the ultimate book, which we can neither close nor reopen at will; when we want to return to the page on which we love, the page on which we die is already between our fingers.

I met Philippe Toussaint at the Tibourin, a nightclub in Charleville-Mézières, in 1985.

He was leaning on his elbows at the bar. And me, I was a bartender. I was doing several casual jobs by lying about my age. A friend at the hostel I lived in had doctored my papers to make me old enough.

I looked ageless. I could have been fourteen as easily as twenty-five. I only ever wore jeans and T-shirts, had short hair, and piercings everywhere. Even in my nose. I was slight, and I put smoky shadow around my eyes to give myself a Nina Hagen look. I'd just left school. I was no good at reading or writing. But I could count. I'd already lived several lives and my one aim was to work to pay my own rent, to leave the hostel as soon as possible. After that, I would see.

In 1985, the only thing that was straight about me was my teeth. Throughout my childhood, I'd had this obsession with having lovely white teeth like the girls in the magazines. When child-welfare workers visited my foster homes and asked me if I needed anything, I always requested an appointment with the dentist, as if my future, my whole life, would depend on the smile I had.

I didn't have any friends who were girls—I looked too much like a boy. I'd been close with a few surrogate sisters, but the continual separations, the changes of foster home, had killed me. *Never become attached.* I told myself that having a shaved head would protect me, give me the heart and guts of a boy. So, girls avoided me. I'd already slept with boys, to be like everyone else, but it was no big deal, I was disappointed. It wasn't really my thing. I did it to allay suspicion, or get clothes, a gram of dope, entrance to somewhere, a hand that would hold mine. I preferred the love in the children's stories, the ones I'd never been told. "They got married and had many, many, many . . . "

Leaning on his elbows at the bar, Philippe Toussaint was watching his friends bopping on the dance floor while sipping a whiskey-and-Coke with no ice. He had the face of an angel. Like the singer Michel Berger, but in color. Long blond curls, blue eyes, fair skin, aquiline nose, mouth like a strawberry . . . ready to eat, a lovely ripe, July strawberry. He wore jeans, a white T-shirt, and a black-leather biker jacket. He was tall, well built, perfect. The moment I saw him, my heart went "*boum*," as my imaginary uncle-by-marriage, Charles Trenet, sings. With me, Philippe Toussaint would get everything for free, even his glasses of whiskey-and-Coke.

He didn't need to do a thing to get to kiss the pretty blondes that hovered around him. Like flies circling a piece of meat. Philippe Toussaint appeared not to give a damn about anything. He went with the flow. He didn't have to lift a finger to get what he wanted, apart from raising his glass to his lips from time to time, between two fluorescent kisses.

He had his back to me. All I could see of him were the blond curls that turned from green to red to blue under the revolving lights. My eyes had been lingering on his hair for a good hour. Occasionally, he would lean towards the mouth of a girl as she whispered something in his ear, and I would study his perfect profile.

And then he spun around to the bar and his eyes landed on me, never to let go. From that moment on, I became his favorite toy.

At first, I thought his interest in me was down to the free

shots of alcohol I poured into his glass. When serving him, I made sure he couldn't see my bitten nails, just my white and perfectly straight teeth. I thought he looked like he came from a good family. To me, apart from the youths at the hostel, everyone looked like they came from a good family.

There was a traffic jam of girls behind him. Like at a toll-booth on the Highway of the Sun at the start of the holidays. But he continued to ogle me, eyes full of desire. I leaned against the bar, facing him, to be sure that it really was me he was looking at. I popped a straw in his glass. I looked up. It really was me.

I said to him: "Would you like something else to drink?" I didn't hear his reply. I moved closer to him, shouting, "Sorry?" He said, "You," to me, in my ear.

I poured myself a glass of bourbon behind the boss's back. After a mouthful, I stopped blushing, after two I felt good, after three I was bold as brass. I went back over to his ear and replied, "After my shift, we could have a drink together."

He smiled. His teeth were like mine, white and straight.

I reckoned my life was going to change when Philippe Toussaint moved his arm across the bar, lightly to touch mine. I felt my skin tighten, like it had a premonition. He was ten years older than me. That age difference gave him stature. I felt like a butterfly gazing at a star.

6.

*For the hour is coming, in which all that are in the graves
shall hear his voice, and shall come forth.*

Someone's gently knocking on my door. I'm not expecting
anyone; indeed, I stopped expecting anyone long ago.

There are two entrances to my house, one from the
cemetery, the other from the road. Eliane starts yapping as she
heads for the road-side door. Her mistress, Marianne Ferry
(1953–2007) is buried in the Spindles section. Eliane turned
up on the day of her burial and never left. For the first few
weeks, I fed her on her mistress's tomb, and gradually she followed me to the house. Nono named her Eliane after Isabelle
Adjani's role in the film *One Deadly Summer*, because she has
beautiful blue eyes and her mistress died in August.

In twenty years, I've had three dogs that arrived along with
their owners and became mine by force of circumstance, but
only she remains with me.

Someone knocks again. I hesitate to open. It's only 7 A.M. I'm
just sipping my tea and spreading my biscottes with salted butter
and strawberry jam, given to me by Suzanne Clerc, whose husband (1933–2007) is buried in the Cedars section. I'm listening to
music. Outside cemetery opening hours, I always listen to music.

I get up and switch off the radio.

"Who is it?"

A masculine voice hesitates, then replies:

"Forgive me, madam, I saw some light."

I can hear him wiping his feet on the doormat.

"I have some questions about someone who's buried in the
cemetery."

I could tell him to come back at 8 A.M., opening time. "Two minutes, I'm just coming!"

I go up to my bedroom and open the winter wardrobe to put on a dressing gown. I have two wardrobes. One I call "winter," the other "summer." It has nothing to do with the seasons, but rather the circumstances. The winter wardrobe contains only classic, somber clothes, for the eyes of others. The summer wardrobe contains only light, colorful clothes meant only for me. I wear summer under winter, and I take off winter when I'm alone.

So, I slip a gray, quilted dressing gown over my pink-silk négligée. I go back down to open the door and find a man of around forty. At first, I see only his dark eyes, staring at me.

"Good morning, forgive me for disturbing you so early."

It's still dark and cold. Behind him, I can see that the night has left a covering of frost. Condensation is coming out of his mouth as if he were puffing on an early-morning cigarette. He smells of tobacco, cinnamon, and vanilla.

I'm incapable of uttering a word. As though I've found someone long lost. I'm thinking that he's burst in on me too late. That if he could have turned up on my doorstep twenty years ago, *everything* would have been different. Why do I say that to myself? Because it's been years since anyone knocked on my road-side door, apart from sloshed kids? Because all my visitors arrive from the cemetery?

I make him come in, he thanks me, seeming embarrassed. I serve him coffee.

In Brancion-en-Chalon, I know everybody. Even the locals who don't yet have any dead at my place. All of them have passed through my avenues at least once for the burial of a friend, a neighbor, a colleague's mother.

But him, I've never seen. He has a slight accent, something Mediterranean in his way of punctuating sentences. His hair is very dark, so dark that his few white hairs stand out in the mess of the rest. He has a large nose, thick lips, bags under his eyes. He looks a bit like the singer Serge Gainsbourg. You can tell he's at odds with his razor, but not with grace. He has fine hands, long fingers. He drinks his coffee piping hot, in small sips, blows on it, and warms his hands on the china.

I still don't know why he's here. I let him into my home because it isn't really my home. This room, it belongs to everyone. It's like a municipal waiting room that I've turned into a kitchen-cum-living room. It belongs to anyone passing through, and to the regulars.

He seems to be studying the walls. This twenty-five-square-meter room has a similar look to my winter wardrobe. Nothing on the walls. No colorful tablecloth or blue sofa. Just lots of plywood, and chairs to sit on. Nothing showy. A pot of coffee always at the ready, white cups, and spirits for desperate cases. It's here that I get tears, confidences, anger, sighs, despair, and the laughter of the gravediggers.

My bedroom is upstairs. It's my secret courtyard, my real home. My bedroom and bathroom are two pastel boudoirs. Powder pink, almond green, and sky blue, like I'd personally modified the colors of spring. At the first ray of sunshine, I open the windows wide, and, other than with a ladder, it's impossible to see anything from outside.

No one has ever set foot in my bedroom as it looks today. Just after Philippe Toussaint's disappearance, I completely repainted it, added curtains, lace, white furniture, and a big bed with a Swiss mattress that molds itself to the contours of your body. My body, so I'd no longer have to sleep in the imprint left by Philippe Toussaint.

The stranger is still blowing into his cup. He finally says to me: "I've come from Marseilles. Do you know Marseilles?"

"I go to Sormiou every year."

"In the Calanque?"

"Yes."

"Strange coincidence."

"I don't believe in coincidences."

He seems to be looking for something in the pocket of his jeans. My men don't wear jeans. Nono, Elvis, and Gaston are always in overalls, the Lucchini brothers and Father Cédric in Terylene trousers. He takes off his scarf, stretches his neck, places his empty cup on the table.

"I'm like you, I'm quite rational . . . And I'm a detective."

"Like Columbo?"

He replies with a smile for the first time:

"No, he was a lieutenant. I'm a captain."

He presses his index finger on a few sugar grains scattered on the table.

"My mother wishes to be buried in this cemetery, and I don't know why."

"She lives around here?"

"No, in Marseilles. She died two months ago. Being buried here is one of her final wishes."

"I'm so sorry. Would you like a drop of something stronger in your coffee?"

"Do you often get people drunk so early in the morning?"

"Sometimes. What is your mother's name?"

"Irène Fayolle. She wished to be cremated . . . and her ashes to be placed at the tomb of a certain Gabriel Prudent."

"Gabriel Prudent? Gabriel Prudent, 1931–2009. He's buried on avenue 19, in the Cedars section."

"You know all the dead by heart?"

"Almost."

"The date of their death, their location, and everything?"

"Almost."

"Who was Gabriel Prudent?"

"A woman comes by from time to time . . . His daughter, I believe. He was a lawyer. There's no epitaph on his black-marble tomb, or photo. I can no longer remember the date of the burial. But I can look in my registers, if you'd like me to."

"Your registers?"

"I record all burials and exhumations."

"I didn't know that was part of your job."

"It isn't. But if we had to do only what was part of our job, life would be sad."

"It's funny to hear that from the mouth of a . . . what's the name of your job? 'Cemetery keeper'?"

"Why? You think I weep from dawn to dusk? That I'm all tears and grief?"

I serve him more coffee while he asks me, twice: "You live alone?"

I eventually answer yes.

I open my register drawers and consult the 2009 volume. I look through the surnames and immediately find that of Prudent, Gabriel. I start reading:

February 18th, 2009, burial of Gabriel Prudent, torrential rain.

There were a hundred and twenty-eight people for the interment. His ex-wife was present, as were his two daughters, Marthe Dubreuil and Cloé Prudent.

At the deceased's request, no flowers or wreaths.

The family had a plaque engraved that reads: "In homage to Gabriel Prudent, a courageous lawyer. 'Courage, for a lawyer, is essential; without it, the rest doesn't count: talent, culture, knowledge of the law, everything is useful to the lawyer. But without courage, at the decisive moment, there are but words, sentences that follow each other, that dazzle and then die.' (Robert Badinter)."

No priest. No cross. The cortege only stayed for half an hour. When the two undertakers had finished taking the coffin down into the vault, everyone left. Still raining heavily.

*

I close the register. The detective looks dazed, lost in thought. He runs a hand through his hair.

"I wonder why my mother wants to be laid to rest beside this man."

For a time, he returns to studying my white walls, on which there's absolutely nothing to study. Then he returns to me, as if he didn't believe me. He indicates the 2009 register with his eyes.

"Can I read it?"

Normally, I only entrust my notes to the families concerned. I hesitate for a few seconds, and end up handing it to him. He starts leafing through it. Between each page, he stares at me as if the words of 2009 were written on my forehead. As if the volume he held in his hands were an excuse to look at me.

"And you do that for every funeral?"

"Not every, but almost. That way, when those who were unable to attend come to see me, I can tell them about it from my notes . . . Have you ever killed anyone? I mean, in connection with your job . . . "

"No."

"Do you have a gun?"

"Sometimes I do. But now, this morning, no."

"Did you come with your mother's ashes?"

"No. For now, they're at the crematorium . . . I'm not going to place her ashes on the tomb of a stranger."

"To you he's a stranger, not to her."

He gets up. "Can I see this man's grave?"

"Yes. Could you come back in about half an hour ? I never go into my cemetery in a dressing gown."

He smiles for the second time, and leaves the kitchen-cum-living room. Instinctively, I switch on the ceiling light. I never switch it on when someone enters my place, but when they leave. To replace their presence with light. An old habit of a child given up at birth.

*

Half an hour later, he was waiting for me in his car, parked outside the gates. I saw the registration on the number plate: 13, for Bouches-du-Rhône. He must have dozed off against his scarf; his cheek was marked, as though creased.

I had put on a navy-blue coat over a crimson dress. I'd buttoned my coat up to my neck. I looked like the night, and yet, underneath, I was wearing the day. I would have only had to open my coat for him to start blinking again.

We walked along the avenues. I told him that my cemetery had four sections—Bays, Spindles, Cedars, and Yews—two columbaria, and two gardens of remembrance. He asked me if I'd been doing "this" for a long time; I replied: "Twenty years." That before, I'd been a level-crossing keeper. He asked how it felt to go from trains to hearses. I didn't know how to reply. Too much had happened between those two lives. I just thought what strange questions he asked, for a rational detective.

When we reached Gabriel Prudent's tomb, he went pale. As if he were coming to pay his respects at the grave of a man he'd never heard of, but who could very well be a father, an uncle, a brother. We remained still for a long while. I ended up blowing into my hands, it was that cold.

Normally, I never remain with visitors. I accompany them and then withdraw. But then, I don't know why, I just couldn't have left him on his own. After a while, which seemed like an eternity to me, he said he was going to get back on the road. Return to Marseilles. I asked him when he thought he'd be back to place his mother's ashes on Mr. Prudent's headstone. He didn't reply.

*There'll always be someone missing
to make my life smile: you.*

I'm repotting some plants on the tomb of Jacqueline Victor, married name Dancoisne (1928–2008), and Maurice René Dancoisne (1911–1997). Two beautiful white heathers, like two pieces of coastal cliff in pots. One of the rare plants that can withstand winter, along with chrysanthemums and succulents. Madame Dancoisne loved white flowers. She came every week to visit her husband's tomb. We'd have a chat. Well, in the end, once she'd got a little more used to the loss of her Maurice. For the first few years, she was devastated. Being unhappy, it leaves you speechless. Or it makes you talk nonsense. Then, little by little, she found her way back to forming simple sentences, to asking for news of others, news of the living.

I don't know why one says "on the tomb." One should really say "beside the tomb," or "against the tomb." Apart from ivy, lizards, cats, or dogs, nothing goes on top of a tomb. Madame Dancoisne rejoined her husband without warning. On the Monday she was cleaning her beloved's headstone; the following Thursday, I was arranging flowers around hers. Since her burial, her children visit once a year, and ask me to look after things the rest of the time.

I like putting my hands into the heathers' soil, even if it is midday and this pale October sun is struggling to warm things up. And although my fingers are frozen, they love it. Just like when I plunge them into the soil of my garden.

A few meters away from me, Gaston and Nono are digging

a grave with shovels while telling each other how their evening went. From where I am, I hear snatches of their conversation, depending on the direction of the wind. "My wife says to me . . . on the TV . . . itching . . . mustn't . . . the boss is coming . . . an omelette at Violette's . . . I knew him . . . he was a good guy . . . curly hair, right? . . . Yeah, must've been about our age . . . that was nice, that was . . . his wife . . . stuck-up . . . Brel song . . . 'mustn't play it rich if one hasn't a bean' . . . just dying to piss . . . scared stiff . . . prostate . . . get the shopping before it closes . . . eggs for Violette . . . it just ain't right . . . "

Tomorrow, there's a burial at 4 P.M. A new resident for my cemetery. A man of fifty-five, died from smoking too much. Well, that's what the doctors said. They never say that a man of fifty-five can die from not having been loved, not having been heard, getting too many bills, buying too much on credit, seeing his children grow up and leave home without really saying goodbye. A life of reproach, a life of grimacing. So, his little cigarette and his little drink to drown that knot in his stomach, he was fond of them.

No one ever says that you can die from having been too fed up, too often.

A bit further along, two little ladies, Madame Pinto and Madame Degrange, are cleaning the graves of their men. And since they come every day, they invent what needs cleaning. Around their tombs, it's as clean as a flooring display in a DIY store.

These folks who visit graves daily, they're the ones who look like ghosts. Who are between life and death.

Madame Pinto and Madame Degrange are as slight as sparrows at winter's end. As if it were their husbands who fed them when they were still alive. I've known them since I've worked here. More than twenty years now that, on their way to the shops, every morning, they've made a detour, like some inescapable ritual. I don't know whether it's love or submissiveness. Or both. Whether it's for appearances, or out of affection.

Madame Pinto is Portuguese. And like most of the Portuguese living in Brancion, in summer she's back off to Portugal. It means a lot of work for her, come autumn. At the beginning of September, she returns, still as thin, but with tanned skin, and knees grazed from having cleaned the graves of those who had died back home. In her absence, I've watered the French flowers. So, to thank me, she gives me a folk-costume doll in a plastic box. Every year, I'm entitled to my doll. And every year I say: "Thank you, Madame Pinto, thank you, you SHOULDN'T have. For me, flowers are a pleasure, not work."

There are hundreds of folk costumes in Portugal. So, if Madame Pinto lives another thirty years, and I do, too, I'll be entitled to thirty new creepy dolls who close their eyes when you lay down the boxes that serve as their sarcophagi, to do the dusting.

Since Madame Pinto comes to my home from time to time, I can't hide the dolls she gives me. But I don't want them in my bedroom, and I can't put them where people come seeking comfort, either. They're too ugly. So, I "display" them on the steps leading up to my bedroom. The staircase is behind a glass door. You can see it from the kitchen. When she comes to mine for a coffee, Madame Pinto looks over at them, to check that they are in their proper place. In winter, when it's dark at 5 P.M. and I see them with their black eyes glinting and their frilly costumes, I imagine they're going to open their boxes and trip me up so I fall down the stairs.

I've noticed that, unlike many others, Madame Pinto and Madame Degrange never talk to their husbands. They clean in silence. As if they'd ceased talking to them well before they were dead. That this silence, it's a kind of continuity. They never cry, either. Their eyes have long been dry. Sometimes, they converge to chat about the fine weather, the children, the grandchildren, and even, soon, can you believe it, their great-grandchildren.

I saw them laugh once. One single time. When Madame Pinto told the other one that her granddaughter had asked her this question: "Granny, what's All Saints? Is it like holidays?"

8.

May your rest be as sweet as your heart was kind.

November 22nd, 2016, blue sky, 10C, 4 P.M. Burial of Thierry Teissier (1960–2016). Mahogany coffin. No marble. Grave dug straight into soil. Alone.

Around thirty people present. Including Nono, Elvis, Pierre Lucchini, and me.

Around fifteen of Thierry Teissier's colleagues from the DIM factories laid a spray of lilies: "To our dear colleague."

An employee named Claire, from Mâcon's oncology unit, holds a bouquet of white roses.

The wife of the deceased is present, as are their two children, a boy and a girl aged, respectively, thirty and twenty-six. On a funerary plaque they have had engraved: "To our father."

No photograph of Thierry Teissier.

On another funerary plaque: "To my husband." With a little warbler etched above the word "husband."

A large cross made of olive wood has been embedded in the soil.

Three school friends take turns reading a poem for him, by Jacques Prévert.

A distraught village listens
To the song of a wounded bird
It's the only bird in the village
And it's the only cat in the village
Who has half-devoured it
And the bird stops singing

The cat stops purring
And licking its muzzle
And the village gives the bird
A marvelous funeral
And the cat who is invited
Walks behind the little straw coffin
In which the dead bird lies
Carried by a little girl
Who doesn't stop crying
If I'd known it would upset you so
The cat said to her
I'd have eaten all of it
And then I'd have told you
That I'd seen it fly off
Fly off to the ends of the earth
To a place so far away
That one never returns
You'd have had less grief
Just sadness and regrets
One must never do things by halves.

Before the coffin is lowered into the ground, Father Cédric speaks:

"Let us recall the words of Jesus to the sister of Lazarus, just after her brother's death: 'I am the resurrection, and the life: he that believeth in me, though he were dead, yet shall he live.'"

Claire places the bouquet of white roses beside the cross. Everyone leaves at the same time.

I didn't know this man. But the way some people looked at his grave makes me think he was kind.

9

His beauty, his youth smiled upon the world
in which he would have lived. Then from his hands
fell the book of which he has read not a word.

There are more than a thousand photographs scattered across my cemetery. Photos in black-and-white, sepia, color that's vivid or faded.

On the day all these photos were taken, none of the men, children, women who posed innocently in front of the camera could have thought that that moment would represent them for all eternity. It was the day of a birthday or a family meal. A walk in the park one Sunday, a photo at a wedding, at a promotion party, one New Year. A day when they were at their best, a day when they were all gathered together, a particular day when they were wearing their finest. Or then in their military, baptism, or First Communion attire. Such innocence in the eyes of all these people who smile from their tombs.

Often, the day before a funeral, there's an article in the newspaper. An article that sums up the life of the deceased in a few sentences. Briefly. A life doesn't take up much space in the local paper. A little more if it was a storekeeper, a doctor, or a football coach.

It's important to put photos on tombs. Otherwise, you just become a name. Death takes away faces, too.

The loveliest couple in my cemetery is Anna Lave, married name Dahan (1914–1987), and Benjamin Dahan (1912–1992). We see them in a tinted photograph taken on their wedding day in the thirties. Two wonderful faces smiling at the photographer. She, blonde like a sun, translucent skin; he, a fine face, almost carved; and their eyes sparkling like starry sapphires. Two smiles they offer up to eternity.

In January, I give the photos in my cemetery a wipe with a cloth. I only do so on tombs that are abandoned or very rarely visited. A cloth soaked in water containing a drop of methylated spirits. I do the same thing to the plaques, but with a cloth dipped in white vinegar.

I have around five to six weeks of cleaning ahead of me. When Nono, Gaston, and Elvis want to help me, I tell them no. That they've already got enough to do with the general maintenance.

I didn't hear him arrive. That's rare. I notice people's steps on the gravel of the avenues immediately. I even know whether it's a man, a woman, or a child. A walker or a regular. But him, he moves without making a sound.

I'm in the middle of cleaning the nine faces of the Hesme family—Etienne (1876–1915), Lorraine (1887–1928), Françoise (1949–2000), Gilles (1947–2002), Nathalie (1959–1970), Théo (1961–1993), Isabelle (1969–2001), Fabrice (1972–2003), Sébastien (1974–2011)—when I feel his eyes on my back. I turn around. He's standing against the light, I don't recognize him immediately.

It's from his "Good morning," from his voice, that I grasp that it's actually him. And just after his voice, with two or three seconds' delay, from his cinnamon and vanilla smell. I didn't think he'd come back. It's been more than two months since he came knocking on my road-side door. My heart quickens a little. I sense it whispering to me: *Beware*.

Since Philippe Toussaint's disappearance, no man has made my heart beat a little faster. Since Philippe Toussaint, its rhythm never changes, like an old clock nonchalantly humming away.

Except for on All Saints' Day, when its rate speeds up: I can sell up to a hundred pots of chrysanthemums, and I have to guide the many occasional visitors who get lost in the avenues. But this morning, although it isn't the day of the dead, my heart quickens. And it's due to *him*. I think I detect fear; my own.

I still have my cloth in my hand. The detective looks at the faces I'm in the middle of polishing. He smiles shyly at me.

"Are they members of your family?"

"No. I'm maintaining the tombs, that's all."

Not knowing what to do with the words buzzing in my head, I say to him:

"In the Hesme family, people die young. As if they were allergic to life, or it didn't want them."

He nods his head, draws in the collar of his coat, and says to me, with a smile:

"It's bitter in your parts."

"It's certainly colder here than in Marseilles."

"Are you going there this summer?"

"Yes, like every summer. I see my daughter over there."

"She lives in Marseilles?"

"No, she travels around a bit."

"What does she do?"

"She's a magician. Professional."

As though to interrupt us, a young blackbird lands on the Hesme family tomb and starts singing its head off. I don't feel like polishing faces anymore. I tip my bucket of water onto the gravel and tidy away my cloths and cleaner. As I bend down, my long gray coat opens a little, allowing my pretty crimson floral dress to be seen. I see that it doesn't go unnoticed by the detective. He doesn't look at me like the others. There's something different about him.

To divert his attention, I remind him that, to place his mother's ashes at Gabriel Prudent's tomb, the authorization of the family will have to be requested.

"No need. Before dying, Gabriel Prudent informed the town hall that my mother would be laid to rest with him . . . They'd thought of everything."

He seems embarrassed. He rubs his unshaven jaw. I can't see his hands, he's wearing gloves. He stares at me for a little too long.

"I would like you to organize something for the day I'll be laying her ashes to rest. Something that's like a celebration, but without celebration."

The blackbird flies away. It was scared off by Eliane, who's come to rub against me in the hope of a pet.

"Ah, but I don't do that. You'll need to speak to Pierre Lucchini at the undertaker's, Le Tourneurs du Val, on rue de la République."

"Undertakers are for funerals. All I would like is for you to help me write a little speech for the day I place her ashes on that guy's tomb. There'll be no one there. Just her and me . . . I'd like to say a few words to her that remain between us."

He crouches down to pet Eliane himself. He looks at her while speaking to me.

"I saw that in your . . . registers, well, your burial note-books, I don't know what you call them, you had copied out speeches. I could perhaps lift bits here and there . . . from others' speeches, to write the one for my mother."

He runs a hand through his hair. He's got more gray hair than last time. Maybe it's because the light's different. Today, the sky is blue, the light white. The first time I saw this man, the sky was overcast.

Madame Pinto goes past us. She says: "Morning, Violette," and looks at the detective suspiciously. Around here, as soon as a stranger goes past a door, a gate, a porch, they're looked at suspiciously.

"I have a burial at 4 P.M., come and see me after 7 P.M., at the keeper's house. We'll write a few lines together."

He seems relieved. Like a weight's been lifted. He takes a pack of cigarettes from his pocket and puts one in his mouth without lighting it, while asking me where the nearest hotel is.

"Twenty-five kilometers away. Otherwise, just behind the church you'll see a little house with red shutters. That's Madame Bréant's place, and she does bed and breakfast. Just one bedroom, but it's never taken."

He's not listening to me anymore. He's looking elsewhere. He's gone, lost in thought. He comes back to me.

"Brancion-en-Chalon . . . Wasn't there some tragedy here?"

"There are tragedies all around you. Every death is someone's tragedy."

He seems to search his memory, without finding what he's after. He blows into his hands and murmurs: "See you later" and "Thank you very much." He goes back along the main avenue to the gates. His steps are still silent.

Madame Pinto goes past me again to fill up her watering can. Behind her, Claire, the woman from Mâcon's oncology unit, makes for Thierry Teissier's grave, clutching a potted rosebush. I go over to her.

"Good morning, madame, I would like to plant this rosebush at Thierry Teissier's grave."

I call out to Nono, who is in his hut. The gravediggers have a hut where they get changed, take a shower at midday and in the evening, and wash their work clothes. Nono says that the smell of death cannot cling to his clothes, but no detergent exists to stop it sullying the inside of his noggin.

While Nono digs where Claire wants to plant the rosebush, Elvis sings: *Always on my mind, always on my mind* . . . Nono puts in a little peat and a stake so the rosebush grows straight. He tells Claire that he knew Thierry, and that he was a good guy.

Claire wanted to give me money for watering Thierry's

rosebush from time to time. I told her that I would water it, but that I never accepted money. That she could slip some change into the ladybird-shaped moneybox in my kitchen, on top of the fridge, and that such cash donations went toward buying food for the cemetery's animals.

She said, "Fine." And that, normally, she never did this, attend the funerals of patients from her unit. That it was the first time. That Thierry Teissier, he was too nice to be buried under the ground, like that, with nothing around him. That she'd chosen a red rosebush for what it symbolized, and she wanted Thierry to live on through it. She added that the flowers would keep him company.

I took her to see one of the loveliest tombs in the cemetery, that of Juliette Montrachet (1898–1962), around which various plants and shrubs have grown, combining colors and foliage harmoniously, while never being maintained. A garden tomb. As though chance and nature had come to an amicable agreement.

Claire said: "These flowers, they're a bit like ladders up to heaven." She thanked me, too. She drank a glass of water at my place, slipped a few notes into the ladybird moneybox, and off she went.

10.

Talking about you is making you exist,
saying nothing would be forgetting you.

I met Philippe Toussaint on July 28th, 1985, the day that Michel Audiard, the great screenwriter, died. Perhaps that's why Philippe Toussaint and I never had much to say to each other. Why our dialogues were as flat as Tutankhamun's brain scan. When he said to me, "That drink, shall we have it at my place?" I immediately said, "Yes."

Before leaving the Tibourin club, I felt the looks of the other girls. The ones kicking their heels in the endless line behind him, since he had turned his back on them to look at me. I felt their eyes, covered in shadow and mascara, killing me, cursing me, condemning me to death when the music stopped.

No sooner had I said yes than we were on his motorbike, a too-big helmet on my head and his hand on my left knee. I closed my eyes. It began to rain on us. I felt raindrops on my face.

His parents rented a studio for him in the center of Charleville-Mézières. As we went up in the lift, I was still hiding my bitten nails under my sleeves.

As soon as we were inside his place, he threw himself on me without saying a word. I also stayed silent. Philippe Toussaint was so handsome that he took my breath away. Like when my primary-school teacher had done a lesson on Picasso and his Blue Period. The paintings she'd shown us, using her ruler on a book, had taken my breath away, and I'd decided that the rest of my life would be blue.

I slept at his place, dazed with the pleasure he'd given my body. For the first time, I'd enjoyed making love; I hadn't done it in exchange for something. I began to hope that it would start again. And we did start again. I didn't leave, I continued to sleep at his place. One day, two days, then three. After that, everything merged together. Days became fused, one to the next. Like a train whose carriages my memory can't distinguish anymore. All that's left is the memory of the journey.

Philippe Toussaint turned me into a dreamy sort. An entranced little girl who, looking at the photo of a blond, blue-eyed boy in a magazine, thinks: *This picture belongs to me, I can put it in my pocket.* I spent hours caressing him, one of my hands forever lingering on some part of him. There's a saying that beauty can't be eaten as a salad, but me, well, I dined on his beauty like a three-course meal. And if there were any left-overs, I helped myself again. He went along with it. I seemed to appeal to him, as did my caresses. He possessed me, and that's all that mattered.

I fell in love. Thank goodness I'd never had a family, I would've abandoned it myself. Philippe Toussaint became my sole focus. I directed all that I was and all that I had at him. My entire being for just one person. If I could have lived in him, inside of him, I wouldn't have hesitated.

One morning, he said to me, "Come and live here." He said nothing more. Just that, "Come and live here." I left the hostel over the top of a wall—I was still underage. I turned up at Philippe Toussaint's with a suitcase containing all that I owned. Meaning, not much. Some clothes and my first doll, Caroline. She spoke when she was given to me ("Hello, Mommy, my name is Caroline, come and play with me," and then she laughed), but the batteries, the damp circuits, the moves, the foster families, the social workers, the caseworkers, it had all taken her breath away, too. School photos; four LPs, two of Etienne Daho (*Mythomane* and *La Notte, la Notte*), one

11

Soothe his rest with your sweetest singing.

A fly is swimming in my glass of port. I deposit it on the outside ledge of my window. As I'm closing it, I see the detective walking up the road, the light of the street-lamps on his coat. The path leading to the cemetery is lined with trees. Down below is Father Cédric's church. And behind the church, the few streets that make up the town center. The detective walks fast. He looks frozen stiff.

I feel like being alone. Like every evening. Speak to no one. Read, listen to the radio, have a bath. Close the shutters. Wrap myself in a pink silk kimono. Just feel good.

Once the gates have been shut, time belongs to me. I'm its sole owner. It's a luxury to be the owner of one's time. I think it's one of the greatest luxuries human beings can afford themselves.

I'm still wearing winter over summer, when normally, at this hour, I wear summer. I'm a bit annoyed with myself for suggesting to the detective that he come to mine, for offering him my help.

He knocks on the door, like the first time. Eliane doesn't move. She's already settled in for the night, curled in a ball under the countless blankets in her basket.

He smiles at me, says good evening to me. A sharp chill enters as he does. Quickly, I close the door. I pull out a chair for him to sit on. He doesn't take his coat off. A good sign. It means he won't stay long.

Without asking him a thing, I take out a crystal glass and

pour him some of my port—1983 vintage—the one José-Luis Fernandez brings me. When he sees the collection of bottles inside the cupboard that serves as my bar, my visitor's big brown eyes get even bigger. There are hundreds of them. Fortified wines, malts, liqueurs, eaux-de-vie, spirits.

"I don't traffic alcohol, they're gifts. People don't dare give me flowers. One doesn't give flowers to cemetery keepers, especially since I sell them. One doesn't give flowers to florists, either. Apart from Madame Pinto, who brings me vacuum-packed dolls every year, the others all go for bottles or pots of jam. I'd need several lives to down it all. So, I give a lot of it to the gravediggers."

He takes off his gloves and has a first sip of port.

"What you're drinking there, it's the finest I have."

"Divine."

I don't know why, but I'd never have imagined him coming out with the word "divine" while sipping my port. Aside from his hair, which goes off in all directions, there's nothing frivolous about him. He looks just as sad as the clothes he wears.

I take a notebook and pen, sit facing him, and ask him to tell me about his mother. He appears to think for a few moments, breathes in, and replies:

"She was blonde. It was natural."

And then nothing more. He's back studying my blank walls as if there were masterpieces hanging on them. From time to time, he raises the crystal glass to his lips and swallows the liquid in small sips. I can see that he's savoring it. And that he's relaxing as he drinks.

"I've never known how to do speeches. I think and speak like a police report, or an identity document. I know how to tell you whether a person has a scar, a beauty spot, a growth . . . whether they limp, their shoe size . . . At a glance, I know the height, weight, color of the eyes, of the skin, the distinguishing feature of an individual. But when it comes to what they feel . . . I'm incapable of knowing. Unless they have something to hide . . . "

He finished his drink. Immediately, I pour him another and cut some slices of comté cheese, which I arrange on a porcelain plate.

"When it comes to secrets, I have a good nose. I'm a real hound . . . I immediately spot the giveaway gesture. Well, that's what I thought . . . before discovering the final wishes of my mother."

My port has the same effect on everyone. It's like a truth serum.

"And you? You're not drinking?"

I pour myself a teardrop and clink glasses with him.

"That's all you're drinking?"

"I'm a cemetery keeper. I drink only teardrops . . . We could talk about your mother's passions. When I say 'passions,' it doesn't have to mean for the theater or bungee jumping. Just what her favorite color was, where she liked to walk, the music she listened to, films she watched, whether she owned cats, dogs, trees, how she spent her time, whether she liked the rain, the wind, or the sun, her favorite season . . . "

He remains silent for a long while. He looks as if he's searching for words, like a lost walker searches for the path. He finishes his drink and says to me:

"She liked the snow and roses."

And that's it. He has nothing else to say about her. He seems both ashamed and helpless. It's as if he's just admitted to me that he's afflicted with some obscure ailment. Not knowing how to speak about a loved one.

I get up and go over to my register cupboard. I take out the one for 2015 and open it at the first page.

"This is a speech that was written on January 1st, 2015, for Marie Géant. Her granddaughter was unable to attend the burial because she was abroad for work. She sent it to me and asked me to read it at the funeral. I think it will help you. Take the register, read the speech, write notes, and you can return it to me tomorrow morning."

He immediately got up, tucking the register under his arm. It's the first time a register has ever left my house.

"Thank you, thank you for everything."

"Are you sleeping at Madame Béant's?"

"Yes."

"Have you had supper?"

"She prepared something for me."

"You're setting off for Marseilles tomorrow?"

"At the crack of dawn. I'll bring you the register before I go."

"Leave it on the ledge, behind the blue window box."

12.

Sleep, Nana, sleep, but may you
still hear our childish laughter
up there in highest Heaven.

SPEECH FOR MARIE GÉANT

S he didn't know how to walk, she ran. She couldn't keep
still. "Jamboter" is the verb for what she did, an expression from eastern France. Say to someone, "Arrête de jamboter," and it means: "Sit yourself down, once and for all." Well,
it's done now, she's sat herself down, once and for all.

She went to bed early and got up at five in the morning. She
was first to arrive at the shops so she wouldn't have to wait in
line. She had an almighty horror of waiting in line. By 9 A.M.,
she'd already got all her groceries for the day in her string bag.

She died during the night between December 31st and
January 1st, a public holiday, she who had slaved away her entire
life. I hope she didn't have to wait too long in line at the gates of
Heaven with all those revelers and road-accident victims.

For the holidays, at my request, she would get two knitting
needles and a ball of wool ready for me. I never got further than
ten rows. Put the years end to end, and I must have finally made
an imaginary scarf, which she'll wrap around my neck when I'll
join her in Heaven. If Heaven's what I deserve.

When she phoned, she'd say, with a chuckle, "It's the old dear
here."

She sent letters to her children every week. Her children who
had moved far away from her home. She wrote just like she
thought.

She sent parcels and checks for every birthday, name day,
Christmas, Easter, for the "poppets." For her, all children were
"poppets."

She liked beer and wine.

She did the sign of the Cross over bread before slicing it.

She said, "Jesus and Mary." Frequently. It was a form of punctuation. A kind of period she put at the end of her sentences.

On the sideboard, there was always a large wireless that stayed on all morning. Since she'd been widowed very early on, I often thought that the radio announcers' masculine voices kept her company.

From midday, the TV took over. To kill the silence. All the inane game shows would be on, until she dozed off in front of The Flames of Love. She commented on what every character said, as if they existed in real life.

Two or three years before she tripped and was obliged to leave her flat for the retirement home, someone stole her Christmas garlands and ornaments from her cellar. She phoned me in tears, as if her lifetime of Christmases had been stolen.

She often sang. Very often. Even at the end of her life, she said, "I feel like singing." She also said, "I feel like dying."

She went to Mass every Sunday.

She threw nothing away. Especially not leftovers. She reheated them and ate them. Sometimes, she made herself sick from eating the same thing, again and again, until it was all gone. But she'd rather vomit than chuck a crust of bread in the bin. An old leftover itself from the war, in her stomach.

She bought mustard in cartoon-covered glasses, which she saved for her grandchildren—her poppets—when they came to stay with her during the holidays.

There was always something tasty simmering in a cast-iron pot on her gas stove. Chicken with rice did her for the week. And she saved the chicken stock for her evening meals. In her kitchen, there were also two or three onions sweating in a pan, or a sauce, that made your mouth water.

She was always a tenant. Never an owner. The only place that ever belonged to her was her family vault.

When she knew we were coming for the holidays she would

wait for us at her kitchen window. She looked out for cars park-
ing in the little lot down below. We could see her white hair
through the window. No sooner had we arrived at hers than she
would say, "When will you be coming back to see the old dear?"
As if she wanted us to leave again.

These last years, she no longer waited for us. If we made the
mistake of being five minutes late at the retirement home to take
her out for lunch, we'd find her in the dining room with the
other old folk.

She slept wearing a hairnet to preserve her perm.

She drank the juice of a lemon in warm water every morning.

Her bedcover was red.

During the war, she was the soldier's pen pal of my grandfa-
ther, Lucien. When he returned from Buchenwald, she couldn't
recognize him. There was a photo of Lucien on her bedside table.
Then the photo was moved, along with her, to the retirement
home.

I used to love wearing her nylon slips. Because she bought
everything by mail order, she received lots of gifts, knickknacks
of all kinds. As soon as I arrived at her flat, I would ask her if I
could go and rummage in her cupboard. She would say: "Of
course, off you go." And I would rummage for hours. I would
find prayer books, Yves Rocher creams, sheets, lead soldiers,
balls of wool, dresses, scarves, brooches, china dolls.

The skin on her hands was rough.

A few times, I did her perm for her.

To save money, she never let the tap run to rinse the dishes.

Towards the end of her life, she would say: "What did I ever
do to the Good Lord to end up here?" referring to the retirement
home.

I started to desert her little flat when I was seventeen to sleep
at my aunt's, about 300 meters away. A fine apartment above a
large café, and also a cinema popular with youngsters, with its
table football, video games, and choc-ices. I still went to eat with

*the old dear, but I preferred to sleep at my aunt's for the ciga-
rettes we'd smoke on the sly, the all-day cinema, and the bar.*

*I'd always seen Madame Fève, a sweet lady, doing the house-
work and ironing at my aunt's. Then one day, I came face to face
with my grandmother as she was vacuuming the bedrooms. She
was replacing Madame Fève, who was on holiday or unwell. It
happened occasionally. So I discovered.*

*The day she died, I couldn't sleep all night because of "that."
Because of the awkwardness there had been between us at that
moment. When I pushed open a door, laughing, and came face to
face with my grandmother doing the housework. Doubled over a
vacuum cleaner to supplement her income. I tried to remember
what we'd said to each other that day. It stopped me from sleeping. I kept revisiting the scene, a scene I had completely forgotten until the day she died. All night long, I pushed open that
door and saw her behind it, doing the housework in other people's homes. All night long, I carried on laughing with my
cousins, and she carried on vacuum cleaning.*

*Next time I see her, I'll ask her this question, "Old dear, do
you remember the day when I saw you doing the housework at
my aunt's?" She'll probably shrug her shoulders and reply, "And
the poppets, are the poppets well?"*

13

*There's something stronger than death, and that's the
presence of those absent in the memory of the living.*

I've just found the 2015 register slipped behind my blue
window box. The detective has scribbled, "Thanks a
lot. I'll phone you," on the back of a leaflet for a gym in
Marseilles's 8th arrondissement. There's a photo of a smiling
girl on it. Her dream body is torn at knee level.

He wrote nothing else, no comment on the speech for
Marie Géant, not a word about his mother. I wonder whether
he's far from Marseilles. Whether he's already arrived. When
did he set off? Does he live close to the sea? Does he gaze at it,
or no longer pay any attention to it? Like those who've lived
together so long that it's separated them.

Nono and Elvis arrive just as I'm opening the gates. They
call out, "Hi, Violette!" and park the municipal truck on the
main avenue to go into the hut and put on their work clothes.
I can hear their laughter from the side avenues I'm surveying
to check that all's well. That everyone's in their place.

The cats come and rub themselves against my legs. At the
moment, there are eleven of them living in the cemetery. Five
of those belonged to the deceased, at least I think they did.
They appeared on the day of the burial of Charlotte Boivin
(1954–2010), Olivier Feige (1965–2012), Virginie Teyssandier
(1928–2004), Bertrand Witman (1947–2003), and Florence
Leroux (1931–2009). Charlotte is white, Olivier black, Virginie
an alley cat, Bertrand grey, and Florence (a tomcat) mottled
white, black, and brown. The other six turned up over time.
They come and go. Because people know that the cats at the

cemetery are fed and sterilized, cats are abandoned, even thrown over the walls.

It's Elvis who names them as he finds them. There's Spanish Eyes, Kentucky Rain, Moody Blue, Love Me, Tutti Frutti, and My Way. My Way was left on my doormat in a shoebox for a size 43.

When Nono sees a new little one turn up at the cemetery, he tells it like it is, "I warn you, the boss's specialty is getting balls chopped off." But that doesn't stop the cats from staying close to me.

Nono put a cat-flap on the door of my house for whoever wants to come in. But most of them slip inside the mortuary chapels. They have their habits and their preferences. Apart from My Way and Florence, who are always curled up in a ball somewhere in my bedroom, the others follow me as far as the landing, but don't come in. As though Philippe Toussaint were still there, inside. Do they see his ghost? They say that cats converse with souls. Philippe Toussaint didn't like animals. As for me, I've loved them since a tender age, although my childhood was only ever tough.

Generally, visitors like stumbling across the cemetery cats. Many tell themselves that their lost loved one is using these feline creatures to give them a sign. On the tomb of Micheline Clément (1957–2013) it says: "If Heaven there is, Heaven it will only be if I'm welcomed in by my dogs and cats."

I return to the house, followed by Moody Blue and Virginie. When I push open the door, Nono is just talking to Father Cédric about Gaston. He's speaking of his notorious clumsiness, of the permanent earthquake Gaston seems to be living through. Of the day when, during an exhumation, Gaston turned his wheelbarrow full of bones around, right in the middle of the cemetery, and a skull rolled under a bench without him noticing. And how Nono had called him back to tell him that he'd forgotten a "billiard ball" under the bench.

Unlike the priests who came before him, Cédric drops by at the house every morning. As he listens to Nono's stories, Father Cédric keeps saying: "My God, there's no way, my God, no way." But every morning, he returns and questions Nono, who feeds him with stories. Between each sentence, he bursts out laughing, and we join him. Starting with me.

I love to laugh about death, to make fun of it. It's my way of putting it down. That way, it pushes its weight around less. By making light of it, I let life have the upper hand, have the power.

Nono uses the familiar "*tu*" with Father Cédric, but calls him "Father."

"Once, we took out a body that was almost in one piece. After more than seventy years, Father, in one piece! . . . Problem was, the opening for putting stiffs into the ossuary, it's really small. Elvis ran off to find me, Elvis with his constantly dripping nose, who says to me, 'Nono, come quick, come quick!' And I says, 'But what is it?' And Elvis screams, 'It's Gaston who's got a feller stuck in the thingamajig!' And I says, 'But what thingamajig?' I arrives at the ossuary at a run, and I sees Gaston shoving the body to get it into the ossuary! I says to them, 'God's sake, guys, we're not with the Germans in the war here . . . ' The best one, yes, the very best, I'm always telling it to the mayor, and the mayor, hell, does it crack him up . . . the town hall gave us a cylinder of gas on a little four-wheeled trolley with a blowtorch on the end for burning away weeds. So, of course, that Elvis, he puts the blowtorch on and Gaston turns on the gas . . . just to clarify, Father, you have to turn the gas on very gently, except that Gaston, he turns it on hard when Elvis comes with his lighter, and it goes BOOM right across the cemetery! You'd have thought there was a war going on in there . . . And, wait for it! They even managed to . . . "

Nono starts splitting his sides. He gets back to his story, nose in a handkerchief:

"There's a woman who's cleaning her tomb, she's put her handbag on top of it, and they bloody set fire to the lady's bag . . . I swear on the head of my grandson, Father, it's true! Let me die on the spot if I tell a lie. Elvis started jumping with both feet on the lady's handbag to put out the flames, with both feet on the bag!"

Propped against a window, with My Way on his knees, Elvis starts gently singing, "I *feel my temperature rising, higher, higher, it's burning through to my soul . . .* "

"Elvis, tell Father how the lady's glasses were in the bag, and how you smashed the lenses! You should've seen the job he did, Father! And Elvis who was saying, 'That Gaston bloody set fire to the bag . . . ' And the little old lady who was screaming, 'He's smashed my glasses! He's smashed my glasses!'"

Father Cédric, in fits of laughter, is weeping into his cup. "My God, there's no way, my God, there's no way!"

Nono spots his boss through my windows. He's up like a shot. Elvis follows suit.

"Talk of the devil, and you always sees his tail. And that one definitely uses his tail. Sorry, Father! May God forgive me, and if he doesn't, no matter. Well, cheerio, folks!"

Nono and Elvis leave my place and head for their boss. As the manager of technical services for the town, it's Jean-Louis Darmonville who supervises the gravediggers. Apparently, he has as many mistresses in my cemetery as down Brancion high street. And yet he's not much to look at. From time to time, he makes an appearance, and paces up and down my avenues. Does he remember all the women he barely held close? The ones who gave him a blow job? Does he look at their portraits? Does he remember their names? Their faces? Their voices? Their laughter? Their smell? What remains of his non-love affairs? I've never seen him paying his respects. Just strolling around, nose in the air. Does he come to reassure himself that none of them will ever talk about him?

As for me, I don't have a boss. Only the mayor. The same one for twenty years. And I only see the mayor for the funerals of his people. Storekeepers, the military, municipal employees, people of influence, the "bigwigs," as we call them here. Once, he buried a childhood friend, and his face was so contorted by grief that I didn't recognize him.

Father Cédric also gets up to leave.

"Good day, Violette. Thank you for the coffee and the good cheer. It's such a tonic."

"Good day, Father."

He places his hand on the handle of my door and reconsiders.

"Violette, do you ever doubt, sometimes?"

I weigh my words before replying to him. I always weigh my words. You never know. Particularly when I'm addressing a servant of God.

"In recent years, less so. But that's because I feel at home here."

He pauses awhile before continuing:

"I fear not being equal to the task. I hear confessions, I marry, I christen, I preach, I teach catechism. It's a weighty responsibility. I often feel as if I'm betraying those who place their trust in me. Starting with God."

At that, I quit weighing anything, and reply to him:

"Don't you think God is the first to betray men?"

Father Cédric seems shocked by my remark.

"God is only love."

"If God is only love, he inevitably betrays: betrayal is part of love."

"Violette, do you really believe what you're saying?"

"I always believe what I say, Father. God is in man's image. That means he lies, he gives, he loves, he takes back, he betrays, just like each and every one of us."

"God is a universal love. Across his entire creation, God

evolves thanks to you, thanks to us, thanks to all the hierarchies of light, he feels and lives all that is lived and he wants to create ever more perfection, ever more beauty . . . It's myself that I doubt, never him."

"Why do you doubt?"

Not a sound comes from his mouth. He looks at me, distraught.

"You can speak, Father. There are two confessionals in Brancion, the one in your church, and this room. I'm told many things here."

He smiles, sadly.

"I feel more and more the desire to be a father . . . It wakes me in the night . . . At first, I took this desire for fatherhood as pride, vanity. But . . . "

He approaches the table, mindlessly opens and closes the sugar bowl. My Way comes to rub up against his legs. He bends to pet him.

"Have you thought about adoption?"

"I have absolutely no right to do so, Violette. All laws prohibit me from doing so. Terrestrial ones as much as divine ones."

He turns around and automatically looks toward the window. A shadow passes.

"Forgive me, Father, but have you ever fallen in love?"

"I love only God."

14.

The day someone loves you, the weather's marvelous.

During the first months of our life together in Charleville-Mézières, I wrote, in red felt-tip, on each day: MADLY IN LOVE. And that was right up to December 31st, 1985. My shadow was still wrapped in Philippe Toussaint's. Apart from when I was working. He inhaled me. Drank me. Enveloped me. He was wildly sensual. He made me melt in his mouth like a caramel, like icing sugar. I was on a perpetual high. When I think of that period of my life, I'm at a fun fair.

He always knew where to place his hands, his mouth, his kisses. He never got lost. He had a roadmap of my body, routes that he knew by heart and I didn't even know existed.

When we'd finished making love, our legs and our lips trembled in unison. We inhabited each other's burning desire. Philippe Toussaint always said, "Violette, bloody hell, bloody fucking hell, Violette, I've never known anything like it! You're a sorceress, I'm sure you're a sorceress!"

I think he was already cheating on me that first year. I think he always cheated on me. Lied. That he drove off to others as soon as my back was turned.

Philippe Toussaint was like one of those swans that are so handsome on water and yet hobble on land. He turned our bed into a paradise, was considerate and sensual when making love, but as soon as he got up, was vertical, left our horizontal love behind, he lost a good deal of color. He had nothing to say, and was interested only in his motorbike and video games.

He didn't want me to be a bartender at the Tibourin anymore because he was too jealous of the men who approached me. I'd had to hand in my notice straight after we met. From then on, I worked as a waitress in a brasserie. I started at 10 A.M., to prepare for the lunch service, and finished at 6 P.M.

When I left our studio in the morning, Philippe Toussaint was still asleep. I found it a wrench to leave our cozy nest for the cold streets. He told me that during the day, he went for rides on his motorbike. When I got back in the evening, he was stretched out in front of the television. I pushed the door shut and stretched out on top of him. Just as if, after work, I dived into a vast, warm swimming pool, bathed in sunlight. I'd wanted to inject some blue into my life, so this hit the spot.

I would have done absolutely anything for him to touch me. Just that. Touch me. I felt like I belonged to him, body and soul, and I adored it, belonging to him body and soul. I was seventeen and, in my head, had a lot of overdue happiness to catch up on. If he'd left me, my body surely couldn't have withstood the shock of a second separation, after that from my mother.

Philippe Toussaint only worked occasionally. When his parents got mad. His father always found a friend to take him on. And he did it all. House painter, mechanic, deliveryman, night watchman, maintenance man. Philippe Toussaint would show up on time the first day, but usually didn't finish out the week. He always had some excuse for not going back. We lived on my salary, which I had transferred into his account—since I was underage, it was easier. I just kept the tips for myself.

Sometimes, his parents would turn up during the day, without warning. They had copies of the keys to the studio. They came to lecture their unemployed, twenty-seven-year-old only son, and fill up his fridge.

I never saw them because I was working. But on one day off, they suddenly appeared. We'd just been making love. I was naked, lying on the sofa. Philippe Toussaint was taking a shower. I didn't hear them come in. I was singing a Lio song at the top of my lungs, "And you, tell me you love me! Even if it's a lie! Since I know you lie! Life is so sad! Tell me you love me! Every day's the same! I need romaaaance!" When I did see them, I thought: Philippe Toussaint doesn't look at all like his parents.

I'll never forget the look Mother Toussaint gave me, her grimace. I'll never forget the disdain in her eyes. Even I, who could barely read, who stumbled on words, could interpret it. As if a malicious mirror were reflecting back at me the image of a degraded, diminished, valueless young woman. A piece of trash, a slut, a bad seed, a girl from the gutter.

Her hair was auburn. It was pulled and gripped so tightly in her chignon, you could see the veins of her temples under her thin skin. Her mouth was a line of disapproval. Her eyelids, always covered in green shadow over her blue eyes, were a lapse of taste she took everywhere with her. Like an evil spell. She had a nose like the beak of some endangered bird and skin so white it had surely never been kissed by the sun. When she lowered her shadow-caked eyes and saw my little rounded belly, she had to grab a kitchen chair to sit down on.

Father Toussaint, a cowed man who was born submissive, started to talk to me as if we were in a catechism lesson. I can remember the words "irresponsible" and "thoughtless." I think he even spoke of Jesus Christ. I wondered what on earth Jesus would be doing here, in this studio. What he would say if he saw the Toussaint parents wrapped in all their contempt and finery, and me, stark naked, wrapped in a blanket with skyscrapers and "New York City" emblazoned in red.

When Philippe Toussaint emerged from the bathroom, with a towel around his waist, he didn't look at me. Carried on as if I didn't exist. As if only his mother was in the room. Eyes just for her. I felt even more wretched. The runt of a stray. The nothing. Like Father Toussaint. The mother and son started talking about me as if I couldn't hear them. The mother in particular.

"But are you the father? Are you quite sure of that? You were tricked, weren't you? Where did you meet *that girl*? Do you want us dead? Is that it? Abortion wasn't just invented for dogs! Where's your head gone, my poor boy!"

As for the father, he continued to spread the good word:

"Everything is possible, nothing is impossible, one can change, one just needs to believe it, never give up. . ."

Wrapped in my skyscrapers, I wanted to laugh and cry at the same time. I felt as if I were in an Italian farce, but without the beauty of the Italians. With the social workers and caseworkers, I was used to people talking about me, about my life, about my future as though it didn't concern me. As though I were absent from my story, from my existence. As though I were a problem to be solved, not a person.

The Toussaint parents were coiffed and shod as though going to a wedding. Occasionally, the mother would glance at me for a second; any longer and she'd have tainted her cornea.

When they left without saying goodbye to me, Philip Toussaint started shouting, "Shit! They make me sick!" while kicking wildly at the walls. He asked me to leave while he calmed himself down. Otherwise, those kicks, they'd end up landing on me. He looked traumatized, when it's me who should have been. I was no stranger to violence. I'd grown up close to it, without it ever physically touching me. I'd always come through without a scratch.

I went out into the street, it was cold. I walked fast to warm myself up. Our daily life was totally carefree; it had taken Father and Mother Toussaint opening our door to shatter everything. I returned to the studio an hour later. Philippe Toussaint had fallen asleep. I didn't wake him.

The following day, I was eighteen years old. By way of a

birthday present, Philippe Toussaint announced to me that his father had found work for both of us. We were going to become level-crossing keepers. We'd have to wait for the position to become vacant, soon, close to Nancy.

15

Sweet butterfly, spread your lovely wings
and go to his tomb to tell him I love him.

O nce again, Gaston has tumbled into a grave. I can't count the number of times it's happened now. Two years ago, during an exhumation, he fell into the coffin on all fours and found himself facedown on the bones. How many times, during funerals, has he tripped on imaginary ropes?

Nono had turned his back on him for a few minutes to push a wheelbarrow of soil some forty meters away. Gaston was talking to Countess de Darrieux, and when Nono returned, Gaston had disappeared. The soil had slipped and Gaston was swimming in the grave and screaming, "Fetch Violette!" To which Nono responded, "Violette isn't a lifeguard!" And yet Nono had warned him, the soil is crumbly during this season. While he helped Gaston out of his predicament, Elvis sang: *Facedown on the street, in the ghetto, in the ghetto . . .* Sometimes, I feel as if I'm living with the Marx Brothers. But reality catches up with me every day.

Tomorrow, there's a burial. Dr. Guyennot. Even doctors end up dying. A natural death at ninety-one, in his bed. He cared for all of Brancion-en-Chalon, and its vicinity, for fifty years. Should be a good turnout for his funeral.

Countess de Darrieux is recovering from her shock by sipping a little plum brandy, given to me by Mademoiselle Brulier, whose parents are buried in the Cedars section. The countess got a real fright when she saw Gaston diving into the grave. She says to me, with a mischievous smile, "I thought I was back watching the world swimming championships." I adore this woman. She's one of those visitors who do me good.

Both her husband and her lover are laid to rest in my cemetery. From spring to autumn, Countess de Darrieux maintains plants and flowers on the two graves. Succulents for her husband and a bunch of sunflowers in a vase for her lover, whom she calls her "true love." Trouble is, her true love was married. And when the widow of this true love finds the countess's sunflowers in their vase, she throws them into the bin.

I've tried before to save these poor flowers, to put them on another grave, but it's impossible because the widow tears off all the petals. And she definitely isn't murmuring, "He loves me, he loves me not," while she strips the countess's sunflowers.

In twenty years, I've seen plenty of widows weeping on the day of their husband's funeral, never to set foot in the cemetery again. I've also encountered many widowers who remarried while their wife's body was still warm. At first, they slip a few cents into the ladybird so I carry on looking after the flowers.

I know a few ladies from Brancion who specialize in widowers. They prowl the avenues, dressed all in black, and locate the solitary men watering the flowers on the tombs of their late spouses. I observed, over a long period, the little game played by a certain Clotilde C., who, every week, invented new dead people to cherish in my cemetery. The first inconsolable widower she spotted, she hooked by starting a conversation about the weather, about life going on, and would get herself invited to "have an apéritif one of these evenings." She finally got herself hitched to Armand Bernigal, whose wife (Marie-Pierre Vernier, married name Bernigal, 1967–2002) lies in the Yews section.

I've found and picked up dozens of new funerary plaques thrown in the bin or hidden under the bushes by outraged families. Plaques with the words, "To my beloved for eternity," placed by a lover.

And every day, I see the illicit discreetly coming in to pay their respects. Especially mistresses. It's mainly women who haunt cemeteries, because they live longer. Lovers never come on the weekends, at the times when they might run into someone. Always when the gates are just opening or closing. How many have I already locked in? Bent over tombs, I don't see them, and they have to come and knock on my door for me to release them.

I remember Emilie B. Ever since her lover, Laurent D., had passed away, she always arrived half an hour before opening time. When I'd see her waiting behind the gates, I'd slip a black coat over my nightdress, and go and open them for her in my slippers. She's the only person I did that for, but I just felt so sorry for her. I'd give her a cup of sweetened coffee, with a little milk, every morning. We'd exchange a few words. She'd talk to me about her passionate love for Laurent. She spoke of him as if he were present. She'd say to me, "Memory is stronger than death. I can still feel his hands on me. I know he's watching me from where he is." Before setting off, she'd leave her empty cup on the window ledge. When visitors came to pay their respects at Laurent's grave—his wife, his parents, or his children—Emilie would change tombs, waiting, hiding in a corner. As soon as they'd all gone, she'd return to Laurent to think about him, to talk to him.

One morning, Emilie didn't come. I thought she must have finished mourning. Because, most of the time, a person does eventually finish mourning. Time unravels grief. However immense it is. Apart from the grief of a mother or a father who has lost a child.

I was wrong. Emilie never finished mourning. She returned to my cemetery between four planks of wood. Surrounded by her loved ones. I don't think anyone ever knew that she and Laurent had loved each other. Of course, Emilie wasn't buried close to him.

On the day of her burial, once everyone had left, just as one plants a tree on the day of a birth, I took a cutting. Emilie had planted a lavender bush at Laurent's tomb. I cut a long stem of that lavender, made lots of little incisions to favor root growth, cut off the top, and stuck it through the pierced base of a bottle that was filled with soil and a little compost. A month later, the stem had sprouted roots.

Laurent's lavender would also become Emilie's. They would have that for years, that plant in common, offspring of the mother plant. I nurtured the cutting all winter, and replanted it in the spring at Emilie's tomb. As Barbara sings, "spring is lovely for talking about love." Laurent's and Emilie's lavenders are still splendid today, and perfume all the neighboring tombs.

*We never meet people by chance. They are destined to
cross our paths for a reason.*

L éonine."

"What did you say?"

"Léonine."

"No, you really are nuts . . . What kind of name is that? A
brand of detergent?"

"I love that name. And anyway, people will call her Léo. I
like girls who have boys' names."

"Call her Henri, while you're at it."

"Léonine Toussaint . . . it's very pretty."

"It's 1986! You could find something more modern,
like . . . Jennifer or Jessica."

"No, please, Léonine . . . "

"In any case, you do what you like. If it's a girl, you choose.
If it's a boy, I do."

"And what would you call our son?"

"Jason."

"I hope it's a girl."

"I don't."

"Shall we make love?"

I hear your voice in the world's every sound.

January 19th, 2017, gray sky, 8 degrees, 3 P.M. Burial of Dr. Philippe Guyennot (1925–2017). Oak coffin, yellow and white roses on top. Black marble. Small gilt cross on headstone.

Around fifty sprays, wreaths, casket tributes, plants (lilies, roses, cyclamens, chrysanthemums, orchids.)

Funeral ribbons saying, "To our dear father," "To my dear husband," "To our dear grandfather," "Thoughts from the class of 1924," "Retailers of Brancion-en-Chalon," "To our friend," "To our friend," "To our friend."

On the funerary plaques: "Time passes, memories remain"; "To my dear husband"; "From your friends who will never forget you"; "To our father"; "To our grandfather"; "To our great-great-uncle"; "To our godfather"; "Thus all passes on earth, intellect, beauty, grace, and talent, like an ephemeral flower felled by a puff of wind."

About a hundred people are present around the grave. Including Nono, Gaston, Elvis, and me. Before the burial, more than four hundred people congregated at Father Cédric's little church. Not everyone could fit inside and sit in pews, so the elderly were allowed in first, to be seated together. Many people remained standing, gathered on the church's small forecourt.

Countess de Darrieux told me she had thought back to when the good doctor would arrive at her home after midnight, his shirt all crumpled, and, after traveling across the countryside, he would return to make sure that her youngest's fever had abated since morning. She said to me, "Each one of us thought back to their anginas, their mumps, their influenzas, and to the death certificates he had filled in, leaning over the kitchen table, because when Dr. Guyennot started practicing, one still died in one's own bed, not in a hospital."

Philippe Guyennot leaves a very fine legacy behind him. During his speech, his son said, "My father was a devoted man, who charged for just one consultation, even when he visited several times on the same day, or had placed his stethoscope over the hearts of an entire family. He was a great doctor, who made the correct diagnosis after asking three questions and looking deep into the patient's eyes. In a world where the world hadn't yet invented *generic* drugs."

A medallion depicting Philippe Guyennot was soldered onto the headstone. The family chose a holiday snapshot where the doctor is around fifty. He's beaming, he's tanned, and one can see the sea behind him. A summer when he must have got a replacement, and left behind countryside and coughing fits to close his eyes in the sun.

Before blessing the coffin, Father Cédric's last words are, "Philippe Guyennot, as the Father has loved me, I have loved you. There is no greater love than dedicating one's life to those one loves."

Drinks have been organized in the function room at the town hall, in honor of the deceased. I'm always invited, but I never go. Everyone leaves, except Pierre Lucchini and me.

While the stonemasons close up the family vault, Pierre Lucchini tells me that the deceased met his wife on the day of her marriage to another man. During the first dance, she had sprained her ankle. Philippe was urgently called to attend to her. When the doctor saw his future wife in her wedding dress, ankle in ice bucket, he fell in love with her. He carried her off to get an X-ray done at the hospital, and never returned her to her new, and short-lived, husband. Smiling, Pierre adds, "It's while fixing her ankle that he asked for her hand."

Before closing time, Philippe's two children return. They watch the stonemasons at work. They remove the condolence cards attached to the flowers. They give me a wave before getting in a car and heading back to Paris.

The dead leaves are shoveled away,
the memories and regrets are, too.

I talk on my own. I talk to the dead, to the cats, to the lizards, to the flowers, to God (not always nicely). I talk to myself. I question myself. I shout at myself. I buck myself up.

I don't fit into boxes. I've never fitted into boxes. When I do a test in a women's magazine—"Get to know yourself," or "Know yourself better"—there's no clear result for me. I'm always a bit of everything.

In Brancion-en-Chalon, there are people who don't like me, who are wary or scared of me. Perhaps because I seem to be forever dressed in mourning garb. If they knew that, underneath, there's the summer, maybe they'd burn me at the stake. All jobs connected with death seem suspect.

And then, my husband disappeared. Just like that, from one day to the next. "You must admit, it is strange. He goes off on his bike and, snap, he's disappeared. Never to be seen again. A handsome man, too, more's the pity. And the police just do nothing. She's never been investigated, never questioned. And she doesn't seem upset about it. Dry eyed. If you ask me, she's hiding something. Always dressed in black, and up to the nines . . . she's sinister, that woman. There are some dodgy goings on in that cemetery, I wouldn't trust her. The gravediggers are always round at her place. And just look at her, talking to herself. Don't tell me it's normal, talking to yourself."

And then there are the others. "A good woman. Generous. Dedicated. Always smiling, discreet. Such a hard job. Nobody wants to do a job like that anymore. And all alone, too. Her husband abandoned her. She deserves credit. Always a little glass of something on hand for the most distraught. Always a kind word. And well turned out, so elegant . . . Polite, friendly, compassionate. Can't knock her. A real hard worker. The cemetery's shipshape. A simple woman who doesn't rock the boat. Head's a bit in the clouds, but having one's head in the clouds never killed anyone."

I'm the main cause of their civil war.

Once, the mayor received a letter requesting my dismissal from the cemetery. He politely replied that I'd never done anything wrong.

Occasionally, youngsters chuck stones at the shutters of my bedroom to scare me, or start banging on my door in the middle of the night. I can hear their giggling from my bed. When Eliane starts barking, or I ring my startlingly loud bell, they're off as fast as their legs can carry them.

I prefer youngsters to be full of life, annoying, noisy, drunk, stupid, rather than in coffins, followed by people bowed with grief.

In the summer, adolescents do sometimes climb over the cemetery walls. They wait until midnight. They come in a group and have fun scaring themselves. They hide behind the crosses, howling, or slam the doors of the mortuary chapels. Some also hold spiritualism seances to terrify, or impress, their girlfriends. "Spirit, are you there?" During these seances, I hear girls screaming and then bolting at the slightest "supernatural manifestation." Manifestations that are really the cats chasing moths between the graves, hedgehogs knocking over the bowls of cat food, or me, hidden behind a tomb, aiming a pistol full of red-dyed water at them.

I won't tolerate the resting place of the dead not being respected. At first, I switch on the lights outside my house and ring my bell. If that doesn't work, I get out my water pistol and pursue them around the avenues. There's no light in the cemetery at night. I can move around without ever being spotted. I know it off by heart. I know my way with my eyes closed.

Leaving aside those who come to make love, one night I discovered a group who were watching a horror film, sitting on the tomb of Diane de Vigneron, the first to be interred in the cemetery. It's her ghost that, for centuries, some inhabitants of Brancion have claimed to have seen. I crept up behind the intruders and blew a whistle as hard as I could. They bolted like rabbits. Leaving their computer behind on the tomb.

In 2007, I had serious problems with a gang of youths on holiday. People just passing through. Parisians, or suchlike. From July 1st through 30th, they came every evening, over the cemetery walls, to sleep on the tombs, under the stars. I called the police several times; Nono gave them a few kicks up the backside, explaining that the cemetery wasn't an adventure playground, but they'd be back the following night. I could switch on all the lights outside my house, shake my bell, target them with my water pistol, impossible to make them clear off. Nothing seemed to have any effect on them.

Fortunately, on the morning of July 31st, they left. But the following year, they returned. On the evening of July 1st, there they were. I heard them at around midnight. They settled down on the tomb of Cécile Delaserbe (1956–2003). And, unlike the previous year, they were smoking and drinking a good deal, leaving their bottles all over the cemetery. Every morning, we had to collect the cigarette butts from the potted plants.

And then a miracle occurred: during the night of July 8th to 9th, they left. I'll never forget their screams of terror. They said they had seen "something."

The following day, Nono told me he'd found "little blue pills" near the ossuary, an overly strong drug that must have distorted the sight of a will-o'-the-wisp, in their altered minds, into some sort of specter. I don't know whether it was the ghost of Diane de Vigneron or Reine Ducha, the white lady, that rid me of those young idiots, but I'm eternally grateful to it.

19.

*If a flower grew every time I thought of you, the earth
would be one massive garden.*

I was about to push open the main door beneath our studio,
when I saw a red apple in the shopwindow, on the cover
of a book, *L'Oeuvre de Dieu, la part du Diable*, a French
translation of John Irving's *The Cider House Rules*. I couldn't
understand the title. It was too complicated for me. In 1986, I
was eighteen, with the educational level of a six-year-old. Teacher, sch-ool, I go, I have, you have, I am go-ing home, it is,
good mor-ning Miss, Panzani, Babybel, Boursin, Skip, Oasis,
Ballantine's.

I bought that eight-hundred-and-twenty-one-page book,
even though just reading one sentence and understanding it
could take hours. As if I were a size 50 and had bought myself
size-36 jeans. But buy it I did, because the apple made my
mouth water. And for a few months, I had lost my desire. It
started with Philippe Toussaint's breath on the nape of my
neck. That breath that meant he was ready, that he wanted me.
Philippe Toussaint always wanted me, never desired me. I didn't
move. I pretended to be asleep. To breathe heavily.

It was the first time my body didn't respond to the call of
his. And then the lack of desire passed, once, twice. Then it
returned, like the hoarfrost that reappears from time to time.

I'd always been at one with life, I'd always seen the fine side
of things, rarely their darker side. Like those waterfront
houses, facades gleaming in the sun. From the boat, you can
see the bright color of the walls, the picket fences white as mirrors, and the verdant gardens. I rarely saw the back of these

buildings, the side along the road, the shadowy side where trash cans and septic tanks are hidden.

Before Philippe Toussaint, despite the foster families and my bitten nails, I saw the sunlight on the facades, rarely the shadows. With him, I came to understand what disillusion means. That it wasn't enough to derive pleasure from a man to love him. The gorgeous guy's picture on glossy paper had become dog-eared. His laziness, his lack of courage when facing his parents, his latent violence, and the smell of other girls on his fingertips, had stolen something from me.

He's the one who wanted a child from me. He's the one who said, "We're going to make babies." The same man, ten years my senior, who whispered to his mother that he'd "picked me up," that I was a "lost cause," and that he was "so sorry." And when his mother had turned her back after writing him the umpteenth check, had kissed me on the neck, explaining that he always told his "old folks" anything to get rid of them. But the words were cast, loaded.

I, too, pretended that day. I smiled, I said, "Fine, of course, I understand." This disillusion produced something else inside of me. Something strong. As I saw my belly gradually expanding, I yearned to learn again. To know what "mouthwatering" really meant. Not through somebody, but through words. The ones that are in books, and that I'd run away from because they scared me.

I waited until Philippe Toussaint had left, on his bike, to read the back cover of *L'Oeuvre de Dieu, la part du Diable*. I had to read out loud: to understand the meaning of the words, I had to hear them. As though telling myself a story. I was my double: the one who wanted to learn and the one who would learn. My present and my future bent over the same book.

Why do books attract us the way people do? Why are we drawn to covers like we are to a look, a voice that seems familiar, heard before, a voice that diverts us from our path, makes us look up, attracts our attention, and could change the course of our life?

After more than two hours, I was only on the tenth page and I'd managed to understand one word in five. I read and reread, out loud, the French translation of this sentence, "An orphan is simply more of a child than other children in that central appreciation of the things that happen daily, on schedule. For everything that promises to last, to stay the same, the orphan is a sucker." In French, "sucker" had been translated as "*avide.*" What on earth could this word mean? I would buy a dictionary and learn how to use it.

Until then, I knew the words of the songs printed inside the covers of my LPs. I listened to them and attempted to read them at the same time, but I didn't understand them.

It was while thinking about buying my dictionary that I felt Léonine move for the first time. The words I'd read out loud must have woken her. I took her slow movements as encouragement.

The following day, we moved to Malgrange-sur-Nancy to become level-crossing keepers. But before that, I went down to buy a dictionary, to find the word "*avide*" inside it, "A person who desires something voraciously."

20.

*If life is nothing but a passage,
our memory will preserve your image.*

I'm dusting the plastic boxes containing my Portuguese dolls. I lay them down as often as possible to avoid seeing their tiny, black pinhead eyes.

I heard that garden gnomes have been disappearing from properties . . . What if I convinced Madame Pinto that all my dolls had been stolen?

Nono and Father Cédric are deep in conversation behind me. Especially Nono. Elvis is leaning at the kitchen window, watching the visitors go by and singing "Tutti Frutti" very softly. Nono's voice is drowning his out.

"I was a painter. A house painter, not a painter like Picasso. And then my wife left me all alone with three young kids . . . and I found myself without a job. I was laid off. And then, in 1982, I was employed by the town as a gravedigger."

"How old were your children?" Father Cédric asks.

"Not very old. The older ones seven and five, the little'un six months. I raised 'em on my own. Later, I had another daughter . . . I was born nearby, behind the first block of houses next to your church. In the old days, the midwife would come to the home. And you, Father, where were you born?"

"In Brittany."

"Rains all the time over there."

"That may be so, but it doesn't stop children from being born. I didn't remain long in Brittany, my father was a soldier. He was always being transferred."

"A soldier producing a priest. Well, that ain't too common."

Father Cédric's laughter echoes around my walls. Elvis carries on humming. I've never know him to have a sweetheart, even though he spends his days singing love songs.

Nono calls me, "Violette! Stop playing with your dolls, someone's knocking on the door."

I throw my cloth on the stairs and go to open to this visitor, who's probably looking for a grave.

I open the cemetery-side door, it's the detective. It's the first time he's arrived at this door. He doesn't have the urn. His hair's still a mess. He still smells of cinnamon and vanilla. His eyes are glistening as if he'd been crying; probably tiredness. He smiles shyly at me. Elvis closes the window, and the noise he makes drowns my hello.

The detective notices Nono and Father Cédric sitting at the table. He says to me, "Am I disturbing you? Would you like me to come by later?" I reply no. That in two hours there's a burial, I'll no longer have time.

He comes in. He greets Nono, Elvis, and Father Cédric with a firm handshake.

"Let me introduce you to Norbert and Elvis, my colleagues, and our priest, Cédric Duras."

The detective introduces himself, too; it's the first time I hear him saying his name: Julien Seul. My three acolytes all leave at once, as if the detective's name had scared them. Nono calls out, "See you later, Violette!"

I introduce myself for the first time, "And me, I'm called Violette. Violette Toussaint." The detective replies:

"I know."

"Oh really, you know?"

"At first I thought it was a nickname, a kind of joke."

"A joke?"

"Admit it, for a cemetery keeper, it's unusual to be called Toussaint."

"In fact, I'm called Trenet. Violette Trenet."

"Trenet, that suits you better than Toussaint."

"Toussaint was my husband's name."

"Why 'was'?"

"He disappeared. He vanished into thin air from one day to the next. Well, not really from one day to the next . . . Let's say he prolonged one of his absences."

With embarrassment, he says to me:

"That I also know."

"You know?"

"Madame Bréant has red shutters and a ready tongue."

I go to wash my hands, I let some liquid soap run into my palms, a sweet rose-scented soap. At my place, everything smells of powdery rose: my candles, perfume, linen, tea, even the little cakes I dip in my coffee. I smooth rose cream over my hands. I spend hours with my fingers in the earth, gardening, I have to protect them. I like to have lovely hands. It's been years now since I stopped biting my nails.

Meanwhile, Julien Seul is again studying my white walls. He seems preoccupied. Eliane rubs her muzzle against him, he pets her, smiling.

As I serve him a cup of coffee, I wonder what exactly Madame Bréant might have told him.

"I've written the speech for my mother."

He takes an envelope out of his inside pocket and leans it against the ladybird moneybox.

"You've just done four hundred kilometers to bring me the speech for your mother? Why not send it to me by mail?"

"No, that's not really what I've come for."

"You have her ashes?"

"No again."

He pauses awhile. He seems increasingly uncomfortable.

"Could I smoke by the window?"

"Yes."

He takes a squashed packet from his pocket and pulls out a cigarette, a light one. Before striking a match, he says to me:

"There's something else."

He goes over to the window and half-opens it. He turns his back on me. Takes a drag and blows the smoke outside.

I think I hear him say, through a curl of smoke:

"I know where your husband is."

"Sorry?"

He stubs his cigarette out on the low outside wall and puts the butt in his pocket. He turns to face me and repeats:

"I know where your husband is."

"What husband?"

I feel sick. I really don't want to understand what he's saying. It's as if he'd just gone up to my bedroom without my permission and opened all my drawers to rummage through them and pull out what's inside without my being able to stop him. He looks down and, in a barely audible voice, whispers:

"Philippe Toussaint . . . I know where he is."

21.

*The darkness is never total; at the end of
the path, there's always an open window.*

The only ghosts I believe in are memories. Whether real or imagined. For me, entities, specters, spirits, all such supernatural things only exist in the mind of the living. Some people communicate with the dead, and I believe they are sincere, but when a person is dead, they're dead. If they return, it's a living person making them return through thought. If they speak, it's a living person lending them their voice; if they appear, it's a living person projecting them with their mind, like a hologram, a 3-D printer.

Loss, pain, the unbearable can make a person experience and feel things that are beyond the imagination. When someone has gone, they've gone. Except in the minds of those who remain. And the mind of just one man is much bigger than the universe.

At first, I told myself that the hardest thing would be learning to ride a unicycle. But I was wrong. The hardest thing was the fear. Controlling it, on the night I did it. Slowing my heartbeat. Not shaking. Not chickening out. Closing my eyes and going for it. I had to get rid of the problem. Otherwise, there'd be no end to it.

I'd tried everything. Kindness, intimidation, other people. I wasn't sleeping anymore. That's all I thought about: getting rid of the problem. But how?

On a bike, whether there's one wheel or two, it's almost the same, it's a question of balance. On the other hand, to practice cycling on the gravel of the cemetery, it was best for me to do it at night. No one should see the keeper unicycling along the graves. So, I practiced once night had fallen, and the gates were closed, several days in a row. I had to work on the slowing down and the accelerating. It was unthinkable that, when the time came, I should fall.

What took longest, and was most fiddly, was sewing the shroud, that piece of material used to wrap around corpses. I collected meters and meters of white fabric: muslin, silk, cotton sheets, tulle. I spent a lot of time stitching it all, to make the ensemble both realistic and surreal. On the nights I was making the "thing," I thought, with amusement, that it was the wedding dress I hadn't worn on the day of my union with Philippe Toussaint. I'm sure we end up laughing at everything. Smiling, at any rate. We end up smiling at everything.

Next, I put the shroud through the washing machine, on cold, along with five hundred grams of sodium bicarbonate, so it would be fluorescent. Before sewing the lining, I stuck on photoluminescent strips that recharge when exposed to light. I had nicked several meters from the van of the highway maintenance men. Normally, they use them for outdoor signposting. They are highly luminescent. You only have to put them in the light just before using them. In sunshine, or, for longer, under a lamp.

My face and hair had to be completely concealed. I took one of Nono's black hats from the hut. I cut into it at eye level, and slipped a bride's veil over it. A visiting undertaker had given me a key ring in the form of an angel. It gave out a pretty strong light when you pinched the edges. A kind of safety flashlight, but small and soft. I wedged it between my lips.

When I saw myself in the mirror, I thought I looked scary. Really scary. I looked like something out of the horror film those youngsters were watching on Diane de Vigneron's tomb, the day they left their computer behind after my whistleblowing. In this getup—long, white, ghostly dress, face hidden under bridal veil, body shining like snow in headlights, mouth lighting up, depending on whether I closed or pinched my lips—in a particular setting, that is, a cemetery at night, where the smallest twig snapping can assume irrational proportions, I could give someone a heart attack.

I was missing sound. I had the image, but not the sound-track. That's what I told myself once I'd finished laughing away, all on my own. There are several sounds that would ter-rify anyone in a cemetery at night. Groans, moans, a creak, the sound of the wind, footsteps, slowed-down music. I opted for a little radio on the wrong frequency. I hung it on my bike. When the time came, I'd switch it on.

At around 10 P.M., I hid inside a mortuary chapel, heart pounding under my getup, clutching my bike.

I didn't have to wait long. Their voices preceded their steps. They came over the wall on the eastern side of the cemetery. There were five of them that evening. Three boys and two girls. It varied.

I waited for them to "settle in." For them to start opening their cans of beer and using the potted plants as ashtrays. They stretched out on the tomb of Madame Cedilleau, a nice woman I'd got to know well when she came to put flowers on her daughter's grave. The thought of them stretching out on that mother and daughter spurred me on.

I started by getting on my bike and arranging my long dress correctly—it mustn't get caught in the wheels. My outfit could be seen from far away, I'd exposed my strips for two hours under a halogen lamp. I pushed open the door of the mortuary chapel, making a lot of noise, a grating noise. Their voices fell silent. I was several hundred meters away from the group. I began to pedal. Gently. As if carried by the breeze.

I was about four hundred meters away from them when one of the boys spotted me. I was petrified. I could feel the clam-miness of my hands, the fabric around my legs, the heat of my head. The boy was incapable of uttering a word. But his expression, his horrified stupor, made one of the girls turn toward me, cigarette in mouth, and she, well, she screamed. She screamed so loud that my mouth went dry, very dry. Her screaming made the other three jump. They who, until then, had been laughing their heads off, stopped laughing.

All five of them stared at me. It lasted one or two seconds, no longer. I stopped abruptly, two hundred meters from them. I pinched my lips and the light shone right at them. I stretched my arms into a cross and again went straight for them, but this time much faster, more threateningly.

In my memory, all that happened in slow motion, and I had time to analyze every second. If I didn't pull it off, if I was unmasked, if they, in turn, pursued me, I was done for. But they didn't think. Once they realized that a fluttering ghost was heading straight for them, at a good clip, arms in a cross, they bolted quicker than lightning. Never has anyone got up so fast. Three of them headed for the gates, screaming, two for the back of the cemetery.

I opted to pursue the trio. One of them fell, but got back up immediately.

I don't know how they managed to scale the gates, despite them being three-and-a-half meters high. Proof that fear gives you wings.

I never saw them again. I know that they told anyone who would listen that the cemetery was haunted. I collected their cigarette butts and empty beer cans. I doused Madame Cedilleau's tomb with hot water.

I found it hard to get to sleep, I couldn't stop laughing. As soon as I closed my eyes, I saw them again, bolting like rabbits.

The following morning, I put the bike and my ghoulish disguise up in the attic. Before hiding it in a trunk, I thanked it. I put it away like you'd put away your wedding dress, taking it out from time to time to see if you can still get into it.

22

Little flower of life. Your scent is eternal,
even if humanity picked you too soon.

P hilippe Toussaint is dead. The only difference between
him and the deceased in this cemetery is that I do occasionally pay my respects at their graves."

"Philippe Toussaint is in the phone book. Well, the name of
his garage is in the phone book."

It has been more than nineteen years since anyone has spoken his first name and surname aloud in front of me. Even in
the speech of others, Philippe Toussaint had disappeared.

"His garage?"

"I thought you would want to know, that you'd looked for
him."

I'm incapable of responding to the detective. I haven't
looked for Philippe Toussaint. I waited for him for a long time,
which is different.

"I noticed that there'd been some movement on Mr.
Toussaint's bank account."

"His bank account . . . "

"His current account was emptied in 1998. I went to check
on the spot where the money had been withdrawn, to find out
whether it was fraud, identity theft, or Toussaint himself who
had withdrawn that money."

I feel chilled from head to toe. Every time he says his name,
I want him to shut up. I want him never to have entered my
house.

"Your husband hasn't disappeared. He lives a hundred
kilometers from here."

"A hundred kilometers . . . "

And yet, that day had started off well: Nono's arrival, Father Cédric, Elvis singing at the window, good humor, the smell of coffee, the men's laughter, my ghastly dolls, the dust to remove, the cloth, the warmth in the stairs . . .

"But why have you been investigating Philippe Toussaint?"

"When Madame Bréant told me he'd disappeared, I wanted to know, to help you."

"Monsieur Seul, if there's a key in the door of our cupboards, it's so that no one opens them."

23.

*If life is but a passage, let us at least
scatter flowers on that passage.*

We arrived at the Malgrange-sur-Nancy level crossing at the end of spring 1986. In spring, everything seems possible, the light and the promises. You can sense that the trial of strength between winter and summer has already been won. That the dice are loaded. A game decided in advance, even if it rains.

"Girls in care are happy with very little." That's what a caseworker had said to my third foster family when I was seven years old, as if I couldn't hear, as if I didn't exist. Being abandoned at birth must make me invisible. And anyhow, what is this "very little"?

As for me, I felt I had everything: my youth, my desire to learn to read *L'Oeuvre de Dieu, la part du Diable*, a dictionary, a child in the belly, a house, work, a family that would be my first family. A rickety family, but a family all the same. Since my birth, I'd never had anything, apart from my smile, some clothes, my doll Caroline, my LPs of Daho, Indochine, and Trenet, and my *Tintin* books. At eighteen, I was going to have a legal job, a bank account, and my very own key. A key I'd load with jangly charms, to remind me that I had a key.

Our house was square, with a tile roof covered in moss, just like nursery-school children draw. Two forsythias were in bloom on either side of the house. They made the little white house with red windows seem to have blond curls. A hedge of red rosebushes, still in bud, separated the back of the house from the railway line. The main road, crossed by the tracks, twisted around two meters from the landing, where a tired doormat lay.

The level-crossing keepers, Monsieur and Madame Lestrille, were leaving for their retirement two days later. They had two days to train us. Show us the ropes of the job: lowering and raising the barrier.

The Lestrilles were leaving their dated furniture, their linoleum, and their blackened bars of soap. Picture frames that had hung on the walls for years had just been removed: the flowery wallpaper was left with lighter rectangles in places. They'd left a canvas *Mona Lisa* beside the kitchen window.

In the kitchen, no kitchen. Just a greasy room boasting an old gas cooker and three units held together with rusty screws. When I opened the tiny fridge, seemingly forgotten behind a door, I found some badly wrapped, rancid butter.

Despite the decrepitude and dirtiness of the place, I managed to picture what I'd do with it. How I'd transform these rooms with a lick of paint. I managed to smile at the color of the repainted walls hiding behind the faded flowers of this pre-war wallpaper. I was going to put everything right. Especially the shelves, which would help me to support our future life. Philippe Toussaint promised, in my ear, to repaper all the walls as soon as the Lestrilles' backs were turned.

Before leaving, the old couple left us a list of emergency phone numbers in case the barrier got stuck.

"Now that we don't raise the barrier with a crank anymore, the circuits can get jammed, and this sort of nonsense comes up several times a year."

They left us the train timetables. Summer timetables. Winter timetables. There wasn't much more to add. On public holidays, strike days, and Sundays, there were fewer crossings and fewer trains. They hoped we'd been warned that the hours would be hard and the rhythm of work tiring. It took at least two people to do it. Ah, yes, they almost forgot: we would have three minutes between the start of the signal sounding and the train passing through to lower the barrier. Three minutes to press the switch on the control panel that activated the barrier and blocked the traffic. Once the train had gone through, regulations demanded a one-minute waiting period before raising the barrier.

As he put his overcoat on, Monsieur Lestrille said to us:

"It's possible that one train might conceal another, but we, in thirty years at the barrier, have never seen that happen."

On the doorstep, Madame Lestrille turned around to warn us:

"Beware of vehicles trying to cross when the barrier is down. There'll always be nutters. And drunkards, too."

In a hurry to get going on their retirement, they wished us good luck and added, without a smile:

"It's our turn to take the train."

And we never saw them again.

As soon as they had gone out the door, instead of repapering all the walls, Philippe Toussaint put his arms around me and said:

"Oh, my Violette, how comfortable we'll be here once you've arranged everything."

I don't know whether it was *L'Oeuvre de Dieu, la part du Diable*, which I'd started the day before, or the dictionary I'd bought that very morning, that gave me strength, but, for the first time, I felt brave enough to ask him for money. For a year and a half, my wages had been deposited into his account, and I'd managed on my waitress tips, but right then, I no longer had a penny to my name.

He generously gave me three ten-franc notes, which it pained him to take from his wallet. A wallet I never had access to. Every day, he would count his money to be sure nothing was missing. When he did this, he lost me a little. Not me, but the love I was made of.

In the mind of Philippe Toussaint, everything was simple: I was a lost girl he'd picked up in a nightclub, and he made me work in exchange for board and lodgings. And I was young and pretty, easygoing, good-natured, quite plucky, and he loved possessing me, physically. And in a more devious part of his mind, he had picked up that I was scared stiff of being abandoned, so I would never leave. And now with his child, he knew he had me stuck right there, at his beck and call.

I had an hour and a quarter before the next train. I crossed the road with my thirty francs in my pocket and went into the Casino store to buy a bucket, mop, sponges, and detergents. I bought whatever I found and whatever was cheapest. I was eighteen, I knew nothing about cleaning products. Normally, at that age, you're buying yourself music. I introduced myself to the checkout girl:

"Hi, I'm Violette Trenet, I'm the new level-crossing keeper, from across the road. I'm replacing the Lestrilles."

The cash-desk girl, whose name, Stéphanie, was on her badge, wasn't listening to me. She was mesmerized by my round belly, and asked me:

"Are you the daughter of the new level-crossing keepers?"

"No, I'm the daughter of nobody. I am the new level-crossing keeper."

Everything about Stéphanie was round, her body, her face, her eyes. She might have been drawn for a comic strip to personify a not very bright heroine, naïve and kind, with a permanent look of surprise. Forever staring wide-eyed.

"But how old are you?"

"Eighteen."

"Ah, I see. And the baby, when's it due?"

September."

"Right, nice one. We'll see each other often, then."

"Yes, we'll see each other often. Goodbye."

I started by washing the shelves in the bedroom, then put our clothes away.

I looked under the grubby carpet, there were tiles. I was in the middle of pulling it away when the alarm for the barrier started ringing. The 15:06 train was on its way.

I ran to the level crossing. I pressed the red switch that lowered the barrier. I was relieved when I saw it going down. A car had slowed down and stopped alongside me. A long, white car whose driver gave me a dirty look, as if I were responsible for the train timetables. The 15:06 went by. The tracks shook. The passengers were Saturday ones. Gaggles of girls off to Nancy, to spend the afternoon shopping or flirting.

I thought: *Maybe girls in care, the ones who are happy with very little.* As I pressed the green switch to raise the barrier, I smiled: I had a job, keys, a house to repaint, a child in my belly, a carpet to remove, a rickety man, to whom I mustn't forget to give the change from the shopping, a dictionary, music, and *L'Oeuvre de Dieu, la part du Diable* to read.

24

You must learn to be generous with your absence to those who haven't understood the importance of your presence.

Death never takes a break. It knows neither summer holidays, nor public holidays, nor dentist appointments. Slack periods, mass departures, the Highway to the Sun, the thirty-five-hour working week, paid leave, the festive season, happiness, youth, heedlessness, lovely weather—it couldn't care less about all that. It's there, everywhere, all the time. No one really thinks about it, or they'd go mad. It's like a dog that's forever weaving around our legs, but whose presence we only notice the day it bites us. Or, worse, bites a loved one.

There's a cenotaph in my cemetery. It's on avenue 3, Cedars section. A cenotaph is a memorial erected over a void. A void left by someone who died at sea, on a mountain, in a plane, or in a natural disaster. A living person who just vanished, but whose death seems indisputable. The cenotaph in Brancion no longer has a plaque. It's very old and I've never known in whose memory it was erected. Yesterday, by chance, Jacques Lucchini told me that it was put up in 1967 for a young couple who disappeared in the mountains. Before getting back into his hearse, Jacques said to me, "Youngsters who went mountain climbing, and apparently fell."

I often hear, "Losing a child is the worst." But I also hear it said that the worst is not knowing. That there's something more horrendous than a grave, and that's the face of a missing person plastered across posts, walls, shopwindows, newspapers, a TV screen. Photos that age, but the face they depict never does. That there's something more terrible than a funeral, and that's the anniversary of the disappearance, the TV news, the releasing of balloons, the silent tribute march.

A few kilometers from Brancion, a child simply vanished thirty years ago. His mother, Camille Laforêt, comes to the cemetery every week. The town hall made an exception and permitted her a tomb on which she could have inscribed the name of her missing son: Denis Laforêt. There's no proof that Denis is dead. He was eleven when he just vanished between his classroom and the bus stop opposite his school. Denis had left class an hour earlier than his friends. He was supposed to go to a study period. And then nothing. His mother looked everywhere for him. As did the police. Every family in the area knows Denis's face. It's "the missing child of 1985."

Camille Laforêt has often told me that having Denis's name inscribed on that false tomb saved her life. That having that name engraved on the marble kept her between the possible and the impossible: imagining that he might still be alive, somewhere, alone, without love, suffering. And every time she pushes open my door, sits at my table, has a coffee, says to me, "How are you, Violette?" she adds, "There's worse than death, there's disappearance."

As for me, I'd really got used to Philippe Toussaint's disappearance. I'd never have wanted to know.

I open the envelope containing the speech Julien Seul has written for his mother. The one he'll read on the day he finally agrees to place her ashes at Gabriel Prudent's tomb. A cursed meeting, that of those two. If Irène Fayolle hadn't met Gabriel Prudent, Julien Seul would never have set foot in my cemetery.

Irène Fayolle was my mother. She smelled lovely. She wore the perfume "L'Heure bleue."

Although born in Marseilles on April 27th, 1941, she never had a Midi accent. She didn't have the South in her genes. She was reserved, distant, spoke little. She always preferred the cold to the heat, skies that blocked out the sun. Even her physical appearance singled her out. She had a pale complexion, freckles, and blond hair.

She liked beige. I never saw her wearing colorful clothes or sandals, apart from a yellow dress in a photo taken on holiday in Sweden, before I was born. A garment that's like a wrong turn.

She loved English teas. She loved the snow. She took photos of it. In our family photo albums, there are only pictures taken in the snow.

She rarely smiled. She was often lost in her own thoughts.

By marrying my father, she became Madame Seul. Since she felt as if she were making a spelling mistake by not writing "Seule," to agree with "Madame," she stuck to her maiden name.

She only had one child, me. For a long time, I wondered whether it was me or our surname that made my parents stop wanting to reproduce.

First, she was a hairdresser, then she became a horticulturist. She created different varieties of rose that thrived in winter. Roses in her own image.

One day, she told me that she liked selling flowers even when they were for decorating tombs. That a rose was a rose, and whether it was destined for a wedding or a cemetery was of no importance. That on all florists' windows it said, "Weddings and funerals." That you couldn't have the one without the other.

I don't know whether she was thinking of the unknown man she'd chosen to spend eternity with, on the day she said that to me.

I respect her choice, just as she always respected my choices.

Rest in peace, dear Mom.

25.

*A mother's love is a treasure
that God gives only once.*

Léonine waited until I had finished painting all the walls in the level-crossing keeper's house to make her appearance.

During the night of September 2nd to 3rd, 1986, I had a first contraction that woke me up. Philippe Toussaint was sleeping against me. My daughter chose the right night to arrive: on the Saturday, there was a nine-hour break between the last train and the Sunday morning one. I woke up Philippe Toussaint. He had four hours ahead of him to take me to the maternity hospital and return to lower the barrier for the 7:10 train.

Léonine took too long for her father to be there when she let out her first cry. It was midday when I pushed her toward life.

Waves of love and terror engulfed me. A life that would count for much more than my own, and that I was responsible for. I struggled to breathe. I can say that Léo took my breath away. I started shaking from head to toe. Emotion and fear made my teeth chatter.

She looked like a little old woman. Within seconds, I felt that she was the elder and I the child.

Her skin against mine, her mouth seeking my breast. Her little head in the palm of my hand. Her fontanel, her dark hair, green slime on her skin, a heart-shaped mouth. The word "seismic" isn't too strong.

When Léonine appeared, my youth shattered as violently as

a porcelain vase on a tiled floor. It's she who buried my carefree girl's life. Within minutes, I went from laughter to tears, from fine weather to rain. Like a March sky, I was sunny spells and sudden showers all at once. My every sense was awakened, heightened, like those of a blind woman.

All my life, when coming across my reflection in the mirror, I wondered which of my two parents I looked like. When her big eyes stared at me, I thought she looked like the sky, the universe, a monster. I found her ugly and beautiful. Furious and gentle. Intensely close and unfamiliar. A marvel and venom within the same person. I spoke to her as if we were continuing a conversation begun a very long time ago.

I welcomed her. I caressed her. I devoured her with my eyes, I breathed her in, I spat her out. I inspected every centimeter of her skin, I licked her with my eyes.

When she was taken from me to be weighed, measured, washed, I clenched my fists. As soon as she had disappeared from my sight, I felt like a child, very small, helpless, useless. I called out to my mother. I didn't have a fever, and yet I called out to her.

I saw my childhood again, speeded up. How could I make sure that my daughter never had to live what I had lived? Were they going to take her away from me? As soon as Léo arrived in my life, I was scared that we would be separated. I was scared that she would abandon me. And, paradoxically, I wanted her to disappear and come back later, when I'd be grown up.

Philippe Toussaint came to see us in the afternoon, between the 15:07 train and the 18:09 one. I'd disappointed him. He wanted a son. He said nothing. He looked at us. He smiled at us. He kissed me through my hair. I found him handsome, with our child in his arms. I asked him to protect us, always. He replied to me, "Obviously."

And then there was the second seismic event. Léo was two

days old. She had just breastfed. I had placed her on my bent thighs, her little head supported by my knees, her little feet against my stomach, her two fists gripping my index fingers. I was looking at her. I was looking for her face's past, as if my parents were going to appear to me. I looked at her so much, the midwives told me I'd end up wearing her out. She stared at me while I spoke to her, I no longer remember what I was telling her. They say that babies don't smile, that they smile at the angels. I don't know which angel she saw through me, but she quite clearly stared at me and smiled.

As if to reassure me. As if to say to me, "Everything's going to be fine." Never have I experienced such a disturbing feeling of love.

The day before we were due to leave, Father and Mother Toussaint came to the maternity hospital in all their finery. She with precious stones on her fingers, he in absurdly expensive tasseled shoes. The father asked me if I would get "the child" baptized, the mother took her in her arms, even though Léonine was sound asleep in her see-through bed. She picked her up awkwardly, without asking me a thing, as if the little one belonged to her. The wicked stepmother made Léo's fontanel disappear into the fabric of her blouse. Hatred engulfed me. I bit the inside of my mouth hard so as not to cry with rage.

It's on that day that I understood that anything could be done and said to me, that my skin and my soul as Violette had become impervious, at my daughter's birth, to any form of annihilation. On the other hand, everything that would touch my daughter would permeate me. I would absorb everything that would concern her, a porous mother.

While cradling my child, Mother Toussaint spoke to her, calling her Catherine. I corrected her, "She's called Léonine." Mother Toussaint replied, "Catherine is much prettier." At that, Father Toussaint spoke to his wife, "Chantal, you're going too far." And that's how I learnt that Mother Toussaint had a first name . . .

Léo started to cry, probably due to the smell of the old woman, her voice, her tense fingers, her rough skin. I asked Mother Toussaint to give her back to me. Which she didn't do. She placed the screaming Léo in her bed, not in my arms.

And then we went home to the "train house," as she later named it. I held her tight, in our bed, in our bedroom. Philippe Toussaint slept on the right side, I on the left side, and Léo even further to the left. For the first two months of our lives together, I left her only to raise and lower the barrier. I changed her under the covers. I overheated our bathroom to bathe her every day.

Then there was winter, hats, scarves, her muffled up in her pram. Teething, fits of giggles, the first ear infection. Me taking her for walks between two trains. The people who leant over to look at her. Who said, "She looks like you," and me replying, "No, she looks like her father."

Then there was her first spring, a blanket laid on the grass, between the house and the tracks, shaded from the sun. Her toys, her starting to sit up well, and putting everything in her mouth between smiles, the barrier to raise and lower, Philippe Toussaint going off on his motorbike, but always returning in time to put his feet under the table. And then going off on his motorbike again. Léo greatly amused him, but for no more than ten minutes.

I think I succeeded in looking after my daughter, despite my young age. I managed to find the gestures, the voice, the touch, the attention. As the years went by, the fear of losing her went quiet. I finally understood that there would be no reason for us to abandon each other.

26

Nothing opposes the night, nothing justifies it.

S ince darkness is winning
  Since there's no mountain
  Beyond the winds higher than the marches of oblivion
Since we must learn
For want of understanding it
To dream our desires and live with "so be it"
And since you think
It's entirely obvious
That sometimes even giving everything isn't necessarily
enough
Since it's elsewhere
That your heart will beat better
And since we love you too much to keep you
Since you're leaving . . .

This is the song that is most played at funerals. In church and at the cemetery.

In twenty years, I've heard it all. From *Ave Maria* to "The Desire to Desire" by Johnny Hallyday. For a burial, a family once requested Pierre Perret's song, "The Willy," because it was the deceased's favorite. Pierre Lucchini and our previous priest refused. Pierre explained that not all final wishes could be fulfilled, either in the house of God or in the "garden of souls"—that's what he calls my cemetery. The family found funerary etiquette's lack of humor baffling.

Regularly, a visitor will place a CD player on a tomb. The

volume is never very high, as though to avoid disturbing the neighbors.

I've also seen a lady placing her little radio on her husband's tomb, "so he can hear the news." A very young girl putting speakers on either side of the cross on the tomb of a schoolboy, to make him listen to the latest Coldplay album.

There are also the birthdays that people come to celebrate, by laying flowers on the tomb or playing music from a mobile phone.

Every June 25th, a woman named Olivia comes to sing for a man whose ashes were scattered in the garden of remembrance. She arrives when the gates open. She drinks a tea without sugar in my kitchen without saying a word, apart from maybe a remark about the weather. At around 9:10, she makes her way to the garden of remembrance. I never accompany her, she knows the way only too well. If it's fine and my windows are open, I can hear her voice right inside the house. She always sings the same song, "Blue Room" by Chet Baker: *We'll have a blue room, a new room for two room, where ev'ry day's a holiday because you're married to me . . .*

She takes her time singing it. She sings it loudly but slowly, to make it last. There are long silences between each verse, as though someone were replying to her, echoing her. Then she sits down for a few moments on the ground.

Last June, I had to lend her an umbrella because it was pouring with rain. When she came over to the house to return it to me, I asked her if she was a singer, because her voice was so beautiful. She took off her coat and sat down close to me. She started talking to me as if I had asked her lots of questions, even though in twenty years, I had asked her just the one.

She spoke to me of the man, François, she came to sing for every year. She was a schoolgirl in Mâcon when she had met him, he was her French teacher. She had fallen in love with him, immediately, at the first lesson. She had lost her appetite over it. She lived only for when she would see him next. The school holidays were bottomless pits. Of course, she always made sure she was at the front, in the first row. She now focused only on French, in which she excelled. She was rediscovering her mother tongue. During that year, she had got 19/20 for some creative writing. She had chosen as her subject, "Is love a trap?" She had written ten brilliant pages on the love a man, a teacher, felt for one of his pupils. A love he dismissed out of hand. Olivia had written her piece in the form of a detective novel, in which the guilty party was none other than her. She had changed the names of all her characters (the pupils in her class) and the setting of the story. She had made it all happen at an English school. Cheekily, she had asked François:

"Sir, why 19? Why not 20?"

He had replied:

"Because perfection doesn't exist, *mademoiselle*."

"But then," she insisted, "why was the 20 score invented, if perfection doesn't exist?"

"For mathematics, for resolving problems. In French, as a subject, there are very few infallible solutions."

As a comment beside the 19/20, he had scribbled in red pen, "Excellent direct speech. You have applied your fertile imagination to serve an implacable literary construct. The subject is fascinating and handled with flair, lightness, humor, and seriousness. Bravo, your writing shows great maturity."

Countless times she had caught him watching her when she had her nose in her notebooks. And she'd chewed many a pen cap that year while watching him offer explanations for Emma Bovary's feelings.

She was sure this love was reciprocal. And, weirdly, they both had the same surname. This had troubled her, although their name, Leroy, was a common one.

A few days before sitting the French exam for the baccalauréat,

Olivia, one of a small group of pupils revising with François, had dared to say to him:

"Monsieur Leroy, if we married each other, nothing would change. We'd have no admin to go through, neither for our ID papers nor for the bills."

The whole group burst out laughing, and François blushed.

Olivia passed her French bac, getting 19 for the oral, and 19 for the written part. She sent a note to François, "Monsieur, I didn't get 20 because you haven't yet found a solution to our problem."

He had waited until after the bac to ask to see her for a one-on-one meeting. After a long silence, which she took as a symptom of love, he had said to her:

"Olivia, a brother and a sister don't marry each other."

Initially, she had laughed. She had laughed because he'd said her first name, when before he'd always called her *mademoiselle*. And then she had stopped laughing while he stared at her, intensely. She had remained speechless when François had informed her that they both had the same father. François had been born of a previous union, near Nice, twenty years before Olivia. Their father and François's mother had lived together for two years, and then separated, painfully. The years had passed by.

François had done some research much later and learnt that his father had remarried and was the father of a little girl called Olivia.

The father had concealed François's existence from his second family. They had seen each other again. François got himself transferred to Mâcon to be closer to him.

He had been shocked to discover that his sister was a pupil in his class. When her name was called, on the first day of term, he'd thought it an unfortunate coincidence when she had stopped whispering in her neighbor's ear to raise her hand at her name and whisper, "Present," while looking him straight in the eye. He had recognized her because they looked alike. He had noticed her because he knew; she hadn't noticed him because she knew nothing.

At first, Olivia hadn't wanted to believe it. To believe that her father could have concealed François's existence. She had thought that he was inventing this story to put an end to the seduction games of a capricious child. And then, when she understood that the story was true, she had said, with feigned light-heartedness, to François:

"We don't come from the same stomach, it doesn't count. I really love you."

Controlling his anger, he had replied to her:

"No, forget it, forget that right now."

Then there had been the final year. Their paths would cross in the school corridors. Every time she caught sight of him, she wanted to throw herself into his arms. But not like a sister into the arms of her brother.

He avoided her, bowed his head. Annoyed, she would do a detour to confront him and virtually shout at him:

"Hello, Monsieur Leroy!"

And he would reply, shyly:

"Hello, Mademoiselle Leroy."

She hadn't dared to ask her father anything. She hadn't needed to. She had seen how he had looked at François on the day the diplomas were handed out at the end of the year.

Olivia had caught a smile between François and their father. She'd felt like grabbing one to kill the other. Her tears and her anger welled up. She could see no way out, other than to forget.

After the diploma ceremony, there had been a celebration. Pupils and teachers took turns performing onstage. After some covers of songs by the groups Trust and Téléphone, François had sung "Blue Room" a cappella, with the same intensity as Chet Baker: *We'll have a blue room, a new room for two room, where ev'ry day's a holiday because you're married to me . . .*

He had sung it for her, gazing into her eyes. She had understood that she would never love any man but him. And that this impossible love was reciprocal.

And then off she had gone. Had been around the world more than once, and had qualified to become a teacher of literature herself. She had married elsewhere, to someone else. She had changed her name.

Seven years later, at the age of twenty-five, she returned to live with François. She knocked on his door one morning, and said to him, "Now we can live together, I don't have the same name as you. We won't get married, we won't have a child, but at least we will live together." François replied, "O.K."

They had continued to use the formal "*vous*" with each other, always. As though to keep a distance between them. To remain at the beginning, like a first date. Life had given them twenty years together. The same number as the years that separated them.

While drinking some port, Olivia said to me, "Our family rejected us, but we didn't suffer from it that much, our family was us. When François died, as if to punish us, his mother had him cremated here, in Brancion-en-Chalon, the town she was born in. To make her son disappear completely, she had his ashes scattered in the garden of remembrance. But he will never disappear, I will carry him forever within me. He was my soul brother."

27

*A weak dawn spills across the fields
the melancholy of setting suns.*

As soon as Léonine was born, I ordered a textbook to relearn to read: *The Little Ones' Day Out—Boscher Method*, by M. Boscher, V. Boscher, J. Chapron (primary-school teachers), and M. J. Carré. Toward the end of my pregnancy, I heard a primary-school teacher talking about it on the radio. She talked about how one of her pupils had had to redo his first year in primary school twice due to his illiteracy. How he didn't try to read, but rather to guess. He might say any old thing, or use his memory to pretend to read when he was actually reciting by heart. That is exactly what I had always done. So, the teacher had made him follow this reading method, and in six months, her pupil was reading almost as well as the rest of the class. This old method of reading was entirely syllabic. It didn't allow word recognition: it was impossible to cheat, to attempt to recognize or guess words or sentences.

For hours, while Léonine was still an infant in her pram, I read words out loud to her, "The street at midday, i ee i i ee ee i ee, feet, pin, beetroot, bin. Christmas holidays. ee o a i o ee a o, olives, hand, dominoes, apples, bottle. Toto tidied the table. To. Ti. Ta. Eric. The peel. The potato. The pram. The pig. Eric was polite at school. Cool. Pool. Stool. Tool. Fool. Wool. Mood i er. Poo dle. Coo ler. Noo dles. Soo ner. The doo dl er. The boo k shop. Sm oo th. Foot step. Ella hears a cuckoo, I look for you, my mother will loop the wool and knit a hood."

Léonine opened her big eyes and listened to me without

passing judgment on the slowness of my reading, the repetition, the pronunciation mistakes, the words I got stuck on, or what they meant. Every day I repeated the same syllables to her, until they just slipped out on their own.

The illustrations were colorful, cheery, and simple. Before long she was putting her little fingers on them. My textbook was stained as soon as Léonine could grab hold of it and crumple it. Spit, chocolate, tomato sauce, felt pen. She even cut her teeth on the cover. She put it in her mouth like she wanted to swallow it whole.

For the first few years, I hid this book. I didn't want Philippe Toussaint to fall on it by chance. If he'd discovered that I was learning to read properly, it would have been unbearable. It would have meant that I really was the poor, uneducated girl so despised by his mother.

I would take it out again as soon as he went off on his bike. When Léonine saw the reader, she squealed with joy, she knew that reading was about to begin. She would let herself be lulled by my voice, and look at the illustrations that she knew by heart. Little girls with blond hair and red dresses, hens, ducks, Christmas trees, grass, flowers, scenes of daily life aimed at very young children. Simplified, happy lives.

I told myself that I had three years to read fluently, that when she started nursery school, I would be able to do so. I managed much sooner than that. When Léonine blew out her first candle, I was on page 60.

I learned to read properly, without stumbling on words, thanks to this Boscher Method. I would have liked to tell this to the teacher on the radio, to tell her that her story had altered the course of my life. I phoned RTL, told an operator that I'd heard a teacher talking in one of Fabrice's programmes in August 1986, but the response was that it was impossible to trace if I didn't have the exact date, which I didn't.

Learning to read is like learning to swim. Once you've

learnt the arm movements, and got over the fear of drowning, crossing a swimming pool or an ocean comes to the same thing. It's just a question of breathing and training.

Very soon, I reached the page before last, and the story told there became Léonine's favorite. It's taken from a Hans Christian Andersen tale, *The Fir Tree*:

"In the forest there was once the sweetest little fir tree imaginable. It grew in a good place, where the sun could warm it, with good friends all around it: fir trees and pine trees. And yet it had but one aim: to be big very soon. The children would sit close to it; looking at it, they would say, 'How sweet this little fir tree is.' And the little fir tree couldn't bear that. To grow, to grow; to become tall and mature, that's the only happiness on earth, it thought . . . At the end of the year, the woodcutters always came to fell a few trees, always the finest ones. 'Where are they going?' the little fir tree wondered . . . A stork told it, 'I believe I saw them; they were standing tall, heads held high, on splendid new boats, and travelling the world.' When Christmas came, every year some very young trees would also be felled, selected from among the finest and sturdiest. 'Where might they be going?' the fir tree wondered. Finally, its turn came. And off it was carried, into a large and beautiful room with lovely armchairs; on all of its branches toys gleamed and lights twinkled. What brightness! What splendor! Only joy! The following day, the fir tree was carried off to a corner where it was forgotten. It had time to think. Looking back at its happy youth in the woods, and the joyous Christmas Eve, it sighed, 'Over, all that is over! Oh, if only I had been able to appreciate the fresh air and the warm sun when there was still time!"

I bought some children's books, some real ones. I read them, and reread them, a hundred times to Léonine. She's probably had more stories read to her than any other little girl.

It became a daily ritual, she never fell asleep without a story. Even during the day, she would run after me clutching books and stammering, "Story, story," until I sat her on my knees and we opened a book together. And then she wouldn't budge, fascinated by the words.

I'd closed *L'Oeuvre de Dieu, la part du Diable* at page 25. I'd hidden it in a drawer, like a promise. A postponed holiday. I reopened it the year Léonine was two. I've never closed it since. And still today, I reread it several times a year. I return to the characters as though returning to an adoptive family. Dr. Wilbur Larch is my dream father. I've made the Saint Cloud's Orphanage, in Maine, my childhood home. The orphan Homer Wells is my big brother, and Nurse Edna and Nurse Angela are my two imaginary aunts. That's the prerogative of orphans. They can do what they want. They, too, can decide who their parents will be.

L'Oeuvre de Dieu, la part du Diable is the book that adopted me. I don't know why I was never adopted. Why I was left to traipse from foster family to foster family, rather than being put up for adoption. Did my biological mother inquire after me occasionally, so I never would be?

I returned to Charleville-Mézières in 2003 to consult my file, that of a child given up at birth. As I was expecting, it was empty. Not a letter, not a trinket, not a photo, not an excuse. A file that could also be consulted by my mother, if she so wished. I slipped my adoptive novel inside it.

28.

There's no solitude that isn't shared.

This morning, we buried Victor Benjamin (1937–2017). Father Cédric wasn't there. Victor Benjamin wanted a civil burial. Jacques Lucchini set up his sound system close to the tomb and everyone gathered to listen to the song "My Old Man," by Daniel Guichard.

"In his scruffy old overcoat, off he'd go, winter and summer, in the chilly wee hours, my old man . . . "

No cross, or flowers, or wreaths, at Victor's request. Just a few funerary plaques placed by his friends and colleagues, his wife, and his children. One of Victor's children held their dog on a lead. He attended the burial of his master, sat when Daniel Guichard sang:

"Us, we'd heard it all before, no one was spared, the bourgeoisie, the bosses, the left, the right, even the good Lord, with my old man."

The family left on foot, followed by the dog, who seemed to appeal to Eliane. She followed them a little, and then returned to curl up in her basket. Too old for love affairs.

When I got home, I had the blues. Nono sensed it. He went off to buy a crusty baguette and farm eggs, and we made a nice omelette with some comté cheese I'd grated. We found some jazz on the radio.

On my table, among the leaflets from purveyors of salad seeds and cypress saplings, bills for plants, catalogues from Willem & Jardins, the postman had left a letter. I looked at its stamp of the Château d'If. It had been posted in Marseilles.

Violette Trenet-Toussaint,
Cimetière de Brancion-en-Chalon (71)
Saône-et-Loire.

I waited until Nono had left to open it.
No "Dear Violette" or "Madame." Julien Seul began his letter without any niceties.

The solicitor opened a letter that was addressed to me. My mother can't have had much faith in me. She wanted things to be "official." She wanted it to be him who read her final wishes to me, so that I couldn't renege on them, I imagine.

There was just one wish. To rest beside Gabriel Prudent in your cemetery. I asked the solicitor to repeat the name of this man I didn't know. Gabriel Prudent.

I told him that he must be mistaken. My mother was married to my father, Paul Seul, who is buried in the Saint-Pierre cemetery in Marseilles. The solicitor told me that there was no mistake. This was the final wish of Irène Fayolle, married name Seul, born April 27th, 1941, in Marseilles.

I got into my car, and entered "Brancion-en-Chalon, cemetery road" into my GPS, because "cemetery" didn't appear on the list of options. Three hundred and ninety-seven kilometers. I'd have to drive up France, it was a direct route. No detours or deviations, the motorway to Mâcon. Exit near Sancé, and drive ten kilometers along country roads. What had my mother been doing up there?

For the rest of the day, I tried to work, but it was useless. I hit the road at around 9 P.M. I drove for hours. I stopped near Lyons to have a coffee, fill up, and type "Gabriel Prudent" in the browser of my mobile phone. All I found was a definition of "prudence" on Wikipedia: "Founded on an aversion to risk and danger."

As I was driving toward this dead and buried man, I tried to recall my mother, the times I'd spent with her in recent years. The few Sunday lunches, an occasional coffee when I was passing through her neighborhood, rue Paradis. She would comment on the news, never asked me if I was happy. I never asked her if she was, either. She asked me questions about work. She seemed disappointed by my replies; she was expecting blood and tales of crimes of passion, when all I gave her was drug trafficking, lowlife crimes, and pickpocketing. Before I left, as she kissed me goodbye in the corridor, because of my job she always said, "Do take care, all the same."

I tried to think of any glimpse she might have given me of her private life—nothing. I found not the slightest trace of that man in my memories, not even a shadow.

I arrived at Brancion-en-Chalon at two in the morning. I parked in front of the cemetery, where the gates were locked, and fell asleep. I had nightmares. I was cold. I restarted the engine to warm up. I fell asleep again. I opened my eyes at around 7 A.M.

I saw some light inside your house. I knocked on your door. I wasn't remotely expecting you. When I knocked on a cemetery keeper's door, I expected to find a ruddy-faced, potbellied old man. I know, preconceptions are stupid. But who could have expected you? With your piercing, fearful, gentle, and wary eyes?

You made me come in and offered me coffee. It felt good in your house, and it smelled good and you smelled good. You were wearing a gray dressing gown, an old lady's thing, whereas you radiated something like youth. I can't find the words. A certain energy, something that time hadn't spoiled. It was as if you were disguised in your dressing gown. That's it, you were like a child who has borrowed an adult's clothing.

Your hair was gathered into a bun. I don't know if it was the shock I'd had at the solicitor's, the night driving, or tiredness that disturbed my vision, but I found you incredibly unreal. A bit like a ghost, an apparition.

In finding you, I felt for the first time like my mother was sharing her bizarre parallel life with me, that she'd brought me to where she really was.

And then you pulled out your burial registers. That was the moment I realized you were different. That women do exist who resemble no other women. You weren't a copy of someone, you were someone.

While you were getting ready, I returned to my car, ran the engine, and closed my eyes. I couldn't sleep. I saw you again, behind that door. You had opened it to me for an hour. Like part of a film I kept replaying to hear again the music of the scene I'd just lived through.

When I got out of my car and saw you in your long navy-blue coat, waiting for me behind the gate, I thought: I have to know where she comes from and what she's doing here.

Next, you took me over to the tomb of Gabriel Prudent. You held yourself straight and your profile was lovely. At each of your steps, I glimpsed the red under your coat. As if you were hiding secrets under your shoes. And I thought again: I have to know where she comes from and what she's doing here. *I should have felt sad that October morning in your gloomy, chilly cemetery, but I felt quite the opposite.*

It struck me, in front of Gabriel Prudent's tomb, that I was like a man who falls in love with a guest at his own wedding.

During my second visit, I watched you for a long time. You were cleaning the portraits of the dead, on their tombs, while talking to them. And I thought, for the third time: I have to know where she comes from and what she's doing here.

I didn't need to question Madame Bréant, the bed-and-breakfast owner, who told me that you lived alone, that your husband had "disappeared." I thought that "disappeared" meant "died." And I'll admit to you that, at that, I felt joy. A strange joy at thinking: She's alone. *When Madame Bréant specified that your husband had just vanished, from one day to the next, twenty years ago, I felt that he could come back. That the unreal state I had found you in behind your door, the first time, was perhaps due to that. To all those hours in limbo that this disappearance had imposed on you, between one life and another. A waiting room you'd been sitting in for years without anyone ever coming to call you or saying your name. As if Toussaint and Trenet were knocking the ball back and forth. It must have been that, that impression of disguise, your youth under a gray dressing gown.*

I wanted to know for you. I wanted to rescue the princess. Play the comic-strip hero. Take off that navy-blue coat to see you in your red dress. Did I seek to know through you what I didn't know about my own mother, and thus my own life? Probably. I broke into your private life to soothe my own. And for that I am sorry.

Sorry.

Within twenty-four hours, I knew what you seemed not to have known for twenty years. It wasn't hard for me to get hold of a copy of the statement you gave at the police station. I read in the notes of the sergeant you spoke to, in 1998, that your husband regularly deserted you. That it wasn't unusual for him to go off for several days, several weeks even, without telling you where he was staying during these periods of absence. No inquiry had been carried out. His disappearance hadn't been considered concerning. His psychological and moral profile, and state of health seemed to indicate that he had left of his own accord. I discovered that this disappearance was just a legend. Yours, and that of the inhabitants of Brancion.

An adult is free to stop contact with his or her family, and if their address is discovered, it will only be passed on with their consent. I don't have the right to give you Philippe Toussaint's details, but I'm taking it. It's you yourself who said to me, "If we had to do only what was part of our job, life would be sad."

Do what you want with this address. I've written it down and slipped it into the enclosed envelope. Open it if you wish to.

Yours ever,

Julien Seul

It's the first love letter I've received in my whole life. A strange love letter, but a love letter all the same. He only wrote a few lines to pay homage to his mother. Words he seems to have struggled like hell to get out. And he sends me pages. It's decidedly easier to pour one's heart out to a perfect stranger than at a family reunion.

I look at the enclosed sealed envelope that contains Philippe Toussaint's address. I slip it between the pages of a copy of *Roses Magazine*. I don't know yet what I'm going to do with it. Keep it in the sealed envelope, throw it away, or open it. Philippe Toussaint lives a hundred kilometers from my cemetery, I can't believe it. I imagined him being abroad, on the other side of the world. A world that's not been mine for a very long time.

29

The leaves fall, the seasons pass,
only memory is eternal.

Philippe Toussaint married me on September 3rd, 1989, the day of Léonine's third birthday. He didn't propose to me on bended knee and all that. He just said to me one evening, between one "I'm going for a ride" and another that "It'd be good if we were married for the little one's sake." End of story.

A few weeks later, he asked me if I'd called the town hall to schedule a date. He said exactly that, "schedule a date." The word "schedule" wasn't in his vocabulary. That's how I realized that he was just repeating a sentence that had been said to him. Philippe Toussaint married me at the request of his mother. So I couldn't have custody of Léonine if we separated. Or take off, from one day to the next, without a trace, as "those girls" do. Yes, in the eyes of Mother Toussaint, I would always be "the other one," "she," "that girl." I'd never have a first name. Just as she would never be Chantal for me.

For the afternoon of the wedding, we'd got ourselves replaced at the level-crossing for the first time since our arrival at Malgrange-sur-Nancy. We'd taken our time off in turns, but we'd never left our barrier together. It suited Philippe Toussaint, that way we could never go away on holiday. And during my time off, since he didn't change his habits, I worked.

The town hall was just three hundred meters from our level-crossing, in the Grand-Rue. We went there on foot: Philippe Toussaint, his parents, Stéphanie—the Casino checkout girl—

Léonine, and me. Mother Toussaint was her son's witness, Stéphanie mine.

Since Léo's birth, the Toussaint parents came to see us twice a year. When they parked their big car outside our home, our little place disappeared. Their affluence swallowed up our impoverishment as they reversed in. We weren't poor, but we weren't rich either. As a couple, that is. Over the years, I learnt that Philippe Toussaint had lots of money, but it was deposited in a separate account and his mother had power of attorney over it. Of course, we married with a prenuptial agreement. And we didn't go near a church, much to his father's dismay. But Philippe Toussaint wouldn't compromise.

Mother Toussaint phoned us regularly, usually at the wrong time: when the little one was in her bath, when we were about to eat, when the barrier had to be lowered outside AND Léo was in her bath. She would call several times a day to try to reach her son, who was often out, "going for a ride." Since I answered most of the time, I would hear her annoyed sigh followed by her voice, snapping like a whip, "Hand me over to Philippe." No time to waste. Too busy. When she did finally manage to get hold of her son, and the conversation ended by touching on me, Philippe Toussaint would leave the room. I could hear him lowering his voice as if I were an enemy, as if he had to be wary. What could he say about me? I still wonder today what on earth he could say to his mother. How did he see me? Indeed, did he see me? I was the person who fed him, did his work for him, washed things, repainted the walls, brought up his daughter. Did he reinvent Violette Trenet? Did he attribute habits to me? Obsessions? Did he conflate all his mistresses just to speak about one woman, his wife? Did he take a bit of one, a bit of another, a bit of both to piece me together?

The ceremony was led by the deputy mayor's deputy, who read three sentences from the Civil Code. When he said the words "that you do promise fidelity and support 'til death you do part," the 14:07 train drowned out his voice and Léonine cried out, "Mommy, the train!" She couldn't understand why I wasn't going out to lower the barrier. Philippe Toussaint replied yes. I replied yes. He leaned toward me to kiss me. The deputy, while slipping his jacket on because he was due elsewhere, said, "I declare you joined together by the bonds of marriage." Deputies of deputies doubtless do the bare minimum when the bride is not in white. As can be seen in the only photo taken by Stéphanie, and that I have left, of this union, Philippe Toussaint and I looked pretty good.

We all went for lunch at Gino's, a pizzeria run by Alsatians who have never set foot in Italy. Léonine blew out her three candles between two fits of giggles. The light shining in her eyes. Her amazed expression when she saw the big birthday cake I'd had made for her. I can still feel, and feel again, that moment, relive it on demand. Léo, and the same curls as her father.

Léo made me a loving mother. I always had her in my arms. Philippe Toussaint often said to me, "Can't you let go of that kid a bit?"

My daughter and I mixed up our wedding and birthday presents, and we opened them at random. It was joyful. Well, I, at any rate, was joyful. I wasn't in white on my wedding day, but, thanks to Léo's smile, I wore the most beautiful gown of all, that of my daughter's childhood.

Inside our gift-wrapped packages there was a doll, kitchen utensils, modeling clay, a recipe book, crayons, a year's subscription to *France Loisirs*, a princess outfit, and a magic wand.

I borrowed the magic wand from Léo and, with one wave, just one, I said to the little gathering as they tucked into the daily special, "May the fairy Léonine bless this marriage." No one heard me, except Léo, who burst out laughing and, reaching out for her magic wand, said, "My turn, my turn, my turn!"

30

Along this river where you loved to dream,
the silvery fish slipped by so lightly,
keep our memories, which can never die.

There's quite a crowd at my place this morning. Nono is telling his stories to Father Cédric and the three apostles. It's very rare for the Lucchini brothers to be together. One of them is always busy at the funeral parlor, but for the past ten days, no one's been dying.

My Way is sleeping curled up on Elvis's lap, and he, as usual, is looking out of the window and singing to himself.

Nono is making everyone laugh:

"And when pumping the water, sometimes we'd open graves or a vault, and they'd be full of water, and I mean to the brim. We'd put a hose inside to drain them, and I mean a hose like that!"

Nono gesticulates to demonstrate the diameter of the hose.

"When you switched the pump on, you had to hold on to it, that hose! Well, that Gaston, he'd left the hose on the avenue . . . just like that, down with the daisies . . . the hose swelled, and swelled, and then, BANG, water everywhere! And when that water had burst out like cannon fire, Gaston and Elvis, they'd drenched a posh lady! Straight in the chignon! Everything flying in all directions! The woman, her glasses, her chignon, and her crocodile handbag! Should have seen the state of her! First time in three years she was visiting her late husband, well, we never saw her again!"

Elvis turns around and sings: *With the rain in my shoes, rain in my shoes, searchin' for you.*

Pierre Lucchini joins in:

"I remember it! I was there! Good god, how I laughed! She was the wife of a foreman! The uptight sort who laughs as they burn. Stiff as a poker. While he was alive, her husband called her Mary Poppins because he dreamt she'd disappear and she never did, she was always breathing down his neck."

"But still, no one funeral is ever like another funeral," Nono continues.

"Just like the sunsets beside the sea," Elvis sings.

"And you've seen the sea, have you?" Nono asks him.

Elvis turns back to the window, without replying.

"Me," Jacques Lucchini picks up, "I've seen burials with masses of people, and others with five or six. But anyhow, as I say, they get buried all the same . . . But it's true that at funerals, there have been slanging matches over an inheritance, rowing in front of the coffin . . . The worst I saw was two biddies who had to be separated because they were tearing each other's hair out . . . Two hysterical lunatics . . . And my father, God rest his soul, took a few knocks that day . . . they were screaming, 'You're a thief, why did you take that, why do you want that,' they were hurling insults . . . how sad is that."

"Right in the middle of a funeral . . . nice . . . " Nono sighs.

"That was before you, Violette," Jacques Lucchini tells me. "It was still the old cemetery keeper, Sasha."

Hearing the name Sasha makes me have to sit down. Nobody had said it out loud in front of me for years.

"What's become of Sasha, anyway?" Paul Lucchini asks. "Anyone heard any news?"

Quick as a flash, Nono changes the subject:

"About ten years ago, a really old tomb was sold off . . . Everything on it had to be thrown away. We cleaned it all up, put everything into a skip, although we do return things to people if they want them. But that one, it was really ancient, a wreck, you know. I found an old plaque with the words, 'To my dear departed ones.' So, I chuck it into the skip. And then

I see a lady, well dressed, I won't say her name out of respect because she's a nice one, a brave one . . . She pulls that plaque, 'To my dear departed ones,' out of the skip and stuffs it in a plastic bag. I say to her, 'What on earth are you going to do with that?' And, like a shot, she answers, totally seriously, 'My husband's got no balls, I'm going to give it to him as a present!'

The men make such a noise laughing that My Way takes fright and goes up to my bedroom.

"And God in all that?" Father Cédric asks. "Do all these people believe in God?"

Nono hesitates before replying.

"There's those who believe in God the day he rids them of jerks. Me, I've seen joyful widows and happy widowers, and I can tell you that, in such cases, your God is mightily thanked, Father . . . Ah, come on, I'm just kidding, don't make that face. Your God, he does relieve plenty of suffering. It's simple, if he didn't exist, he'd have to be invented."

Father Cédric smiles at Nono.

"You see it all, in our line of work," Paul Lucchini steps in. "Sadness, happiness, believers, time passing, the unbearable, the unjust, the intolerable . . . in other words, life. Basically, us undertakers, we deal with life. Maybe even more so than in other lines of work. Because those who come to see us, it's them that remain, them that remain alive . . . Our father, God rest his soul, always said to us, 'Sons, we're the midwives of death. We deliver death, so make the most of living, and earn a good one.'"

31.

We were two loving each other,
Only I remain to grieve for you.

hilippe Toussaint's motorbike didn't take him very far
from Brancion. He lives exactly one hundred and ten
kilometers from my cemetery. He just switched regions.

I often asked myself a whole load of questions: *What made
him stop in another life and stay there? Did he fall off his bike,
or in love? Why didn't he warn me? Why didn't he send me a
letter of dismissal, of resignation, of desertion? What happened
on the day he left? Did he know he wouldn't come back? Did I
say something I shouldn't have, or was it that I didn't say anything?* Toward the end, I no longer said a thing. I got meals
ready.

He hadn't packed a bag. He'd taken nothing. No clothing,
no bits and bobs, no photograph of our daughter.

At first, I thought he was just lingering in another woman's
bed. One who spoke to him.

After a month, I thought he'd had an accident. After two
months, I reported him missing to the police. How could I
have known that Philippe Toussaint had emptied his bank
accounts, I had no access to them. Only his mother had power
of attorney over all of it.

After six months, I was scared he'd come back. Once I'd
got used to his absence, I got my breath back. As if I'd been
underwater for a long time, at the bottom of a swimming pool.
His departure allowed me to push off and rise back up to the
surface to breathe.

After a year, I said to myself: *If he comes back, I'll kill him.*

After two years, I said to myself: *If he comes back, I won't let him in.*

After three years: *If he comes back, I'll call the police.*

After four years: *If he comes back, I'll call Nono.*

After five years: *If he comes back, I'll call the Lucchini brothers.* More specifically, Paul, the one who's an embalmer.

After six years: *If he comes back, I'll ask him a few questions before killing him.*

After seven years: *If he comes back, it's me who's leaving.*

After eight years: *He won't come back.*

***

I've just visited Mr. Rouault, Brancion's solicitor, for him to send a letter to Philippe Toussaint. He told me that he couldn't do anything. That I must contact a solicitor specializing in family law, that was the procedure.

Since I know Mr. Rouault very well, I dared to ask him to do that on my behalf. To call a solicitor of his choosing and write the letter for me, without me having to explain, justify, beg for, or order anything. Simply to inform Philippe Toussaint that I wished to return to using my maiden name, Trenet. I told Mr. Rouault that there was no question of claiming alimony or anything like that, it would just be a formality. Mr. Rouault spoke to me about "compensatory allowance for desertion," and I replied, "No. Nothing."

I want nothing.

Mr. Rouault told me that, in my old age, it could make things easier for me, more comfortable. My old age, I'll spend it in my cemetery. I won't need more comfort than I already have. He persisted, saying:

"You know, dear Violette, maybe one day you won't be able to work anymore, and you'll have to retire, take it easy."

"No, nothing."

"O.K., Violette, I'll take care of everything."

He wrote down Philippe Toussaint's address, the one Julien Seul had scribbled inside the sealed envelope that I'd ended up opening.

Mr. Philippe Toussaint, c/o Mme Françoise Pelletier
13, avenue Franklin-Roosevelt
69500 Bron

"I hope you don't mind me asking how you found him again. I thought your husband had disappeared. After all this time, he must have had to work, must have had a social security number!"

It was true. The town hall had stopped paying him as a cemetery keeper a few months after his disappearance. That, too, I only discovered much later. The Toussaint parents received his paychecks and completed his tax returns. As level-crossing keepers and cemetery keepers, we'd never paid rent or utilities. I did the daily shopping with my salary. Philippe Toussaint used to say, "I give you a roof, I keep you warm, I give you light, and in exchange, you feed me."

Apart from paying for the upkeep of his motorbike, he'd not touched his pay for all the years we'd lived together. It was always me who bought his and Léonine's clothes.

"Are you sure this is really him? Toussaint is a common name. It could be his namesake. Or someone who looks like him."

I explained to Mr. Rouault that anyone could make a mistake, but not when you actually see the man you spent so many years married to. That even if he had lost his hair and put on weight, I could never confuse Philippe Toussaint with another man.

I told Mr. Rouault about the detective, Julien Seul, that he really *was* called Julien Seul, how he turned up at my cemetery, his mother's ashes, Gabriel Prudent, the research he'd done into Philippe Toussaint without asking my permission because of a red dress peeping under my coat, and the revival of Philippe Toussaint, who was living just a hundred and ten kilometers from my cemetery. That I'd borrowed Nono's car— "Norbert Jolivet, the gravedigger," I specified—that I'd driven to Bron, that I'd parked beside 13, avenue Franklin-Roosevelt, that No. 13 was a house not unlike the one I'd lived in previously, in Malgrange-sur-Nancy, when I was a level-crossing keeper in the east of France, except that it had nice curtains at the windows, an extra floor, and double-paned windows with oak frames. That opposite No. 13 there was the Carnot brasserie. That I drank three coffees there while waiting. Waiting for what, I had no idea. And then I saw him crossing the avenue.

He was with another man. They were smiling. They were walking in my direction. They came into the brasserie. I'd put my head down.

I'd had to grip the bar counter when Philippe Toussaint passed behind me. I'd recognized his smell, his particular scent, a mix of Caron's "*Pour un Homme*" and that of other women. He always wore their smell like a loathed garment. Must be the smell of his former mistresses that had clung like bad memories, and that I alone noticed. Even after all those years.

The two men had ordered two daily specials. I'd watched him eating his lunch, in the mirror opposite me. I'd said to myself that anything was possible, that he was smiling and that anyone could start a new life, that neither Léonine nor I had heard a word from him for a long time, and that no one knew that in his present life. That anyone could appear in one life and disappear in another. Here or elsewhere, anyone was capable of completely changing, of starting over. Anyone could be Philippe Toussaint, who went off for a ride and didn't come back.

Philippe Toussaint had got fatter, but he smiled openly. I'd never seen him smiling like that, back when we'd lived together. His eyes still showed no curiosity. He lived on avenue Franklin-Roosevelt and I knew that, even in this present life, the one in which he smiled more than before, he didn't know who Roosevelt was, that even if he'd changed his life, if, in that one, someone had asked him who Franklin Roosevelt was, he would have answered, "The name of my street."

Gripping on to my bar, I'd realized that I'd been very lucky that he'd gone and never returned. I hadn't moved. I hadn't turned around. I had my back to him. All I could see of him was his smiling reflection in the mirror.

The waiter had called him "Monsieur Pelletier," but the guy I took to be his friend had called him "boss" twice, and the waiter had said, "Everything on the account as usual, Monsieur Pelletier?" And Philippe Toussaint had replied, "Yup."

I'd followed him in the street. The two men were walking side by side. They had entered a garage that was about two hundred meters from the brasserie, the Pelletier Garage.

I'd hidden behind a car that looked as much of a wreck as I did when Philippe Toussaint had disappeared. Broken down, dented, scratched, left to one side until someone decided what to do with it. There must surely be a few motor parts to salvage. A bit of gasoline left in the tank. Enough to set off again. Finish the trip.

Philippe Toussaint went into an office shielded by glass partitions. He made a phone call. He seemed like the boss. But when Françoise Pelletier arrived ten minutes later, he seemed like the husband of the boss. He looked at her with a smile. He looked at her lovingly. He looked at her.

I left.

I returned to Nono's car. A parking ticket was wedged between the windscreen and the wiper, a fine of a hundred-and-thirty-five euros, because I was parked in the wrong place.

"The story of my life," I said, smiling at the solicitor.

Mr. Rouault remained speechless for a few seconds.

"My dear Violette, I've seen it all, in my time as a solicitor. Uncles who pretend to be sons, sisters who disown each other, false widows, false widowers, false children, false parents, false affidavits, false wills, but I have never been told a story such as that."

And then he showed me out.

Before I left his office, he promised to take care of everything. The solicitor, the letter, the formalities of the divorce.

Mr. Rouault is fond of me because whenever frost is likely, I take care of covering the plants, native to Africa, that he planted for his wife. Marie Dardenne, married name Rouault (1949-1999).

32.

My dear friends, when I die, plant
a willow in the cemetery. I love its weeping foliage.
Its paleness is sweet and dear to me, and its shadow
will fall lightly upon the earth in which I sleep.

In April, I put ladybird larvae on my rosebushes, and on those of the deceased, to combat greenfly. I'm the one who places the ladybirds, one by one, with a little paintbrush, on the plants. It's as though I repainted my garden in the spring. As if I planted stairways between earth and sky. I don't believe in phantoms or ghosts, but I do believe in ladybirds.

I am convinced that when a ladybird settles on me, it's a soul getting in touch with me. As a child, I imagined that it was my father coming to see me. That my mother had abandoned me because my father was dead. And since we tell ourselves the stories we feel like telling ourselves, I always imagined that my father looked like Robert Conrad, the hero in *The Wild Wild West*. That he was handsome, powerful, tender, and that he adored me from up in heaven. That he protected me from where he was.

I invented my guardian angel for myself. The one who arrived late on the day of my birth. And then I grew up. And I understood that my guardian angel would never have a permanent contract. That he would often have to sign on at the employment agency, and, as Brel sings, would get drunk "every night, on bad wine." My Robert Conrad aged badly.

Placing my ladybirds, one by one, keeps me busy for ten days, if I do only that. If there's no funeral in the meantime. Putting them on the rosebushes feels like opening the doors to the sun, letting it in over my cemetery. It's like giving it permission. A permit. That doesn't stop anyone from dying during the month of April, or from visiting me.

Once again, I didn't hear him arriving. He is behind me. Julien Seul is behind me. He watches me without moving. How long has he been there? He hugs the urn containing his mother's ashes. His eyes shine like black marble covered in frost, when the winter sun glints on it. I'm speechless.

Seeing him has the same effect on me as my closets: a black wool dress over a pink silk slip. I don't smile at him, but my heart is pounding like that of a child arriving late at the door of a favorite pâtisserie.

"I've come back to tell you why my mother wanted to be laid to rest at the tomb of Gabriel Prudent."

"I'm used to men who disappear."

That's all I'm capable of saying to him.

"Would you mind accompanying me to his tomb?"

I put my paintbrush down carefully on the Monfort family vault, and head for Gabriel Prudent.

Julien Seul follows me, and then says:

"I have no sense of direction, so in a cemetery . . . "

We walk side by side, in silence, toward avenue 19. When we arrive at Gabriel Prudent's tomb, Julien Seul puts the urn down and then moves it several times, as if he can't get it right, as if trying to find the right place for a piece in a jigsaw puzzle. He finally sets it against the headstone, in the shade.

"Since my mother preferred the shade to the sun . . . "

"Would you like to read her the speech you wrote? Would you like to be alone?"

"No, I'd prefer you to read it, later. When the cemetery is closed. I'm sure you know how to do that very well."

The urn is a forest-green color. "Irène Fayolle (1941–2016)" is engraved in gold. He gathers his thoughts for a few moments, I remain beside him.

"I've never known how to pray . . . I've forgotten the flowers. Do you still sell them?"

"Yes."

*

While choosing a pot of daffodils, he tells me he wants to go into town to buy a plaque. He asks me if I could accompany him to Le Tourneurs du Val, the Lucchini brothers' funeral parlor. I agree to, without thinking. I've never been to Le Tourneurs du Val. For twenty years now, I've been telling others how to get there, having never set foot in it myself.

I get into the detective's car, which smells of stale smoke. He is silent. As am I. When he switches on the ignition, an already inserted CD blares out "Elsass Blues," by Alain Bashung, at full volume. We jump. He turns it off. We start laughing. It's the first time Alain Bashung has made anyone laugh with this magnificent, but terribly sad, song.

We park in front of Le Tourneurs du Val. The Lucchini brothers' funeral parlor is right next to the morgue, but also to Le Phénix, the Chinese restaurant of Brancion-en-Chalon. It's the locals' favorite joke. But that doesn't stop Le Phénix being full to bursting at lunchtime.

We push open the door. In the window there are funerary plaques and bouquets of artificial flowers. I loathe artificial flowers. A plastic or polyester rose is like a bedside lamp trying to imitate the sun. Inside, various woods for coffins are displayed like in a DIY store, where you can choose the color of your flooring. There are the precious woods for making very special coffins. And then the woods of inferior quality—soft, hard, tropical—and plywood. I hope the love we feel for a living person isn't measured by the quality of wood we choose.

On nearly all of the plaques in the window are the words, "Warbler, if you fly around this tomb, sing him your most beautiful song." After reading a few of the texts Pierre Lucchini showed him, Julien Seul chooses, "To my mother" in brass lettering on a black plaque. No poem or epitaph.

Pierre is amazed to see me in his funeral parlor. He doesn't know what to say to me, even though he's been visiting my place several times a week for years, and wouldn't dream of entering my cemetery without coming to say hello.

I know almost everything about Pierre, his bags of marbles, his first love, his wife, his children's tonsillitis, his grief at losing his father, the products he applies to his scalp for hair loss, and now, it's like I'm a stranger in the middle of his plastic flowers and his plaques that speak only of eternity.

Julien Seul pays and we leave.

On the way back to my cemetery, Julien Seul asks me if he can invite me to dinner. He wants to tell me the story of his mother and Gabriel Prudent.

And to thank me for everything. And also in the hope of being forgiven for having researched Philippe Toussaint without asking me. I reply to him, "Fine, but I'd rather we ate at my place."

Because we'll have time, and won't be disturbed by a waiter between every dish. There will be no meat for dinner, but it will still be good. He tells me that he's going to book his room with Madame Bréant, even though it's never taken, and that he'll be back at my place at 8 P.M.

33

*Along with time, goes, everything goes, you forget
the passions and you forget the voices, telling you
quietly what pathetic folk say: don't get in
too late, above all, don't catch cold.*

Irène Fayolle and Gabriel Prudent met in Aix-en-Provence in 1981. She was forty, he fifty. He was defending a prisoner who had helped another prisoner escape. Irène Fayolle had found herself in this court at the request of her employee and friend, Nadia Ramirès. She was the wife of an accomplice of the defendant. "We don't choose who we fall in love with," she had said to Irène, between a root-lift and a blow-dry, "that would be too easy."

Irène Fayolle attended the trial on the day of Mr. Prudent's speech for the defence. He spoke of the sound of keys, of freedom, of this need to extricate oneself from ageless walls, to rediscover the sky, the forgotten horizon, the smell of coffee in a bistro. He spoke of the solidarity among prisoners. He said that close confinement could prompt a true brotherhood between the men, that freedom to speak was an escape route. That to lose freedom was to lose a loved one. That it was like a grieving process. That no one could understand this if they hadn't lived through it.

Just like in Stefan Zweig's *Twenty-four Hours in the Life of a Woman*, Irène Fayolle looked only at Mr. Prudent's hands during the speech for the defense. Large hands, which opened and closed. With pale, perfectly buffed nails. Irène Fayolle said to herself: *It's strange, this man's hands haven't aged. They have remained childlike, they are those of a young man. Pianist's hands.* When Gabriel Prudent was addressing the jury, his hands opened up; when addressing the counsel for the prosecution, they closed again, clenching so much that they seemed shriveled, as if resuming their true age. When he focused on the magistrate, they froze, when he turned to the public, they couldn't keep still, like two overexcited teenagers, and when he returned to the accused, they came back together, curled up like two kittens seeking warmth. In but a few seconds, his hands went from confinement to joy, restraint to freedom, and then to a kind of praying, or entreaty. In fact, his hands were just miming his words.

After the speech for the defense, everyone had to leave the court to go and have a drink in Aix while the jury was deliberating. The weather was lovely, as always in Aix, and that neither gladdened nor saddened Irène. Lovely weather had never had any effect on her. She didn't give a hoot about it.

Nadia Ramirès went off to the Saint-Esprit church to light a candle. Irène went into a random café, not fancying sitting at a terrace like all the others. She went upstairs to have peace. She wanted to read. The previous evening, when Paul, her husband, was already asleep, she had started a novel, which she now longed to get back to.

Mr. Prudent, who liked the sun but not the crowds, was there alone, sitting in a corner. Waiting for the verdict on his client, leaning against a closed window. Staring into space, he smoked one cigarette after another. Although he was alone upstairs, a smoky fug filled the room, right up to the lights. Before stubbing one out, he would use it to light the next. Once again, Irène froze at the sight of his right hand as it crushed the butt in the ashtray.

In the novel from the previous day, she had read that an invisible thread links those who are destined to meet, that this thread can become tangled, but never break.

When Gabriel Prudent saw Irène Fayolle at the top of the stairs, he said to her, "You were in court earlier." It wasn't a question, merely a comment. There had been many people in

the court. And she had been at the back, on the second-to-last
bench. How had he noticed her? She didn't ask. She sat in a
corner, in silence.

And as if he had heard her thoughts, he began to describe
to her the outfits worn by each member of the jury and the
deputies, by the defendants, and by all those in the public
gallery. One after the other. He used strange words to describe
the color of some trousers, a skirt, or a sweater, "amaranthine,"
"ultramarine," "whiting," "chartreuse," "coral." He might
have been a dyer, or a fabric seller at the Saint-Pierre market.
He had even noticed that the lady at the far left of the third
bench, "the one with a jet-black bun, poppy scarf, and linen-
gray outfit," was wearing a brooch in the form of a scarab.
During this extraordinary sartorial description, he flapped his
hands at certain moments. Especially when he needed to say
the word "green," which he hadn't said. As if this word were
forbidden him, he had used the words "emerald," "pepper-
mint cordial," pistachio," and "olive."

Still silent, Irène Fayolle wondered what, for a lawyer, was
the point of identifying each person's clothing

Once again, as if he had heard her think, he told her that,
in a court, everything was written in the clothing. Innocence,
regrets, guilt, hatred, or forgiveness. That each person chose
exactly what he or she wore on the day of a verdict, whether it
was on them or on someone else. Like for one's funeral or one's
marriage. That there was no room for chance. And that
according to what each individual wore, he was able to predict
whether it was someone from the plaintiff's side or the opposite side, the prosecution or the defense, a father, brother,
mother, neighbor, witness, lover, friend, enemy, or busybody.
And that he adapted his speech for the defense according to
the clothing and appearance of each individual when he
directed his words and eyes at them. And that, for example,
she, Irène Fayolle, from the way she was dressed today, it was

clear that she was not implicated in this business. That she was totally unbiased. That she was there as a dilettante.

"As a dilettante." He actually used those words.

She didn't have time to respond because Nadia Ramirès had just joined her. She told Irène that she was crazy to shut herself away in this bistro in such beautiful weather, that her man, he would have dreamt of sitting at a terrace. And that if he were acquitted, they would sit at every terrace in Aix, one after the other, to celebrate. And Irène Fayolle thought: *Well, my dream is to continue reading the novel at the bottom of my bag . . . or to set off for Iceland with the man* with the hands *who is chain smoking at the end of this room.*

Nadia greeted Mr. Prudent, told him that his defense speech was outstanding, that, as agreed, she would pay him a little every month, that *her Jules* would surely be acquitted thanks to him. And the lawyer replied, between two drags, in a deep voice:

"We'll know that later, after the deliberations. You're looking lovely, I really like the dragée-pink dress you're wearing. I'm sure it must have raised your husband's spirits."

Irène had a tea, Nadia an apricot juice, and Gabriel a draft beer with no foam. He paid for it all and left before them. Irène looked at his hands one last time; they were clutching his files. Two great pincers gripping the case in progress.

Irène Fayolle couldn't access the public gallery for the verdict; only family members were admitted. But she waited outside the court, at the end of the walkway, to observe the color of people's clothes as they came out. She saw the ultramarine sweater, the coral dress, the mint-cordial skirt, and the scarab of the woman with the jet-black bun. She clocked them all, one after the other.

Irène returned alone to Marseilles. Nadia Ramirès stayed in Aix to celebrate the acquittal of her Jules from terrace to terrace.

A few weeks later, Irène closed her hairdressing salon and took up horticulture. She felt that she wanted to do something else with her hands, she'd had enough of cutting hair, products full of ammonia, shampooing sinks, and, most of all, chatter. Irène Fayolle was, by nature, taciturn, too secretive to be a hairdresser. To be a good hairdresser, you have to be curious, amusing, and generous. She didn't think she possessed any of these attributes.

For years, soil and roses had obsessed her. With the money from her salon, she bought a plot of land in Marseilles's seventh arrondissement, which she turned into a rose-nursery. She learned how to plant, grow, water, pick. She also learned how to create new varieties of rose in tones of carmine, raspberry, grenadine, and "maiden's blush," all while thinking of Gabriel Prudent's hands.

She created flowers as though creating hands that open and close, depending on the weather.

A year later, Irène Fayolle accompanied Nadia Ramirès back to Aix-en-Provence for a second trial. Her husband had again got caught over some drugs business. Before leaving, Irène wondered how to dress so as not to look like a "dilettante."

She was disappointed. Mr. Prudent wasn't there anymore. He had left the area.

Irène discovered this in the car on the way from Marseilles to Aix when Nadia told her that she was worried because this time it wouldn't be Mr. Prudent pleading in her Jules's defense, but a colleague.

"But why?" Irène asked, like a child going on holiday who discovers that there won't be any sea there.

A divorce situation, he had moved. Nadia knew nothing more.

The months passed, until the day a woman entered Irène Fayolle's rose-nursery to order a spray of white roses to be delivered to Aix-en-Provence. As she filled in the delivery note, Irène saw that the roses were to be taken to Aix's Saint-Pierre cemetery, for Mme Martine Robin, wife of Gabriel Prudent.

For the first time, it was Irène who did the delivery, on the morning of February 5th, 1984, to Aix-en-Provence, where frost had appeared overnight. She took special care of the spray of flowers to be delivered. It took up all the space in the back of her Peugeot van.

At the Saint-Pierre cemetery, a municipal employee allowed her to drive along the avenues to deliver the roses close to the tomb of Martine Robin, who hadn't yet been buried. It was only 10 A.M. and the burial wasn't until the afternoon.

Into the marble had been engraved, "Martine Robin, married name Prudent (1932–1984)." Under her name, her photo had already been soldered: a beautiful, dark-haired woman smiling straight at the camera. The photo must have been taken when she was around thirty.

Irène went off to wait. She wanted to see Gabriel Prudent again. Even from a distance. Even from a hiding place. She wanted to know if he was the widower, if it was his wife being buried. She looked through the death notices, but found no actual mention of him.

"It is with great sadness that we announce the sudden death of Martine Robin, at the age of fifty-two, in Aix-en-Provence. Martine was the daughter of the late Gaston Robin and the late Micheline Bolduc. She leaves behind, in grief, her daughter Marthe Dubreuil, her brother Richard and sister Mauricette, her aunt Claudine Bolduc-Babé, her mother-in-law Louise, numerous cousins, nephews and nieces, and her close friends, Nathalie, Stéphane, Mathias, and Ninon, along with several others."

No mention of Gabriel Prudent. As if he had been crossed off the list of those permitted to grieve.

Irène left the cemetery and drove to the first bistro she found, about three hundred meters away. A transport café. She thought to herself: *Strange, this transport café stuck between the cemetery and Aix's municipal swimming pool. As if it lost its way.*

She parked, and then almost turned back because the windows were filthy and the curtains hanging behind them beyond old. But a shadow stopped her. Inside, a hunched silhouette. She recognized him despite the dirty glass. He was there. Really there. Leaning against a closed window, smoking a cigarette, staring into space.

For a few seconds, she thought she was hallucinating, getting confused, taking her desires for reality, in a novel rather than in life, real life. The one that's less fun than the life you promise yourself at fourteen. And also, she had only seen him once, three years ago.

He looked up when she entered. There were three men leaning on the bar and just Gabriel Prudent sitting at a table. He said to her:

"You were in Aix for the trial of Jean-Pierre Reyman and Jules Ramirès the year Mitterrand was elected . . . You're the dilettante."

She wasn't surprised that he recognized her. As if it stood to reason.

"Yes, hello, I'm a friend of Nadia Ramirès."

He shook his head, lit another cigarette with the dying embers of his butt, and replied:

"I remember."

And without inviting her to join him at his table, as if that were obvious, he ordered two coffees and two "calvas" by pointing his index finger at the ceiling and then the waitress. Once again, Irène Fayolle, who had never drunk coffee in her life—just tea—and even less so, calvados at ten in the morning, stared at Gabriel's large hands and sat in front of him. His hands still hadn't aged.

He was the first to speak, a lot. He said that he'd returned to Aix to bury Martine, his wife, well, his ex-wife, and that he couldn't stand stoups, priests, and guilt. So he wouldn't go to the religious service, just the burial, that he'd wait here, that he'd lived with another woman in Mâcon for two years, that he'd never seen Martine, his wife, well, his ex-wife, again since he'd left, that since he'd left her because he'd met someone else, his kid—who wasn't one anymore—wasn't speaking to him, that he'd been devastated by the news—Martine, dead!— but that no one would understand, that he would forever be the total bastard who had abandoned a wife, his own. And as postmortem revenge, Martine, his wife, well, his ex-wife, or his daughter, he no longer really knew, had had his name engraved on the tombstone. She had taken him with her to her eternity.

"And you? Would you have done that?"

"I don't know."

"You live in Aix?"

"No, Marseilles, I delivered some flowers this morning, to the cemetery, for your wife, well, your ex-wife. Before going back, I wanted to have a tea, it's cold, not that the cold really bothers me, on the contrary, but I was cold. Now, at least, calvados warms one up, I think it's gone to my head, in fact, I don't just think, it *has* gone to my head, I won't be able to hit the road straight away, it's strong stuff, calvados . . . Forgive me if I'm being indiscreet, I'm not normally, but how did you meet your new wife?"

"Oh, nothing original, because of a man I defended for years; through preparing his defense, explaining it to his wife, through returning to the prison year after year, we were the ones who ended up falling in love with each other. What about you, has that ever happened to you?"

"What?"

"Falling in love."

"Yes, with my husband, Paul Seul, we have a son, Julien, who is ten."

"You work?"

"I'm a horticulturist. Before, I was a hairdresser, but I don't only sell flowers, I cultivate them, too, I do some hybridization."

"Some what?"

"Some hybridization. I combine varieties of roses to create new ones."

"Why?"

"Because I like it . . . Cross-breeding."

"And what kind of colors does it produce? Two more coffee-calvas, please!"

"Carmine, raspberry, grenadine, or even 'maiden's blush.' I do varieties of white, too."

"What kind of white?"

"Snow. I adore the snow. My rosebushes also have the particularity of not being affected by the cold."

"And you, you never wear any colors yourself? Back in Aix, during the trial, you were all beige."

"I prefer bright colors on flowers and pretty girls."

"But you're worse than pretty. Your face has its whole life ahead of it. Why do you smile?"

"I'm not smiling. I'm drunk."

Toward midday, they ordered two omelettes with salad and a plate of fries to share. And a tea for her. He said, "I'm not sure tea and omelette go well together," to which she replied, "Tea goes with everything, it's like black and white, it goes with everything."

During the meal, he licked his fingers, he licked the salt off the fries. He drank a draft beer. As she combined English tea and her nth glass of calvados, he said, "Normandy and England are like black and white, they go well together."

He got up twice. She watched the dust, the static electricity around him. In the sunbeams, it looked like snow. And they ordered more fries, tea, and calva. Usually, in such a grimy place, Irène would have wiped the glasses on the lapel of her jacket, but not this time.

When the hearse drove past the café, it was ten past three. She hadn't noticed the time pass. It was like she'd entered this transport café 10 minutes ago. They'd been together for five hours.

They got up in a hurry, he paid in a hurry, and Irène told him to get in her van, she would take him there. She knew where Martine Robin's tomb was.

In the van, he asked her what her first name was. He said he'd had enough of addressing her as "*vous*."

"Irène."

"And I'm Gabriel."

They arrived at the gate that led to Martine Robin. He didn't get out. He said:

"We're going to wait here, Irène. What matters is that Martine knows I'm here. I couldn't care less about the others."

He asked if he could smoke in the car, she said of course, he lowered the window, he leaned back on the headrest, took Irène's left hand into his own, and closed his eyes. They waited in silence. They watched the people coming and going along the avenues. At one moment, they thought they heard music.

When everyone had left, when the empty hearse had driven past them, Gabriel got out of the car. He asked Irène to come with him, she hesitated, he said, "Please." They walked side by side.

"I told Martine that I was leaving her for another woman, I lied. To you, Irène, I can tell the truth, I left Martine because of Martine. The people you leave someone for, they're excuses, alibis. We leave people because of people, nothing more complicated than that. Of course, I'll never tell her that. And certainly not today."

When they reached the tomb, Gabriel kissed the photo. His

hands gripped the cross that stood proud on the headstone. He whispered words that Irène didn't hear and didn't try to hear.

Her white roses were at the center of the tomb. There were many flowers, loving words, and even a granite bird.

* * *

"But who told you all that?"

"I read it in the diary my mother kept."

"She kept a diary?"

"Yes. I found it in some boxes last week, while sorting her belongings."

Julien Seul gets up.

"It's two in the morning, I must go. I'm tired. Tomorrow, I'm hitting the road very early. Thank you for that dinner, it was delicious. Thank you. It's been a long time since I've eaten so well. And had such a delightful time. I'm repeating myself, but when I feel good, I repeat myself."

"But . . . what did they do after the burial? You must tell me the ending of this story."

"Perhaps this story doesn't have an ending."

He takes my hand and plants a kiss on it. I know of nothing more arousing than a gallant man.

"You always smell nice."

"'*Eau du Ciel*' by Annick Goutal."

He smiles.

"Well, don't ever change it. Good night."

He puts his coat on and leaves the house, road-side. Before closing the door behind him, he says to me:

"I'll come back to tell you the ending. If I tell it to you now, you won't want to see me anymore."

As I go to bed, I think how awful it would be to die in the middle of reading a good novel.

34

In our hearts you remain forever.

Three years after our marriage, in June 1992, the French railway came to a standstill. In Malgrange, the 6:29 train became the 10:20 one, which became the 12:05 one, until the 13:30 one stopped on the tracks at 16:00 and didn't move again for forty-eight hours. Strikers put up a barricade about two hundred meters from our barrier. The train was packed. It had been particularly hot that day. The passengers soon had to open the windows and doors of the Nancy-Epinal train.

The Casino supermarket had never seen so many customers. The stocks of bottled water had all been sold within a few hours. Toward the end of the afternoon, Stéphanie stopped checking the bottles through the register, instead distributing them personally on the steps of the train. No one made a distinction anymore between first and second class. Everyone was outside, in the shade of the train, around the tracks. The SNCF ticket inspectors and driver had disappeared at the same time.

Once the passengers realized that the train wasn't going anywhere, cars started to arrive, belonging to neighbors and friends. Some travelers phoned from our place to be collected. Others used the phone box. Within a few hours, the train and its surroundings had emptied.

All traffic in Malgrange-sur-Nancy was cut off. People came as far as the closed barrier, picked up the passengers, and turned back. By 9 P.M., the Grand-Rue was silent, and the

Casino was closing its doors. When Stéphanie lowered the shutters, she was bright red. In the distance, all you could hear now were the voices of the strikers. They were going to sleep right there, behind their barricade.

When night had already fallen and Philippe Toussaint had long since gone for a ride, I noticed that, inside the front carriage, there were still two passengers: a woman and a little girl, who must have been Léonine's age. I asked the woman if there was someone who could come and pick her up, but she replied that she lived seven hundred and twenty kilometers from Malgrange, that it was very complicated, that she was coming from Germany where she had just collected her granddaughter, and was going to Paris. She couldn't contact anyone before the following day, and even that wasn't certain.

I invited her to come and have supper at my house. She declined. I insisted. I took their suitcases without asking what she thought, and they followed me.

Léo was already sound asleep.

I opened all the windows, for once; it could get warm inside the house.

I gave some supper to little Emmy, who was exhausted. During the meal, she played with one of Léo's dolls, and then I lay her down beside Léo. Watching them sleeping side by side, I thought how I would like to have a second child. But Philippe Toussaint wouldn't agree to it. I could already hear him telling me that our place was too small to have a second kid. I thought how it was our love that was too confined to welcome a new child, not the house.

I told Emmy's grandmother, who was called Célia, that she must sleep at my place, that I wouldn't let her return to an empty train, that it was too dangerous. And I also told her that, for the first time in years, thanks to this strike, I was on holiday, that I had a guest, and that I hoped this railway line would be down for as long as possible, that at last I would be able to sleep more than eight hours in a row without being disturbed by the barrier alarm.

Célia asked me if I lived alone with my daughter. That made me smile. Instead of replying, I opened a very good bottle of red wine that I was keeping for "a special occasion," but until that day, there had never been one.

We started drinking. After two glasses, Célia accepted my invitation to sleep over. I would put her in our bedroom and we, my husband and I, would sleep on the sofa bed. We slept on the sofa bed when Philippe Toussaint's parents visited us— twice a year since our marriage. They would come to collect Léo to take her on holiday. One week between Christmas and the New Year, and ten days in the summer to go to the seaside.

After the third glass, my guest said that she accepted my invitation on the condition that she slept on the sofa bed.

Célia was around fifty. She had beautiful, very gentle blue eyes. She spoke softly, with a reassuring voice and a lovely Midi accent.

I said, "O.K. for the sofa bed," and I was right to. When Philippe Toussaint finally returned, he made a beeline for our room to collapse on the bed. He didn't even look in our direction.

I said to Célia, as Philippe Toussaint went past, "That's my husband." She smiled at me, without comment.

Célia and I carried on talking in the sitting room until one in the morning. The windows were still open. It was the first time since our arrival that the rooms had been so warm. Célia lived in Marseilles. I told her she must've brought the sun right into the house. That usually, the heat didn't get in, that there was an invisible barrier that prevented it from doing so.

When we had finished the bottle of wine, I told her that she could sleep on my sofa bed on condition that I sleep with her, because I had never had a female friend or sister, and that apart from my daughter when she was a baby, I had never slept with a girlfriend like real girlfriends do. Célia replied, "OK, girlfriend, we'll sleep together."

That night, I made a wish come true by making up a little for what I'd missed of friendship. All those nights when I would have liked to sleep at a best friend's, with her parents nearby, all those nights when I would have liked to jump over the wall with her to meet up with boys sitting on their mopeds at the end of the road, I made up for them a little.

I think we spoke until six in the morning. It had been light for a short while when I finally dropped off. At 9 A.M., Léo came to wake me up to tell me that there was a little girl who couldn't talk in her bed. Emmy was German, and spoke not a word of French. Then Léo asked a stream of questions:

"And why are you sleeping in the sitting room? Why's Daddy sleeping all dressed on the bed? Who is the lady? Why aren't there any more trains? Who are they, Mommy, these people? Who is that little girl? Is she from our family? Are they going to stay here?"

Sadly, no. Célia and Emmy left us two days later.

When they got back on the train, I thought I would die of sadness. As if I'd always known them. All strikes come to an end. Holidays, too. But I had met someone, my first girlfriend. Through the half-open window of the train, carriage 7, Célia said to me:

"Come and live with us in Marseilles. You'll be happy there, I'll find you some work . . . Usually, I don't pass judgment, but since France is on strike, let's say that I, too, am on strike and I'm going to tell you what I really think: Violette, it's obvious that your husband isn't right for you. Leave him."

I replied that I had already been deprived of my parents, that I would never deprive Léonine of her father. Even if Philippe Toussaint was a father in quotation marks, he was still a father.

A week after their departure, I received a long letter from Célia. In this letter, she had slipped three round-trip Malgrange-sur-Nancy–Marseilles train tickets.

She had a chalet in the Calanque de Sormiou and was putting it at our disposal. The fridge would be full. It should be enjoyed, at last. She had written that, "Enjoy it, at last. You will be able to have a proper holiday, Violette, and see the sea with your daughter." She also wrote that she would never forget that I had welcomed her into my home. That in exchange for those two days I had given her, it would be holidays every year in Marseilles.

Philippe Toussaint said he wouldn't go. That he had "better things to fucking do than going to a dyke's place." That's what he called all women he wasn't sleeping with, "dykes."

As for me, I told him that it was perfect that he wasn't going, that way he could work the barrier while Léo and I went there. He can't have liked the thought of us having a good time without him. He had a sudden fit of love: for the first time in six years, at his request, the SNCF found replacements for us within a matter of hours.

A fortnight later, on August 1st, 1992, we discovered Marseilles. Célia was waiting for us at the end of the platform at Saint-Charles station. I threw myself into her arms. It was even sunny on the platform, I remember saying that to Célia, "It's even sunny on the platform . . . "

When I saw the Mediterranean for the first time, I was in the back of Célia's car. I lowered my window and sobbed like a child. I think I'd had the shock of my life. The shock of the *majestic*.

35.

Everything fades away, everything passes,
except for memory.

Love letters, a watch, a lipstick, a necklace, a novel, children's stories, a mobile phone, a coat, family photos, a calendar for 1966, a doll, a bottle of rum, a pair of shoes, a pen, a bunch of dried flowers, a harmonica, a silver medal, a handbag, sunglasses, a coffee cup, a hunting gun, an amulet, an LP, a magazine with Johnny Hallyday on the cover. You find all sorts of things in a coffin.

Today, Jeanne Ferney (1968–2017) was buried. Paul Lucchini told me that he'd slipped a portrait of her children inside her coffin, as she had requested. Last wishes are often respected. We don't dare thwart the dead, we're too scared that they will bring us bad luck from the beyond if we disobey them.

I've just closed the gates of the cemetery. I pass in front of Jeanne's tomb, decked with fresh floral tributes. I remove the cellophane from around the flowers so they can breathe.

Rest in peace, dear Jeanne.

Maybe you've already been born elsewhere, in another town, on the other side of the world. There's your new family around you. Celebrating your birth. They are looking at you, kissing you, showering you with gifts, saying that you look like your mother, while here you are being mourned. And you, you are sleeping, you are preparing yourself for a new life with everything to be done again, while here you are dead. Here you are a memory, over there, the future is you.

***

When Célia's car took the steep little road down to the Calanque de Sormiou, I looked beauty in the eye. Léo told me that she felt sick; I took her on my lap and said, "Look, can you see the sea down there? We're nearly there."

We opened the chalet's shutters, we let in the sun, the light, and the aromas.

The cicadas were singing. I'd only ever heard them on the television. They drowned out our voices.

We pulled on our bathing suits without bothering to unpack our suitcases. The sea awaited us! We walked a hundred meters and, already, we had our feet in the limpid, pale-green water. From afar, the Mediterranean was blue, close up crystal-clear. All I had ever known was the chlorinated water of municipal swimming pools.

I inflated Léo's swan-shaped rubber ring and we entered the cool water, squealing with joy.

Philippe Toussaint made us laugh, he splashed us. He kissed me. He left salt on my lips. Léo said, "Daddy gave Mommy a kiss."

Léo's laughter on her father's shoulders, the cicadas, the coolness of the water, and the sun—it all made me giddy. It was like a merry-go-round going round too fast. I plunged my head under the water and opened my eyes. The salt stung me. I was ecstatic.

We stayed for ten days. I barely slept. Something within me refused to let my eyes close, a surplus of happiness, my emotions were off the scale. I had never seen my daughter so full of joy.

Whatever the time, it was daylight. Whatever the time, we swam. Or we ate. Or we listened. Or we contemplated. Or we breathed. Now, only three sentences left our lips, "That smells good," "The water's good," "That's good." Bliss makes idiots of us. It's as if we had changed worlds, as if we'd just been born elsewhere, into a blinding light.

During these ten days, Philippe Toussaint didn't go off for a ride. He stayed with us. He made love to me and I returned the favor. We exchanged our sun-drenched skin for a semblance of happiness. We were back to how we'd started, but without the love. It was simply for the pleasure, to revel in it all. Everything was far away. The Eastern sky, and the others.

Léo resisted when I covered her in sun lotion. She also resisted when I wanted to keep her in the shade. She had decided to live naked, in the water. She had decided to turn herself into a little mermaid. Like in the cartoons.

Over the ten days, I don't think we put shoes on. That's it, I've understood what holidays are about: not putting shoes on anymore.

Holidays are like a reward, a first prize, a gold medal. One has to merit them. And Célia had decided that I had several lives' worth of merit. One life for each foster family, and the one with Philippe Toussaint.

From time to time, Célia came down to see us. She came to inspect our happiness. And like a satisfied foreman, she would leave with a smile on her face, after having a coffee with me.

I showered her with thanks like others shower their wives with jewelry. I created entire parures of thanks for her. And I was far from done. It wasn't me who closed the chalet's shutters on the day we left. I asked Philippe Toussaint to do it. If I'd closed the shutters myself, I would have felt as if I were burying myself alive, closing up my own tomb. As Jacques Brel sings, "I'll make up crazy words for you that you'll understand." That's what I did so that Léo didn't cry when it was time to go, so that she didn't cling to the doors of the chalet screaming. I made up crazy words for her. The childhood ones, the simplest ones.

"Sweetheart, we have to leave because in a hundred-and-twenty days, it's Christmas, and a hundred-and-twenty days go very quickly. So we'll have to start that list for Father Christmas immediately. Here, there's no pen, no crayon, no paper. There's only the sea. And so we must go back home. Then, we'll need to decorate the Christmas tree, hang ornaments of every color at the ends of the branches, and this year, we're going to hang paper garlands that we're going to make ourselves, yes, all by ourselves! That's why we need to get back home very quickly, there's no more time to lose. And if you're really good, we'll repaint the walls of your bedroom. In pink? If you like. And then before Christmas, what's coming up before Christmas? Your BIRTHDAY! And that's in almost no time at all. We're going to blow up balloons, oh, quick, quick, quick, we must get back home! We've got so many fun things to do there. Put your shoes back on, sweetheart. Quick, quick, quick, let's pack the suitcases! We're going to see the trains again—and maybe they might even stop running them! And Célia will be in one of them. Quick, quick, quick, we're going home! And in any case, we'll come back to Marseilles next year. With all your presents."

36

All those who knew you miss you and mourn you.

Irène Fayolle and Gabriel Prudent left the tomb of Martine Robin, married name Prudent. Before leaving, Gabriel Prudent stroked her name engraved on the stone. He said to Irène: "It does feel strange to see your own name written on a tomb."

They walked along the avenues of the Saint-Pierre cemetery, stopping from time to time in front of other tombs, in front of strangers. To look at photographs or dates. Irène said:

"Personally, I'd want to be cremated."

In the car park, outside the cemetery, Gabriel said:

"What would you like to do?"

"What can you do, really, after that?"

"Make love. I'd like to take off all your beige and make you see all the colors of the rainbow, Irène Fayolle."

She didn't respond. They got into the van and drove as best they could, with all that love, alcohol, and sorrow in their blood. Irène drove and dropped Gabriel outside Aix's railway station.

"You don't want to make love?"

"A hotel room, like two thieves in the night . . . we deserve better than that, don't we? And anyhow, who would we be stealing from, apart from ourselves?"

"Would you like to marry me?"

"I'm already married."

"So, I've come too late, then."

"Yes."

"Why don't you use your husband's name?"

"Because he's called Seul. Paul Seul. If I used his name, I'd be called Irène Seul. It would be a spelling mistake."

They hugged each other. Didn't kiss. Didn't say goodbye. He got out of the van, his widower's suit all creased. She looked at his hands one last time. She told herself that it was the last time. He waved to her before turning and walking off down the platform.

She took the road back to Marseilles. Access to the motorway wasn't that far from the station. The traffic was moving well. In just under an hour, she would park in front of the house where Paul was waiting for her. And the years would go by.

Irène would see Gabriel on the television, he would be talking about a criminal case, someone he would defend, and of whose innocence he would be certain. He would say, "This whole case is built around an injustice that I will dismantle, piece by piece." He would say, "I will prove it!" He would appear agitated, the other man's innocence would gnaw away at him, it would show. She would think he looked tired, his eyes shadowed, that he'd aged, perhaps.

On the radio, Irène would hear a song by Nicole Croisille, "He was cheery as an Italian when he knows he'll have love and wine." And then she would have to sit down. Those words would knock her off her feet, would suddenly take her back to the transport café on February 5th, 1984. She would recall snatches of conversation between the fries, the gross curtains, the beer, the funeral, the white roses, the omelettes, and the calvados.

"What do you love most of all?"

"The snow."

"The snow?"

"Yes, it's beautiful. It's silent. When it's snowed, the world stops. It's like a giant shroud of white powder is covering it . . . I find that extraordinary. It's like magic, you know? And you? What do you love most of all?"

"You. Well, I think I love you most of all. It's strange to meet the woman of one's life on the day of the funeral of one's wife. Perhaps she died so I could meet you . . . "

"That's a dreadful thing to say."

"Perhaps. Perhaps not. I've always loved life. I love eating, I love fucking. I'm all for movement, amazement. If you fancy sharing my pitiful existence, to shed some light on it, you're most welcome."

When Irène Fayolle would think about Gabriel Prudent, she would think: *panache*.

Irène told herself that she didn't want to live in the conditional, but in the present. She put her turn signal on. She changed direction. She took the Luynes exit, drove past a shopping complex, and started driving very fast in the direction of Aix. Faster than the train timetables.

When she arrived in front of Aix station, she parked her van in a space reserved for staff. She ran to the platform. The train for Lyons had already left, but Gabriel hadn't got on it. He was smoking in the "Au Depart" brasserie. Since it was forbidden, the waitress had said to him, twice, "Sir, we don't allow smoking here." He had replied, "I'm not acquainted with this 'we.'"

When he saw her, he smiled and said:

"I'm going to go through your pockets, Irène Fayolle."

37.

I loved you, I love you, and I will love you.

Elvis is singing "Don't Be Cruel" to Jeanne Ferney (1968–2017). I can hear it from a distance. Gaston has gone off to do some shopping. It's 3 P.M., the cemetery is empty, only Elvis's song fills the avenues, *"Don't be cruel to a heart that's true, I don't want no other love, baby, it's just you I'm thinking of . . . "*

He often befriends a freshly buried person, as if he feels he must help them on their way.

The weather's really lovely. I'm making the most of it to plant my chrysanthemum seedlings. They have five months to grow, five months to burst into color for All Saints' Day.

I don't hear him going in and closing the door behind him. Crossing the kitchen, going up to my bedroom, lying down on my bed, going back down, kicking my dolls, going out through the garden behind the house, my private garden, where I grow the flowers that I sell every day to meet our needs, because he never did protect us.

"Baby, if I made you mad, for something I might have said, please, let's forget the past . . . "

Did he know that, today, Nono wouldn't be here? Did he know that this week, the Lucchini brothers wouldn't be coming? That no one had died? That he would be alone with me?

"The future looks bright ahead . . . "

I don't have time to react, I stand up, hands covered in soil, the seedlings and watering can at my feet, I turn around when I see his shadow, huge and menacing . . . a sword of ice cuts right through me. I freeze. Philippe Toussaint is there, motorbike helmet on head, visor raised, his eyes looking straight into mine.

I say to myself that he's come back to kill me, to finish me off. I say to myself that he's come back. I say to myself that I promised myself I'd never suffer again.

I have time to say all that to myself. I think of Léo. I don't want her to see this. Not a sound comes out of my mouth.

Nightmare or reality?

"Don't be cruel to a heart that's true, I don't want no other love, baby, it's just you I'm thinking of . . . "

I can't see whether the look in his eyes is one of disdain, fear, or hatred. I think he's looking me up and down as if I were even less than less than nothing. As if I had shrunk with time. Just as his parents looked me up and down, especially the mother. I had forgotten that I'd been looked at in that way.

He grabs me by the arm and grips it very hard. He hurts me. I don't struggle. I can't cry out. I'm paralysed. I never thought that, one day, he would lay his hands on me again.

"Don't stop thinking of me, don't make me feel this way, come on over here and love me . . . "

It's when living through what I'm living through now that you know everything's fine, that nothing's serious, that human beings have an extraordinary ability to rebuild themselves, to cauterize themselves, as if they had several layers of skin, one on top of the other. Lives one on top of the other. Other lives in store. That the business of forgetting has no limits.

"You know what I want you to say, don't be cruel to a heart that's true . . . "

I close my eyes. I don't wish to see him. Hearing him will be quite enough. Breathing him is unbearable. He grips my arm even harder, and says into my ear:

"I received a solicitor's letter, I'm returning it to you . . . Listen to me carefully, very carefully, NEVER write to me again at that address, do you hear? Not you, not your solicitor, NEVER. I don't want to read your name anywhere anymore, otherwise I will . . . I will . . . "

"*Why should we be apart? I really love you, baby, cross my heart . . .*"

He stuffs the envelope into my apron pocket and then leaves. I fall to my knees. I hear him starting up his motorbike. He's gone. He won't come back again. Now, I'm sure of it, he won't come back. He's just said goodbye to me. It's finished, over.

I look at the letter he's crumpled up. The solicitor instructed by Mr. Rouault is called Gilles Legardinier, like the author. The letter informs Philippe Toussaint that a request for divorce by mutual consent has been submitted on behalf of Violette Trenet, married name Toussaint, to the registrar at the court of Mâcon.

I go upstairs to have a shower. I scrub away the soil from under my nails. He's passed his hatred on to me. Transmitted it to me like a virus, an inflammation. I pick up my dolls, and put my bedcover into a plastic bag to take it to the dry cleaners. As if a crime had taken place in my house and I wanted to erase the evidence.

The crime is him. His footsteps in mine. His presence in my rooms. The air he inhaled and exhaled between my walls. I air everything. I spray a scent of assorted roses.

In the bathroom mirror, I'm scarily pale, almost translucent. It's as if my blood has stopped circulating. That it's all gone to my arm, which is blue. He has left imprints of his fingers on my skin. That's all I'll have left of him: bruises. I'll cover it up very quickly with a new skin. As I have always done.

I ask Elvis to stand in for me for an hour. He looks at me as if he can't hear me.

"Do you hear me, Elvis?"

"You're white, Violette. Very white."

I think of those youngsters I terrified a few years ago. Today, I wouldn't need any disguise to make them bolt.

38

The memory of the happy days soothes the pain.

And so, we returned home to get the garlands ready for the Christmas tree, cutting up bits of paper in the middle of August. We turned our backs on the sea, we did the same journey in reverse.

In the trains that brought us back to our barrier at Malgrange-sur-Nancy, Léo and I drew boats on the sea with turquoise felt-tip pens bought at the station, and suns, and fish and cicadas, while Philippe Toussaint tried out his tan on the girls he came across, on platforms we stopped at, in the train's bar, from one compartment to the next. He seemed delighted by all the looks he was getting.

When we arrived, our replacements were waiting for us on the doorstep. They barely greeted us. They didn't allow us time to open our suitcases. They told us that everything had gone smoothly, that there was nothing to report, and then left us just like that, leaving an unbelievable mess behind them, too.

Fortunately, they hadn't set foot in Léo's bedroom. She sat on her little bed and wrote two lists: one for her birthday and another for Father Christmas.

I started putting things away while Philippe Toussaint went off on a ride. He had to make up for lost time. The time he'd wasted with me in the bed at the chalet.

By the following day, I had cleaned everything and life returned to normal. I raised and lowered the barrier to the trains' rhythm, Philippe Toussaint continued to go off on rides, and I to do the shopping.

Léo and I went back to sharing bubble baths, and we looked at our holiday photos a hundred times. We pinned them up all over the house. So as not to forget, so as to be back there now and then, just for a glance.

In September, between two trains, I repainted her walls pink. She helped me, she wanted to do the skirting boards. I had to go over them after her, without her noticing.

Léo started primary school, and very soon we were back in our woolly cardigans.

We made our paper garlands and bought a synthetic Christmas tree, so it would do all our Christmases to come and avoid a real one being killed every year.

I thought to myself that it was the last year she would believe in Father Christmas, the following year it would be over. Some older kid would tell her that he didn't exist. All through life, we encounter older kids who inform us that Father Christmas doesn't exist, we stumble from one disappointment to the next.

I could have found it intolerable, Philippe Toussaint chasing anything in a skirt, but it suited me. I no longer wanted him to touch me. I needed sleep. I slept little between the last train at night and the first in the morning. I needed peace and quiet. And his body on mine was a disturbance that I had once liked, but no longer liked at all.

Sometimes I dreamt of a prince when I listened to songs on the radio. Male and female voices coming out with sweet, crazy, coarse words. Voices full of promise. Or when I told stories to Léonine in the evening. Her bedroom was my refuge, an earthly paradise in which dolls, bears, dresses, necklaces of glassy beads, felt-tip pens, and books slept, all mixed together, jumbled up, in a magical mess.

I could have found it intolerable, not speaking to anyone apart from my daughter and Stéphanie, the checkout girl at the

Casino. Stéphanie who commented on my purchases, which were always the same. Recommended a new dish soap to me, or said to me, "Did you see the ad on TV? You spray the product on the bath, you wait a good five minutes, and all the grime washes away. Well, it works, you should try it."

We had absolutely nothing to say to each other. We would never be friends. We would remain two lives that brushed against one another every day. Sometimes she dropped by to have a coffee at mine during her lunch break. I liked it when she came, she was gentle. She gave me samples of shampoo and body lotion. She often said to me, "You're a good mother, that's for sure, really nice as a mother." And off she'd go in her smock, back to her register and her shelves to be stacked.

Every week, Célia wrote me a long letter. I could read her smile in her words. And when we didn't have time to write to each other, we phoned each other on Saturday evening.

Philippe Toussaint would have supper with me once I had put Léo, an early sleeper, to bed. We'd chat about this and that, but never shout at each other. Our relations were at once cordial and nonexistent. Our relations were silent, but never violent. Although, couples who don't shout, never get angry, are indifferent towards each other, are sometimes suffering the worst violence of all. No smashing of china at our place. Or closing of windows to avoid disturbing the neighbors. Just silence.

After supper, when he didn't go off on a ride, he would switch the television on, and me, I would open *L'Oeuvre de Dieu, la part du Diable.* In ten years of living together, Philippe Toussaint never noticed that I was still reading the same book. When I didn't read, we'd watch a film together, but that very rarely brought us any closer. We didn't even share television. He often fell asleep in front of it.

As for me, I waited for the last train, the Nancy-Strasbourg at 23:04, and went to bed until the Strasbourg-Nancy at 04:50.

When I raised the barrier after the 04:50, I would go to Léo's bedroom to watch her sleep. It was my favorite thing. Some people treat themselves to a sea view, but me, I had my daughter.

During those years, I didn't hold it against Philippe Toussaint, leaving me in solitude, because I didn't feel it, didn't experience it, it just slid over me. I think solitude and boredom touch the emptiness in people. But I was full to the brim. I had several lives that took up all the space: my daughter, reading, music, and my imagination. When Léo was at school, and my novel was closed, I never did the washing, cleaning, or cooking without listening to music and dreaming. I invented myself a thousand lives during that particular life, at Malgrange-sur-Nancy.

Léonine was the bonus of the everyday. The bonus of my life. Philippe Toussaint had given me the most wonderful of presents. And, cherry on the cake, he'd given her his looks. Léo is totally beautiful, like her father. With grace and joy on top. Whether she was horizontal or vertical, I gobbled her up with my eyes.

Philippe Toussaint had the same rapport with his daughter as with me. I never heard him raise his voice at her. But Léo didn't interest him for long. She amused him for five minutes, but very quickly, he moved on to something else. When she asked him a question, it was me who answered her. I completed the sentences that her father didn't bother to finish. He didn't have a father's rapport with her, but rather a friend's. The only thing he liked to share with his child was his motorbike. He would put her behind the engine and go once around the block of houses, very slowly, to entertain her for ten minutes. And then, as soon as he accelerated a little, she was scared, she screamed.

He may have found the right buttons to press more easily with a boy. For Philippe Toussaint, a chick was a chick.

Whether she was six years old or thirty. And could never be better than a guy, a real one. One who plays football and races a supersonic truck. One who doesn't cry when he falls down, who gets his knees dirty, and can handle throttle levers and steering wheels. The complete opposite of Léonine, who was a candy-pink-with-sequins little girl.

She belonged to the Malgrange-sur-Nancy library. It was a room adjoining the town hall that was open twice a week, Wednesday afternoon included. Every Wednesday, between the 13:27 train and the 16:05 one, we would dash, hand in hand, to get Léo's quota of books for the week, and return those borrowed the previous week. On our way back from the library, we would stop at the Casino, where Stéphanie would give Léo a lollipop as I picked up a Papy Brossard "Savane" marbled cake. I would dunk mine in my tea, and she would dunk hers in an orange-blossom infusion after I had raised the barrier for the 16:05 train.

As soon as Léo was three years old, whenever a train was due, she would go out onto the landing to greet the passengers as the train went past our house. She would wave at them. It had become her favorite game. And some passengers waited for this moment. They knew they would see "the little girl."

Malgrange-sur-Nancy was just a level crossing, the trains went through without stopping; there were another seven kilometers to the next station, Brangy. Several times, Stéphanie took us in the car so that we could do the Brangy-Nancy round trip together. Léo wanted to ride in the train she saw going by every day, she wanted a ride on that merry-go-round.

Her cries of joy the first time we did this strange, pointless journey, I will never forget. To this day, I still sometimes dream of them. She would have been less thrilled going around an amusement park. We, of course, took the train that went past our house, where her father was waiting on the doorstep to wave at her as it went by. It's funny how happy children can be when you reverse the roles.

The three of us celebrated Christmas 1992 together. Like every year, Philippe Toussaint gave me a check for me to buy "whatever you want, but nothing too expensive, all the same." As for me, I gave him his scent, "*Pour un Homme*" by Caron, and some nice clothes.

Sometimes, I felt as if I were making him smell nice and dressing him for others, so that he continued to appeal elsewhere. And especially so that he continued to appeal to himself. Because as long as he liked what he saw, as long as he admired himself in mirrors or in the eyes of other women, he paid no attention to me. And I wanted him to pay no attention to me. You don't leave a woman that you no longer see, who doesn't make scenes, who doesn't make a noise, who doesn't slam doors—it's far too convenient.

For Philippe Toussaint, I was an ideal woman, one who is no trouble. He wouldn't have left me for passion. He wasn't in love with his conquests, I could smell it. He had their odor on his fingertips, but not their love.

I think I have always had this reflex, of being no trouble. As a child, in my foster families, I said to myself: *Don't make any noise, that way, this time, you'll stay, they'll keep you.* I knew very well that love had visited us a long time ago and had gone elsewhere, between other walls that would never again be ours. The chalet had been an interlude for our two salty bodies. I looked after Philippe Toussaint like you look after a housemate you have to play up to, for fear that one day he would disappear, taking Léo with him.

For Christmas, Léo received everything she'd written on her list. Books that were exclusively *hers*, including *Blue Dog* by Nadja. A princess dress, videos, a doll with red hair, and a new magician's kit. Even better than the one she got last

Christmas. With two new wands, magical playing cards, and mystical cards. Léo has always adored doing magic tricks. Even when tiny, she wanted to be a magician. She wanted to make everything vanish inside hats.

The following day, since it was a public holiday, there were fewer trains. Just one in four. I could rest, play with her. She made her hands disappear behind multicolored scarves.

In the evening, I packed her suitcase. On the morning of December 26th, as in previous years, Philippe Toussaint's parents came to collect my daughter to take her for a week in the Alps. They didn't stay long, but the mother and son had time to shut themselves in the kitchen to talk to each other in muted voices. She must have given him a check for Christmas, and me, like every year, I was entitled to dark chocolates filled with a cherry in liqueur. Not the Mon Chéri ones, but a lesser brand in pink packaging called Mon Trésor.

This time I was the one who went out onto the doorstep to wave at Léo when Mother and Father Toussaint's car drove off. She had a smile on her lips and her magician's kit in her lap. She lowered the window and we said to each other, "Until in a week." She blew me kisses. I kept them.

Every time I saw their very big car taking away my very little girl, I was scared that they wouldn't bring her back to me. I tried not to think about it, but my body thought about it for me—I fell ill, I was feverish.

Like every time Léo went away, I spent the week tidying up her room. Being in the middle of her dolls and her pink walls soothed me.

On December 31st, Philippe Toussaint and I rang in the New Year in front of the television. We ate all his favorite things. Like every year, Stéphanie had given us unsold hampers of food. "Violette, you must eat them before tomorrow because after that it'll be too late, O.K."

Léonine called us on January 1st, in the morning.

"Happy New Year, Mommy. Happy New Year, Daddy. Happy New Year, Daddy, Mommy. I'm going to try for my first star!"

She returned on January 3rd, glowing with health. My fever subsided. The Toussaint parents stayed for an hour. Léo had pinned her first star onto her sweater.

"Mummy, I got my first star!"

"Well done, darling."

"I know how to slalom."

"Well done, sweetheart."

"Mummy, can I go on holiday with Anaïs?"

"Who's Anaïs?"

39.

The essential is invisible to the eyes.

No one's dying right now."

Father Cédric, Nono, Elvis, Gaston, Pierre, Paul, and Jacques are deep in conversation in my kitchen. The Lucchini brothers have been going round in circles. It has been more than a month since anyone set foot in their funeral parlor. All the men are having a coffee around my table. I made them a chocolate marbled cake, which they are all sharing while chattering like little girls around a birthday cake.

I'm finishing planting my chrysanthemum seedlings in my garden. The doors are open. Their voices carry to where I am.

"It's because the weather's good. People die less when the weather's good."

"Got the parent-teacher meeting this evening. Can't stand it. Any case, they're all going to tell me my kid does bugger all there. Thinks of nothing but clowning around."

"Our business is all about the human. We encounter living people who are lost, who attach enormous importance to the ceremony going well because it will allow them to mourn, so it's a true service occupation, there's no room for error."

"I baptized two children last Sunday, twins, it was very moving."

"What makes our work different from all the rest is that we deal with the emotional, not the rational."

"Oh, we had a jolly good laugh!"

"Meaning?"

"That there's no room for error. For each family, there will be something that really matters. What suits one family won't necessarily suit another. It's all in the details. For example, for my last deceased person, there was just one thing that mattered: the watch being on the right-hand wrist."

"Saw a good film yesterday evening on the TV, with that actor, you know, the one who's blondish, his name's on the tip of my tongue . . . "

"And we can't make spelling mistakes on the death notices, either, there'll always be someone who is called Kristof with a K, or Chrystine with a Y."

"What time does Bricomarché close? I've got to go and get a part for the lawnmower."

"And it's all about the relations with the deceased. Between the husband and the wife, the children and the parents, in short, it's about dealing with the human."

"Hey, I ran into that little lady, what's she called . . . Madame Degrange, her husband worked for Toutagri."

"Gaston, watch out, you're spilling coffee everywhere."

"And we have to take care of the religious questions, and the whole emotional aspect."

"There's the hairdresser, too, that Jeannot, he told me he's had health worries with his wife."

"Paradoxically, very few people are in tears when they come through our door, they're just thinking coffin, church, cemetery."

"And you, dear old Eliane, what do you think? Are you after a bit of cake, or a stroke?"

"And when we talk to them about selecting music, readings, about what you can do, in homage, in memory, because there's plenty you can do, they do give us pretty free rein."

"It's been a while now that we haven't seen Violette's detective."

"Personally, I always find it strange when people come to

thank me and say, 'It was really beautiful.' We are talking about a funeral, after all."

"Personally, I reckon he's got the hots for her, have you seen how he looks at our Violette?"

"People have been buried for five thousand years, but the market's very recent. What we're doing is ridding the trade of its cobwebs."

"Yesterday evening, Odile made us caramelized chicken."

"Our funeral rites have changed. Before, everyone systematically went to put flowers on graves on All Saints' Day, but now people no longer live where their parents and grandparents live."

"I do wonder who on earth we're going to have as our next president . . . As long as it isn't the blonde."

"Nowadays, the management of memory is different: the dead are burnt. Customs change, the financial costs do, too; people organize their own funerals."

"It comes to the same thing. Left, Right, all they think about is lining their own pockets . . . All that matters is what we've got left in our wallets at the end of the month, and that, that will never change for the likes of us."

"Do you realize that in 2040, twenty-five percent of French people will organize their own funerals?"

"I disagree, never forget that they're the ones who vote the laws in."

"But that, that depends on the family, there are families that don't talk about death. It's like sex, it's taboo."

"But for you, Father, it amounts to the same thing."

"We're death's representatives on Earth. So to other people, we're bound to be sad."

"A nice, warm goat-cheese salad, with pine nuts and a drizzle of honey."

"You say 'funeral chamber' if it's private, and 'mortuary chamber' if it's public."

"For me, that's it, I've got the barbecue out again."

"Cleansing, dressing, complete preservation care. The law doesn't impose that yet, but it shouldn't be long, for reasons of hygiene."

"And a new shop's opening there, instead of Carnat's. A bakery, I believe."

"Proposed law: keeping the deceased in the home is no longer permitted."

"And all the fuses blew yesterday evening, I think it's the washing machine that's acting up and short-circuiting everything."

"I say that there's a place for the living and one for the dead. When you keep a dead person in the house, you risk not being able to mourn properly."

"She sure has a great figure. I'd have her in my bed, wouldn't be sleeping in the bath."

"For me, there's just one rule: to follow your heart."

"You going away on a little holiday this summer?"

"When I started, I told myself: *I will not do expensive coffins for cremations.* A rookie mistake. My father told me, 'Why, you think there's more point three meters under the ground? A family wanting to pay a fortune for a coffin that's heading for the flames, of course it's irrational, but you can't stop them from choosing an outrageously expensive coffin. You know nothing about people's lives, it's not for you to decide.'"

"Me, I say retirement is the beginning of the end."

"Over time, as I've dealt with more families, I realize that our father was right . . . There are many people who want to spend astronomical sums on the coffin, for what reason? I don't know . . . "

"We're going to Brittany, to the brother-in-law's."

"It's the guys from the council who are organizing it, it'll be early July. I, for one, really like fishing, I bother no one, apart from the fish, and even then, I chuck 'em back in the river."

"We have six days to bury someone, that's the law."

"He gives piano lessons. Been around for at least three years now. A tall fellow, always dressed like he's on TV."

"We're not permitted to split up ashes because, in the eyes of the law, they're a body."

"A little onion, and then you cook the mushrooms in the cream, delicious."

"Scattering ashes in the sea, you only see that at the cinema. The boat rocks, it's windy, and the ashes rise to the surface. The truth is, ashes must be thrown, in a biodegradable urn, about a kilometer from the coastline."

"So, how many kids still come to catechism, Father? Can't be a ton of them."

"With funerary contracts, people no longer want to spend thousands of euros on a family vault when their children live in Lyons or Marseilles. Lots of people say to us, 'We weren't keen on cremation, but after thinking about it, we prefer our children to benefit from the money while we're alive.' I tell them they're absolutely right."

"I have three weddings scheduled for July, and two for August."

"It's still a bit weird, organizing your own funeral. Seeing your name on a tombstone when you're not yet in the box."

"What I said to the mayor was, when it comes to roads with that level of traffic, we should do something. One day's never the same as another."

"People who plan their own funeral, they're not grieving, there isn't the shock of loss. So they spend half as much money."

"Well, the vet will be pleased!"

"In the funeral business, it's forbidden to forbid. But I do advise families against attending exhumations."

"Did you see it? That second goal, a masterpiece . . . Straight into the top corner."

"We must preserve a nice image of a person we've loved. It's hard enough to lose a loved one, to bury them . . . Fortunately, embalming has improved a great deal. Nine times out of ten, the result is really very attractive, the person appears to be sleeping. I apply a little makeup, so the skin looks natural again, I dress them up, and I use the deceased's usual perfume, which I request from the family."

"Don't know, have to see, maybe the cylinder-head gasket. If it's that, it'll cost an arm and a leg."

"It's serious, but not very, very serious, because I know what serious is now. Two weeks ago, I ripped the fender off the hearse, broke my phone, had leaks in the house—it's annoying, but it ain't serious."

"The other day, that Elvis, he opens the door of the technical office, and he comes face to face with the boss, that Darmonville, who was having it off with Mother Rémy. Sorry, Father. That Elvis, he about-turned and legged it."

"Tell people we love them, make the most of them while they're alive. I think I have more *joie de vivre* now than before. A perspective on things."

"*Love me tender . . .* "

"I'm not saying one should become a cold-blooded creature. I understand grief, but I'm not grieving. I don't know the deceased."

"It's harder when you have memories of the deceased. When you've known them personally."

40.

My grandmother taught me early on how to pick stars: at night, just place a basin of water in the middle of the courtyard, and you'll have them at your feet.

I went to Mr. Rouault's office to ask him to stop everything. I told him that he was probably right, that Philippe Toussaint had disappeared, that we'd leave it at that. That I didn't want to stir up the past anymore.

Mr. Rouault didn't ask me any questions. He phoned Mr. Legardinier in front of me, to tell him to stop proceedings. Not to follow up on my request. Today, whether I'm called Trenet or Toussaint really doesn't matter. People call me Violette or "Mademoiselle Violette." The word "*mademoiselle*" may have been erased from the French language, but not from my cemetery.

On my way home, I stopped at the tomb of Gabriel Prudent. One of my pine trees was giving shade to Irène Fayolle's urn. Eliane joined me, growled something, and then sat at my feet. Then, from nowhere, Moody Blue and Florence appeared, rubbed up against me, and then stretched right out on the tombstone. I bent down to pet them. Their bellies and the marble were warm.

I wondered whether Gabriel and Irène were using the cats to give me a sign. Like when Léo went on the steps to wave at the passengers in the trains. I imagined the two of them, when Irène had returned to Gabriel at Aix station. I wondered why she hadn't left Paul Seul, why she had gone back home. And what her final wish, to rest beside this man, really meant. Did she imagine that, although they hadn't had a life together, they would have eternity? Would Julien Seul return to tell me the rest of this story? These thoughts led me to Sasha, toward Sasha.

Nono turned up beside me.

"Dreaming, Violette?"

"If you like . . . "

"At last, there's a client at the Lucchini brothers'."

"Who?"

"A road-accident victim . . . in a bad state, apparently."

"Who is it? Did you know him?"

"No one knows who he is. He had no papers on him."

"That's strange."

"It's the guys from the council who found him in a ditch, apparently he'd been there for three days."

"Three days?"

"Yes, a biker."

In the funeral chamber, Pierre and Paul Lucchini explain to me that they are waiting for the police requisition order. In a few hours' time, the biker's body will go to Mâcon. The pathologist had put some forensic obstacle in place so an autopsy would be carried out.

Like in a bad TV series, with bad lighting and bad actors, Paul presents the body of the victim to me. Only the body, not the face. "There's no longer a face," Paul says. He also says that he doesn't have the right to show me the deceased.

"But for you, Violette, it's not the same. We won't mention it. Do you think you know him?"

"No."

"Why do you want to see him then?"

"To be totally sure of it. He wasn't wearing a helmet?"

"He was, but he hadn't fastened it."

The man is naked. Paul has placed a cloth on his genitals and on his head. The body is covered in bruises. It's the first time I've ever seen a dead person. Usually, when I deal with them, they are already "in the box," as Nono puts it. I feel unwell, my legs buckle, a black veil falls over my eyes.

41

The earth conceals you, but my heart still sees you.

On January 3rd, 1993, Mother Toussaint gave me a brochure before she left. Anaïs was Catherine's friend (my mother-in-law never called Léonine by her real name), she was the daughter of "very nice people" they had befriended during their holiday in the Alps. The father was a doctor, the mother a radiologist. When Mother Toussaint said the words "doctor" or "lawyer," she was ecstatic. Like me when I swam in the Mediterranean with a diving mask. To her, "frequenting" doctors and lawyers was the pinnacle of happiness.

Anaïs was in Léo's skiing group. They had gained their first stars together. By happy coincidence, Anaïs's family lived in Maxeville, near Nancy.

Every year, little Anaïs went on holiday to La Clayette, in Saône-et-Loire, and it would be nice if Léonine went with her in July. Anaïs's parents had even offered to come and collect Léonine on the way, and Mother Toussaint had said yes, without asking us, because "poor little Catherine, spending a whole month stuck beside a railway line . . . " Mother Toussaint always spoke about Léo as if she felt sorry for her. As if she had to take things in hand to save her from the great misfortune of being my daughter.

I didn't reply that the "poor little girl" wasn't unhappy beside the railway line, whatever the season. That between each train, we did plenty of things in the summer; that we inflated a swimming pool in the garden—of course, our swimming pool was small, but we could still swim in it, and we had great fun. We laughed in our plastic pool. But the verb "to laugh" didn't feature in Philippe Toussaint's parents' vocabulary.

I merely said that in August we were going back to Sormiou, but if Léo wanted to go away with a friend in July, why not.

Once the Toussaint parents had gone, I looked at the brochure for the Notre-Dame-des-Prés holiday camp in La Clayette. "Only our reliability never takes a holiday." Beneath the slogan, there were the general conditions for enrollment, and in the photos, a blue sky. Rain must have been banned by the person who had compiled the promotional brochure. On the first page, there was a photo of a very fine château and a large lake. On the next page, a refectory where children aged about ten were eating; a studio with the same children painting; the lakeside beach with the same children swimming; and finally, in the biggest picture, some impressive countryside where the same children were riding ponies.

Why is it that all little girls dream of riding a pony?

Personally, I was wary of ponies after seeing the film *Gone with the Wind*. I was more fearful of Léo riding a pony than of her riding on the back of Philippe Toussaint's motorbike.

Mother Toussaint had drummed the idea into Léo's head, "This summer, you're going to go pony riding in the countryside with Anaïs." The magic words, the words that make all seven-year-old little girls dream.

The months and the trains went by. Léonine learned to tell the difference between a tale, a diary, a dictionary, a poem, and an essay. She solved some problems, "I get 30 francs for Christmas, I buy a sweater for 10 francs, a cake for 2 francs, and then Mommy gives me 5 francs in pocket money, how much do I have left at Easter?" She learnt about France, its position on the map, its major cities, its place in Europe, in the world. She drew a red spot on Marseilles. She did magic tricks. She made everything vanish, apart from the mess in her room.

Then, on her report card, she proudly showed me, "Promote to next grade."

On July 13th, 1993, Anaïs's parents came to our place to take away my daughter.

They were charming. They were like the holiday-camp brochure. There was only blue sky in their eyes. Léo threw herself into the arms of Anaïs. The little girls couldn't stop laughing. I even thought to myself: *Léo doesn't laugh as much with me.*

"I'm tired, I'd like to rest . . . "

Julien Seul is facing me. He looks drawn. Perhaps it's the wan light from the walls of the hospital room. It was Nono who called him after paramedics picked me up from the Lucchini brothers' floor. Nono thinks we're lovers and that Julien Seul will take care of me. Nono is wrong, no one will take care of me apart from me.

All that I'm able to say to the detective, who seems concerned for me, is, "I'm tired, I'd like to rest."

If Irène Fayolle hadn't turned back between Aix and Marseilles to rejoin Gabriel Prudent at the station, Julien Seul would never have entered my cemetery. If Julien Seul hadn't noticed my red dress peeping out from under my coat on the morning I took him to Gabriel Prudent's tomb, he would never have got mixed up in my life. If he hadn't got mixed up in my life, he wouldn't have found Philippe Toussaint. And if Philippe Toussaint hadn't received my request for a divorce, he would never have returned to Brancion. That's all it takes.

I told no one that Philippe Toussaint had come to my house last week, not even Nono.

The first thing Julien Seul noticed, on entering my hospital room, was my arms. He doesn't miss a thing. He said nothing, but I felt his eyes focusing on my bruises.

But there's something crazier: when he left my place, Philippe Toussaint was killed at exactly the same spot as Reine Ducha (1961–1982), the young woman who died in an accident about three hundred meters from the cemetery, and who, some say, appears at the side of the road on summer nights.

Did Philippe Toussaint see her? Why hadn't he fastened his helmet, when he hadn't removed it between arriving at and leaving my place? Why didn't he have any identity papers?

Julien Seul gets up, telling me he'll be back later. Before leaving my room, he asks me if I need anything. I shake my head and close my eyes. And I go over everything for the thousandth time, maybe more, maybe less.

Anaïs's parents didn't set off immediately. They wanted to "get acquainted." Give the girls time to catch up. We went to Gino's, the pizzeria run by the Alsatians who have never set foot in Italy. Philippe Toussaint stayed at home to take care of the barrier and the "midday trains": 12:14, 13:08, and 14:06. It suited him fine. He loathed making conversation with people he didn't know, and for him, talking about holidays, children, and ponies, that was chick stuff.

The girls had a pizza topped with a fried egg, while chatting about ponies, swimming suits, school, that first star, magic tricks, and sun cream.

Anaïs's parents, Armelle and Jean-Louis Caussin, went for the daily special. I copied them, thinking that it should be me paying the bill. That that was the least I could do, since they were covering Léonine's transport. Since I had just finished paying for the holiday camp, I risked going into the red.

I thought about that all through the meal, between each mouthful. I wondered how I was going to deal with this overdraft at the bank, with it not being authorized. I was adding everything up in my head: *Three daily specials, plus two children's meals, plus five drinks.* I remember saying to myself: *Thank goodness they're driving, there won't be any wine.* Philippe Toussaint still gave me nothing. All three of us lived on my salary. I had to count every centime.

I also remember that they said to me: "You're so young, at what age did you have Catherine?" They didn't know that Léonine was called Léonine. And I remember Léo dipping her pizza dough into the egg yolk. She said, "A poke in the eye for you!" And she laughed.

And I remember thinking to myself: *That's it, she's a big girl now, she has a real friend. My first friend, it took a train strike for me to meet her at the age of twenty-four.*

I was saying, "Yes . . . no . . . oh . . . ah . . . O.K. . . . that's wonderful," while gazing now and then at the Caussins' beautiful blue eyes, but I wasn't listening to them. I was finding it hard to tear my eyes away from Léo. And I was counting: *Three daily specials, plus two children's meals, plus five drinks.*

Léo punctuated her sentences with laughter. She'd just lost two teeth. Her smile was like a piano abandoned in an attic. I'd done her hair in two braids, more practical for traveling.

Before leaving the restaurant, she made the paper napkins vanish. I would have loved her to make the bill vanish. I paid by check, quaking with fear. Thinking that if it bounced, I would die of shame. It's strange, I presume that all of Malgrange knew that my husband was cheating on me, but people's looks in Grand-Rue didn't bother me. On the other hand, if it had been known that I wrote bouncing checks, I would never have left the house again.

We made our way back to the barrier. Léo got into the Caussins' car, in the back, next to Anaïs. She almost forgot her *doudou*; she'd hidden it in my handbag so Anaïs wouldn't know she needed it for the journey. I made her take some Cocculine because she got carsick and there were three hundred and forty-eight kilometers to be covered. I slipped the tube in her pocket for the return journey.

They would be arriving late afternoon, they would call me when they did.

During the afternoon, while tidying Léo's things, I found the list I'd written a fortnight earlier so I wouldn't forget anything when packing her suitcase.

Pocket money, 2 swimming suits, 7 undershirts, 7 pairs of underwear, sandals, sneakers (riding boots supplied), sun cream, hat, sunglasses, 3 dresses, 2 dungarees, 2 shorts, 3 trousers, 5 T-shirts (sheets and towels supplied), 2 swimming towels, 3 comics, mild + anti-lice shampoo, toothbrush, strawberry toothpaste, 1 warm sweater and 1 cardigan for evening + rain cape + 1 pen and sketchbook. Disposable camera + magician's kit.
Doudou.

Close to 9 P.M., Léo phoned me, overexcited, everything was REALLY great. When she'd arrived at the camp, she'd seen the really cute ponies, she'd given them some bread and carrots, which was really cool, the weather was really lovely, the bedrooms were really pretty, there were two bunk beds in each room, Anaïs would sleep in the bottom bed and she in the top. After eating she'd done some magic tricks, everyone had really laughed. The supervisors were really nice, there was one who really looked like me. No, I couldn't hand her over to Daddy, he'd gone for a ride. "Love you, Mommy, big kiss. Big kiss to Daddy."

After hanging up, I went out into my little patch of garden. I saw a Barbie swimming on her back in the plastic swimming pool. The water had turned green. I emptied it out. The water ran along the rose bushes. I would fill it again the following week, when Léo would be back home.

42

Love is when you meet someone who gives you news about yourself.

J ulien Seul came to pick me up from the hospital. We drove in silence. He left for Marseilles immediately after dropping me off outside my house. Detective Seul told me he'd be back soon. He took my right hand and placed a kiss on it. It was the second one since we've known each other.

I returned to my cemetery with a prescription for tonic and vitamin D. And test results that were good. Eliane was waiting for me at the door. In the house, Elvis, Gaston, and Nono were also waiting for me. Gaston's wife had prepared a meal for me that just needed heating up. They gently teased me because I had passed out at the sight of a dead body, and "for the keeper of a cemetery, that really takes the cake!"

I asked for news of the dead man like one asks for news of a retired colleague. The body of the "unknown biker" was taken to Mâcon. No one knew who he was. His bike wasn't registered, and it was a standard model from which the serial number had been removed. Probably a stolen bike. The police had issued a description.

Nono showed me the article in the *Journal de Saône-et-Loire*, headlined: "Cursed bend."

It's been described as a tragic accident in the very place that Reine Ducha met her death in 1982. The biker hadn't fastened his helmet and was riding at high speed. He was disfigured. Hence the impossibility of taking a photograph for identification, and using an Identikit picture instead.

*

I look at the Identikit, which has been sketched. Philippe Toussaint is unrecognizable. In the caption it says, "Man of around fifty-five years old, light skin, brown hair, blue eyes, 1.88m, no tattoos or distinguishing features. No jewelry. White T-shirt. Levi's jeans. Black boots and black leather biker jacket with Furygan label. For all inquiries, go to nearest police station, or telephone 17 (emergency services and police stations)."

Who is going to look for him? Françoise Pelletier, I imagine. Did he have friends apart from her? When we lived together, he had mistresses, but not friends. Two or three fellow bikers in Charleville and Malgrange. And his parents. But his parents are dead now.

I don't dwell on the pages of the newspaper. I go up to my bedroom to have a shower and change. When I open my summer and winter wardrobe, I wonder whether to put on my pink dress under my raincoat, or wear a black dress. I'm a widow and no one knows it.

I did recognize him in the mortuary chamber. I recognized his body. I think that, after the horror, it was disgust that made me fall to the ground. Disgust at him. The hatred, when he came to terrorize me in my garden, the hatred of him, which he passed on to me through my arm that he gripped too hard. So hard that I still have some marks.

I've always worn colors under my dark clothes to cock a snook at death. Like the women who wear makeup under their burka. Today, I feel like doing the opposite. I feel like putting on a black dress, and slipping a pink coat over it. But I would never do that, out of respect for others, for those who remain, and who pace up and down the avenues of my cemetery. And I've never owned a pink coat.

I go back down to the kitchen, avoiding tripping on my

vacuum-packed dolls, pour myself a drop of port at the bottom of a glass, and wish myself good health.

I set off to do the tour of my cemetery. Eliane follows me. I cover all four wings, Bays, Spindles, Cedars, and Yews. All in perfect order. The ladybirds are starting to appear. The tomb of Juliette Montrachet (1898–1962) is just as beautiful.

From time to time, I pick up pots of flowers that have fallen over. José-Luis Fernandez is there. He's watering his wife's flowers. Tutti Frutti is keeping him company. Madames Pinto and Degrange, too. They are each scratching the surrounds of their husbands' tombs in silence. They are scratching at earth that can't take any more scratching. The weeds surrendered long ago.

I come across a couple I know by sight. The woman comes occasionally to visit the tomb of her sister, Nadine Ribeau (1954–2007). We exchange greetings.

It's not raining anymore. It's pleasant. I'm hungry. Philippe Toussaint's death hasn't ruined my appetite. I feel the silk of my pink dress brushing against my thighs. I say to myself that Léo won't have to go through that. Burying her father. Me neither.

By choosing to disappear from my life, Philippe Toussaint chose to disappear from his death. I won't have to scratch around his tomb, or buy flowers for him. I think back to the love we made when we were young. It's been years since I made love. In the Yew wing, I make for the children's section.

Most of the tombs are white. There are angels everywhere, on the plaques, on the banks of flowers, on the tombstones. There are pink hearts and teddy bears, many candles, and an abundance of poems.

Today, no parents. When they come, it's often after work, at around five or six o'clock, and often the same parents. At first, they spend all day there. Numb. Dazed with grief. Dead drunk. More dead than alive. After a few years, they space out their visits, and it's better that way, because life goes on. And death is elsewhere.

And then, in this section, there are children who would be a hundred-and-fifty years old. As the song goes:

And in a hundred-and-fifty years' time, we'll no longer even
think
About those we have loved, about those we have lost,
Come on, let's empty our coffins for the thieves in the street!
All ending up in the earth, my God, what a letdown!
And look at these skeletons giving us dirty looks
And don't sulk, don't wage war on them
There'll be nothing left of us, any more than of them
I'd stake more than my life on it
So smile.

I crouch down in front of the tombs of:

Anaïs Caussin (1986–1993)
Nadège Gardon (1985–1993)
Océane Degas (1984–1993)
Léonine Toussaint (1986–1993)

43

Like a flower crushed by the wind of the storm,
death snatched him away in the spring of his life.

My daughter, you cannot imagine how bitterly I regretted giving you that magician's kit for Christmas. Your trick worked, you really did vanish. And you made three of your friends, including Anaïs, vanish, too.

The other rooms in the castle weren't affected. Or they were evacuated in time. I don't know anymore, that I have forgotten.

Only yours. Only yours and your friends'. Your particular room was the one closest to the kitchens.

A short circuit. Or a hot plate not quite turned off.

Or food that might have caught fire in the oven.

Or a gas leak.

Or a cigarette end.

Later, I'll know what it was later.

No trickery in your magic trick. No trapdoor hidden in the floor, no applause, no dramatic reappearance with music and bowing.

Nothingness, ashes, the end of the world.

Four small lives obliterated, turned to dust. All of you, placed end to end, you don't even measure three meters; thirty-one years of little girls.

After that night, you all flew away.

One finds consolation where one can: you didn't suffer. You were asphyxiated in your sleep. When the flames started to reach you, you were already gone. You were dreaming and that's how you all remained.

I hope you were riding a pony, my darling, or in the Calanque, being a mermaid.

*

After the 5:50 train, I'd stretched out on the sofa, and had just dozed off. My heart raced when the phone rang—I thought I'd forgotten the 7:04. I answered it. I'd just been dreaming that Mother Toussaint gave me a teddy bear with no eyes and no mouth, and I was drawing them in with one of your felt-tip pens.

A policeman spoke to me, asked me to confirm my particulars, I heard your name, "Château Notre-Dame-des-Prés . . . La Clayette . . . four unidentified bodies."

I heard the words "tragedy," "fire," "children."

I heard, "I'm so sorry," your name again, "arrived too late . . . firemen unable to do anything."

I saw you again, bursting your egg with the pizza dough and making the napkins vanish while I counted: *Three daily specials, plus two children's meals, plus five drinks.*

I could have not believed the man speaking to me on the phone. I could have said to him, "You are mistaken, Léonine is a magician, she will reappear," I could have told him, "It's a stunt by Mother Toussaint, she's taken her from me and replaced her with a rag doll that has burnt in bed," I could have asked for proof, hung up, told him, "Your joke is in very poor taste," I could have said to him . . . But I instantly knew that what he was telling me was true.

Ever since my childhood, I had never made a noise, so that I would be kept, so that I wouldn't be abandoned anymore. I left yours, your childhood, screaming.

Philippe Toussaint appeared, took the phone, spoke some more with the policeman, and then he started to scream, too. But not like me. He insulted him. All the bad words we forbade you from saying, your father said them. In a single sentence. Me, your death destroyed me. After that yelp, I stopped speaking for a long time. Him, your death enraged him.

When the 7:04 went by, neither of us went out to lower the barrier.

God, who had deserted the château of Notre-Dame-des-Prés that night, at least deigned to make an appearance around our barrier because one tragedy, on the list of our lives, must have been enough. No car came by, no car came to smash into the 7:04. At that time, that road is usually very busy.

For the following barriers, Philippe Toussaint went and alerted someone, asked for help. I'll never know who came.

As for me, I lay down in your room and never left it.

Dr. Prudhomme arrived—I know, you don't like him, you called him "smelly" when he treated your tonsillitis, your chicken pox, your ear infections.

He gave me an injection.

And then another one. And yet another one.

But not on the same day.

Philippe Toussaint called Célia for help. He didn't know what to do with my pain. He passed it on to someone else.

Apparently, Philippe Toussaint's parents arrived. They didn't come to see me in your room. They did the right thing. For the first and last time, they did the right thing. They left me alone. They set off for La Clayette, all three of them. They set off toward you, toward your nonexistent remains.

Célia arrived, after, later, I don't know, I'd lost all notion of time.

I remember that it was dark, that she pushed open the door. She said, "It's me, I'm here, I'm here, Violette." Her voice had lost all its sunniness. Yes, even in Celia's voice, darkness descended when you died.

She didn't dare touch me. I was in a heap, on your bed. A heap of nothing. Célia gently forced me to eat something. I vomited. She gently forced me to drink something. I vomited.

Philippe Toussaint phoned to tell Célia that nothing remained of the four bodies. That it was total devastation. That you had all been reduced to ashes. That it wouldn't be possible to identify you, one from the other. That he was going to issue a formal complaint. That we would be compensated. That all the other children had gone home. That instead of them, there were cops everywhere. That you were all going to be buried in the children's section, together, with our permission. He repeated that, "buried together." And that to avoid the journalists, the crowds, the chaos, it would take place in the strictest privacy, in the little cemetery of Brancion-en-Chalon, a few kilometers from La Clayette.

I asked Célia to call Philippe Toussaint back, so he would recover your suitcase.

Célia told me that the suitcase had burned. Célia repeated, "They didn't suffer, they died while they slept." I replied, "We will suffer for them." Célia asked me if I'd like an object or item of clothing to be slipped inside the coffin. I replied, "Me."

Three days went by. Célia told me that the following day we would set off early. That she must take me to Brancion-en-Chalon for the funeral ceremony. Célia asked me what I would like to wear, if I would like her to go and buy me some clothes. I refused the shopping and I refused to go to the funeral. Célia told me that that wasn't possible. That it was unthinkable. I replied that, yes, it was possible, that I wouldn't attend the funeral of my daughter reduced to ashes. That she was already far away, elsewhere. Célia said to me, "For you to grieve, it's crucial. You must say a final goodbye to Léonine." I replied that no, I wouldn't go, that I wanted to go to Sormiou, to the Calanque. That was where I would say goodbye to you. The sea would bring me close to you, one last time.

I left with Célia, in her car. I don't remember the journey. I was in a haze due to medication. I didn't sleep; I wasn't awake, either. I was floating in a kind of dense fog, in the trance of a permanent nightmare in which all senses are anesthetized, all except for pain. Like those people who are put under for an operation, but can feel the surgeon's every incision. The level of grief crushing my bones was pushed to the maximum of unbearable. Breathing hurt me.

"On a scale of 1 to 10, how would you rate your level of pain?" On "indeterminate, infinite, perpetual."

I felt as if I were being amputated all day long.

I told myself, "*My heart will give way, it will give way, as fast as possible,*" I hoped it would be as fast as possible. My only hope was to die.

I was clutching two old bottles of plum brandy to my chest. Bottles that Philippe Toussaint had already had back in the studio. From time to time, I downed a mouthful, which burned me inside, just where I had carried you.

We took the steep road down to the Calanque de Sormiou. It's known as "the road of fire." I hadn't noticed that the previous year.

I didn't undress before going into the sea. I went under the water, I closed my eyes, and I heard the silence, and I heard our last holidays, the happiness, the opposite of tears.

I immediately sensed you, I sensed your presence. Like a dolphin's strokes, brushing against my stomach, my thighs, my shoulders, my face. Something gentle that came and went in the currents of the water around me. I sensed that you were fine where you were. I sensed that you were not afraid. I sensed that you were not alone.

Before Célia grabbed me by the shoulders and got me back up to the surface, I heard your voice clearly. You had the voice of a woman, a voice that I would never hear. I think I heard, "Mommy, you must know what happened that night." I didn't have time to reply to you. Celia screamed:

"Violette, Violette!!!"

Some people, vacationers in bathing suits, like us last year, helped her bring me back to the shore, just to the shore.

44.

*Warbler, if you fly above this tomb,
sing him your sweetest song.*

The weather is magnificent. The May sun caresses the soil I'm turning over. Three of the older cats rediscover their youth in the middle of the nasturtium leaves and chase after imaginary mice together. A few wary blackbirds sing, a bit further along. Eliane sleeps on her back, all four legs in the air.

Squatting in my garden, I finish planting my tomato seedlings while listening to a program on Frédéric Chopin. I had put my little battery radio on a wooden bench I picked up in a yard sale a few years ago. I repaint it blue or green, from time to time. The passing years have given it a fine patina.

Nono, Gaston, and Elvis have gone for lunch. The cemetery seems empty. Although it's lower than my garden, there are certain avenues I can't see due to the stone wall separating them.

I've taken off my grey-jersey top to liberate the flowers on my cotton dress. I've pulled on my old boots.

I like giving life. Sowing, watering, harvesting. And starting again every year. I like life just as it is today. Bathed in sunshine. I like being at the essence of things. It's Sasha who taught me how.

I've set the table in my garden. I've made a salad of multi-colored tomatoes, and a lentil one, bought a few cheeses and a large baguette. And I've opened a bottle of white wine, which I've placed in an ice bucket.

I like fine china and cotton tablecloths. I like crystal glasses and silver cutlery. I like the beauty of objects because I don't believe in the beauty of souls. I like life just as it is today, but it's worthless if it isn't shared with a friend. While watering my seedlings, I think of Father Cédric, who is such a friend, and whom I'm expecting. We lunch together every Tuesday. It's our ritual. Unless there's a burial.

Father Cédric doesn't know that my daughter rests in my cemetery. Apart from Nono, nobody knows. Even the mayor is unaware of it.

I often speak of Léonine to others because not speaking of her would be to make her die all over again. Not to speak her name would make the silence win. I live with my memory of her, but I tell no one that she is a memory. I make her live elsewhere.

When I'm asked for a photo of her, I show her as a child, with her gappy smile. People say she looks like me. No, Léonine looked like Philippe Toussaint. She had nothing of me.

"Hello, Violette."

Father Cédric has just arrived. He has a pastry box in his hands and says to me, smiling:

"A love of fine food is very naughty, but it's not a sin."

His clothes have a whiff of incense from his church, and mine of powdery roses.

We never shake hands or embrace, but we do clink our glasses.

I go to wash my hands and then rejoin him. He's poured us both a glass of wine. We sit facing the vegetable garden and, as usual, we speak first of God, as of a mutual old friend not seen for a while: for me, a villain I give no credit to, and for him, an extraordinary person, exemplary and devoted. Then we discuss international and Burgundian news. And then we always end with the best, novels and music.

Usually, we never transgress into the personal. Even after

two glasses of wine. I don't know if he has ever fallen in love with anyone. I don't know if he has ever made love. And he knows nothing about my private life.

That day, for the first time, while stroking My Way, he dares to ask me if Julien Seul is "just a friend," or if there's more between us. I reply to him that there's nothing between us apart from a story that he started telling me and that I'm waiting to hear the ending of. The story of Irène Fayolle and Gabriel Prudent. I don't say their names. I just say that I'm waiting for Julien Seul to tell me the end of a story.

"You mean to say that when he's finished telling you this story, you won't see him anymore?"

"Yes, probably."

I go to get the dessert plates. The air is sweet. The wine has gone to my head.

"Do you still want to have a child?"

He pours himself another glass of wine and puts My Way down by his feet.

"It wakes me up at night. Yesterday evening, I saw *The Well-Digger's Daughter* on TV, and as it just deals with that, basically, just with fatherhood, love, and filiation, I cried all evening."

"Father, you're a very handsome man. You could meet someone and have a child."

"And leave God? Never."

We plunge the backs of our dessert forks into the sugar-fondant and ground-almond topping of one of our pastries. He can hear my disapproval, but says nothing. He simply smiles.

Often, he says to me, "Violette, I don't know what you and God said to each other over breakfast this morning, but you seem very angry with him." And I always reply, "It's because he never wipes his feet before entering my house."

"I am united with God. I committed myself to his path. I'm on Earth to serve him, but you, Violette, why not start over?"

"Because in life, one can never just start over. Take a piece of paper and tear it, you can stick each piece back together as much as you like, the tears will always remain, and the folds and the scotch tape."

"Sure, but when the pieces are stuck back together, you can continue to write on that sheet."

"Yes, if you own a good felt-tip pen."

We burst into laughter.

"What are you going to do about your desire for a child?"

"Forget it."

"A desire can't be forgotten, especially when it's visceral."

"I'll grow older, like everyone, and it will pass."

"And if it doesn't pass? It's not because one grows older that one forgets."

Father Cedric breaks into song:

"Along with time, along with time, goes, everything goes. The other whom one adored, for whom one searched in the rain, the other whose mind one could read, with just a glance . . . "

"Have you ever adored someone?"

"God."

"Someone?"

He replies to me, with a mouth full of crème pâtissière:

"God."

45.

We think that death is an absence,
when in fact it's a secret presence.

Léonine continued to make her belongings disappear. Her room emptied, bit by bit. Her clothes and toys went to the charity Emmaüs. Every time Paulo, that was his name, parked his truck with its picture of l'Abbé Pierre, the charity's founder, outside my house, and I passed him bags full of pink, I felt as if I were donating one of Léo's organs for another child's benefit. For life to go on through her dolls, her skirts, her shoes, her castles, her beads, her cuddly toys, her crayons.

She made Christmas disappear. We never had a tree again. The famous synthetic tree, to avoid killing living ones, will probably remain the worst investment of my life. Easter, New Year, Mother's Day, Father's Day, birthdays . . . I never again blew out a candle on a cake after her death.

I lived in a kind of permanent alcoholic coma. As if my body, to protect itself from the pain, had put itself into a state of inebriation without my swallowing the slightest drop of alcohol. Well, not always. Sometimes I drank like a bottomless pit. And that's what I was, a bottomless pit. I lived in cotton wool, my movements were stilted, as if in slow motion. Like Tintin, when he was still hanging on the wall of Léonine's room: I walked on the Moon.

I finished off the grenadine. I finished off the Prince biscuits, the Savane cakes, the pasta shells, the Advil Drops. Meanwhile, I got up, I lowered the barrier, I went back to bed, I got up again, I made food for Philippe Toussaint, I raised the barrier, I went back to bed again.

I said thank you to all the "Sincere condolences" in the Grand-Rue. I replied thank you to numerous letters. I filed the countless drawings by classmates in my choice of a blue folder. As if Léo had been a boy. As if she hadn't really existed.

The worst of the worst was meeting the horrified eyes of Stéphanie, behind her register, every time I went through the door of the Casino. That and nights, that's what I dreaded the most. I steeled myself for hours to manage to leave the house, cross the road, and open the door to the mini-market. I looked down while pushing my little shopping cart along the narrow aisles, until Stéphanie's eyes met mine. The sorrow, the despair that clouded her eyes like a fog as soon as she caught sight of me. It was more than a mirror, it was desolation. She didn't bat an eyelid when she saw what I was placing on the register's conveyor belt. The bottles of alcohol. She announced the total, followed by "please." I held out my debit card, entered my PIN, goodbye, see you tomorrow.

She no longer suggested the latest products to me, "the tops," as she put it. All that stuff she'd tried out. The dish soap that softens your hands; the washing powder that smells nice and washes well even at thirty degrees, even in cold water; the delicious vegetable couscous from the frozen section; the magic duster; the omega-3 oil. You don't suggest anything any-more to a mother who has lost her child. Not special offers, not savings coupons. You leave her to buy whiskey, eyes down. I could still feel Stéphanie's eyes on my back as I opened my front door.

We dealt with insurers, lawyers. There would be legal pro-ceedings, the management of Notre-Dame-des-Prés would be sued, we'd get the establishment closed down for good. Of course, we would receive compensation.

How much does a life weighing seven-and-a-half years cost?

Every night, I heard Léo's voice again, her woman's voice,

saying to me, "Mommy, you must know what happened that night, you must know why my room burned down." It was those words that made me keep going. But it took me years to act on them. I wasn't physically able to. And the pain was far too strong for me to manage to resuscitate myself.

I needed time. Not time to feel better, I would never feel better. Time to be able to move once again, to be on the move.

Every year, from August 3rd to 16th, the SNCF sent people to replace us. Philippe Toussaint, who refused to follow me in my "morbid delirium," left on his bike to meet up with Charleville friends, and I left for Sarmiou. Célia came to pick me up at Saint-Charles station, took me down to the chalet, and then left me alone with my memories. From time to time, she would visit me and we would drink Cassis wine while contemplating the sea.

For me, All Souls' Day was in August. I immersed myself and I felt the presence of my daughter who was no longer there.

I never heard a thing from Armelle and Jean-Louis Caussin, Anaïs's parents. Not a phone call, not a letter, not a sign. They must have held it against me, not going to the burial of our children's ashes.

The old Toussaints returned to the cemetery several times. Each time, they brought their son with them. I never saw them again, either, after Léonine's death. They no longer came inside my home. It was like a tacit agreement between us.

Anger, and the promise of substantial compensation, kept Philippe Toussaint going. His obsession was that those who caused the fire should pay. But he was repeatedly told that no one "caused" the fire, that it was an accident. Which made him even angrier. A silent anger. He wanted compensation. He thought our daughter's ashes were worth their weight in gold.

He started to change physically, his features hardened, his hair whitened.

When, twice a year, he returned from the Brancion-sur-Chalon cemetery, and his parents dropped him off outside the house without ever coming in, he said nothing to me. When he got up in the morning, he said nothing to me. When he went off on a ride, he said nothing to me. When he got back, hours later, he said nothing to me. At the table, he said nothing to me. Only the video games he played with his joysticks, sitting in front of the television, made a racket. And from time to time, when the police or the lawyers or the insurers phoned, he shouted and demanded an explanation.

We still slept together, but I no longer slept. I was terrified by my nightmares. At night he stuck himself to me. And I imagined that it was my daughter, there, behind me.

Once or twice, he said to me, "We'll have another kid," and I replied yes, but I took a contraceptive as well as the antidepressants and tranquilizers. My stomach was done for. Carry life in the death that was now my body? Never. Léo had made that disappear, too: the possibility of another child.

I could have left, dumped Philippe Toussaint after the death of our child, but I had neither the strength nor the courage to do so. Philippe Toussaint was the only family I had left. Remaining close to this man was also staying close to Léonine. To see her father's features every day was also to see her own features. Going past the door of her room was to be close to her world, her footprints, her passage on Earth. I would forever be a woman who would never leave, but who would be left.

In September 1995, I received a parcel with no sender's name. It had been posted from Brancion-en-Chalon. At first, I thought it could only come from my dear Célia. That she had been *over there*, at the cemetery. But I didn't recognize her writing.

When I opened the parcel, I had to sit down. I had in my

hands a white funerary plaque with a lovely dolphin engraved to one side and these words: "My darling, you were born on September 3rd, died on July 13th, but to me, you will always be my August 15th."

I could have written those few words. Who had sent me this plaque? Someone wanted me to go and place it on Léonine's tomb, but who?

I put it back in the packaging and put it away in the cupboard in my room under a pile of towels we never used.

While folding the laundry, I found a list of names and positions slipped between two sheets:

Edith Croquevieille, director.
Swan Letellier, cook.
Geneviève Magnan, dinner lady.
Eloïse Petit and Lucie Lindon, supervisors.
Alain Fontanel, maintenance man.

The list of the staff of Notre-Dame-des-Prés, scribbled by Philippe Toussaint. He must have noted down their names during the week of the court case. The list had been written on the back of a bill, a meal for three people in the café at the law courts, the year of the lawsuit, at Mâcon. Three people: Philippe Toussaint and, presumably, his parents.

I took that as a sign coming from Léonine. On the same day, I received that plaque and I had before my eyes the list of the people who had seen her for the last time.

It's from that day on that I started to go out of my house, to wave at passengers in the trains from my barrier. And it's from that day on that Philippe Toussaint started to look at me as if I'd lost my mind. But he didn't understand me: I was finding it again.

I started by ripping up my chemical life jacket. I stopped the medication, little by little. The alcohol completely. All the pains would lay into me, ruthlessly no doubt, but I would no longer die of them.

I left the house, through the glass my eyes met Stéphanie's, behind her register, and she gave me a sad smile. I walked for a good ten minutes, reflecting that before, when I went this way, past the houses, I had my daughter's hand in my pocket. My pockets would always be empty from now on, but Léonine's hands would continue to guide me. I pushed open the door of Bernard's Driving School, to sign up for the written and road tests for a license.

46.

You're no longer where you were,
but you're everywhere that I am.

I'm gradually waking up while taking small sips of my piping-hot tea. The morning sun gets a few rays through the kitchen's drawn curtains. A little dust floats in the room, I find it beautiful, almost magical. I've put some music on, quietly, Georges Delerue, the theme song of Truffaut's film, *Day for Night*. I hold my cup in my right hand, and my left hand pets Eliane, who stretches her neck and closes her eyes. I love feeling her warmth under my fingers.

Nono knocks, and comes in. Like Father Cédric, he never kisses me, or shakes my hand. Just good morning or good evening "my Violette." Before pouring himself a coffee, he places the *Journal de Saône-et-Loire* on the table for me to read: "Brancion-en-Chalon: Road Tragedy, Biker Identified." I hear myself saying to Nono, in a flat voice:

"Could you read me the article, please, I don't have my glasses."

Eliane, who senses the tension in my fingers, rubs up a little against Nono, as if to say hello, and then scratches on the door to be let out. Nono pets her, lets her out, and then returns to me. He pulls a chair over to sit opposite me, fumbles in his pocket, puts on his glasses, which are reimbursed one hundred percent by social security, and begins to read, a bit like a child in primary school, emphasizing each syllable. Like when Léonine was a baby and I read to her from the Boscher Method, "If all the girls in the world wanted to hold hands, all around the sea, they could dance in a ring." But the words are not the same as in my colorful book.

"*The victim of the fatal accident in Brancion-en-Chalon is said to have been identified by his partner. He apparently lived in the Lyons area. The man was found lifeless on April 23rd in Brancion-en-Chalon. According to the initial police reports, his motorbike, a striking black 650cc Hyosung Aquila—its serial number had been removed—had hit the verge, causing the driver, who was wearing an unfastened helmet, to fall. On the day following his disappearance, his partner had alerted police stations and hospitals in the area, and that is how the connection could be established.*"

We're interrupted by some family members of a deceased person, arriving at the cemetery in clusters. Some are playing acoustic guitars. Everyone is holding a balloon in one hand.

Nono puts the newspaper down and says to me:

"I'll go."

"Me, too."

As I put on my black overcoat, I wonder whether I should tell the police that Philippe Toussaint had come from my place.

"Only silence," Sasha often said.

Haven't I given enough already? Don't I deserve some peace?

Even dead, Philippe Toussaint continues to torment me. I remember his final words and the bruises he left on my arms.

I want to live in peace. I want to live how Sasha taught me to. Here and now. I want Life. And not to churn up a man who contributed nothing to mine. Whose parents took away my only sun.

The hearse enters the cemetery and drives as far as the Gambini family vault. Today, a well-known fairground entertainer is being buried, Marcel Gambini, born one day in 1942 in the municipality of Brancion-en-Chalon. His deported parents only just had time to hide him in the village church.

I found myself almost wishing that desperate people would come and hide their children at Father Cédric's. The lottery of life sometimes just doesn't work. I would have so liked to be brought up by a man like Father Cédric, instead of going from family to family.

There are at least three hundred people at Marcel's funeral, including guitarists, violinists, and a bassist, who play some Django Reinhardt around his coffin. Their music contrasts with the grief, the tears that flow, the somber looks, the lost, bowed figures. Everyone falls silent when Marcel's granddaughter, Marie Gambini, a young girl of sixteen, starts to speak:

"My grandfather had a soft spot for cotton candy, the crunch of toffee apples, the smell of pancakes and waffles, the sweetness of marshmallow, nougat, and churros. Chips dipped in the salt of life, fingers sticky with simple pleasures. He will forever have the smile of the boy triumphantly holding his goldfish in a bag of water. Fishing rod in one hand, balloon in the other, perched on a carousel horse. That was the struggle of his life: giving us a shooting gallery, cuddly tigers invading the bedcovers, hours of playing peek-a-boo with a child in the plane, fire engine, or racing car of a merry-go-round. My grandfather was about hitting the jackpot and first thrills, that first kiss in a conga, a haunted castle, a maze. That icing-sugary kiss that gave us an enduring foretaste of the roller coasters the future had in store for us. My grandfather was also a voice, music, the god of the Gypsy women who can read the lines of a palm. He had Gypsy jazz in his blood, and he has gone off to play new chords, where we can no longer hear him. The line on his palm has broken. I don't ask you to rest in peace, dear Grandfather, because you're incapable of resting. I simply say to you: have fun and see you later."

She kisses the coffin. The rest of the family follows suit.

While Pierre and Jacques Lucchini lower Marcel Gambini's coffin into his vault with the help of ropes and pulleys, all the musicians play Django Reinhardt's "Minor Swing" again. Everyone releases their balloons, which float up into the sky. Then each member of the family scatters lottery tickets and soft toys onto the coffin.

This evening, I won't close the gates of my cemetery at 7 P.M.; the Gambini family asked my permission to remain beside the grave for supper. I gave them permission to stay until midnight. To thank me, they gave me dozens of tickets for bigthrill attractions at the next fun fair in Mâcon, in a fortnight. I didn't dare turn them down. I'll give them to Nono's grandchildren.

I don't know if you can judge the life of a man by the beauty of his funeral, but Marcel Gambini's is one of the most beautiful I've had the privilege to attend.

47

*The darkness has to intensify
for the first star to appear.*

In January of 1996, four months after receiving the funerary plaque, I put it in my bag and told Philippe Toussaint that, for once, he was going to have to work, and take care of the barrier for two days. I didn't give him time to react, I had already left, behind the steering wheel of Stéphanie's car, a red Fiat Panda, with a stuffed white tiger dangling from the rearview mirror to keep me company.

Normally, I would have had a three-and-a-half-hour drive ahead of me. It took me six. Nothing would be normal anymore. I had to stop several times. During the journey, I listened to the radio. I sang for Léonine, whom I imagined, two and a half years earlier, sitting in the back of the Caussins' car, Cocculine in pocket, clutching *doudou*.

"Like the bee, like the bird, swiftly, the dream flies away, like a cloud, like the wind, night falls as the moon tiptoes in, the fires in the hearths die down, even the embers will hide, the flower closes on the dew, only the mist will rise . . . "

As I scanned the houses, the trees, the lanes, the landscapes, I tried to imagine what had held her attention. Did she doze off? Did she do some magic tricks?

On the rare occasions we had been together in a car, it was in Célia's or Stéphanie's. Otherwise, we took the train. We didn't have a car, Philippe Toussaint just had his motorbike. That way, he didn't have to take us anywhere. In any case, where would he have taken us?

I arrived at Brancion-en-Chalon at around 4 P.M. *Teatime*, I thought. The door of the cemetery-keeper's house was ajar. I saw no one. I asked for nothing. I wanted to find Léonine all on my own.

This cemetery, it was like a treasure-hunt map, but the wrong way round. Harrowing, the right way round.

After half an hour of weaving between the graves, clutching the white plaque, I finally found the children's section, in the Yews wing. I thought to myself: *I should be busy preparing for Léonine to start middle school, buying stationery, filling in enrollment forms, forbidding her from wearing eye makeup, and here I am, like a lost soul, a wandering soul, deader than the dead, hunting for her name on a tomb.*

For a long time, I asked myself what wrong I had done to deserve *this*. For a long time, I asked myself what *someone* had wanted to punish me for. I reviewed all my mistakes. When I hadn't managed to understand her, when I'd been annoyed with her, when I hadn't listened to her, when I hadn't believed her, when I hadn't realized that she was cold or hot, or really did have a sore throat.

I kissed her surname and first name, engraved on the white marble. I didn't ask her to forgive me for not having come sooner. I didn't promise her to come back often. I told her that I preferred to be back with her in the Mediterranean in August, that it was much more like her than this place of silence and tears. I promised her that I would find out what had happened that night, why her room had burned down.

And I placed my funerary plaque, "My darling, you were born on September 3rd, died on July 13th, but to me, you will always be my August 15th." Among the flowers, poems, hearts and angels. Beside another one with the words: "The sun set too soon."

I couldn't say how long I stayed there, but when it was time to leave, the cemetery gates were locked.

I had to knock on the keeper's door. There was some light

inside the house. A soft, indirect light. I tried looking through the windows, but the drawn curtains stopped me from seeing anything. I had to knock again and again, on the door, on the windows, no one came. I ended up pushing open the door, which was already ajar. I went in, calling out, "Anyone at home?" No one answered me.

I heard a noise from upstairs, footsteps above my head, and music, too. Some Bach, interrupted by a presenter's voice, coming from a radio.

I immediately liked this house. The walls and the aromas. I closed the door behind me and I waited, just standing there and looking at the furniture around me. The kitchen had been turned into a tea store. On the shelves there were around fifty labeled tea caddies. The names had been handwritten in ink. Terra-cotta teapots, also labeled, corresponded to the names on the caddies. Perfumed candles had been lit.

Moments before, I was confronting my daughter's ashes, and by pushing open a door, I had changed continents.

I believe I waited a long time before hearing footsteps on the stairs. I saw some black mules, black linen trousers, and a white shirt. The man must have been around sixty-five. He was of mixed race, probably a combination of Vietnam and France. He wasn't surprised to see me standing there, in front of his door, he simply said:

"Sorry, I was taking a shower, do sit down, please."

His voice reminded me of the actor Jean-Louis Trintignant's. Emotional, melancholic, gentle, and sensual. With that voice, he said, "Sorry, I was taking a shower, do sit down, please," as if we had an appointment. I thought he was mistaking me for someone else. I wasn't able to reply because he continued:

"I'm going to make you a glass of soy milk with ground almonds and orange blossom."

I would have preferred a shot of vodka, but I didn't let on. I watched him pouring the milk, orange blossom, and ground almonds into a blender and filling a large glass with his concoction and sticking in a colorful straw, as if at a child's birthday party. Then he handed it to me. As he did so, he smiled at me as no one had ever smiled at me, not even Célia.

Everything about him was elongated. His legs, arms, hands, neck, eyes, mouth. His limbs and features had been drawn with a two-meter ruler. Like they have in primary schools to measure the world on maps.

I started drinking through the straw, I found it delicious—it reminded me of the childhood I'd never had, and of Léonine's, it reminded me of something infinitely gentle. I dissolved into tears. It was the first time I was enjoying swallowing something. Since July 14th, 1993, I had lost my sense of taste. Léonine had done that, too, made my sense of taste disappear.

I said to him, "Forgive me, the gates were locked." He replied, "No harm done. Take a seat." He took a chair and brought it to me.

I couldn't stay. I couldn't leave. I couldn't speak. I was incapable of doing so. Léo's death had also taken words away from me. I read, but I was no longer able to say. I stored things up, but nothing came out. The life of my words boiled down to, "Thank you . . . hello . . . goodbye . . . it's ready . . . sorry, I'm going to bed." Even to do the tests for my driving license, I hadn't needed to speak, I'd just had to tick the right boxes and parallel park.

I was still standing. My tears were rolling down into my glass of milk. He dabbed a cotton handkerchief with a perfume called "*Rêve d'Ossian*" and made me breathe it in. I carried on crying as if the floodgates had given way, but the tears I shed did me good. They cleansed me of nasty things, like bad sweat, like poisonous toxins oozing out of me. I thought I had cried all my tears, but there were more left. The dirty tears, the muddy ones. Like stagnant water, the sort that just festers at the bottom of a hole, long after the rain has stopped.

The man made me sit down and, when his hands touched me, I felt a shock wave. He stood behind me and started to massage my shoulders, trapezius muscles, nape, and head. He touched me as if he were healing me, as if he were placing deep-heat plasters all along my back and on the top of my head. He murmured, "Your back is harder than a wall. One could abseil down it."

I had never been touched like this. His hands were really hot and radiated an extraordinary energy that penetrated me, as if he were trailing a slight burning sensation over my skin. I didn't resist. I didn't understand. I was in a cemetery house, the cemetery where my daughter's ashes were buried. A house that reminded me of a voyage I'd never made. Later, I would learn that he was a healer. "A kind of bonesetter," as he liked to describe it.

I closed my eyes under the pressure of his hands and dozed off. A deep sleep, dark, with no painful images, no wet sheets, no nightmares, no rats devouring me, no Léonine whispering in my ear, "Mommy, wake up, I'm not dead."

I woke up the following morning, lying on the sofa under a thick, soft blanket. As I opened my eyes, I struggled to surface, to know where I was. I saw the tea caddies. And the chair I'd sat on was still in the middle of the room.

The house was empty. A very hot teapot had been placed on a low table opposite the sofa. I helped myself and sipped the jasmine tea, which was delicious. Beside the teapot, on a porcelain plate, the master of the house had arranged dainty almond cakes, which I dipped into my cup of tea.

In the daylight, I immediately saw that the cemetery house was as modest as my own. But the man who had received me the previous day had transformed it into a palace, thanks to his smile, his kindness, his almond milk, his candles, and his perfumes.

He came in from outside. He hung his big coat on the peg

and blew into his hands. He turned his head in my direction and smiled at me.

"Good morning."

"I must go."

"Where to?"

"Home."

"Where's that?"

"In the east of France, near Nancy."

"You are Léonine's mother?"

" . . . "

"I saw you at her tomb yesterday afternoon. I know the mothers of Anaïs, Nadège, and Océane. You, it's the first time . . . "

"My daughter isn't in your cemetery. There are only ashes here."

"I'm not the owner of this cemetery, just the keeper."

"I don't know how you're able to do that . . . This job. Yours is a funny job, well, not funny. At all."

He smiled again. There was no judgment in his eyes. Later, I would also discover that he always put himself on the same level as the people he was addressing.

"And you, what kind of job do you do?"

"I'm a level-crossing keeper."

"So, you stop people from crossing to the other side—me, I help them a little in getting there."

I tried my best to return his smile. But I didn't know how to smile anymore. He was all goodness, I was all in pieces. I was a wreck.

"You'll be back?"

"Yes. I have to know why the children's room burned down that night . . . Do you know them?"

I took out and handed him the list of the staff of Notre-Dame-des-Prés, scribbled on the back of a bill by Philippe Toussaint.

"Edith Croquevieille, director; Swan Letellier, cook; Geneviève Magnan, dinner lady; Eloïse Petit and Lucie Lindon, supervisors; Alain Fontanel, maintenance man."

He read the names carefully. Then looked at me.

"You'll be back to visit Léonine's tomb?"

"I don't know."

Eight days after our meeting, I received a letter from him:

"*Madame Violette Toussaint,*

Please find enclosed the list of names you forgot on my table. Also, I have prepared a packet of blended tea—a green tea with almond and jasmine and rose petals. If I'm not there, take it, the door is always open. I've put it on the yellow shelf, to the right of the cast-iron teapots. Your name is on it: 'Tea for Violette.'

Yours truly,

Sasha H."

To me, this man seemed like he was straight out of a novel, or an asylum. Which comes to same thing. What was he doing in a cemetery? I didn't even know the job of cemetery keeper existed. For me, the death business was just about being an undertaker, waxen faced and clad in black, with a crow perched on one shoulder, if not a coffin.

But there was something much more disturbing. I recognized his handwriting on the envelope and the note. He's was the one who'd sent me the "My darling, you were born on September 3rd, died on July 13th, but to me, you will always be my August 15th" plaque to place on my little Léo's tomb.

How did he know I existed? How did he know these dates, particularly the happy one? Was he already here when the children were buried? Why was he interested in them? In me? Why had he lured me to the cemetery? What did it have to do with him? I began to wonder whether he hadn't knowingly locked me in the cemetery so I would come into his house.

My life was a bombsite, to which an unknown soldier had sent me a funerary plaque and a letter.

Yes, the war was drawing to a close. I sensed it. I would never recover from the death of my daughter, but the bombing had stopped. I would live through the postwar period. The longest, the hardest, the most pernicious . . . You pick yourself up, and then find yourself face to face with a girl of her age. When the enemy has gone, and there's nothing left but those who are left. Desolation. Empty cupboards. Photos that freeze her in childhood. All the others growing, even the trees, even the flowers, without her.

In January of 1996, I announced to Philippe Toussaint that, from then on, I would be going to the cemetery in Brancion-en-Chalon two Sundays a month. I'd set off in the morning and return in the evening.

He sighed. He rolled his eyes, as if to say, "I'm going to have to work two days a month." He added that he didn't understand, that I hadn't been to the funeral, and then now, all of a sudden, this fancy takes me. I didn't respond. How could one respond to that? To the word "fancy"? According to him, going to visit my daughter's tomb was a caprice, a whim.

The writer Christian Bobin said, "Words left unspoken go off to scream deep inside us."

Those weren't his exact words. But me, I was full of silences that screamed deep inside me. That woke me up at night. That made me put on weight, lose weight, age, cry, sleep all day, drink like a bottomless pit, bang my head against doors and walls. But I survived.

The playwright Prosper Crébillon said, "The greater the misfortune, the greater one is for living." In dying, Léonine had made everything around me disappear, except me.

Like a flight of swallows as winter approaches,
Your soul flew away with no hope of return.

J ulien Seul is standing at my doorstep. The one beside my
vegetable garden, at the back of the house.

"It's the first time I've seen you in a T-shirt. You look like
a young man."

"And you, it's the first time I've seen you in colors."

"That's because I'm at home, in my garden. No one comes
across me behind this wall. Are you staying long?"

"Until tomorrow morning. How are you?"

"Like a cemetery keeper."

He smiles at me.

"It's lovely, your garden."

"That's down to the fertilizers. Close to cemeteries, everything grows very fast."

"I've never known you to be so caustic."

"That's because you don't know me."

"Maybe I know you better than you think I do."

"Poking around in people's lives doesn't mean you know
them, detective."

"May I invite you to dinner?"

"On condition that you tell me the end of the story."

"Which story?"

"The one about Gabriel Prudent and your mother."

"I'll come and pick you up at 8 P.M. And whatever you do,
don't change, stay in colors."

These few flowers, in memory of times gone by.

I went inside Sasha's house. I opened the packet of tea, closed my eyes, and inhaled its contents. Would I come back to life in this cemetery house? It was my second time inside it, and already I could smell that aroma that pulled me, almost by force, out of the blackness of my shadow of a life since Léo's death.

As Sasha had indicated in his letter, the packet of tea was on the yellow shelf beside the cast-iron teapots. He'd stuck on a label like those on school workbooks: Tea for Violette. But what he hadn't mentioned in his letter was that, under the packet, there was also a brown envelope with my name on it. It wasn't sealed. I discovered that he had slipped several pages inside it.

Initially, I thought it was a list of people who had died recently, and the "Toussaint" written on the envelope might refer to tombs requiring flowers for All Saints' Day. Then I understood.

Sasha had put together the contact details of all the staff present at the château of Notre-Dame-des-Prés on the night of July 13th to 14th, 1993. The director, Edith Croquevieille; the cook, Swan Letellier; the dinner lady, Geneviève Magnan; the two supervisors, Eloïse Petit and Lucie Lindon; the maintenance man, Alain Fontanel.

Apart from the director's face, it was the first time I was seeing the faces of those who had seen my daughter for the last time.

The tragedy had been covered on the 8 P.M. TV news bulletin. On every channel. They had shown a picture of the château of Notre-Dame-des-Prés, the lake, the ponies. And they had kept repeating the same key words: tragedy, accidental fire, four children perished, holiday camp. The children had been front-page news in the *Journal de Saône-et-Loire* for several days. I had skimmed through the articles that Philippe Toussaint brought back for me the day after the funeral. Pictures of the children, smiles full of gaps, teeth the fairy had taken away, lucky thing. We, the parents, had nothing anymore. I would have given my life to know where her fairyland was, to get Léo's little teeth back, get a little of her smile back. But these articles had no photos of the staff from the establishment.

The director, Edith Croquevieille, had gray hair gathered in a chignon, wore glasses, and smiled sagely at the camera. One sensed that the photographer had given her these directions, "Smile, but not too much, you need to look friendly, trustworthy and reassuring." I knew that photo. It was at the back of the publicity brochure that Mother Toussaint had handed me, years earlier. That brochure full of blue skies. Like in the brochures of undertakers.

"Only our reliability never takes a holiday." How often did I berate myself for not reading between those lines?

Beneath the portrait of Edith Croquevieille, her address had been written.

The photo of Swan Letellier was from an automatic booth. How had Sasha got hold of it? Just as for the director, Sasha had written the cook's address. But it didn't seem to be his personal address. The name of a restaurant in Mâcon, "Le Terroir des Souches." Swan must have been about thirty-five. He seemed thin, almond-shaped eyes, handsome and disturbing at the same time, a strange face, fine lips, a shifty look.

The photo of Geneviève Magnan, the dinner lady, must

have been taken at a wedding. She was wearing a ridiculous hat, like the mothers of the bride and groom sometimes wear. She had put too much makeup on, and badly. Geneviève Magnan must have been about fifty. It was probably this plump little woman, squeezed into her blue flowery suit, who had served Léo her last meal. I'm sure Léo thanked her, because she was well brought up. I had taught Léo that—it had been my priority—always to say hello, goodbye, thank you.

The two supervisors, Eloïse Petit and Lucie Lindon, were posing together in front of their school. In the photograph, they must have been sixteen. Two cheeky and carefree young girls. Did they eat at the same table as the children? On the phone, Léo had told me that one of the supervisors "really" looked like me. And yet neither Eloïse nor Lucie, both blonde with blue eyes, looked like me.

The face of the maintenance man, Alain Fontanel, had been cut out from a newspaper. He was wearing a football jersey. He must have been posing, squatting with other players, in front of a ball. There was something of the rocker Eddy Mitchell about him.

Always an address, jotted down in blue ink, under each portrait. Those of Geneviève Magnan and Alain Fontanel were identical. And always the same writing as on the parcel containing the funerary plaque, the letter, and the labels on the tea caddies.

But who was this cemetery keeper who'd lured me here? And why?

I waited for him, he didn't come home. I put the tea in my bag, along with the envelope containing the portraits and names of those present *that evening*. And I went around the cemetery to find Sasha. I came across unknown people watering plants, and walkers. I wondered who was buried here of theirs. I tried to guess by looking at their faces. A mother? A cousin? A brother? A husband?

50.

*For me, it's been years now, forever, that your dazzling smile
has sustained the same rose with its glorious summer.*

Irène Fayolle and Gabriel Prudent went into the first hotel
they saw, a few kilometers from Aix station. The Hôtel du
Passage. They chose the Blue Room. Like the title of the
novel by Georges Simenon. There were others: the Joséphine
Room, the Amadeus Room, the Renoir Room.

At reception, Gabriel Prudent ordered pasta and red wine
for four people, to be served in the room. He thought making
love would make them hungry. Irène Fayolle asked him:

"Why four people? There's just two of us."

"You're bound to think about your husband, I about my
wife, so we might as well invite them for a bite from the get-
go. It will avoid unspoken resentment, lamentment, and all
that."

"What's 'lamentment'?"

"It's a word I invented to combine melancholy, guilt,
regrets, steps forward, and steps backward. Everything that
really bugs us in life, in other words. That holds us back."

They kissed. They undressed, she wanted to make love in
the dark, he said that there was no point, that since the trial he
had undressed her several times with his eyes, that he already
knew her curves, her body.

She insisted. She said:

"You're a smooth talker."

He replied:

"Obviously."

He closed the blue curtains of the Blue Room.

There was a knock on the door, room service. They ate, drank, made love, ate, drank, made love, ate, drank, made love. They enjoyed each other, the wine made them laugh, they enjoyed, laughed, cried.

They decided, by mutual consent, never to leave this room ever again. They told themselves that dying together, there, then, that could be *the* solution. They envisaged running away, disappearing, a stolen car, a train, a plane. They went on quite a journey.

They decided they would go and live in Argentina. Like war criminals did. She fell asleep. He stayed awake, smoked cigarettes, ordered a second bottle of white wine and five desserts.

She opened her eyes, asked him who the third guest was, beside her husband and his wife, he replied, "Our love."

They went to the bathroom. Returning to bed, they decided to dance. They switched on the alarm-clock radio, heard that Klaus Barbie was going to be extradited to France to be tried. Gabriel Prudent said these words, "At last, justice. Got to celebrate that." He ordered champagne. She said, "I've known you for twenty-four hours and I haven't been sober. It might be a good idea for us to meet again on an empty stomach."

They danced to Gilbert Bécaud's "I'm coming back for you."

She fell asleep at around 4 A.M. and opened her eyes again at 6 A.M. He had just fallen asleep.

The room smelled of stale smoke and alcohol. She heard the birds singing. She hated them for it.

"Hold back the night." Those are the words that came to her. Johnny Hallyday at six in the morning in the Blue Room. She tried to remember the words, "Hold back the night, today, until the end of the world, hold back the night . . ." And she couldn't remember what came next.

He had his back to her, she caressed him, breathed him in. It woke him up, they made love. Fell back to sleep.

They were rung at 10 A.M., to know if they were keeping the room or checking out. If the latter, the room had to be vacated by midday.

51.

*Each day that passes weaves the invisible thread
of your memory.*

On the ground floor of the left wing, one main corridor,
three adjacent bedrooms, each with two bunk beds and
toilets and basins, for boarders, and a bedroom reserved
for staff. On the second floor, three adjacent rooms, each with
two bunk beds and toilets and basins, for boarders, and five bedrooms reserved for staff.

On the night of July 13th to 14th, 1993, all the rooms were
occupied.

The bedrooms of Edith Croquevieille (director and supervisor), Swan Letellier (domestic staff), Geneviève Magnan (domestic staff and supervisor), Alain Fontanel (domestic staff), and
Eloïse Petit (supervisor) were on the second floor. The bedroom
of Lucie Lindon (supervisor) was on the ground floor.

Anaïs Caussin (aged seven), Léonine Toussaint (aged seven),
Nadège Gardon (aged eight), and Océane Degas (aged nine) were
in Room 1, situated on the ground floor. They left their room
without permission, and without making any noise so as not to
wake up their supervisor (Lucie Lindon), who was sleeping in
one of the rooms adjoining theirs. They went to the kitchen,
located five meters from their bedroom, at the end of the main
corridor. They opened one of the fridges and poured milk into a
two-liter stainless-steel saucepan in order to warm it up. They
used a gas cooker with eight rings (two electric, six gas). They lit
one of the gas rings with household matches. They searched in the
storeroom at the back of the kitchen to find cocoa powder and in
the cupboard for four mugs, into which they poured the hot milk.

They each carried their mug of hot milk back to their bedroom. (*The four mugs were found in Room 1—non-flammable ceramic.*)

The four victims had placed the stainless-steel saucepan back on the gas ring, which, mistakenly, hadn't been switched off but turned down to low.

The plastic handle of the stainless-steel saucepan began to melt, then to catch fire. (*Saucepan found, stainless-steel non-flammable.*)

Ten minutes later (estimated approximate time), the flames coming from the plastic handle began to reach the kitchen units located above and to the right of the gas cooker.

The plastic-coated cladding covering these kitchen units proved to be highly toxic. Organic compounds (lacquers and varnishes) that are very volatile.

It was also noted that the four children hadn't closed the door to the kitchen, or to their bedroom.

Between the moment when the four victims left the kitchen and the moment when the toxic gases had invaded the kitchen, the corridor, and their bedroom, between twenty-five and thirty minutes had gone by.

As previously stated, Room 1 was located around five meters from the kitchen. The emanation of toxic gases produced by the combustion of the kitchen units must have rapidly plunged the four children into a coma, and caused their deaths by asphyxiation and poisoning.

The bodies of the four victims were found burned to ashes in their beds. They were asleep when they inhaled the toxic gases, and that proved fatal to them.

Room 1 caught fire when one of the windows in that same room exploded due to the heat, creating a draft.

Due to the explosion and the extreme temperature, all the windows in the room exploded, allowing some of the toxic gases to escape outside. The other bedrooms (to which all doors were closed) on the ground floor were not affected.

The supervisor (Lucie Lindon), who occupied the room adjoining that of the four victims, immediately evacuated the two bedrooms on the ground floor, in which eight children were sleeping (unharmed), and which weren't affected by the fire.

It was not possible for Lucie Lindon to enter Room 1.

After ensuring that all the occupants on the first floor (twelve children and five adults) were safe and sound, Lucie Lindon alerted the fire brigade.

It was harder than usual to reach the latter as it had been commandeered to keep people safe at a firework display, ten kilometers from the place known as La Clayette.

Alain Fontanel and Swan Letellier again attempted to enter Room 1 by any means, but in vain. The heat and the height of the flames were too extensive.

Between Lucie Lindon's telephone alert and the arrival of the fire brigade, twenty-five minutes elapsed. The call was made at 23:25, and the fire brigade arrived at the location of the fire at 23:50.

A large part of the left wing had already been devastated by the flames.

It took three hours to get the fire under control.

Due to the young age of the four victims, and the advanced level of calcination of the bodies, identification using dental records was not possible.

This is what the investigation revealed.

It's roughly what was written in the police report, drawn up for the public prosecutor.

It's what was said during the trial (which I didn't attend), as repeated to me by Philippe Toussaint.

It's what was written in the newspapers (which I didn't read).

Detached words, devoid of pathos, precise. "Without drama, without a tear, those pathetic and derisory arms, because there are certain pains that weep only on the inside," as the song goes.

Edith Croquevieille was sent down for two years, one without remission, because the kitchen door had not been locked, and the surfaces of floors, walls, and ceilings at Notre-Dame-des-Prés were in a bad state of repair. It was never explicitly said, or written, that the children were responsible. One can't accuse four little victims of seven, eight, and nine years old. But to me, it was implied in the director's sentence.

What immediately struck me as problematic, in these experts' reports, is that Léonine didn't drink milk. She absolutely hated it. A single sip was enough to make her vomit.

52.

Here lies my garden's most beautiful flower.

W hile watching the colorful fish in the huge aquarium, covering an entire wall in the Chinese restaurant, Le Phénix, I'm reminded of the Calanque de Sormiou. Of the sunshine, of the beauty in that light.

"Do you swim often in Marseilles?"

"When I was a kid I did."

Julien Seul pours me another glass of wine.

"The Hôtel du Passage, the Blue Room, the wine, the pasta, the lovemaking with Gabriel Prudent, all that is written in your mother's journal?"

"Yes."

He takes a notebook out of his inside pocket. With its stiff navy-blue cover, it looks like the Prix Goncourt winner of 1990, *Les Champs d'honneur*, which Célia gave me.

"I brought it for you. I've slipped some colored sheets between the pages that concern you."

"What do you mean?"

"My mother mentions you in her journal. She saw you, several times."

I open the notebook at random, look furtively at her handwriting in blue ink.

"Keep it. You can return it to me later."

I put it away, at the bottom of my handbag.

"I'll take care of it . . . How does it make you feel, discovering your mother's other life in her journal?"

"It's as if I were reading someone else's story, a stranger's.

And my father did die a long time ago. 'It's ancient history,' as they say."

"It doesn't bother you that she's not buried alongside your father?"

"At first, I found it hard. Now it's fine. And also, I would never have got to know you."

"Once again, I'm not sure that we know each other. We've met, that's all."

"Then let's get to know each other."

"I think I need a drink."

I down the wine he's just poured me, in one.

"Usually, I don't drink much, but right now, that's impossible. And that way you have of looking at me. I never know whether you want to arrest me or marry me."

He bursts into laughter.

"Marry or arrest, comes to the same thing, right?"

"Are you married?"

"Divorced."

"Do you have children?"

"A son."

"How old is he?"

"Seven."

An awkward silence.

"Would you like us to get to know each other at a hotel?"

He seems surprised by my question. He strokes the cotton tablecloth with his fingertips. He smiles at me again.

"You and me at a hotel, that was one of my medium- or long-range plans . . . But, since you're suggesting it, we can reduce the waiting time."

"The hotel, it's the start of the journey."

"No, the hotel is already the journey."

53

Don't cry over my death. Celebrate my life.

The second time I saw Sasha, he was in his vegetable garden.

When I entered his house, it was in a mess. Saucepans spilling out of the sink, cups scattered everywhere, empty teapots, too. Numerous papers spread across the low table. The tea caddies covered in dust. But the walls still smelled as good.

I heard some noise at the back of the house. Classical music coming from outside. The door that led to the vegetable garden, at the back of the kitchen, was wide open. I saw the sunlight.

Sasha was at the top of a ladder that was leaning against a cherry-plum tree. He was collecting the sweet fruit in a potato sack. When he saw me, he smiled at me with his matchless smile. And I wondered how it was possible to seem so happy in such a sad place.

I immediately thanked him for the packet of tea and the list of Notre-Dame-des-Prés staff. He replied, "Oh, you're welcome."

"How did you manage to find the photos and addresses of those people?"

"Oh, wasn't difficult."

"Edith Croquevieille and the others, do you know them?"

"I know everyone."

I wanted to ask him questions about *those people*. But I couldn't.

As he came down his ladder, he said to me:

"You look like a sparrow, a fledgling that's fallen from the nest. You're a sorry sight. Come here, I'm going to tell you something."

"How did you get my address? Why did you send me the funerary plaque?"

"It was your friend Célia who gave it to me."

"You know Célia?"

"A few months ago, she came to the cemetery to place a plaque on the tomb of your little girl. She asked me where it was, I accompanied her. She told me she'd imagined the words you would have had engraved if you'd come here, in person. She'd chosen the words for you. She just couldn't understand why you had never set foot in the cemetery. She said it would probably do you good. She spoke to me about you for a long while. She told me you were in a bad way. So, the idea came to me. I asked her permission to send you the plaque so you would come and place it yourself. She hesitated for a long time, and then agreed."

He grabbed a Thermos left at the end of one of his garden's paths, and poured me some tea in a glass from the kitchen, murmuring, "Jasmine and honey."

"I had my first garden at nine years old. One square meter of flowers. It was my mother who taught me how to sow, water, harvest. I sensed that it would be my thing. She always said to me, 'Don't judge each day by what you can pick, but by the seeds you sow.'"

He went quiet for a few moments, then grabbed my arm and looked into my eyes.

"You see this garden? Twenty years I've had it. You see how beautiful it is? You see all these vegetables? These colors? This garden is seven hundred square meters, that's seven hundred square meters of joy, love, sweat, endeavor, determination, and patience. I'm going to teach you how to look after it, and once you know, I'll entrust it to you."

I said that I didn't understand. He pulled off his gloves and showed me the wedding ring on his finger.

"You see this wedding ring? I found it in my first vegetable garden."

He led me under an arbor of climbing ivy and made me sit down on an old chair. He sat facing me.

"It was a Sunday, I must have been around twenty, and I was walking my little dog not far from the social housing I lived in, in the suburbs of Lyons. I left the car park behind me and took a random path. There was some so-called 'country-side' a bit higher up, a few meadows that had ended up in the midst of the concrete, arid meadows, not very attractive, and a cluster of old trees. At the end of the path, I fell upon a group of people sitting under an oak tree and cleaning beans at an old, oilcloth-covered table. I was struck by how happy they looked. They were neighbors, people who lived in the social housing whom I knew by sight, people who didn't smile like that when I passed them in the stairwell. All around them, I could see their hodgepodge gardens. They grew fruit and vegetables. I realized that it was those little plots of land and the well that put those smiles on their faces. I asked them if I, too, could have a garden like them. They told me to phone the town hall, that they rented the plots for peanuts, that there were a few left, back there.

"I proudly dug up my plot in October and covered it with manure. The following winter, I grew my seedlings in empty yogurt pots. Squashes, basil, peppers, eggplants, tomatoes, zucchini. I had grand ideas. I was ambitious for my vegetables. I planted them in spring. I followed the gardening manuals, I gardened with my head, not my heart. Without paying attention to the lunar cycles, the frost, the rain, the sun. I also planted some carrots and potatoes directly into the soil. I waited for it all to grow. I dropped by occasionally to do some watering. I was counting on the rain.

"Of course, nothing grew. I didn't realize that you have to spend days in the garden for the magic to work. I didn't realize that the weeds, the ones that grow around vegetables, if you don't remove them every day, they drink all the water, they kill off everything."

He got up to go into his kitchen and returned with almond cakes on a china plate.

"Eat, you're looking thin."

I said I wasn't hungry, he replied, "Don't care." We enjoyed his cakes, smiling at each other, and then he picked up his story:

"By September, as if my garden were mocking me, only one carrot had appeared. Just one! I saw its yellowing top, alone in the middle of the dry, badly aerated soil. Soil I hadn't remotely understood. Mortified, I pulled the carrot up, ready to throw it to the hens, when I saw there was a silver wedding ring wedged onto my pathetic, deformed vegetable. A real silver wedding ring someone must have lost years before, in the soil of my garden. I rinsed my carrot, took a bite out of it, and pulled the wedding ring off. I took it as a sign. It was as if I'd failed my first year of marriage by not understanding my wife at all, but still had dozens more ahead of me to make up for it."

54.

She hid her tears but shared her smiles.

Wash his clothes with powder detergent, dry them, except for the sweaters, fold while still warm, put away, according to color, on his shelves. Do the shopping: fluoride toothpaste, *Auto-moto* magazine, Gillette razorblades, chamomile anti-dandruff shampoo, shaving foam for tough stubble, fabric softener, polish for the biking leathers, Dove soap, packs of lager, milk chocolate, vanilla yogurts.

The things he likes. The brands he prefers.

In the bathroom, clean hairbrush and combs. Tweezers and nail-clippers ready for use.

Baguette, crusty. Everything cherry-flavored. Meat to chop up without breathing through the nose. Brown it and braise in a cast-iron casserole. Lift lid and check pieces of dead animal, add flour, put on a plate, bay leaves soaking in onion sauce.

Serve.

Eat only the vegetables, pasta, mashed potato. Eat only the side dishes. Which is what I am. A side dish.

Clear the table.

Wash the floor, the kitchen. Vacuum clean. Air the place. Dust. Change the channel immediately when he doesn't like the program. Switch off the music. Never music when he's around: my "moronic" singers give him a headache.

Him going off for a ride, me staying home. Going to bed. Him getting back late. He wakes me up because he makes a racket, doesn't care about the water running in the sink, the stream of pee hitting the toilet, the doors slamming. He sticks himself right behind me. He smells of another woman. Pretend to sleep. But sometimes he wants me anyway. Despite the other woman, the one he's just left. He slides inside me, strains, grunts, I close my eyes. I think of elsewhere, I go for a swim in the Mediterranean.

That's all I knew. Just that particular smell. Just that particular voice, just his words and his habits. The last years of my life with him occupy more of my memories than the early ones, the ones that sped by, the short, lighthearted, and carefree years of love. When our youths were intertwined.

Philippe Toussaint aged me. To be loved is to stay young.

It's the first time I make love with a man who's sensitive. Before Philippe Toussaint, a few guys at the hostel and from Charleville. Just clumsiness, beaten-up lives banging together. Making a noise, jerks who don't know how to caress. Who botched learning French from textbooks, botched learning love.

Julien Seul knows how to love.

He's sleeping. I hear his breathing, it's a new breath. I listen to his skin, I breathe in his gestures, his hands on me, one on my left shoulder, the other around my right hip. He is all over me. Outside of me. But not within me.

He's sleeping. How many lives would I need to fall asleep against someone? To trust enough to close my eyes and let go of the souls that haunt me? I'm naked between the sheets. My body hasn't been naked between sheets since the dawn of time.

I adored this moment of love, this surge of life.

Now I would like to go home. I want to be back with Eliane, the solitude of my bed. I would like to leave this hotel room without waking him, run away, in fact.

Saying goodbye tomorrow morning seems impossible to me. A dialogue almost as unbearable as meeting Stéphanie's eyes when I lost Léonine.

What would I say to him?

We'd downed a bottle of champagne to brace ourselves, finally, to touch each other. We were terrified of each other. Like people truly attracted to each other are. Like Irène Fayolle and Gabriel Prudent.

I'm not after a love story. I'm too old for that. I've missed the boat. My meager love life is an old pair of socks shoved to the back of a closet. That I never got rid of, but that I won't ever wear again. It doesn't matter. Nothing matters apart from the death of a child.

I have life ahead of me, but not the love of a man. Once you've got used to living alone, you can't live as part of a couple anymore. Of that I am certain.

We're twenty kilometers from Brancion-en-Chalon, just near Cluny, at the Hôtel Armance. I'm not going to walk home. I'm going to take a taxi. Go down to reception and call a taxi.

This thought spurs me on. I slip out of bed as gently as possible. Like when I slept with Philippe Toussaint and didn't want to wake him.

I put on my dress, grab my bag, and leave the room, shoes in hand. I know he's watching me leave. He has the good grace to say nothing, and I the bad grace not to turn around.

Irreverent, that's what I think of myself.

In the taxi, I try to read random pages of Irène Fayolle's journal, but can't. It's too dark. As we drive past a block of houses, the streetlamps light up one word in ten.

"Gabriel . . . hands . . . light . . . cigarette . . . roses . . . "

55.

His life is a lovely memory.
His absence a silent agony.

When I left Sasha's cemetery, it was 6 P.M. I drove toward Mâcon, in the Fiat Panda, to catch the motorway. The white tiger, dangling from the rear-view mirror, was watching me out of the corner of its eye while nonchalantly swinging.

I thought again of Sasha, of his garden, of his smile, of his words. I thought of how a strike had sent me Célia, and the death of my daughter this straw-hatted gardener. My own, personal Wilbur Larch. A man between life and the dead, his earth and his cemetery. *L'Oeuvre de Dieu, la part du Diable.*

I thought again of the holiday-camp staff. Decent people, too, no doubt. I saw again the faces of the director, Edith Croquevieille; the cook, Swan Letellier; the dinner lady, Geneviève Magnan; the two young supervisors, Eloïse Petit and Lucie Lindon; the maintenance man, Alain Fontanel. Their faces all lined up.

What was I going to do with their addresses? Was I going to go and see them, one after the other?

As I drove, I recalled that the cook, Swan Letellier, worked at the Terroir des Souches in Mâcon. I had seen on a map that the restaurant was in the town center, on rue de L'Héritan.

I didn't take the motorway, I went into Mâcon, parked in a car park about two hundred meters from the restaurant, close to the town hall. A waitress welcomed me nicely. Two couples were already seated.

The last time I had set foot in a restaurant was at Gino's, the day I'd had lunch with Anaïs's parents, the day Léonine had burst the eggs with a burst of laughter. I've relived that day thousands of times, the meal, the dress she was wearing, her braids, her smile, the magic, what the bill came to, the moment she got in the Caussin's car and waved me goodbye, her *doudou* hidden under her knees—a gray rabbit whose right eye risked falling off, and that I'd put in the wash so often, it had lost an ear. There are hours that should be swiftly forgotten. But events decide otherwise.

I couldn't see Swan Letellier. He must have been in the kitchen. There were just girls busy serving. *Four girls, like in the tomb*, I thought.

I drank a half-bottle of wine, and ate almost nothing. The waitress asked me if I didn't like it. I said that I did, but I wasn't very hungry. She smiled at me, condescendingly. I watched people arriving and leaving. I hadn't drunk for several months, but I felt too alone at this table to drink water.

At around nine, the restaurant was full. After I'd left, unsteadily, I sat on a bench a bit further down and, staring into the dark, waited for Swan Letellier.

Nearby, I could hear the Saône flowing. I felt like throwing myself into it. To be back with Léo. Would I find her again? Wouldn't it be better to throw myself into the sea? Was she still there? In what form? And me, was I still there? What was the point of my life? What use had it been? And to whom? Why had I been put on a radiator on the day I was born? That radiator had stopped working on July 14th, 1993.

What was I going to say to poor old Swan Letellier? What did I want to know, exactly? The room had burned down, what was the point of questioning the present. Stirring shit up.

I couldn't face getting back into Stéphanie's Panda, returning to the barrier, driving through the night.

Just when I wanted to get up, step over the wall behind me, jump into the black water, a Siamese cat came and rubbed itself against my legs, purring. It stared at me with its beautiful blue eyes. I leaned forward to touch it. Its fur was soft, warm, wonderful. It jumped onto my lap, startling me. I didn't dare move. It stretched right out on me. Like a dead weight on my thighs, a safeguard. I was going to lean into the void, and it stopped me from doing so. I think that evening, that cat saved my life. At least, what little was left of it.

Once the last clients had gone and the lights in the restaurant gone out, Swan Letellier was the first to appear.

I didn't move from the bench I was sitting on.

He was wearing a black bomber jacket, its fabric shining under the streetlights, jeans, and sneakers, and walked with a rolling gait.

I called out to him. I didn't recognize my own voice. As though another woman were shouting at him. A stranger I was harboring. Probably the effect of the alcohol. Everything seemed abstract to me.

"Swan Letellier!"

The cat jumped to the ground and sat at my feet. Swan Letellier turned his head and looked at me for a few seconds, before responding, warily:

"Yes?"

"I'm the mother of Léonine Toussaint."

He froze. He had the same look as those youngsters I terrified that evening I turned myself into the white lady. I felt his frightened eyes searching mine. While I was in total darkness, I could see his features clearly where he was standing.

One of the four waitresses came out of the Terroir des Souches. She went up to him and snuggled against his back. He said to her, quite drily:

"Go on ahead, I'll join you."

She immediately saw that he was looking in my direction. She recognized me and whispered something in his ear. No doubt that I'd just knocked back a half-bottle of wine all on my own. The girl gave me a dirty look and then left, almost shouting at Swan:

"I'll be waiting for you at Titi's!"

Swan Letellier moved closer to me. When he reached me, he waited for me to speak:

"Do you know why I'm here?"

He shook his head.

"Do you know who I am?"

He replied, coldly:

"You said: the mother of Léonine Toussaint."

"Do you know who Léonine Toussaint is?"

He hesitated before replying:

"You never came to the funeral, or the trial."

I hadn't expected him to say that to me at all. It's as if he'd slapped me in the face. I clenched my fists until my nails dug into my skin. The Siamese cat was still close to me. Sitting at my feet, staring at me.

"I never believed that the children had gone into the kitchen that night."

He replied, defensively:

"Why?"

"Intuition. And you, what did you see?"

His voice became choked:

"We tried to get into the room, but anyway, it was too late."

"Did you get on well with the rest of the staff?"

He seemed to be struggling to breathe. He took a tube of Ventolin from his pocket and inhaled from it, hard, through his mouth.

"Gotta go, someone's waiting for me."

I detected his fear. People who are afraid can sniff out others' fear more easily. That evening, sitting on that bench, facing that young man who was both worried and worrying, I was afraid. I sensed that the fire that was consuming my child would consume her forever if I didn't discover the truth.

"Don't want to think about all that. You should do the same. It's sad, but that's life. Sometimes, it can be shit. I'm sorry."

He turned his back on me and started walking very fast. Almost running. His reaction merely confirmed my feeling that nothing was true in the report addressed to the public prosecutor.

I looked down. The Siamese cat had gone without my noticing.

56

Sweet are the memories that never fade.

When Jean-Louis and Armelle Caussin come to visit Anaïs's tomb, they don't know who I am. They don't make the connection between the young, shy, scruffy young woman they had lunch with on July 13th, 1993 in Malgrange, and the smart municipal employee who strides purposefully up and down the avenues of Brancion cemetery. They have even bought my flowers without recognizing me.

After my daughter's death, I lost fifteen kilos, my face became both gaunt and puffy. I aged by a hundred years. I had the face and body of a child in crumpled packaging.

An old little girl.

I was seven-and-a-bit.

Sasha said of me, "An old fledgling that's fallen from the nest and got soaked in the rain."

After meeting Sasha, I changed. I grew my hair and wore different clothes. I went off jeans and sweatshirts.

When I rediscovered my body, when I saw it reflected in a shopwindow, it was that of a woman. I put it into dresses, skirts, and blouses. My facial features changed. If I'd been a painting, my face would have gone from an angular Bernard Buffet to an almost ethereal Auguste Renoir.

Sasha made me change century, going backward to keep going forward.

The last time I saw Paulo and his Emmaüs van, I gave him Léonine's remaining possessions, my doll Caroline, my trousers, and my clodhoppers. I filed my nails, drew a fine line along my eyelids, and bought some elegant shoes.

Stéphanie, who had always known me in jeans and no makeup, looked at me suspiciously when I placed powder and blusher on her register's conveyor belt. Even more so than when I was placing bottles of every kind of alcohol under her nose.

People are strange. They can't bear to look in the eye a mother who has lost her child, but they're even more shocked to see her picking herself up, dressing herself up, dolling herself up.

I learned about day cream, night cream, powdery roses, the way others learn how to cook.

The woman who looks after the cemetery looks sad, but she always smiles at passersby. I suppose looking sad goes with the job. She looks like an actress I can't remember the name of. She's pretty, but ageless. I noticed she's always smartly dressed. Yesterday I bought some flowers from her for Gabriel. I didn't feel like giving him my roses. The woman who looks after the cemetery sold me a lovely purple heather. We chatted about flowers together, she seems passionate about gardens. When I told her I owned a rose nursery, she lit up. She became a different person.

That's what Irène Fayolle wrote about me in her journal from 2009. One month after the funeral of Gabriel Prudent. Years after the disappearance of Philippe Toussaint.

If Irène Fayolle had known that, one day, the "woman who looks after the cemetery" would spend a night of love with her son.

I've had no news from Julien Seul. I imagine he'll turn up one morning, silently, like he usually does. Like me when I left the Hôtel Armance.

I think of our night of love as I stand in front of the coffin of Marie Gaillard (1924–2017), which is being interred. It seems that Marie Gaillard was a nasty piece of work. Her housekeeper has just whispered in my ear that she'd come to the funeral of the "old woman" to make sure that she really was dead. I pinched the palm of my hand hard so as not to laugh. There's not a soul around the tomb, not even the cemetery's cats. Not a flower, not a plaque. Marie Gaillard is buried in the family vault. I hope she won't be too vile to those she's joining.

It's not uncommon to see visitors spitting on tombs. I've even seen it more often than I would have believed. When I first started, I thought hostilities died with the hated person. But tombstones don't put the lid on hatred. I've attended funerals with no tears. I've even attended happy funerals. There are some deaths that are convenient for everyone.

After Marie Gaillard's interment, the housekeeper muttered that "nastiness is like manure, its stink hangs in the wind for ages, even once it's been removed."

* * *

Starting in January of 1996, I returned to see Sasha every other Sunday. Like the parent without custody who sees their child every other weekend. I always borrowed Stéphanie's red Fiat Panda, which she lent me willingly. I set off in the morning, at 6 A.M., and returned in the evening. I sensed that it couldn't last. That very soon, Philippe Toussaint would ask me questions, stop me from going. He was very suspicious.

As my visits to Brancion cemetery continued, I changed, physically. Like a woman who has a lover. My only lover was the compost that Sasha taught me to make with horse dung. He taught me to turn it over in October, and then again in spring, depending on the weather. To watch out for earthworms, not to crush them, so they could "do their job."

He taught me to look at the sky and decide whether planting should be done in January or later, if I wanted to harvest in September.

He explained to me that nature took its time, that eggplants planted in January wouldn't emerge before September, and that, on industrial farms, they sprayed vegetables with vast quantities of chemical fertilizer so they would grow fast. A yield not required in the vegetable garden at Brancion cemetery. No one was waiting for these vegetables apart from him, the keeper, and me, his "old fledgling fallen from the nest." He taught me to use only nature to nurture nature. Never fertilizer, unless it was untreated. And to make a nettle slurry and sage infusion for treating the vegetables and flowers. Never pesticides. He said to me, "Violette, the natural way is much more work, but time, as long as one is alive, one finds it. It grows like the mushrooms in the morning dew."

He soon used the informal "*tu*" with me; I never did likewise.

When he saw me, he began by telling me off:

"Have you seen your getup! Can't you dress like the beautiful woman you are? In fact, why is your hair so short? Do you have lice?"

He said this to me as if talking to one of his cats, cats that he adored.

I would arrive on Sunday morning at around 10 A.M. I'd go into the cemetery and straight to Léonine's tomb. I knew that she was no longer *there*. That beneath that marble, there was just emptiness. Like a wasteland, a no-man's-land. I went there to read her first name and her surname. And to kiss them. I didn't leave flowers; Léonine couldn't care less about flowers. At seven years old, a girl prefers toys and magic wands.

When I pushed open the door to Sasha's house, there was always that aroma, that combination of simple cooking, of onions being softened in a pan, of tea, and of "*Rêve d'Ossian*," which he sprayed on handkerchiefs scattered here and there around the room. And me, as soon as I entered, I breathed more easily. I was on holiday.

We would have lunch, sitting opposite each other, and it was always good, colorful, spicy, aromatic, tasty, and without meat. He knew I couldn't stand it.

He would ask me questions about my fortnight, my daily existence, life in Malgrange-sur-Nancy, my work, what I was reading, the music I was listening to, the trains that went by. He never spoke to me of Philippe Toussaint, or, when he did come up, just said "him."

Before long, we would go out into his garden to work together. Whether it was freezing or fine, there was always something to do.

Planting, sorting seedlings, pricking out, positioning stakes, hoeing, weeding, taking cuttings, tidying the avenues, both of us leaning toward the earth, hands in the earth, all the time. On warm days, his favorite game was to target me with the hosepipe. Sasha had a child's-eye view, and the games that went with it.

He had been the keeper of this cemetery for years, he never spoke about his private life. The only wedding ring he wore was the one found in his first vegetable garden, around the carrot.

Sometimes, he would pull *Regain*, the novel by Jean Giono, out of his pocket and read me passages from it. I would recite the bits of *L'Oeuvre de Dieu, la part du Diable* I knew by heart.

Sometimes, we were interrupted by some emergency, someone who'd hurt their back or sprained an ankle. Sasha would say to me, "Carry on, I'll be back." He would disappear for half an hour to look after his patient, and always returned with a cup of tea, a smile on his lips, and the same question, "So, how's it going with our bit of earth?"

How I loved that first time. Hands in the earth, nose in the air, creating a link between the two. Learning that the one never went without the other. Returning two weeks after the first planting and seeing the transformation, approaching the seasons differently, the power of life.

Between those Sundays, the wait felt endless to me. The Sunday I didn't go to Brancion was a desert where only the future counted, the following Sunday on the horizon.

I spent my time reading the notes I had taken, on what I had planted, how I had done this or that cutting, my seedlings. Sasha had entrusted me with some gardening magazines, which I devoured, just as I had devoured *L'Oeuvre de Dieu, la part du Diable*.

After ten days, I felt like a prisoner counting the final hours before being released. From Thursday evening on, I was stamping my feet with impatience. On Friday and Saturday, unable to bear it any longer, I'd take myself for a walk between each train. I needed to, so as to channel my energy without Philippe Toussaint noticing. I took shortcuts that he didn't take on his motorbike. If, by chance, he was around, I told him that I was off to do some quick shopping. On Saturday, late afternoon, I went to pick up Stéphanie's Panda, parked outside her house.

Never has anyone in the world loved a car like I loved Stéphanie's Fiat Panda. No collector, no driver of a Ferrari or an Aston Martin has felt how I felt when placing my trembling hands on the steering wheel. When turning the key, going into first gear, pressing down on the accelerator.

I spoke to the white tiger. I imagined what I was going to find, the plants that had grown; the seedlings to be pricked out; the color of the leaves; the state of the soil, whether loose, dry, or soggy; the bark of the fruit trees; the progress of the buds, the vegetables, the flowers; the threat of frost. I imagined what Sasha had made me for lunch, the tea we would drink, the aroma of his house, his voice. Returning to my Wilbur Larch. My personal doctor.

Stéphanie thought I was impatient to return to my daughter, but I was impatient to return to life after my daughter. Lives other than mine. With the main one extinguished, the volcano was extinct. But I sensed branches, offshoots growing inside me. Whatever I sowed, I could feel it. I was sowing myself. And yet, the arid soil that was me was much poorer than that of the cemetery vegetable garden. A soil full of gravel. But a blade of grass can grow anywhere, and that anywhere was me. Yes, a root can take hold in tar. All that's needed is the tiniest crack for life to penetrate the impossible. A little rain, some sun, and then shoots from who knows where, from the wind perhaps, appear.

The day I squatted to pick the first tomatoes I had planted, six months earlier, Léonine had long been filling the garden with her presence, as if she had brought the Mediterranean to the little vegetable garden of the cemetery in which she was buried. That day, I knew that she was within each little miracle the soil produced.

57.

*Fate followed its path but
it never separated our hearts.*

JUNE 1996, GENEVIÈVE MAGNAN.

I'm so sensitive that whenever I read or hear the word "sour," my tongue hurts and my eyes sting. I burn all over. That's what I tell myself when I see an ad for sour candies on the TV. "You're too sensitive," my mother would spit at me, between wallops.

Must be a balance thing: since my soul's had it, worth only feeding to strays, my body makes up for it.

I change the channel. If only I could change life by flicking my remote. Since I've been unemployed, I'm slumped in my old armchair, not knowing what to do. Telling myself that nothing matters. That it's over. That they can't go back on it. That the matter's closed. They're dead. They're buried.

I was asleep when Swan Letellier phoned me. He left me a message I couldn't understand, his words were confused, he was in a right panic, everything gets jumbled up in his bird brain. I had to listen to it several times to make any sense of his words: Léonine Toussaint's mother was waiting for him outside the restaurant where he works as a cook, she seems crazy, she doesn't believe that the girls went into the kitchen to make themselves hot chocolate that night.

After the trial, I thought I'd never hear mention of Léonine ever again. Just like I'd never hear mention of Anaïs, Océane, and Nadège ever again. Thankfully, it was her, the boss, who got all the blame. Two years in the pen. About time the rich faced the shit, about time for a bit of justice, now and then. Never could stand her, that one, all holier-than-thou.

Léonine Toussaint's mother . . . The families weren't from around here. It's only middle-class types who send their brats to dip their bums in the lake of a château. I thought the parents were just ticking the cemetery-visit box when they came to our parts, and that they hurried back home once they'd left flowers and crucifixes on their kids' tombs.

What's she after? What does she want? Is she going to come to my place? Is she going to ask around? Letellier's panicking, I'm not, I stopped being afraid of anyone ages ago.

There were six of us at the château. Letellier, Croquevieille, Lindon, Fontanel, Petit, and me.

Thinking back on all that, it reminds me of the first time I saw him. Not the last, the first. Usually, I think of the last. And I have hatred burning in my veins, like rivers of sour candies.

The first time, it was an end-of-year party for the local nursery schools. I had sick on my shirt, milk reflux from my youngest, who'd been suffering due to the heat. I'd opened it up a little, so people wouldn't see the stain. He didn't look at me, he just glanced down at my nursing bra. I trembled. The look of a randy dog. He made me want him. Bad.

He didn't see me, but me, "I had eyes only for him," as the rich would say.

The two months of school holidays were a real downer.

Then I was employed as a domestic assistant for the nursery schools. On the first day, I waited for him, like a mutt. When I saw him entering the schoolyard to pick up his offspring, my skin went as hard as the leather of his biker jacket. I'd have liked to be the creature they'd cut into pieces to keep him warm.

He rarely came. It was always the mother who dropped off and picked up the child.

It took him months to say a word to me. He probably had nothing better to do that day. No other girls to do. He was a skirt chaser and, hell, was he dishy. You could tell he was a good screw from a hundred meters, with those T-shirts and tight jeans. With his icy blue eyes, he undressed anything in a skirt, like the mothers who came and went along the corridors that reeked of ammonia.

The windows I cleaned with Ajax after class . . . The brats I took to the toilets . . .

One day, I stopped him, just to say any old thing to him. Some story about glasses I'd supposedly found in a child's locker. Did they belong to him? He was as cold as the freezer in the school shed. He said, "No, they're not mine." He was used to females approaching him, you could see it, you could breathe it. He had the look of a devilish prince, a traitor, a swine, the handsome types, the ones in the old films.

At the end of the school year, after seeing me hanging around the corridors in the hope of bumping into him, cornering him, he finally gave me a date. Not a date to whisper sweet nothings in my ear; no, by giving me the time and place, he'd already undressed me.

He just came out with it, "One evening, and a quickie." Because he was married, like I was. He didn't want any hassle, or a hotel bed. He screwed in nightclub johns, against trees, or on the back seats of cars.

I took hours to get myself ready. Removing the hair from my legs, covering myself in Nivea cream, slapping a clay mask on my face, on my big conk, spraying perfume under my arms, dropping the kids off to a friend who'd keep mum. One who slept around, and whom I'd already covered for. One whose adultery would stop her from talking.

We were supposed to meet near the "little rock," as the locals called a big stone placed at the edge of town, a kind of broken boulder, a dark corner where kids had smashed the streetlights long ago.

He arrived on his motorbike. He placed his helmet on the seat. Like someone not staying long. He didn't say hello, good evening, how are you, to me. I think I barely smiled at him. My heart was pounding. Enough to make my chest burst. My new shoes were sinking in the mud, they'd given me blisters.

He turned me around. Without looking at me. He pulled down my underpants and tights, separated my thighs. No caresses, no gentle words, or rough ones. No words at all. He made me come so strong, I almost died. Started shaking like a dead leaf the tree's in a hurry to get rid of.

After, when he'd gone, my blisters and my eyes started weeping at the same time. Love, my mother had always told me that it was stuff for the rich. "Not for a good-for-nothing."

Every time I met him at the little rock, he screwed me from behind without looking at me. He came and went inside me, making me squeal like a sow having its throat slit. He never knew that my cries, they were heaven and hell, good and evil, pleasure and pain, the beginning of the end.

I felt his breath on the back of my neck, and I loved it. I wanted more. While he was doing up his fly, I'd say to him, "Meet again next week? Same time?" He'd reply, "OK."

The following week, I was there. I was always there. And him, not always, not every time. Sometimes he didn't come. He screwed elsewhere. Me, I waited, leaning against the freezing little rock. I waited for the lights of his motorbike. It went on like that for months.

The last time I saw him, he came by car. He wasn't alone. There was a man in the passenger seat. I panicked, I wanted to leave, but he grabbed me by the arm, gripped me roughly, and hissed between his teeth, "You stay there, you don't move, you're mine." He turned me round, defiled me in his usual way, and I let it be done, squealing. I could hear myself shouting. I heard the car door slam. I could hear my mother saying to me, "Love, that's for the rich." I heard him saying to the car passenger, who was right beside us, "She's yours, help yourself." I said no. But I let it be done.

They both left. I was still turned around, underpants around my ankles. A collapsed puppet. My mouth was pressed against the little rock. The taste of the stone in my mouth, a bit of moss, I thought it was blood.

After that, I moved house, the two kids in tow. Never saw him again.

Someone's knocking on my door, must be her. She didn't go to the funeral. Didn't go to the trial. She was bound to end up going somewhere.

58.

It's the words they didn't say
that make the dead so heavy in their coffins.

June 1996—I'd been visiting Sasha every other Sunday for six months. I'd just left him, still had soil under my fingernails. I put their address on my dashboard. A place known as La Biche aux Chailles, just past Mâcon. I drove for about half an hour, got lost in the small roads, kept going forward, kept reversing, cried with rage. I finally found it. A small house covered in roughcast that was shabby and grubby, stuck between two others that were bigger and more imposing. It looked like a poor little girl between her two parents dressed in their finest.

Both of their names were on the letterbox that hung on the door: "G. Magnan. A. Fontanel."

My heart started racing. I felt nauseous.

It was already late. I thought about how I'd have to drive at night to get back to Malgrange, and how I hated doing that. With my stomach churning, I knocked several times. I must have knocked hard. I hurt my fingers. I saw the soil under my fingernails. My skin was dry.

It was she who opened the door. I didn't instantly make the link between the woman standing before me and the one posing in a ridiculous hat at a wedding, in the photo Sasha had slipped in the envelope. She had seriously aged and put on weight since that photo had been taken. In the picture, she was badly made-up, but she was made-up. In this late-afternoon light, her skin was marked by the years. She had purplish shadows under her eyes and red blotches down her cheeks.

"Hello, I'm Violette Toussaint. I'm the mother of Léonine. Léonine Toussaint."

Saying the first name and surname of my daughter in front of this woman chilled my blood. I thought: *She probably served Léo her last meal.* I thought, for the thousandth time: *How could I have let my seven-year-old daughter go to* that place?

Geneviève Magnan didn't respond. She remained stony-faced and let me go on without opening her mouth. Everything about her was double-locked. No smile, no expression, just her sticky, bloodshot eyes staring at me.

"I would like to know what you saw on that night, the night of the fire."

"What for?"

Her question astounded me. And without thinking, I replied:

"I don't believe that, at seven years old, my daughter went into a kitchen to heat herself some milk."

"Should have said that at the trial, then."

I felt my legs shaking.

"And you, Madame Magnan, what did you say at the trial?"

"I had nothing to say."

She whispered goodbye to me and slammed the door in my face. I believe I remained like that for a long while, breath taken away, in front of her door, looking at the flaking paint and their names written on some plastic tape: "G. Magnan. A. Fontanel."

I got back into Stéphanie's Fiat Panda. My hands were still shaking. I had sensed, when speaking to Swan Letellier, that something wasn't clear about the sequence of events on *that night*, and my "meeting" with Geneviève Magnan had merely confirmed it. Why did these people all seem so elusive? Was it me who was imagining things? Was I going crazy? Even more crazy?

During the return journey, I went from lightness to darkness. I thought of Sasha, and of the staff at the château of

Notre-Dame-des-Prés. I decided that, next time, the Sunday after next, I would go to the château. I had never felt strong enough to go past it. And yet it was only five kilometers from the Brancion cemetery. And I would return to the home of Magnan and Fontanel, and I would kick their door until they finally spoke.

I arrived outside my house at 22:37. I just had enough time to park before lowering the barrier for the 22:40 train. When I opened the door, I saw Philippe Toussaint, who had dropped off on the sofa. I looked at him without waking him, thinking that I had loved him, a long time ago. That if I'd been eighteen with short hair, I would have thrown myself on him, saying: "Shall we make love?" But I was eleven years older and my hair had grown longer.

I went to lie down on my bed. I closed my eyes without finding sleep. Philippe Toussaint came and slid into the bed in the middle of the night. He grumbled, "So, you're back." I thought: *Lucky I am, or who would have lowered the barrier for the 22:40?* I pretended to sleep, not to hear him. I sensed that he was sniffing me, that he was seeking the smell of someone else in my hair. The only smell he must have found was the air freshener from the Fiat Panda. He was soon snoring.

I thought of a story about seeds that Sasha had told me. He had tried to plant melons in his vegetable garden, they had never grown. He had tried two years in a row, nothing doing, the melons refused to grow. The following year, he had thrown the rest of the melon seeds to the birds. Further away, at the back of the vegetable garden, where there were piles of pots, rakes, watering cans, and planters. One of those birds, carelessly or mischievously, must have carried one of the seeds in its beak and dropped it in the middle of a path in the garden. A few months later, a fine plant had grown, and Sasha hadn't pulled it up, just walked around it. It had produced two beautiful melons. Nice and plump, nice and sweet. And every year, it had again produced one, two, three, four, five. Sasha had said to me, "You see, they're melons from heaven, that's what nature is all about, it's she who decides."

I fell asleep on those words.

I dreamt of a memory. I was taking Léonine to school. It was the first day of term at primary school. We were walking along the corridors. Her hand in mine. Then she had let mine go because she was "a big girl now."

I woke up screaming:

"I know her! I've seen her before!"

Philippe Toussaint switched the bedside lamp on.

"What? What's up?"

He rubbed his eyes, looked at me as if I were possessed.

"I know her! She worked at the school. Not in Léonine's class, in the one next door."

"What're you talking about?"

"I saw her. After the cemetery, I stopped by at Geneviève Magnan's."

Philippe Toussaint looked horrified.

"What?"

I looked down.

"I need to understand. To meet the people who were at the château of Notre-Dame-des-Prés that night."

He got up, walked around the bed, grabbed me by the collar, and, choking me, yanked me right up and started screaming:

"You're beginning to seriously piss me off! Carry on, and I'll get you locked up. Do you hear me? And I warn you, you're not going back there! Do you hear me? NEVER set foot over there, ever again!"

Over the years, he had let me sink into a bottomless solitude, a black pit. I could just as well have been someone else, got myself replaced, employed a temp to lower and raise the barrier, do the shopping, make lunch and supper, wash his clothes, and sleep on the left side of the bed, he wouldn't have cared, wouldn't have noticed.

Never had he knocked me about or threatened me. By doing that, he brought me to my senses. I became myself again.

* * *

The following morning, I went to Stephanie's to return the keys to the Panda. On Mondays, the Casino was closed. She lived alone on Grand-Rue, on the first floor of a house. She made me come in and poured me some coffee in a ceramic goblet. She was wearing a long T-shirt with Claudia Schiffer on it, and said, "Monday, at home, it's cleaning day." It seemed odd to me, seeing her head above that supermodel's, but it's her head that moved me to tears, her friendly round face, her lovely rosy cheeks, her tow-colored hair.

"I filled her up for you."

"Oh, well, thanks a lot."

"Looks like it's going to be nice today."

"Oh, well, yes."

"It's good, your coffee . . . My husband doesn't want me to go to Brancion cemetery anymore."

"Oh, right, well, hold on, hey. It's for going to see your kid, after all, isn't it."

"Yes, I know. In any case, thanks for everything."

"Oh, well, it's nothing, hey."

"Yes, Stéphanie, it's everything."

I clasped her in my arms. She didn't dare move. As if no one had ever shown her the slightest sign of affection. Her eyes and mouth became even rounder than normal. Three flying saucers. Stéphanie would remain forever an enigma, the Martian of the Casino. I abandoned her there, arms dangling, in the middle of her sitting room.

Next, I went back along Grand-Rue, heading for the primary

school. Like in Dave's song, "Swann's Way," I took the same route backwards. The one I took every morning with Léo. In her satchel, the Tupperware box took up more space than her textbooks and exercise books. I was obsessive about making her lavish packed snacks, so she never went without. Because I still had that emptiness the foster families had left me with. When we'd go on a school trip, and the others would have chips, bars of chocolate, sandwiches made with farmhouse bread, sweets, and fizzy drinks in their knapsacks. Me, it's not that I went without, but there were no treats in my plastic bag. "Girls in care are happy with very little." It wasn't the fact of having less that upset me, it was not being able to share my frugal lunch. Having just enough. I wanted to give Léonine the chance to share with the others.

It wasn't the children that disturbed me as I entered the covered playground, but the smells, from the canteen, a building adjoining the school, and the bustling corridors. It was lunchtime. I used to collect Léonine at lunchtime. And she often said to me, "You see, Mommy, the canteen doesn't smell very nice, I'm glad I go home."

On the pain scale, if such a shit scale exists, going into Léonine's school was harder than going into the cemetery. In Brancion, my daughter was dead among the dead. Inside her school, she was dead among the living.

The children who had been Léonine's friends were no longer there. They had just started middle school. I would have found seeing them unbearable, recognizing them without really recognizing them. The same figures, with "life" as an added option. Gangly, less baby-faced, mouths full of metal, feet in giants' trainers.

With pockets empty, I made my way along the corridors. I thought how Léonine wouldn't have wanted me to hold her hand anymore on the way to her classroom. A mom had told me that once they went to middle school, you lost a little bit more of them every year. Yes, and when they went to a holiday camp, you could lose them all in one go.

Léonine called her primary-school teacher "Mademoiselle Claire." When gentle Claire Berthier, bent over some exercise books, looked up and saw me coming into the classroom, she turned pale. We hadn't seen each other since my daughter's disappearance. My presence made her feel awkward, she clearly wished that the ground would swallow her up.

The death of a child is a strain on grown-ups, adults, other people, neighbors, storekeepers. They avert their eyes, avoid you, change sidewalks. When a child dies, for many people, the parents die, too.

We exchanged polite greetings. I didn't give her a chance to say anything. I immediately took out the photo of Geneviève Magnan, the one of her in the ridiculous hat.

"Do you know her?"

Surprised by my question, the teacher frowned and stared at the photo, replying that it didn't ring any bells. I persisted:

"I think she worked here."

"Here? You mean at the school?"

"Yes, in a neighboring class."

Claire Berthier turned her lovely green eyes back to the photo and studied Geneviève Magnan's face for longer.

"Ah . . . I think I remember, she was in Madame Piolet's class, with the large nursery groups . . . She arrived in the middle of the year. Didn't stay very long here."

"Thank you."

"Why are you showing me this photo? Are you looking for this lady?"

"No, no, I know where she lives."

Claire smiled at me the way one smiles at a madwoman, a sick woman, a widow, an orphan, an alcoholic, an idiot, a mother-who's-lost-her-child.

"Goodbye, and thank you."

59.

*It's when the tree is lying down that
one gets the measure of its stature.*

I put Irène Fayolle's journal into the drawer of my bedside table. I read the passages that refer to me randomly, never in chronological order. She came to my cemetery occasionally, between 2009 and 2015, to visit Gabriel's tomb. Years during which she made notes on the weather, on Gabriel, the surrounding tombs, the potted flowers, and me.

Julien had slipped colored paper between the pages where his mother talks about "the cemetery lady" in her journal. Like flowers lain over the lines in which she speaks of me. It instantly reminded me of Stefan Zweig's *Letter from an Unknown Woman*.

January 3rd, 2010
Today I noticed that the cemetery lady had been crying . . .

October 6th, 2009
As I was leaving the cemetery, I came across the lady who looks after it, she was smiling, she was accompanied by a gravedigger, a dog, and two cats . . .

July 6th, 2013
The cemetery lady often cleans the tombs, she's not obliged to . . .

September 28th, 2015
I came across the cemetery lady, she smiled at me but her thoughts seemed to be elsewhere . . .

*

April 7th, 2011
I just learned that the cemetery lady's husband
disappeared . . .

September 3rd, 2012
The cemetery lady's house was locked and the shutters
closed. I asked a gravedigger why, he told me that on Christmas
Day and September 3rd, the keeper didn't want to see anyone.
They're the only days of the year when she's replaced, apart
from the summer holidays . . .

June 7th, 2014
Apparently, the cemetery lady records the speeches made for the
deceased in notebooks . . .

August 10th, 2013
When buying some flowers, I learned that the cemetery lady
was on holiday in Marseilles. I could have walked past her . . .

When I read beyond the lines concerning me, when I open
the journal at places where there are no colored markers
slipped in by Julien, I feel as if I'm entering Irène's bedroom
and poking around under her mattress. Like her son when he
started looking for Philippe Toussaint. As for me, it's Gabriel
Prudent I'm looking for when I go out of bounds.

There are some words I can't make out. Irène wrote as illeg-
ibly as doctors do prescriptions. With her ballpoint pen, she
produced a tiny, spidery scrawl.

After their night of love in the Blue Room, Gabriel Prudent
and Irène Fayolle didn't leave the hotel together.

They had to vacate the room by midday. Gabriel called
reception to say that he would be staying another twenty-four

hours. He stroked Irène with his fingertips, murmuring, between drags:

"I need to sober up after all that alcohol, and, even more, I need to sober up after you before leaving here."

She took it badly. It was as if he'd said: "I need to rid myself of you before leaving here."

She got up, had a shower, got dressed. Since she'd been married, she'd never spent the night away from home. When she came out of the bathroom, Gabriel had fallen asleep. In the ashtray, acrid smoke was rising from a badly stubbed-out butt.

She opened the minibar for a bottle of water. Gabriel opened his eyes and watched her drinking from the bottle. She already had her coat on.

"Stay a little longer."

She wiped her mouth with the back of her hand. He loved this gesture. Her skin, her eyes, her hair gathered in a black elastic band.

"I've been away since yesterday morning. I was supposed to deliver flowers to Aix and return straight after . . . I'm sure my husband has already reported my disappearance."

"You're not tempted to disappear?"

"No."

"Come and live with me."

"I'm married and I have a son."

"Get divorced and bring your son with you. I get along pretty well with children."

"One can't get divorced just like that, with the flick of a magic wand. You seem to think everything is easy."

"But everything is easy."

"I don't want to go to my husband's funeral. You abandoned your wife and she died of it."

"You're becoming unpleasant."

She looked for her handbag. Checked her van keys were inside.

"No, realistic. One doesn't just abandon people like that. If you find it easy to pack in everything and start again elsewhere, without worrying about others, about their grief, well . . . that's fine."

"Each to their own life."

"No. The lives of others matter, too."

"I know, I spend mine defending those lives in various courts."

"It's the lives of strangers that you defend. The lives of people you don't know. Not your own life. Not the lives of your loved ones. It's almost . . . easy."

"We're already at the reproaches stage. After a single night of love. We may be going a little too fast, here."

"It's only the truth that hurts."

He raised his voice:

"I abhor the truth! It doesn't exist, the truth! It's like God . . . It's been invented by men!"

She shrugged her shoulders, as if to say what she did say:

"That doesn't surprise me."

He looked at her, sadly.

"Already . . . I don't surprise you anymore."

She agreed. Gave him a faint smile, and slammed the door without saying goodbye.

She went down by the stairs, three floors, looked for her van. She couldn't remember where she had parked the previous day. While searching for it in the streets around the hotel, along shopwindows announcing the final winter sales, she almost went back up to the room, to throw herself in his arms. When she was just about to turn back, she spotted her van, parked at the end of a cul-de-sac, half on a sidewalk, pretty much any old how.

At the end of a cul-de-sac. Any old how. It was all any old thing. She must go home, get back to Paul and Julien.

In the van, there was a smell of stale smoke. She opened the windows wide, despite it being winter. She drove directly to Marseilles. She didn't stop off at the rose nursery. She went straight home.

Paul was waiting for her. When she opened the door, he almost shouted, "Is that you?" He was worried sick, but hadn't reported her disappearance. He knew that his wife could disappear from one day to the next. He'd always known it. Too beautiful, too taciturn, too secretive.

She apologized to him. Told him that she'd had an unexpected encounter at the cemetery, a widower abandoned by his family, anyhow, in short, a strange story, she'd had to look after everything.

"What do you mean, everything?"

"Everything."

Paul never asked questions. For him, questions belonged to the past. Paul lived in the present.

"Next time, call me."

"Have you eaten?"

"No."

"Where's Julien?"

"At school."

"Are you hungry?"

"Yes."

"I'll make some pasta."

"O.K."

She smiled, went to the kitchen, took out a saucepan, filled it with water, put it on the stove, adding salt and herbs. She thought back to the pasta she'd eaten the previous day with Gabriel, to the love they had made.

Paul came into the kitchen, pressed himself to her back, kissed her on the nape of her neck.

She closed her eyes.

60.

A memory never dies, it merely falls asleep.

JUNE 1996, GENEVIÈVE MAGNAN

The Parisian girls arrived in a minibus—suitcases, pigtails, braids, flowery dresses, sick bags, squeals of joy. Lots of chattering, lots of whining: six- to nine-yearolds. Some I knew, already seen them the year before. Only girls. Four will be arriving by car, later. Two kids from Calais, two from Nancy.

I've never liked girls; remind me of my sisters. Couldn't stand 'em. Thankfully, I just had two boys, tough ones. They don't whine, boys. They fight, but they don't whine.

I've never been good at math. Or any other subjects, come to that. But I do know what the scale of probability is—my crap life taught me that only too well, just let me knock that into your thick head. The bigger the number, the bigger the chance of the thing happening. But in this case, the number was minuscule. A godforsaken place of three hundred souls, where I was a replacement for two years.

When I saw her getting out of the car, looking peaky, my first thought was of a resemblance, not of the scale of probability. I said to myself: *Old girl, you're nuts. You see* evil *everywhere*.

I went off to the kitchen to make pancakes for the lot of them. I found them again in the refectory, sitting around jugs of water and bottles of grenadine syrup, and served them a pile of pancakes sprinkled with sugar, which they gobbled up.

When the boss called the register, and the little girl replied, "Present," on hearing her surname, I nearly fainted. A name that goes with the dead.

One of the supervisors gave me a glass of cold water. She said, "Is it the heat making you feel queasy, Geneviève?" I replied, "That must be it."

At that moment, I realized that the Devil existed. God I'd always known was an invention for suckers, but not the Devil. That day, I'd have almost taken my hat off to him, a hat I've never had. In my family, we almost never wore hats.

"Hats, they're just for the bourgeoisie," my mother would say, between wallops.

The kid looked like her father, two peas in a pod. I watched her eating her pancake, and thought back to that last time, that taste of blood in my mouth. It was three years since I'd seen him, and I thought about it all the time. Sometimes, at night, I'd wake up in a sweat, I'd dreamt of missing him, and that yearning to get my revenge, too, have his hide like he'd had mine.

After tea, the brats went out to stretch their legs. I cleared the tables, it was a lovely day, I opened the windows, I saw her playing, running with the others with squeals of joy. I thought to myself that I wouldn't last the week. Seven days of seeing him through her, at morning, midday, and evening meals. I'd have to call in sick. But this work, I needed it. The upkeep of the château gave me a living all year. And I couldn't clear off in full season. The boss had warned us: in July and August, no absences allowed unless you're dying. A right bitch, that one, all holier-than-thou.

I thought of tripping the kid up so she broke a leg on the stairs and got sent back to her father pronto. No one the wiser, return to sender. With a note pinned to her dress, "With my worst memories."

I prepared the grub. Tomato salad, breaded fish, rice pilaf, and creamy desserts. I laid the tables, twenty-nine settings, Fontanel gave me a hand.

"You don't look quite yourself, old girl."

I asked him to shut it. That made him laugh.

He leaned out of the window to ogle the two supervisors, while the brats were playing one, two, three, red light, green light.

One, two, three, red light, green light . . .

61.

We know that you would be with us today if heaven weren't so far away.

When we moved to the cemetery in August of 1997, Sasha had already left the house. As usual, the door was open. He had left a note and the keys for us on the table. He welcomed us, explained where to find the hot-water tank, electricity meter, water mains, lightbulbs, and spare fuses.

The tea caddies were gone. The house was clean. Without him, it was sad, it had lost its soul. Like a girl forsaken by her first love. I went upstairs for the first time, saw the empty bedroom.

The vegetable garden had been watered the previous day.

The head of the municipal technical department came to see us in the evening to check we'd settled in alright.

At first, people came to the house to get treatment for their tendinitis and their chronic pains, not knowing that Sasha had left. He had said goodbye to no one.

* * *

The church bells are ringing. Never a funeral on Sunday, just Mass, to call the living to order.

Usually, at midday on Sunday, it's Elvis who comes to have lunch with me. He brings me vanilla cream puffs, and I make him penne with mushrooms. I add a little fresh parsley on top. Delicious. According to the season, I pick what there is in the vegetable garden, and we have tomatoes, radishes, or a green-bean salad.

Elvis says very little. It doesn't bother me, with him there's no need to make conversation. Elvis is like me, he has no parents. He stayed at a Mâcon hostel until he was twelve, and then was sent to be a farmhand in Brancion-en-Chalon. The farm, just outside the village, is now in ruins.

All the members of that family have been dead and buried in my cemetery for a long time. Elvis never goes near their vault. He's scared of the father, Emilien Fourrier (1909–1983), a brute who hit everything that moved. Around their vault, the paths aren't raked. He has always told me that he doesn't want to be buried with them. He made me promise to see to it. For that I would have to die after him. So, I made him take out a funeral contract with the Lucchini brothers. That way, he would have his own tomb, just for him, with a photo of Elvis Presley soldered on top, and the words *Always on my mind* in golden lettering. Although Elvis looks like a child, as boys who've never known a mother's caresses often do, he'll soon be retiring.

It's Nono and I who do his accounts and fill in his admin papers. His real name is Eric Delpierre, but I've never heard anyone call him that. I think all the Brancion locals are unaware of his true identity. He's always gone by his stage name. He fell in love with Elvis Presley when he was eight. Some people enter religious orders, he entered Elvis, or maybe Elvis entered him. Elvis's songs touched him and stayed with him, like prayers. Father Cédric recites the "Our Father," and Elvis, "Love me Tender." I've never known him to have a girlfriend, and neither has Nono.

While looking for dried bay leaves in my condiments cupboard, I come across a letter from Sasha, slipped between the olive oil and the balsamic vinegar. I scatter Sasha's letters around the house in order to forget them and then finally come across them by chance. This one dates back to March 1997.

"Dear Violette,

My garden has become sadder than my cemetery. As the days go by, they feel like little funerals.

What can I do to see you again? Do you want me to organize your abduction, over there, where the trains are?

Two Sundays a month, it was hardly excessive. No big deal.

But why do you actually obey him? Are you aware that, sometimes, one must be a rebel? And anyhow, who's going to look after my new tomato plants?

Yesterday, Madame Gordon came for me to heal her shingles. She left smiling. When she asked me, "What can I do to thank you?" I almost replied, "Go and get Violette for me."

I'm in the middle of doing my carrot seedlings. I put the seeds in pottery cups. I've spread my seedlings around my sitting room, beside the tea caddies, just behind the windows. That way, when the sun hits, it's directly on them. When it's hot, they grow well. Nothing works like the heat. The ideal would be to put them in front of a fireplace, but my little house doesn't have one. That's why Father Christmas never visits me. Next, when they have grown well, I'll put them under glass. Onions, shallots, and beans you can put straight into the soil. But not carrots. Never forget the ice saints, on May 11th, 12th, and 13th every year. That's when it's make or break, that's when you have to prick them out. In theory. If you want to protect your young shoots, place pots over them at night, or some light clingwrap.

Come back soon. Don't be like Father Christmas.

With all my best wishes,

Sasha."

Elvis knocks on the door and comes in with his vanilla cream puffs wrapped in white paper. I fold up Sasha's letter and put it back in its place, to forget it, and come across it another time, by chance.

"Everything O.K., Elvis?"

"Violette, someone's looking for you. She said, 'I'm looking for Philippe Toussaint's wife.'"

My blood freezes. A shadow follows Elvis. She comes in. She stares at me without saying a word. Next, her eyes sweep around the inside of the house, and then return to me. I can see that she's cried a lot—I'm used to seeing people who have cried a lot, even if it was several days before.

Elvis calls Eliane by slapping both thighs, and takes her outside, as if wanting to protect her. The dog cheerfully follows him. She's used to going off on walks with him.

Now there's only her and me in the house.

"You know who I am?"

"Yes. Françoise Pelletier."

"You know why I'm here?"

"No."

She takes a deep breath to hold back her tears.

"You saw Philippe, on that day?"

"Yes."

She reels from the blow.

"What did he come here for?"

"To return a letter to me."

She feels unwell, she changes color, her forehead is beaded with sweat. She doesn't move an inch, and yet, in her midnight-blue eyes, I see cyclones passing. Her hands are clenched. Her nails digging into the skin.

"Have a seat."

She musters a faint smile of gratitude and pulls over a chair. I serve her a large glass of water.

"What letter?"

"I'd sent him a request for a divorce, to your place, in Bron."

My reply seems to come as a relief to her.

"He wanted to hear nothing more of you."

"Me neither."

"He said he'd gone crazy because of you. He hated this place, this cemetery."

" . . . "

"Why did you stay here once he'd left? Why didn't you move? Make a new life for yourself?"

" . . . "

"You're a pretty woman."

" . . . "

Françoise Pelletier downs her glass of water in one go. She's shaking a lot. The death of the other slows down the movement of the one left behind. Her every movement seemed held back by that slowness. I serve her more water. She gives me a pained smile.

"The first time I saw Philippe, it was in Charleville-Mézières in 1970, the day of his First Communion. He was twelve and I was nineteen. He was wearing a white surplice, and a wooden cross hung from his neck. I've never seen anyone look so wrong in an outfit. I remember saying to myself: 'Doesn't ring true, this kid dressed up as a choirboy.' The sort that drinks the Communion wine and smokes cigarettes in secret. I'd just got engaged to Luc Pelletier, the brother of Chantal Toussaint, Philippe's mother. Luc had insisted that we go to Mass in the morning and have lunch with them. He didn't get on at all with his sister and brother-in-law, he called them 'the stuck-ups,' but he adored his nephew. We had a pretty tedious day. We waited for Philippe to open his presents, and by 3 P.M. we'd already left. Philippe's mother gave me dirty looks all day; we could tell that it infuriated her that her brother had got himself a young girl. I was thirty years younger than Luc.

"That same year, we got married in Lyons, Luc and I; Philippe and his parents came to our wedding, oozing resentment. Philippe got drunk by downing all the dregs in the adults' glasses. He was so drunk that, at the start of the dancing, he kissed me on the lips and hollered, 'I love you, auntie.' He made all the guests laugh. He spent the rest of the evening vomiting in the bathroom, while his mother guarded the door, saying, 'Poor boy, he's had indigestion on and off all week.' She stuck up for him, no matter what. Philippe greatly amused me, I adored his lovely little face.

"After our wedding, Luc and I opened a garage in Bron. At first, we did basic repairs, oil changing, maintenance, body-work, and then we became dealers. The business was always profitable. We worked hard but never struggled. Never. Two years went by and Luc invited 'little Philippe,' as he called him, to come and stay with us during the summer holidays. We lived in a house in the country, about twenty minutes from our garage. Philippe celebrated his fourteenth birthday with us, and as a present, Luc gave him a motorbike, a 50cc. Philippe cried tears of joy. That's when Luc and his sister had a falling out. Chantal insulted her brother over the phone, calling him every name under the sun, asking him what made him think he could give a motorbike to her son, it was too dangerous, he wanted Philippe to kill himself; him, the good-for-nothing who'd never managed to have children. Which was true. He'd never had any. Neither with his first wife nor with me.

"That day, Chantal had touched a nerve. Luc never spoke to his sister again. But despite his parents' disapproval, Philippe returned to our house every summer. And he never wanted to leave. He said he wanted to live with us all year round. He begged us to keep him, but Luc explained that it wasn't possible, that if he did so, it would be his death warrant, his sister would kill him. He was a nice kid, chaotic but nice. Seeing him gave Luc pleasure, he'd transferred his affection to his nephew. Philippe was his surrogate son for a long time. I got on well with him. I spoke to him like I would to a child— he often reproached me for that, saying, 'I'm not a kid.'

"For the summer of his seventeenth birthday, he came on

holiday with us to Biot, near Cannes. We'd rented a villa with a sea view. And we went to the beach every day. We set off in the morning, had lunch in a straw-hut café, and went home in the evening. Philippe went out with girls, a different one every day. Sometimes, one of them would join us on the beach during the day. He would kiss them on his towel, and I found him disturbingly mature and disconcertingly laid-back. He always appeared not to give a damn about anything. He went dancing every evening, came back in the middle of the night. Before setting off, he monopolized the bathroom, and left the caps of his aftershaves lying around. He stole his uncle's razors, always left shaving foam around the edge of the basin, and never closed the toothpaste tube, left bath towels on the floor. That all succeeded in annoying Luc. It annoyed him, but it amused him, too. As for me, I picked up and washed the clothes of the kid that Luc and I would never have together. We liked having Philippe, he brought us youth, a carefreeness. There were just seven years between Philippe and me. They matter, those first twenty years, one's living on two different planets, but with time, the difference becomes less marked, the planets draw closer: a liking for the same films, the same TV series, the same music. One ends up laughing at the same things.

"During this stay in Biot, I had a fling with a bartender, nothing original or particularly risky. Luc and I loved each other. We were always crazy about each other. Luc often said to me, 'I'm an old fool, if you want to have fun with younger men, go for it, as long as I know nothing about it. And above all, you don't fall in love—that I couldn't handle.' With hindsight, I'm convinced that, by almost pushing me into the arms of other men, he hoped I'd end up pregnant. It was subconscious, of course, but I think he hoped for a long time that I'd come home one day with a bun in the oven. A little one he could have stamped with his name. Anyhow, during that summer holiday, we were having a party at the villa, around twenty people, and we'd all had a few drinks, and Philippe caught me with my handsome lover in the swimming pool. I'll never forget the look he gave me. In his eyes, I saw a mix of astonishment and pleasure, a sort of satisfaction. I think that night, he saw me as a woman for the first time. A woman and, therefore, prey. Philippe was a formidable predator. So beautiful, he would tempt a saint in heaven. But I don't need to tell you that . . .

"Of course, he said nothing to Luc, didn't tell on me, but whenever I passed him in the villa, he'd smile at me in a knowing way. A smile that meant: 'We're accomplices.' And I hated that. I could have slapped his face all day long. He became unbearably smug. We stopped laughing together, from one day to the next. I started to find his presence intolerable, the smell of his aftershave, the mess he left everywhere, the noise he made coming in at five in the morning. When I told him to get lost, Luc would say to me, 'Be nice to the boy, he gets enough from his mother to do his head in.' At the table, as soon as Luc had his back turned, Philippe would stare at me, faintly smiling. I'd look down, but I could feel his eyes on me, burning with arrogance.

"On the final evening, he got back earlier than usual, and without a girl. I was on the terrace, alone, lying on a sunlounger, and I'd dozed off. He placed his lips on mine, I woke up, and I slapped his face, saying to him, 'Listen to me carefully, you jerk, do that once more and you'll never set foot in our home again.' He went off to bed without batting an eyelid. The following day, we left the villa. We accompanied him to the station. He was getting a train to Charleville-Mézières. On the platform, he kissed us goodbye, hugging us both, Luc and me, one with each arm. I didn't want his affection, but had no choice. Luc couldn't bear the fact that I couldn't stand his nephew anymore. It made him very unhappy. I was trapped. Philippe thanked us a hundred times. While he was hugging us, he slid his hand down my back and placed it on my bottom, pressing me firmly against his thigh. I couldn't react, Luc was right there with us. Philippe's action chilled me. I thought what an outrageous cheek he had, and the ways of such a cocksure man. Finally, he let us go, 'Bye-bye auntie, bye-bye uncle.' He got on the train, throwing his bag over his shoulder, waved at us, with his angelic smile. And while I was glaring at him, he was smirking, as if to say, 'Got you.'

"We went home to Bron, and got back to work. The following spring, Philippe phoned us to say he wouldn't be with us that summer, he was going away to celebrate his eighteenth birthday in Spain with friends. I admit that it was a relief. I wouldn't have to be near him, or avoid his looks and inappropriate gestures. Luc was very disappointed, but as he hung up, he said, 'It's normal, at his age.' We returned to Biot, spent a month with friends we'd joined there, but Luc missed Philippe being around. He often said to me, 'The house is too tidy, there's not enough noise here.' Actually, it wasn't Philippe himself he was missing, even though Luc was very attached to him, but a child of our own. I remember that, coming home from the holiday, on the return journey, I suggested adopting a child. He said no. Doubtless because he'd thought about it at length. He just told me that we were good together, us two, so good.

"In January of the following year, Luc and Chantal's mother died. We went to the funeral, and despite the circumstances, Luc and his sister didn't say a word to each other. Philippe was there. We hadn't seen him for a year and a half. He had changed a lot. Luc gave him a long hug, pointing out that now, Philippe was a head taller than him. Philippe pretended not to see me for the entire ceremony. Just before getting into the car, while Luc was off saying goodbye to family, he trapped me against the door, looking down at me from his full one-meter-eighty-eight, and saying, 'So, auntie, you were here, didn't see you.' And he kissed me on the mouth before I had time to react, and whispered to me, 'See you next summer.'

"And next summer arrived. The summer of his twentieth birthday. Before he'd even reached his bedroom at the villa, I grabbed him by the collar. He stared wide-eyed, amused; I must have been a funny sight. Me, measuring one meter sixty on tiptoe; him, huge, back to the corridor wall; and my small, shaking hands gripping him with all their might. 'I warn you,' I said to him, 'if you want to have a nice holiday, you give it a rest. You don't come near me, don't look at me, don't even hint at anything, and all will go smoothly.' He replied, sarcastically, 'O.K., auntie, promise, I'll keep my nose clean.'

"From then on, he behaved as if I didn't exist. He remained polite, good morning, good night, thank you, see you later, but our exchanges were limited to those four niceties. We set off for the beach together in the morning, him in the back seat, us two in front. He still went out late, scattered his things around the house. Girls came to find him during the night, or on his beach towel in the afternoon; sometimes, he went off to screw one behind a rock; it was an endless parade of boobs. And furtive giggling wherever we went. It cracked Luc up. Philippe was so handsome, with his angelic face, blond curls, and tanned skin. He had a man's body, neat and muscular; on the beach, all the girls ogled him, the women, too, even the other men envied him. It gave him so much confidence, all those eyes turned to him. Sometimes, Luc would whisper in my ear, 'My sister must have cheated on Father Toussaint, it's not possible that those two horrors could have produced such a beautiful kid.' It made me laugh so much. Luc always made me laugh. I really had a lovely life with him. I was spoiled with love. We were the best friends in the world, I couldn't have survived being apart. He was a friend, a father, a brother. Not much action in our bed anymore, but I made up for that elsewhere, now and then.

"I know what you're thinking: *When did Philippe finally get her?*"

A lengthy silence ensues before Françoise continues her monologue. She removes an imaginary stain from her jeans with the back of her hand. Time has stopped. We're alone, face to face. It's as if Philippe had changed his scent. As if Françoise was introducing a stranger into my kitchen.

"On the evening of his twentieth birthday, Luc and I organized a party for Philippe at the villa. His young friends came. There was music, alcohol, and a buffet set up beside the small swimming pool. It was warm, we all danced together, I don't know what came over me, but I started flirting with one of Philippe's friends, a certain Roland, a young dimwit Philippe hung out with. We went off to make out. We finally rejoined the others for the birthday cake and presents. When we reappeared, Philippe stared daggers at me. I thought he was going to let me have it. He blew out his twenty candles, eyes full of rage. Meanwhile, Luc had his present, festooned with red ribbon, rolled out to his nephew: a gray Honda CB100, and a check for a thousand francs in an envelope, attached to the full-face helmet. There were hugs, champagne glasses raised aloft, cries of joy and amazement. I could see that Philippe was pretending to be relaxed, smiling at everyone, showing off as usual, but his jaw remained clenched. He was seriously annoyed. When the music started up again, and we were all dancing, Roland was all over me again, so Philippe grabbed him by the shoulder, said something in his ear, to which Roland replied, 'Are you serious, man?' And the punches started flying. Luc, who had retired to bed, got up when he heard the racket, and threw Roland out the door, with several kicks up the backside. When it came to his nephew, Luc reacted like his sister: nothing was his fault. Luc asked Philippe what had gone on, Philippe, already pretty tipsy, replied, 'Roland's hunting on my territory . . . my territory is my territory!!!'

"The party just carried on as if nothing had happened. That night, I didn't sleep. Philippe undressed one of his girlfriends and stuck her on the ledge of our bedroom window. I could make out their silhouettes writhing in all directions. I heard the girl groaning and Philippe telling her all sorts of salacious and smutty things, which were very clearly aimed at me. He spoke loud enough for me to hear, but not to wake up Luc. He knew his uncle took sleeping pills at night. He also knew that I was *there*, close to them, eyes wide open, head on pillow, and could hear *everything*. He was getting his revenge. In the days that followed, we barely glimpsed him. He went off to ride his motorbike, from morning to night. Even during the day, he no longer joined us on the beach. His towel stayed dry and unoccupied. Sometimes, I'd doze off, and I'd dream that he was standing beside me, and then lying down, fully stretched out, on my back. I would wake up suffocating.

"About a fortnight after his birthday, he made an appearance on the beach. I'd gone for a swim, far from the shore. I saw him approaching Luc, just as a distant figure. His blondness and his bearing. He embraced him warmly, and sat beside him. Luc ended up pointing me out. Philippe spotted me and got undressed. He dived in the water to join me. He came toward me, swimming the crawl. I couldn't escape. I was trapped, cornered. As he was nearing me, I started to panic, I couldn't swim anymore, I was treading water. I don't know why, but I convinced myself that he was coming to drown me, to harm me. I panicked so much that I started to sob. I started to cry out. But from where I was, no one heard me. I'd passed the lifebelts a while back. In a few minutes, he reached me. He instantly saw that I was in a state. I carried on calling for help, but without looking at him. He tried to help me, but I hit him, screaming, 'Don't touch me!' And gulped a mouthful of water. He heaved me, forcibly, onto his back and brought me, as best he could, as far as a floating buoy. While he was swimming, I was hitting him, and he hit me back to make me calm me down. We finally made it. I clung to the buoy. He was exhausted, too. We got our breath back. He said, 'Now just calm down! Catch your breath, and we'll get back to the beach!' I shouted, 'Don't you touch me!'—'I can't touch you, but all of my friends can screw you, is that it?!'—'You, you're my nephew!'—'No, I'm Luc's nephew.'—'You're just a spoiled brat!'—'I love you!'—'Stop that right now!'—'No, I'll never stop!' I started to feel cold, to shiver. I looked toward the beach, it seemed so far to me. I saw Luc. I longed for his heavy, protective, reassuring arms. I asked Philippe to take me to the shore. He again heaved me onto his back, I put my hands around his neck, and he started to swim the breaststroke, and I let myself be carried. I sensed his muscles under my body, but I felt nothing but fear and loathing.

"I didn't see Philippe again for the two following summers. Luc and I went off to Morocco. He phoned us from time to time to give us his news. He came to see us in May, almost three years after the episode at the beach. The year of his twenty-third birthday. He came on the Honda that Luc had given him with a girlfriend riding behind him. When he took off his helmet, I saw his face, his smile, his eyes, and, to the day I die, I'll remember saying to myself: *I love him*. It was warm that day. We had supper, all four of us, in the garden. We stayed talking for a long while, about everything and nothing. The girlfriend, whose name I've forgotten, was very young. Very intimidated. Luc was thrilled to see his nephew again. Philippe had left school long before, he was drifting from one casual job to another. My heart skipped a beat when Luc suggested employing him at the garage. He told him he would train him, and if all went well, he'd take him on. I've never believed in God. I didn't do any catechism, and I've rarely set foot in a church, but that evening I prayed: *Dear God, please don't let Philippe ever come to work with us*. I immediately felt

Philippe's eyes on me. He replied to his uncle, 'Let me talk to my father, we don't want him kicking up a big fuss.' We all went off to bed. I didn't sleep all night. The following day was a public holiday. Philippe and his girlfriend got up late. We hung around until lunchtime. In the afternoon, Luc had a nap, and I stayed watching television with Philippe's girlfriend, while he went off for a ride on his bike.

"Since their arrival, I'd done all I could not to find myself alone with him. And then it happened at aperitif time. I went down to the cellar to fetch a bottle of champagne, I smelled his aftershave behind me. He wasted no time. He said, 'I'm not going to come and work at your garage, but this evening, at midnight, you must come out to the garden, sit on the low wall, and wait.' Before I'd even opened my mouth, he'd cut in, 'I won't touch you.' He went straight back upstairs. I took the bottle and rejoined Luc and the young girl, sitting at the table waiting for me. Philippe arrived five minutes later, as though coming in from outside. I wondered what he was expecting of me. At the back of the garden, there was a log shed, and behind it, an old, low wall. An old, low wall Philippe had enjoyed skateboarding on as an adolescent. Indeed, Luc called it 'Philippe's wall': 'We should put some planters on Philippe's wall,' 'Must give a lick of paint to Philippe's wall,' 'Saw a lovely angora cat the other day on Philippe's wall . . .'

"The evening went by in a haze, I drank like a fish. At 11 P.M., everyone got up to go to bed. Philippe looked at me, and then said to Luc, 'Uncle, I don't think I'll be able to come and work for you, I spoke to the parents today, they made a big fuss about it.' Luc replied, 'Never mind, dear boy.'

"I opened a book in bed, Luc fell asleep against me. The later it got, the more my heart raced. There wasn't a sound in the house. At 11:55 P.M., I slipped a coat on, and went to sit on the low wall. I was in complete darkness. The garden faced the back of the house, so no street lighting. I remember jumping at the slightest noise. And I was afraid that Luc would wake up and look everywhere for me. I don't know how long I stayed sitting there like that, not moving. I was paralyzed with terror. Nothing happened. Just silence all around me. But I didn't dare move, thinking: *If I move, Philippe will change his mind, he'll come and work for us.* If that had happened, I would have left. I would have got a divorce without saying a thing to Luc. It would have killed him to know that his adored nephew *wanted me.* It would have killed him to know that *I loved him.*

"Philippe and his girlfriend finally turned up. He said to her, 'Say nothing, let yourself be led.' Philippe was holding her by the hand, she didn't know where she was going, she'd been blindfolded. In his other hand, he had a flashlight, which he directed at me. He lit me up. It hurt my eyes. All I could see of them was their silhouettes. He placed the girl with her back to a tree. He was facing me. He put the flashlight down by his feet, still directed at me. It was like being caught in the headlights of a car. He said, 'I want to see your face.' The girl thought he was talking to her. He gave her a whole load of instructions, which she carried out before my eyes, not knowing that I was there, close by. 'Since it's forbidden, I at least want to kiss your face.' He made love to the girl. I didn't see him, I was blinded, but I sensed him staring at me. At one moment, he said, 'Come, come, come.' Until I got up and approached them. She still had her back to me, Philippe was pressed to her, facing her, facing me. I was so close to them that I could smell their bodies. 'Yes, that's it, see how much I love you.' His eyes looking straight into mine, never will I forget it. Or his sad smile. How he held her, his thrusting, his eyes looking straight into mine, his climax, his victory over me.

"I returned to my bedroom, shaking, I fell asleep against Luc. That night, I dreamt of Philippe. And the nights that followed, too. The next day, Philippe and the girl went home. I didn't see them leave. I used a headache as an excuse to stay in bed. When I heard his motorbike start up, and then the sound of the engine fade away, I got up, promising myself never to see him again. But I thought about him. Often. The following summer, I organized a trip to the Seychelles with Luc for a romantic holiday, telling him I felt like having a second honeymoon with him.

"I saw Philippe again the summer he was twenty-five. He turned up at the villa without warning. Luc knew, they wanted to surprise me. I pretended to be pleased, I wanted to vomit, too many emotions, loathing, attraction. That very evening, he was back making love to a girl under my windows, murmuring, 'Come, come, come, see how much I love you.' It went on for a month. I tried to avoid him all day long. When our paths crossed at breakfast, he'd say to me, with feigned cheeriness, 'Good morning, auntie, sleep well?' But he didn't smile anymore. He seemed unhappy. Something had changed. And yet, every night, he was at it again with a different girl. I didn't smile anymore, either. I, too, was unhappy. He had succeeded in contaminating me with an unhealthy love. I was more infected by him than in love with him.

"On the last day of the holidays, I was the one who took him to the station. I told him that I never wanted to see him again. He replied, 'Come, we're leaving together. I feel that with you, everything is possible, with you, I can face anything. If you refuse, I'll become a loser, a good-for-nothing.' He broke my heart. I made him understand, gently, that I would never leave Luc. Never. He asked me if he could kiss me one last time, I said no . . . If I'd let him kiss me, I would have left with him.

"On August 30th, 1983, once his train had disappeared, I knew that I wouldn't see him again. I felt it. Not in that life, anyhow. You know, there are several lives within a life.

"We lost touch with Philippe. At first, he continued to phone us, and then, little by little, as the years went by, nothing anymore. Luc thought that he'd ended up doing his parents' bidding. That he'd sided with them. We returned to our routine, our life. A peaceful, serene life. A year later, we heard that Philippe had met someone, you, that he'd had a child, that he'd got married. That he'd moved. But he never called us to tell us so. I knew it was because of me. But Luc suffered greatly from not hearing from him anymore.

"I think he would have loved to meet you, to meet your . . . Perhaps things would have been different. Easier. And then there was that tragedy. We learned about it almost by chance. The holiday camp. Horrendous. Luc wanted to contact Philippe. He phoned his sister to get your phone number, she slammed the phone down on him. He didn't persist. He put it down to grief. Luc said to me, 'And in any case, what could we say to them? Poor Philippe.'

"In October of 1996, Luc died in my arms, heart attack. And yet it had been a beautiful day. We'd laughed together at breakfast. By late morning, he'd stopped breathing. I screamed to make him open his eyes, I screamed to make his heart restart, but it was no use. Luc couldn't hear me anymore. I blamed myself. For a long time, I told myself that it had happened because of Philippe. Because of that funny, hidden love. That wasn't funny at all.

"I had him buried in the strictest privacy. I didn't tell Philippe's parents. What was the point? Luc couldn't have tolerated seeing them at his funeral. He might even have come back to life for five minutes, to box their ears and tell them to beat it. I didn't tell Philippe, either. What was the point? I decided to keep the garage, but I appointed a manager, I went away for several months, far from Bron. I needed to think, 'time to grieve,' as they say.

"Distancing myself didn't help me. Quite the opposite. I, in turn, nearly died. I had a nervous breakdown. I found myself in a psychiatric hospital under medication. I couldn't even count to ten anymore. Luc's death almost cost me my life, too. In losing my man, I lost my bearings. I was so young when I'd met him. When I began to resurface, I decided to take back control of the business. That garage, it was our whole life, particularly mine. I sold our house in the country to buy one in town, five minutes from the garage. On the day of the sale, when I handed the keys to the new owners, a blackbird was perched on Philippe's wall, singing its head off.

"In 1998, I was busy writing an estimate for a client's vehicle when I saw him enter the garage. I was in my office and, through the glass partition, I saw him arriving by bike. He hadn't yet taken his helmet off, but I already knew it was him. Fifteen years it was, since I'd last seen him. His body had changed, but his bearing was still the same. I thought I would die. I thought my heart, like my man's, was going to stop. I never thought I'd see him again one day. I rarely thought of him. He was part of my nights. I often dreamt of him, but during the day, rarely thought of him. He belonged to my memories. He took his helmet off. He started to belong to the present. He looked awful. Unwell. What a shock. I had left a kid of twenty-five on a station platform, and now I was seeing a somber man. I found him terribly handsome. Tired-looking, but handsome. I felt like running into his arms, like in those Lelouch films. I recalled his last words, 'Come, we're leaving together. I feel that with you, everything is possible, with you, I can face anything. Otherwise I'll become a loser, a good-for-nothing.'

"I walked toward him. And me? I, too, had changed. I was almost forty-seven. I was scrawny. My skin had taken the flak. I'd drunk too much and smoked too much. I don't think he cared a damn about that; when he saw me, he threw himself into my arms. 'Fell into my arms' would be more accurate. He sobbed. For a long time. In the middle of the garage. I took him to my place. Our place. He told me everything."

* * *

Françoise Pelletier has been gone for an hour. Her voice is echoing between my walls. I thought she'd come to find me to hurt me, when in fact, she made me a gift of the truth.

62

I no longer dream, I no longer smoke, I no longer even have a history, I'm dirty without you, I'm ugly without you, I'm like an orphan in a dormitory.

Gabriel Prudent stamped out his cigarette, and went into the rose nursery five minutes before closing time. Irène Fayolle had already switched off the lights in the shop, and access to the gardens was closed. She had lowered the heavy iron shutters. She was in the storeroom when she saw him in front of the counter. He was waiting like an abandoned, neglected customer.

They saw each other at the same time, her in the white light of a halogen lamp, him lit only by a red neon light hung above the entrance door.

She's still as beautiful. What's he doing here? I hope it's a nice surprise. Has he come to say something to me? She hasn't changed. He hasn't changed. How long has it been now? Three years. The last time, rather angry. He looks lost. Left without saying goodbye. Hope he doesn't hold it against me. No, or he wouldn't be here. Is she still with her husband? Has he made a new life for himself? Seems she's changed the color of her hair, it's lighter. Still in his old navy coat. Still all in beige. He looked younger on the television, last time. What has she been doing all this time? What has he seen, defended, known, eaten, lived? Years. Water under the bridge. Will she agree to have a drink with me? Why has he come so late? Does she remember me? He hasn't forgotten me. It's good that she's here. We're lucky, usually on Thursday evening, Paul comes to fetch me. I could just leave without saying a thing. Will he kiss me? Will she have any time for me? There's the parent-teacher meeting tonight.

Maybe I should have followed her into the street. Did he follow me? Pretended to bump into her on a sidewalk by chance. Paul and Julien are waiting for me outside the school at 7:30 P.M. The French teacher wants to talk to us. The first move, I'd like her to make the first move. That's a song, that is. And live, each in our own place. Will we go to the hotel? Will he make me drink like last time? She must have things to tell me. There's the English teacher, too. I must give her that present, I can't leave without giving her that present. What am I doing here? Her skin, the hotel. Her breath. He doesn't smoke anymore. Impossible, he'll never quit smoking. He just doesn't dare to here. His hands . . .

IRÈNE FAYOLLE'S JOURNAL

June 2nd, 1987

I came out of the storeroom, Gabriel followed me, smiling shyly, he the great lawyer, he with all that charisma, that lofty tone, he couldn't speak anymore, like a very small child. He who defended the criminal and the innocent, he couldn't say a thing to defend our love.

We found ourselves out in the street. Gabriel still hadn't given me my present and we hadn't exchanged a single word. I locked up the shop and we walked to my car. Like three years ago, he sat close to me, leaned his neck against the headrest, and I drove aimlessly. I no longer felt like stopping or parking. I didn't want him to get out of my car. I found myself on the motorway, drove towards Toulon, and then along the coast as far as Cap d'Antibes. It was 10 P.M. when, with the tank showing empty, I parked beside the sea, near a hotel, La Baie Dorée. We walked over to the panels displaying the room rates and the restaurant menus. A blonde woman welcomed us with a lovely smile. Gabriel asked if it wasn't too late to dine.

It was the first time I was hearing the sound of his voice since he had entered the rose nursery. In the car, he hadn't said a word. He had just searched for music on the radio.

The woman at reception replied that, in that season, the restaurant was closed during the week. She would have two salads and some club sandwiches sent up to our room.

We hadn't asked for a room.

Without waiting for a response, she handed us a key, for room 7, and asked whether we'd prefer white, red, or rosé to accompany our supper. I looked at Gabriel: when it came to alcohol, he did the choosing.

Finally, the lady at reception asked how many nights we would be staying, and then it was me who replied, "We don't know yet." She took us up to room 7 to show us how the lights and television worked.

On the stairs, Gabriel whispered in my ear, "We must look like we're in love, for her to offer us a room."

Room 7 was pale yellow. Its colors were those of the Midi. Before disappearing, the lady from reception opened a bay window leading to a terrace; the sea was black and the wind gentle. Gabriel placed his navy coat on the back of a chair and took something out of it that he handed to me. A small object covered in wrapping paper.

"I'd come to give it to you. I never thought that, by entering your rose nursery, we'd end up here, in this hotel."

"Are you sorry?"

"Not on your life."

I removed the wrapping paper. I discovered a snow globe. I turned it over several times.

The lady from reception knocked and pushed in a trolley, which she left in the middle of the room. She apologized and left as fast as she'd arrived.

Gabriel cupped my face in his hands and kissed me.

"Not on your life" are the last words he uttered that night. We touched neither the food nor the wine.

The following morning, I called Paul to tell him that I wouldn't be back immediately, and then hung up. Then I informed my employee, asking her to look after the rose nursery on her own for a few days. Somewhat panicked, she said, "I've got to deal with the register, too?" Yes, I replied. And hung up, without saying goodbye.

I thought I would never return. Disappear once and for all. Not face up to anything anymore, particularly Paul's look. Run away like a coward. See Julien again, but later, when he was older, when he would understand.

Neither Gabriel nor I had a change of clothes. The following day, we went to a boutique to buy some. He wouldn't allow me to choose beige, and bought me colorful dresses trimmed with gold. And sandals. I've always hated sandals. People being able to see my toes.

During these few days, I felt as if I were in disguise. Someone else in different clothes. Those of another woman.

For a long time, I wondered whether I was disguised, or whether it was myself that I had found, discovered for the first time.

A week after our arrival in Cap d'Antibes, Gabriel had to attend court in Lyons, to defend a man accused of homicide. Gabriel was certain of his innocence. He begged me to come with him. I thought: One might be able to abandon roses and one's family, but not a man accused of murder.

We returned to Marseilles to collect Gabriel's car, parked a few streets away from my rose nursery. I would leave my van, and the keys hidden on the front left wheel, as I often did, and we'd go to Lyons together.

When I saw Gabriel's car, a red convertible sports car, I thought how I didn't know this man. That I knew nothing about him. I'd just had the most wonderful days of my life, and what then?

I don't know why, but it reminded me of those holiday

romances. The handsome stranger on the beach you fall madly in love with, and see again, all stiff in his clothes, on a gray Paris street in September, having lost all his summer charm.

I thought of Paul. About Paul, I knew everything. His gentleness, his beauty, his refinement, his love, his shyness, our son.

At that very moment, I saw Paul at the wheel of his car. He must have just left the rose nursery. He must have been looking everywhere for me. He was very pale, lost in thought. He didn't see me. I would have liked his eyes to meet mine. By not seeing me, he left me the choice. Return to him, or get into Gabriel's car. I saw myself in a shopwindow. In my green-and-gold dress. I saw that other woman.

I said to Gabriel, who was already at the wheel of his convertible, "Wait for me." I walked to my rose nursery, went past it, there was no one there. My employee must have been in the gardens, at the back.

I started running as though being chased. Never have I run so fast. I went into the first hotel I came to and shut myself in a room to cry in peace.

The following day, I returned to my work at the rose nursery, put my beige clothes back on, placed the snow globe on the counter, and then went home.

My employee told me that a well-known lawyer had come to the rose nursery the day before, that he had looked everywhere for me, like a madman. That he didn't look as good in real life as on television, smaller.

A week later, the newspapers announced that the lawyer Gabriel Prudent had got the Lyons man acquitted.

63

*The absence of a father strengthens the memory
of his presence.*

At the trial, apart from Geneviève Magnan, just one thing had struck him, obsessed him: Fontanel's face. His suit, his gestures, his attitude. Of all those who had come to testify, he could remember only him.

Alain Fontanel had been called last by the plaintiffs' lawyer. After the supervisory staff, the firemen, the experts, the cook. As Fontanel answered the judge's questions in a confident voice, Philippe Toussaint saw Geneviève Magnan lowering her eyes. When he'd caught sight of her in the corridors of the court, on the first day of the trial, and had learned that she had been at Notre-Dame-des-Prés that night, he'd instantly thought: *It's her who set fire to the room, she took her revenge.*

And yet it was when Fontanel was speaking that Philippe Toussaint had felt deeply disturbed. He'd said to himself that he couldn't be the only one feeling that way, that vertigo when faced with a lie. He'd studied the other parents, watched to see if Fontanel had the same effect on them as on him, but saw nothing. The other parents were dead. Like Violette, all dead. Like the director in the stand for the accused, staring into space, she'd listened to Fontanel without listening to him.

Once again, Philippe Toussaint had said to himself: *I'm the only one who's alive.* He'd felt guilty. Léonine's death hadn't destroyed him like it had the others. As if, within their couple, Violette had taken it all for herself. Hadn't shared her grief. But deep down, he knew that it was anger that had picked him up off the floor, kept him above the fray. A subdued, heavy, violent, black anger, which he'd never spoken to anyone about because Françoise was no longer there. Hatred for his parents, hatred for his mother, hatred for those people who hadn't reacted when the fire . . .

He hadn't been a good father. An absent father, a distant father, a seeming father. He was too selfish, too focused on himself to give out love. He'd decided only to take an interest in his motorbike and women. All those women waiting to be consumed, like ripe fruit at the grocer's stall. Over the years, he'd helped himself so liberally to the neighbors that a friend had suggested *L'Adresse* to him, a place for having group fun. Where the women didn't fall in love, didn't take the lead, didn't sulk, and came wanting just what the guys wanted.

The verdict was announced: two years behind bars for the director, one without remission. And compensation, lots of compensation. Which he'd keep for himself. A habit that his bitch of a mother had instilled into him, "Keep everything for yourself. That woman, she's just there to bleed you dry."

When he left the court, his parents were waiting for him outside, stiffer than the proceedings he'd just been through. He'd felt like bolting, leaving thorough a secret door to avoid facing their looks. He couldn't tolerate them at all since Léonine's death. His mother, who always blamed everything on Violette, hadn't been able to lay into her after the tragedy. She'd tried her best, but it was she, after all, who'd insisted that Léonine go on holiday to that wretched place. He had given in and gone to have lunch with them. He'd not been able to swallow a thing or say a thing. On the back of the bill, he'd scribbled, with his father's pen, used for writing the check: "Edith Croquevieille, director; Swan Letellier, cook; Geneviève Magnan, dinner lady; Eloïse Petit and Lucie Lindon, supervisors; Alain Fontanel, maintenance man."

He'd returned home on his motorbike, carrying with him, as his only luggage, Fontanel's testimony: "Me, I was sleeping upstairs. I was woken by Swan Letellier's screams. The women had already started evacuating the other children. The room downstairs was on fire, impossible to go in, it could have been worse."

Violette hadn't reacted when he'd told her the verdict. She had said, "Right," and had gone out to lower the barrier. At that moment he had thought again of Françoise, of those summers in Biot. He often thought of them, returned to the holidays in his memory when the present depressed him too much. And then he had grabbed the controller of his Nintendo game and played until he was exhausted, shouting, getting annoyed when Mario missed an obstacle, or was getting nowhere fast. When he switched the TV off, Violette had been asleep in their room for a long while. He hadn't joined her. He had jumped on his bike to go to *L'Adresse*, to have sex with women who expected what he did: sad sex, climax, a booth. But he couldn't get Fontanel's words out of his head, "Me, I was sleeping upstairs. I was woken by Swan Letellier's screams. The women had already started evacuating the other children. The room downstairs was on fire, impossible to go in, it could have been worse."

What could have been worse?

Léonine's death had been bad news for his navel. The navel his mother had taught him to contemplate, no matter what, "Don't think of others, think of yourself."

Sometimes, he said to Violette, "We'll have another kid." She said yes to get rid of him. Get rid of the man who had abandoned her years ago, the one who cheated on her, not with all the women surrounding him, but with Françoise, the only one he had ever loved. He hadn't married Violette to make her happy, he'd married her to free himself from his mother, who harassed him.

He had felt enormous sorrow for Violette when she had lost their child. He had suffered more over the grief of his wife than over the loss of his child. He had suffered from not having been able to do anything for her. From not having to look after her. From her silence, never managing to speak to her about anything more than a shampoo brand or a TV program. Not having been able to say to his wife, "How are you feeling?" That, too, he had felt guilty about. He hadn't even learned how to suffer. In fact, he had learned nothing. Neither to love, nor to work, nor to give. A good-for-nothing.

He'd fallen for Violette the first time he'd seen her behind the bar. He had been attracted by all the sugar she seemed to be sprinkled with. Like a colorful lollipop at a fun-fair stall. It was nothing like what he had felt, and would always feel, for Françoise, but he'd wanted that particular girl. Her voice, her skin, her smile, her feather-lightness. Her tomboy looks, her fragility, her way of giving herself without restraint. That's why he had got her pregnant so soon, he wanted to keep her for himself, all to himself. Like a pastry you don't want to share. That you gobble in a corner, even if you end up covered in crumbs. And his mother had caught him red-handed, him, the child who could do no wrong, sweater smeared in grease. And a bun in the girl's oven, to boot.

In August of 1996, so nine months after the trial that sent Edith Croquevieille to prison, Violette had left to spend ten days in Marseille at Célia's chalet. That woman he couldn't stand, and he sensed the feeling was mutual. He'd said that, during that time, he would go biking with friends from Charleville, friends from before. Friends he no longer had. Not before, not now.

He had set off for Chalon-sur-Saône, alone. Alain Fontanel worked in a hospital over there. The Sainte-Thérèse Hospital, built in 1979, where he took care of electrical maintenance, plumbing, and paintwork with two other colleagues, since losing his job at Notre-Dame-des-Prés. Philippe Toussaint didn't know how he was going to tackle him. Should he speak nicely to him, or beat him up until he came clean? Fontanel was about twenty years older than him, not hard to overpower, put in an armlock. He hadn't planned anything, apart from having a one-on-one with him. Asking the questions that no one had asked him during the trial.

Philippe Toussaint had gone into the hospital, asked at reception to speak to Alain Fontanel, and been asked, "Do you know his room number?" Philippe Toussaint had stammered, "No, he works here."

"He's a nurse? An intern?"

"No, he does maintenance."

"I'll find out."

As the receptionist was picking up her phone, Philippe Toussaint spotted Fontanel entering the ground-floor cafeteria, about fifty meters away. He was wearing gray overalls. Philippe Toussaint felt just as disturbed as at the trial, he couldn't stomach this guy. Without thinking, he walked very fast toward him, until he was standing behind his back. Fontanel was carrying a tray and waiting in line at the self-service counter. Philippe Toussaint stayed behind him, took a tray himself, and requested the daily special. Fontanel went over to a window, alone. Philippe Toussaint joined him and sat opposite him, not asking if he minded.

"Do we know each other?"

"We've never spoken, but we do know each other."

"Can I help you?"

"No doubt."

The guy cut his meat as if everything was perfectly normal.

"I can't stop thinking about you."

"I usually have that effect on women."

Philippe Toussaint bit his cheek hard to remain calm, not get carried away.

"So, I don't think you said everything at the trial . . . Your testimony, it goes around in circles in my head, like a wildcat in a cage."

Fontanel showed no sign of surprise. He studied Philippe Toussaint for a minute, doubtless trying to remember him from the trial, to place him there, and then he mopped up the sauce from his plate with a hunk of bread.

"And you think I'm going to add something, just like that, for your pretty face?"

"Yup."

"And why would I do that?"

"Because I could become a lot less nice."

"You can do me in, I don't give a damn. To tell you the truth, it would suit me. I don't like my job, don't like my wife, don't like my kids."

Philippe Toussaint clenched his fists so tight, his hands went white.

"I don't give a damn about your life, I want to know what you saw on that night . . . You're lying through your teeth."

"The Magnan woman, do you know the Magnan woman? She's my wife."

" . . . "

"At the trial, she pissed herself every time she laid eyes on you."

The moment Fontanel said her name, he saw Geneviève Magnan again in the school corridors, with sleep in her eyes, running after him like a bitch in heat. He saw himself again screwing her, always in the same place, feet in the mud, in the headlights of his motorbike. It made him heave. Fontanel, the smell of food and hospital combined . . . Had she set fire to the room to take her revenge? That question tormented him.

"What actually happened, for Chrissake . . . "

"It was an accident. Nothing more, nothing less. A fucking accident. Don't bother looking, you'll find out nothing more, I'm telling you."

Philippe Toussaint leapt over the table, grabbed him, and laid into him as if he'd gone crazy. In the face, in the stomach, he was hitting in all directions, randomly. He felt like he was pounding a mattress dumped on a street corner. He struck out, ignoring the cries all around him. Fontanel didn't defend himself. He let it be done to him. Someone pulled Philippe by the arm, to stop him from going further, tried to restrain him, get him on the floor, but he fought back, with superhuman strength, and then took off. His fists were stinging and bleeding, he'd hit that hard.

As he had expected, Fontanel had said nothing, hadn't lodged a complaint for assault and battery. He had stated that he didn't know the identity of his assailant.

64

*Sleep, Daddy, sleep, but may you still hear
our childish laughter in highest Heaven.*

Bron Cemetery, June 2nd, 2017, blue sky, twenty-five degrees, 3 P.M. Funeral of Philippe Toussaint (1958–2017). Oak coffin. Gray marble tomb. No cross.

Three wreaths—"Beautiful flowers for beautiful memories that will never fade"—white lilies—"Accept these flowers as testimony of my deepest sympathy."

Funeral ribbons that read: "To my companion," "To our colleague," "To our friend." On a funerary plaque, beside a golden motorbike: "Gone but never forgotten."

Around twenty people present at the tomb. People from Philippe Toussaint's other life.

As his lawful wife, I authorized Françoise Pelletier to bury Philippe Toussaint in the vault of Luc Pelletier. So he would be back with the uncle I didn't know existed. Just like I didn't know about an entire part of Philippe Toussaint's life.

I wait until everyone has left to go up to the tomb. I place a plaque on Léonine's behalf: "To my father."

65.

Just a little note to tell you we love you.
Just a little note to ask you to help us
overcome the great ordeals down here.

AUGUST 1996, GENEVIÈVE MAGNAN.

I expected him for a long time. I knew he'd end up coming. I knew it well before seeing Fontanel's mug. Done in when he got home. Walking with crutches. Face red and blue, two teeth smashed in.

"What've you done now?" I asked. I thought he'd hit the bottle, got into a brawl with his fellow winos again. He'd always had violence in his blood, rage. He'd also given me some hidings on nights when he was plastered.

But he replied, "Go and ask the guy who was screwing you behind my back."

That sentence, it hurt me much more than any of my mother's and Fontanel's blows. Their hidings, compared with that sentence, no big deal. Just a knife cutting meat.

He's the one who was done in, limping, but it's me who really copped it. So I couldn't even move. Rooted to the spot, I was. Petrified.

I thought of the pig slaughtered the week before at the neighbor's. How it had the jitters, how it had trembled, how it had squealed. From terror and pain. Grotesque. The men who kept at it, their laughter. Afterwards, us women, we were drafted in to make the blood sausage. The smell of death. That day, I wanted to hang myself. It wasn't the first time, that desire to "put an end to it," as the rich say. No, it wasn't the first time. But then, it gripped me for a long time. Longer than usual. I even picked up the money to go and buy the rope at Bricorama. And then I put it down again, thinking of the boys. Four and nine years old. What would they do, all alone with Fontanel?

I knew that one day *he* would come to ask me questions, when I saw the look he gave me in the corridors of the court.

Someone knocked, I thought it was the postman. I was expecting a delivery from La Redoute. But it wasn't the postman. It was him, he was behind the door. His eyes were tired. I saw his sadness. I saw his beauty. And then his disdain. He looked at me like I was a pile of shit.

I tried to shut the door, but he kicked it, violently. He was like a madman. I thought of calling the cops, but what would I have said to them? I'd been afraid of him since *that night*. He didn't touch me, I disgusted him too much. I sensed he was full of both hatred and horror. I managed to say just one thing, "It really was an accident, I did nothing on purpose, I'd never have done any harm to kids."

He looked hard at me, and then he did something I wasn't expecting. He sat at my kitchen table, put his head on his arms, and started blubbering. He was sobbing like a kid who's lost his mother in the crowd.

"D'you want to know what happened?"

He replied no.

"I swear to you it was an accident."

He was a meter away from me. I wanted to touch him, undress him, undress myself, for him to take me, make me squeal like before, against the rock. Never has anyone despised themselves as much as I despised myself at that moment.

Him, distraught, lost in my kitchen, which I hadn't cleaned for ages. Since I've been on the dole, I don't do a damned thing. Me who's responsible. Me the guilty one.

He got up and left without looking at me. After he'd gone, I sat in his seat. His scent remained.

After school, I'll drop my kids off at my sister's. She's much nicer than me, my sister. I'll tell them to be good. To stay put. I'll take the money from the last time. On the way home, I'll buy some rope at Bricorama.

66

*The death of a mother is the first
sorrow one weeps over without her.*

W ould you like a taste?"
"With pleasure."
I pick a few cherry tomatoes and get Mr. Rouault to
try them.

"Delicious. Are you going to stay here?"

"Where do you want me to go?"

"With your inheritance money, you could stop working."

"Ah, no, no. I love my house, I love my cemetery, I love my
work, I love my friends. And anyhow, who would look after my
animals?"

"But come now, all the same, buy yourself a little property,
something, somewhere."

"No way. Then I'd forever be obliged to go there. You
know, second homes put a stop to any other journeys, the ones
you decide on at the last moment. And anyhow, can you imagine me with a second home, honestly?"

"What are you going to do with all that money, if it's not
indiscreet to ask?"

"What does a hundred divided by three come to?"

"33.33333 to infinity."

"Well, I'll give 33.33333 and infinity to *Restos du Coeur*,
Amnesty International, and the *Fondation Bardot*. That will
allow me to save the world a bit, from my little cemetery.
Come, Mr. Rouault, let's have a drink."

He picks up his cane and follows me, smiling. We sit under
my arbor to savor a wonderful chilled Sauterne. Mr. Rouault

takes off his suit jacket and stretches out his legs, while plunging his fingers into the salted peanuts.

"Look how beautiful it is today, every day I'm intoxicated by the world's beauty. Of course, there's death, grief, bad weather, All Saints' Day, but life always gets over it. There's always a morning when the light's beautiful, when the grass sprouts again from the scorched earth."

"I should send you the siblings who insult each other in my office, they could do wisdom internships around you."

"Personally, I think inheritance shouldn't exist. I think we should give everything to the people we love while we're alive. Our time and our money. Inheritances were invented by the Devil, to make families tear themselves apart. I only believe in donations while one is alive. Not in the promises of death."

"Did you know that your husband was rich?"

"My husband wasn't rich. He was too lonely and too unhappy. Luckily, at the end of his life, he lived with the right person."

"How old are you, dear Violette?"

"No idea. Since July 1993, I no longer celebrate my birthday."

"You could make a new life for yourself."

"My life is fine as it is."

67

*On the quicksand into which life has slipped
grows a sweet flower my heart has picked.*

In August of 1996, a year before moving to the cemetery, I left the Sormiou chalet earlier than usual. I took a train to Mâcon, and then a bus that stopped at Brancion-en-Chalon on its way to Tournus. My bus passed through La Clayette, I saw the château of Notre-Dame-des-Prés, in the distance, through the window, for the first time. My bus stopped a few minutes later, in front of the Brancion-en-Chalon town hall, and when I got off, I was shaking from head to toe. My legs struggled to carry me to the cemetery. With every step, I kept seeing the château again, the windows, the white walls. I had glimpsed the lake, just behind, glistening like a sea of sapphires. It was a very hot day.

The door to Sasha's house, on the cemetery side, was half-open; I didn't go in. I went straight to Léonine's tomb, still seeing the walls of the château. Standing in front of the headstone engraved with the names of my daughter and her friends, for the first time I felt bad for not having been to the funeral, for leaving her to depart alone, for not having placed even a white pebble on her tomb. And yet, once again on that day, I knew that Léonine was far more present in the Mediterranean I'd just come from, and among the flowers in Sasha's garden, than beneath this tombstone. I walked over to Sasha's house with an aching heart.

He didn't know I was there, I hadn't told him I was coming. I hadn't seen him for more than two months. Since Philippe Toussaint had forbidden me from doing so. The house was tidy. The door leading to his vegetable garden wide open. I didn't call to him. I went out and saw him lying on a bench, having a nap, a straw hat shading his face. I approached him very gently, he immediately jumped up and hugged me.

"There's nothing more beautiful than the sky seen through a straw hat. I like looking at it through the holes without the sun harming me. My little sparrow, what a lovely surprise . . . Are you staying all day?"

"A little longer."

"That's wonderful! Have you eaten?"

"I'm not hungry."

"I'm going to make you some pasta."

"But I'm not hungry."

"With butter and grated Gruyère, come, follow me, we've got work to do! Have you seen how everything has grown? It's a big year for the garden! A big year!"

At that moment, seeing him bustling about and smiling, I felt a warmth in my belly, a little like happiness. Not something put on, not one of those spurts of life that lasted but seconds, but a plenitude, a smile on the lips not instantly erased, quite simply, desire. I was no longer remote-controlled, I was inhabited.

I would have liked to keep the summer and that moment, the garden, and Sasha forever.

I stayed with him for four days. We started by picking the ripe tomatoes to make preserves. First, we sterilized the jars in a pan of water that Sasha brought to the boil over a wood fire. Next, we chopped and deseeded the tomatoes, before putting them in the jars with freshly picked basil leaves. Sasha taught me the importance of having new rubber washers to seal the jars hermetically. We heated them up for fifteen minutes.

"Now we can keep these jars for at least four years. But you see, all the people lying in this cemetery, they put things aside, and what good did it do them? Us two, we're not going to wait for anything, and this evening we're opening one up just for us."

We did the same thing with the beans. We removed their stalks, put them in the jars with a glass of salted water, sealed them, and brought them to a boil.

"This year, my beans appeared over a single night, just two days ago; they must have sensed you were coming . . . Never underestimate your garden's powers of divination."

On the second day, there was a funeral. Sasha asked me to accompany him. I'd have nothing to do, just be with him. It was my first time attending a funeral. I saw the faces, the grief, the pallor, the smart, dark clothes. I saw hands being shaken, people arm-in-arm, heads bowed. I still remember the speech given by the son of the deceased with tears in his voice:

"Dad, as André Malraux said, the finest tombstone is our memory. You loved life, women, great wine, and Mozart. Every time I open a good bottle or come across a beautiful woman, every time I savor a great wine in the company of a beautiful woman, I'll know that you're not far away. Every time the vines change color, from green to red, and the sky gradually lights up with a gentle glow, I'll know you're not far away. When I listen to a clarinet concerto, I'll know that you're there. Rest, Dad, everything's taken care of."

When everyone had left, and we'd returned to Sasha's, I asked him if he ever kept the eulogies he heard. If he recorded them somewhere.

"What for?"

"I'd like to know what was said on the day of Léonine's funeral."

"I keep nothing. Vegetables don't grow year after year. Every year, you have to start from scratch. Apart from cherry tomatoes: they grow all on their own, pretty messily, pretty much anywhere."

"Why are you telling me that?"

"Life is like a relay race, Violette. You pass the baton to someone, who takes it and passes it to someone else. I passed it to you, and one day you will pass it on."

"But I'm alone in the world."

"No, I'm here, and there will be someone else after me. If you want to know what was said on the day of Léonine's funeral, write it yourself, write it later, before going to bed."

On the third day, I read Léonine her eulogy.

I found Sasha in one of the cemetery's avenues. We walked along the tombs, he spoke to me of the dead, both long-time residents and those who had just moved in.

"Do you have children, Sasha?"

"When I was young, I wanted to do like everyone else, I got married. And there's a bloody stupid mistake, an idiotic idea: doing like everyone else. Good manners, pretenses, and received ideas are all killers. My wife was called Verena, she was very pretty, and had a gentle voice, like you. In fact, you resemble her a little. Like the young, pretentious twit that I was, I thought her beauty would turn me on. On the day of the wedding, when I saw her in her white lace, shy and blushing, when I lifted the veil covering her lovely face, I knew that I was lying to everyone, starting with myself. I placed a cold kiss on her mouth as the guests applauded us, and all that interested me was the muscles under the men's shirts. I got myself drunk before the first dance. The honeymoon night was nightmarish. I tried my best, I thought of my wife's brother, dark with big brown eyes. But it didn't work, I didn't manage to make love to her. Verena put 'it' down to emotions and drunkenness. As the weeks went by, the nights spent close to one another, I finally made it. I finally took her virginity. I can't even tell you how unhappy it made me, her eyes full of love and affection when I had only managed to touch her thanks to my disgusting imagination. Night followed night, and all the men in my village got the same treatment, I touched them all through her.

"Then we moved house. Second stupid mistake: changing address doesn't change your desire. It sticks to the suitcases. Unlike migratory birds and weeds, it doesn't have the ability to adapt to all climates. I changed windows and doormat, but I continued to look at men. I cheated on my wife countless times in public restrooms. What a disgrace . . . Through continually pretending, I became ill. I wasn't pretending to love Verena, I sincerely loved her. I devoured her with my eyes, but only with my eyes. I loved her gestures, her skin, her movements, but I saw the lovely lock of brown hair that fell across her face as barring me. I finally came down with blood cancer. My white blood cells started eating up my red ones. Those white cells, I saw them as women in bridal gowns multiplying in my veins; shame was devouring me. It may seem strange to you, but my stays in hospital came as a relief to me. They relieved me of that obligation to 'honor' Verena in our bed. To 'dishonor' her, more like. Between the sheets, I continued to close my eyes and caress her body while thinking of someone else, anyone else. Even TV presenters.

"Verena became pregnant. I saw this pregnancy as a ray of light, as the only positive to come from the three bleak years since our union. I watched her belly growing, I took up gardening again. I returned to being an almost happy man. That child was my dream. And he was born. A son we baptized Emile. Verena looked at me less, desired me less, she was devoted to her child, and I felt better and better. I had lovers, a gentle wife, the mother of my son, I was almost swimming in happiness, a polluted happiness, but happiness all the same. I'm a great father, you know? And a child is very handy when one no longer wants to touch one's wife. She's tired, vulnerable, often has a headache, hears him crying during the night, too hot, too cold, teething, a nightmare, an ear infection. I made love to Verena just once, after a boozy New Year's Eve, and that was enough for her to get pregnant again. Three years after Emile's birth, Ninon was born. An adorable little girl.

"I had two children with Verena. Two children. I gave life, the real thing, twice over. Which just shows that God has a laugh at everything, even poofs."

"How old are they now?"

"The same age as my wife."

"I don't understand."

"They no longer have an age. They died in 1976, in a car accident. On the Highway to the Sun. I was supposed to join them three days later, by train, at our seaside rental. Do you know why?"

"Why what?"

"Why I was supposed to join them three days later?"

". . ."

"I told Verena I had some work to catch up with. In '76 I was an engineer. The truth was, I'd planned three days of sex with a colleague. When I was told they had died, I went mad. I had to be confined to a mental hospital for a long time. It was there, between those white walls, that I learned how to heal others with my hands. You see, dear Violette, you and me, we've had our share of tragedy, and yet here we are. Between the two of us, we're like all of Victor Hugo's novels put together. An anthology of great woes, small joys and hopes."

"Where are they buried?"

"Close to Valence, in Verena's family vault."

"But how did you wind up here, at this cemetery?"

"After my release from hospital, I was a social misfit. The mayor here has known me forever and he employed me as a roadman. The fellow in blue overalls talking to himself while sweeping around the municipal trash cans, that was me. When I had regained some strength, I applied for the post of cemetery keeper, as it was vacant. My place was among the dead. The dead of others."

Sasha took my arm. We passed a man and a woman, who asked him where a particular tomb was. While he was giving directions, which avenues to take, I watched him. As he had spoken to me of his lost family, he had gradually become a little stooped. I thought how we were two survivors who were still standing. Two shipwrecked people that an ocean of adversity hadn't managed to drown entirely.

Once the man and woman had thanked him, I put my hand in his and we carried on walking.

"At first, the mayor hesitated. But my loved ones had been dead a long time, there was a statute of limitations. You don't need me to tell you that between death and time, there's always a statute of limitations . . . Look, the weather's splendid. Today I'm going to teach you the art of taking rosebush cuttings. Do you know what 'August branches' are?"

"No."

"They're branches that start producing new wood in August. Brown spots appear on the green, the same spots you can see on my hands. They're signs of old age. They're known as 'August branches.' Well, believe it or not, it's with these old branches that you're going to create young shoots. Isn't that incredible? What do you feel like eating this evening? What if I made you avocados with lemon? It's good for you, packed with vitamins and fatty acids."

On the fourth day, he drove me to Mâcon station in his old Peugeot. He had slipped some jars of tomatoes and beans into my suitcase. It was so heavy, I struggled to lug it all the way to Malgrange.

On the way, between the cemetery and the station car park, he told me that he wanted to retire. That he was tired, that it was time for him to hand over to someone else, and that someone could only be me.

68

Of their love that's bluer than the sky around them.

Y ou won't put your teenage years behind you.
You won't celebrate being twenty-five and still unmarried by St. Catherine's Day.
You won't dance any slow dances.
You won't have a handbag or painful periods.
You won't have braces on your teeth.
I won't see you growing taller, getting fatter, suffering, divorcing, dieting, giving birth, breastfeeding, loving.
You won't get acne or an IUD.
I won't hear you lying. I won't have to cover up for you, or stick up for you.
You won't nick coins from my purse. I won't open a savings account for you in case of a rainy day.
You won't be on the Pill.
I won't see your wrinkles and liver spots appearing, or your cellulite and stretch marks.
I won't detect cigarette smoke on your clothes, I won't see you smoking, and then quitting smoking.
I'll never see you drunk or high.
You won't study for your baccalauréat while watching Roland-Garros; you won't have it in for Madame Bovary, "that pathetic female"; or for Marguerite Duras; or for your teachers.
You won't have a scooter or a broken heart.
You won't French-kiss anyone, you won't climax.
We won't celebrate you passing your bac.
We'll never clink glasses together.

You won't use deodorant, you won't get appendicitis.

I won't fret about you getting into a stranger's car. That you've already done.

You won't have toothache.

We won't go to the ER in the middle of the night.

You won't sign on at the employment office.

You won't have a bank account, or a student card, or a young person's discount card, or a social security number, or loyalty cards.

I'll never know your tastes, what appeals to you. Which clothes, which literature, which music, which perfume.

I won't see you sulking, slamming doors, running away, waiting for someone, taking a plane.

You won't leave home. You won't change address.

I'll never know whether you bite your nails, wear nail polish, eye shadow, mascara.

Or whether you have a gift for foreign languages.

You'll never change the color of your hair.

You'll keep Alexandre, your primary-school crush, forever in your heart.

You'll marry no one.

You'll always be Léonine Toussaint. Mademoiselle.

You'll only ever like eating French toast, omelettes, fries, pasta shells, pancakes, breaded fish, floating islands, and Chantilly cream.

You will grow up differently, in the love I will always have for you. You will grow up elsewhere, among the murmurs of the world, in the Mediterranean, in Sasha's garden, in the flight of a bird, at daybreak, at nightfall, through a young girl I will meet by chance, in the foliage of a tree, in the prayer of a woman, in the tears of a man, in the light of a candle, you will be reborn later, one day, in the form of a flower or a little boy, to another mother, you will be everywhere my eyes come to rest. Wherever my heart resides, yours will continue to beat.

69

*Nothing can wilt it, nothing wither it,
this charming flower is called memory.*

"Hello, madame."

"Hello, young man."

An adorable little boy is sucking on his straw to capture the last drops of apple juice in his bottle. He's sitting at my kitchen table, alone.

"Where are your parents?"

He indicates the cemetery to me with a nod of the head.

"My father told me to wait for him here because it's raining."

"What's your name?"

"Nathan."

"Would you like a slice of chocolate cake, Nathan?"

His eyes widen in anticipation.

"Yes, thank you. Is this your house?"

"Yes."

"Do you work here?"

"Yes."

He blinks. He has long, dark eyelashes.

"Is this where you sleep as well?"

"Yes."

He looks at me as if I were his favorite cartoon.

"Aren't you scared at night?"

"No, why would I be scared?"

"Because of the zombies."

"What are zombies?"

He swallows a large piece of chocolate cake.

"The living dead that mega-terrify people. I saw a film, and it was mega-terrifying."

"Aren't you a bit young to watch that kind of film?"

"It was at Antoine's, on his computer, we didn't watch all of it, we were too scared. But I am seven, you know."

"Ah, yes, of course."

"Have you ever seen any zombies?"

"No, never."

He looks terribly disappointed. He pulls a delightful face. Tutti Frutti comes in through the cat flap. His fur is soaked. He joins Eliane in her basket, to share some of her warmth. The dog opens one eye and then goes right back to sleep. Nathan leaves his chair to go and pet them. He yanks up his jeans with both hands, and tugs on the sleeves of his sweatshirt. He's wearing trainers with soles that light up with his every step. They remind me of Michael Jackson's "Billie Jean" video.

"Is the cat yours?"

"Yes."

"What's its name?"

"Tutti Frutti."

He bursts into laughter. He's got chocolate all over his teeth.

"That's a funny name."

Julien Seul knocks on my cemetery-side door and comes in. He's as soaked as the cat.

"Hello."

He glances towards the child, and smiles at me, tenderly. I sense he would like to come over to me, touch me, but he doesn't move. He merely does so with his eyes. I feel him undressing me. Removing winter to see summer.

"Everything O.K., kiddo?"

I freeze.

"Daddy, do you know what the cat's name is?"

Nathan is Julien's son. My heart races as fast as a galloping mustang, as if I'd just charged up and down the stairs several times.

Julien answers straight back:

"Tutti Frutti."

"How come you know?"

"I know the cat. It's not the first time I've been here. Nathan, have you said hello to Violette?"

Nathan stares at me.

"You're called Violette?"

"Yes."

"You've all got funny names around here!"

He returns to the table, sits down, and polishes off his cake. His father watches him with a smile.

"We have to go now, kiddo."

It's my turn to feel terribly disappointed. Like when Nathan heard that I'd never seen a zombie.

"You won't stay a little longer?"

"We're expected in Auvergne. A cousin getting married this afternoon."

He stares at me. Then says to his son:

"Kiddo, go and wait for me in the car, it's open."

"But it's pissing cats and dogs!"

We're so surprised by the child's reply that we both burst out laughing.

"The first one to the car gets to pick the music."

Nathan promptly comes over to kiss me on the cheek.

"If you see any zombies, just call my father, he's a policeman."

He runs out through the cemetery-side door, heading for the car park.

"He's totally adorable."

"He gets that from his mother . . . Have you read mine's journal?"

"I haven't finished it. Would you like to take a coffee with you, for the road?"

He shakes his head.

"I'd rather take you with me, for the road."

This time, he comes over to me and hugs me. I can feel him breathing in my neck. I close my eyes. When I open them, he's already at the door. He's made my clothes damp.

"Violette, I have absolutely no desire that, one day, your ashes end up on my tomb. I couldn't care less, in fact. I want to live with you now, right now. While we can still gaze at the sky together . . . Even when it's pouring like today."

"Live with me?"

"I would like this story . . . this encounter between my mother and that man, to be for that purpose, for us, in fact."

"But I'm not fit for it."

"Fit for it?"

"Yes, fit for it."

"But I'm not talking about you doing military service."

"I'm dysfunctional, broken. Love is impossible for me. I'm unbearable to live with. More dead than the ghosts lurking in my cemetery. Haven't you understood that? It's impossible."

"No one can be expected to do the impossible."

"Yes, they can."

He smiles at me, sadly.

"Shame."

He closes the door behind him, and then comes back in without knocking, two minutes later.

"You're coming with us."

" . . . "

"To the wedding. It's a two-hour drive away."

"But I . . . "

"I'll give you ten minutes to get ready."

"But I can't . . . "

"I've just phoned Nono, he'll be here in five minutes to replace you."

70.

*One day we will come to sit
beside you in the house of God.*

AUGUST 1996.

Philippe had left Geneviève Magnan's place feeling more wretched than the stones—a strange expression his Uncle Luc often used. He had driven to the cemetery. There was a funeral on that day. The mourners were gathered in the heat, in clusters, far from Léonine's tomb. He hadn't brought any flowers. He'd never brought any. Usually, his mother took care of that.

It was the first time he was visiting her on his own. He came twice a year, always with his parents.

His father and mother would park next to the barrier, no longer coming inside for fear of encountering Violette, of facing her despair. He, like a good son, sat at the back of the car, like when he was a child and they set off on holiday, and the back seat seemed vast to him, but at the end of the journey, there was the sea.

Philippe had always told himself that he was an only son because his parents had only made love once, by accident. Philippe had always told himself that he was an accident.

His father, stooped with grief and years of living with his wife, drove badly. Slowed down, no one knew why, accelerated, no one knew why, either. Drove on the left and then too far to the right. Passed when he shouldn't, didn't pass on straight roads. Got lost too often. Seemed to ignore signposts.

The journey between the barrier and the cemetery seemed interminable to Philippe. The first time they had done it, he had picked up the smell of burning when they were still several kilometers from the château. The air smelt as acrid as after a major fire.

First, they had stopped in front of the gates of the château to park. Hadn't felt able to go in straight away, had remained prostrate, all three of them, just like that, in the car. Then they had walked the two hundred meters to the imposing building, its left wing blackened and destroyed. There were firemen, policemen, dazed parents, local councilors. Confusion amidst the horror. Lots of silence, awkward gestures, as though frozen. Everything in slow motion. Not really felt, seen from a distance, wrapped in cotton wool, or wadding. Like when body and mind separate so as not to let go. When the combination is too much to bear. The weight of the pain.

Philippe hadn't been able to get near Room 1. The entire area had been cordoned off—an expression out of an American TV series, but there in Burgundy, and in real life. Lines of red plastic tape to contain the horror. Experts were examining the ground and the walls, taking photographs. Studying the fire's trajectory, rewriting history while looking for what was explicit: evidence, clues, prints. A precise report was required for the public prosecutor, the death of four children couldn't be taken lightly. There would be punishment and sentencing.

He'd heard plenty of "I'm so sorry, we're so sorry, all our condolences, they didn't suffer." He hadn't seen the château staff, or maybe he had but he'd forgotten. The other children, the lucky ones, those spared, had already left. They had been swiftly evacuated.

He didn't have to identify Léonine's body, there was nothing left of it. He didn't have to choose a coffin or readings for the ceremony, his parents had taken care of that. So he'd have nothing to choose. He'd thought: *I never bought a pair of shoes, a dress, a barrette, socks for my daughter. It was Violette who did that, who liked doing that.* But for the coffin, Violette wouldn't be there. Violette would no longer be there. So he wouldn't have to look after anyone.

In the evening, he'd phoned her from the hotel. It was the Marseillaise who'd answered. That's what he called Célia. He'd remembered that he had asked her to come. Violette was sleeping. The doctor had made several visits to give her sedatives.

The funeral took place on July 18th, 1993.

The others, they held each other by the hand or arm, they supported each other. He hadn't touched or spoken to anyone. His mother had tried, he had recoiled, like when she wanted to kiss him when he was fourteen.

The others, they had wept, wailed. The others, they had collapsed. Some women, flattened like reeds in a gale, had to be helped up. During the burial, one might have thought everyone there was drunk, no one could stay upright. He'd stood straight, without tears.

And then, in the huge crowd gathered around the tomb, he'd seen her. Dressed all in black. Very pale. With a faraway look. What the hell was Geneviève Magnan doing there? He had let it go. His heart wasn't in anything anymore. He'd opened his heart to Françoise. He'd opened his heart to Violette and Léonine. That was the end of it.

The only sentence that crossed his mind a thousand times during those four days in Burgundy was: *I didn't even manage to protect my daughter.*

Afterwards, the others, they'd go on holiday. Afterwards, the others, they'd remain there, in that wretched cemetery. And he would go home in his parents' car, on the vast back seat, and at the end of the journey, there wouldn't be the sea, but Violette and her untold grief.

An empty bedroom. A pink bedroom he'd always avoided. From which laughter could be heard, and the words Violette read aloud every evening.

Three years after this tragedy, alone in front of his daughter's tomb, he had said nothing. Uttered not a word, not a prayer for her. And yet he knew plenty of prayers. He'd attended catechism classes, done his First Communion. That was the day he'd seen Françoise for the first time, on the arm of his uncle. The day he'd secretly recited, along with the big brother of a friend, while sipping the Communion wine:

Our Father who farts forever
Hallowed be thy bum
Thy condom come
Thy willy be done
On turds as it is in heaven
Give us this day our daily beer
And forgive us our burps
As we forgive those who burp against us
And lead us not into penetration
But deliver us from perverts. Omen.

They'd laughed until they cried, especially after slipping their white surplices over their T-shirts and jeans. And they'd all mocked each other:

"You look like a priest!"

"And you like a sissy!"

And then he had seen Françoise. And had seen only her from then on.

She looked like his uncle's daughter. She looked like a big sister. She looked like a dream mother. She looked like perfection. She looked like the love of one's life. She looked like the love of his life.

He had wanted to see her again, and the more he saw her again, every year, the more he wanted to see her again.

Three years after the tragedy, standing before his daughter's tomb, he'd thought he wouldn't come to Brancion-en-Chalon anymore, seeing as not a word came out of him. Seeing as he was incapable of talking to Lèonine. He'd wanted to get back on his bike and go and see Françoise, throw himself into her arms. But the years had gone by and she had to be forgotten.

He must return to Violette, fall on his knees before her, beseech her, apologize to her. Seduce her like he'd seduced her at the beginning. Before the barrier and the trains. Try to look after her, make her laugh. Give her another child. After all, she was still so young, Violette. Tell her he was going to find out what really happened that night at the château, admit to her that he'd smashed Fontanel's face in, and, in the past, had sex with Magnan. Admit to her that he was pathetic, but that he would get to the truth. Yes, give her another kid, and this time look after it. Maybe they would have a boy, a little lad, his dream. And he'd keep his nose clean. Stop sleeping around. Move to a new place, perhaps. Change his life with Violette. It was possible to change one's life, he'd seen it on TV.

First, he must go back to see Magnan. "I'd never have done any harm to kids." Why had she said that? He must go back there to make her spit it out; she'd almost spoken earlier on, but he hadn't let her. Wasn't ready.

He looked at Léonine's tomb one last time, failed, once and for all, to open his mouth, like when she was alive and he already didn't say much to her. Never answered her questions. "Daddy, why is the moon switched on?"

When he left Léonine's tomb and was walking briskly to the gate, he saw them. Violette and the old man, on the avenue. Violette was holding his arm. Philippe had seen the deception. He'd heard his mother saying to him: "Trust no one, think only of yourself, of you."

He thought she was in Marseilles, at Célia's chalet. He thought she was on a kind of pilgrimage. And there she was, with another man. She was smiling. Philippe hadn't seen Violette smile once since Léonine's death.

For six months, Violette had come, every other Sunday, to this cemetery. So that was it. She'd borrowed the red car from the twit at the Casino to make Philippe think she was visiting Léonine's tomb. She'd hidden her game very well. She had a lover? This old man? How had she met him? Where? A lover, Violette, impossible.

He hid behind a large stone cross and watched them for a while. They walked arm in arm to the house at the entrance to the cemetery. The old man came back out, at around 7 P.M., to close the gates. So that was it, he was the keeper of this wretched place. His wife was sleeping with the keeper of the cemetery in which their daughter was buried. Philippe heard himself laugh, an evil laugh. An intense desire to kill, to strike, to slaughter.

Violette remained inside. He saw her, through a window, laying the table for two, like she did at their home, with a tea cloth tied around her waist. It hurt him so much, he gnawed his fingers until they bled. Like in the Westerns he watched as a child, when the cowboy bites into a piece of wood while the bullet in his stomach is extracted. Violette had a double life and he hadn't been aware of a thing.

Night fell. The old man and Violette switched off the lights. Closed the shutters. And she had remained inside. She had slept there. No longer any question about it.

Two months previously, he'd forbidden Violette from returning to Burgundy. When she'd spoken to him about that Magnan, told him she'd been to see her, he'd been scared. Scared of being found out. Scared of Violette knowing that she had been her husband's mistress, the very woman who did the cooking at the château.

But the story was very different, she had a lover. That's why she seemed more lighthearted the day before going there. Every other Sunday. She had dared to announce to him, "I will go to the cemetery every other Sunday." And he'd seen nothing; now he understood why his wife seemed to improve from week to week.

He climbed a wall to get out; it was late. He gave a big kick to the road-side door, got on his bike, and sped off like a madman.

It must have been about 10 P.M. when he found himself back on the road of the house Magnan lived in. There were cops inside, their van was parked outside. Neighbors in dressing gowns were talking under the streetlights. He told himself that Fontanel must have hit her too hard.

Philippe turned straight around and headed back east without stopping. Once there, he went directly to *L'Adresse*, where bodies were on the house.

71

*Through the open window, together we looked
at life, love, joy. We listened to the wind.*

Irène Fayolle's Journal

October 22nd, 1992
Yesterday evening, I heard Gabriel's voice on the television news. I heard him talking about "defending a woman who left me." Of course, he didn't say that, my mind distorted his words.

Paul was helping me prepare supper in the kitchen, the television was on in the room next door. I was so surprised to hear the sound of his voice again, the sound of my most wonderful memories, that I dropped the saucepan of boiling water I was carrying. It clattered onto the tiles and my ankles got splashed. It made an almighty racket, Paul panicked. He thought I was shaking because of my burns.

He ushered me into the sitting room and made me sit on the sofa, facing the television, facing Gabriel. There he was, inside that rectangle I never watch. While Paul flapped around, applying wet gauze to my smarting skin, I saw images of Gabriel in court. A journalist said he had been defending in Marseilles that week. That he had got three men acquitted out of five accused of conspiring to escape. The trial had concluded the previous day.

Gabriel was in Marseilles, so close to my life, and I didn't know it. But anyhow, what would I have done? Would I have gone to see him? To say what to him? "Five years ago, I ran away in the street because I didn't want to abandon my family. Five years ago, I was afraid of you, afraid of myself. But you should know that I have never stopped thinking of you"?

Julien emerged from his bedroom, said to his father that I should be taken to hospital. I refused. While my husband and son were debating it, and before I finally found a tube of Biafine cream in the medicine cabinet, I watched Gabriel waving his beautiful hands around in front of the journalists. I saw the passion he put into defending others in his long black robe. I wanted him to pop out from the screen, to be Mia Farrow in that Woody Allen film, The Purple Rose of Cairo.

And me? Would he have defended me? Would he have found mitigating circumstances for me on the day that I dumped him?

How long had he waited for me at the wheel of his car? When had he finally set off? At what moment had he realized that I wouldn't be coming back?

Tears started rolling down my cheeks. Against my will.

Paul switched off the television.

I collapsed in front of the black screen.

My son and husband thought it was due to the pain. They called the family doctor, who inspected my burns and said they were superficial.

I didn't sleep all night.

Seeing Gabriel again, hearing his voice again, I realized that I had missed him too much.

* * *

The following morning, Irène looked up the phone number of Gabriel's office. It was still in Saône-et-Loire, in Mâcon. She asked for an appointment with him, was told that she would have to wait several months, that Mr. Prudent's schedule was very full, but it would be quicker with one of his two associates. Irène said she had the time, she would wait for Mr. Prudent. She left her name and phone number—not the home one, the rose nursery one. She was asked which case it was about, there was an awkward silence, and then Irène replied,

"A case Mr. Prudent already knows about." She was given a date, she would have to wait three months.

Gabriel rang her two days later, at the rose nursery. That morning, Irène was just raising the shutters when the phone rang. She thought it must be a flower order and ran to answer it, out of breath. She had already grabbed her order form and a pen, its lid chewed by her employee. He said, "It's me." And she said, "Hello."

"You called my office?"

"Yes."

"I'm in court all week in Sedan. Want to come?"

"Yes."

"See you later."

And he hung up.

On her order form, Irène had scribbled "Sedan" in the "Message from sender" box.

One thousand two hundred kilometers to cover. She would have to travel the length of France. In a long, straight line.

She left Marseilles at around 10 A.M., took several connecting trains. At Lyon-Perrache station, she powdered her face and dabbed some gloss on her lips using the mirror in the restroom. It was April, she was wearing a beige raincoat. That made her smile. She gathered her blond hair into a black elastic band. She bought a sandwich, a toothbrush, and some lemon-flavored toothpaste.

She arrived in Sedan at around 9 P.M. She got in a taxi and asked the driver to drop her off outside the court. She knew she would find Gabriel in the nearest café or restaurant. Irène knew that Gabriel wasn't the sort to return early to his hotel. He worked on his files on the corner of a table. Between a glass of beer and a plate of fries. Between a glass of wine and the daily special. Gabriel needed to feel life all around him. He hated the silence of hotel rooms, the bedcovers, the curtains, the TV switched on just for a presence.

She caught sight of him through a window, sitting at a table with three other men. Gabriel was talking and smoking at the same time. They had stained the tablecloth, and undone their top buttons. Their ties hung on the armrests of their chairs.

When he saw her come in, Gabriel raised a hand and called out to her:

"Irène! Come and join us!"

He said it to her as if she just happened to be passing by on her way home.

Irène greeted the three other men.

"Let me introduce you to three of my colleagues, Laurent, Jean-Yves, and David. Gentlemen, let me introduce you to Irène, the love of my life."

The men smiled. As if Gabriel were joking. As if Gabriel could only say such a thing as a joke. As if there were many loves of his life in his life.

"Sit down. Are you hungry? Yes, you must eat. Mademoiselle Audrey, the menu, please! What will you have to drink? Tea? No way, one doesn't drink tea in Sedan! Mademoiselle Audrey, another bottle of this, please! A Volnay 1982, you're going to see . . . or rather, drink a marvel. Come and sit beside me."

One of Gabriel's colleagues got up to make room for her. Gabriel took Irène's hand and kissed it with his eyes closed. Irène saw that he was wearing a wedding ring. A white-gold band.

"I'm pleased you're here."

Irène ordered fish and listened to the conversation from afar. She felt like a groupie who has crossed the country to spend the evening with a rock star, who's in no hurry to be alone with her because it's a foregone conclusion. The night of love owed him after the concert.

Irène felt like disappearing. She regretted coming. She wondered how she could get up, find an emergency exit, a door at the back, to run to the station and return home, slip between her clean, aloe vera-scented sheets. Discreetly, she asked the waitress for a green tea. From time to time, Gabriel returned to her, asked her if all was well, if she wasn't cold, thirsty, hungry.

Gabriel and the men finally rose, as one, from the table. Gabriel went to the bar to settle the bill. Irène followed on, in silence.

Outside, it started to rain. Or maybe it had been raining for ages, Irène hadn't noticed. She felt increasingly uncomfortable. She thought about how she had brought nothing with her. Just her handbag, a few banknotes, and a checkbook. She thought that she was crazy and all this wasn't like her. She who was usually so sensible. She felt pathetic, like a cheap groupie.

Gabriel borrowed an umbrella from the restaurant, saying he would return it the following day. He took Irène by the arm and followed close behind the other three. They walked in the same direction. Gabriel gripped her arm very tightly.

In the lobby of the Hôtel des Ardennes, they all picked up their keys at reception, all took the lift. Two of them got out on the third floor. "Good night, guys, see you tomorrow." The third man at the fifth floor. "Good night, David, see you tomorrow."

"7:30 in the breakfast room?"

"O.K."

Between the fifth and seventh floors, they found themselves alone, face to face. Gabriel didn't take his eyes off her.

The lift door opened onto a dark corridor. They walked to room 61. Irène smelt the stale smoke as soon as he opened the door. Orangey walls, faux Moroccan stucco.

He entered before her, saying, "Sorry," went to switch on the lights in every corner of the room, and then disappeared into the bathroom.

Irène didn't know what to do with her raincoat, or herself. She remained frozen at the entrance to the room, like a marble statue, a mannequin in a shopwindow. She looked at Gabriel's half-open suitcase, his spotless shirts. His sweaters, his pairs of socks. She wondered who had ironed his collars, folded his laundry.

Gabriel came out of the bathroom, smiling.

"Come on in, get undressed."

Irène must have made quite a face because he burst out laughing.

"Not completely. Take off your raincoat."

" . . . "

"You seem very quiet."

"Why did you ask me to come?"

"Because I wanted you to. I wanted to see you. I always want to see you."

"And that wedding ring, what's that about?"

He sat on the bed. She took off her raincoat.

"Someone asked me to marry them, I couldn't have said no. It's hard to say no to a woman who asks you to marry her. And bad manners. And you? Still married?"

"Yes."

"So, we're even. One all."

" . . . "

"I often dream of you."

"Same here."

"I miss you. Come closer."

Irène sat close to him, but not touching him. She left a space between them, drew a line.

"Have you ever cheated on your wife?"

"With you, I wouldn't be cheating on her, I would be betraying her."

"Why did you remarry?"

"I told you, my wife asked me to."

"Do you love her?"

"Why ask me that question? Would you leave your husband

for me? I don't have to answer you. You're a shackled woman, Irène, tethered. Get undressed. Completely. I want to look at you."

"Switch off the light."

"No, I want to look at you. No coyness between us."

"Do you think your three friends thought I was your tart?"

"They're not my friends, they're colleagues. Get undressed."

"You get undressed at the same time as me, then."

"Agreed."

72

Jesu, joy of man's desiring.
May the inventor of birds make a hero of me.

It's still raining. The windshield wipers sweep across our faces. On the back seat, Nathan has fallen asleep. I turn frequently to watch him. It's been a long time since I watched a child sleeping. From time to time, we catch songs on the radio, and then, as the road bends, they get lost. Between snatches, Julien and I talk about Irène and Gabriel.

"After the Sedan episode, they saw each other often."

"How does it feel, knowing all that about your mother?"

"Honestly? I feel as if I've read the story of a stranger. In fact, her journal, I'm giving it to you, I don't want it back. You can keep it with your registers."

"But I . . ."

"I insist. Keep it."

"Have you read it all?"

"Yes, several times. Especially the parts where she mentions you. Why didn't you tell me that you knew each other?"

"We didn't really know each other."

"You have an extraordinary way of twisting things, Violette, of playing on words . . . I always want to get you to spit it out. You're worse than the lot I have in custody . . . Honestly, I wouldn't like to arrest you . . . I'd go mad questioning you."

I burst out laughing.

"You remind me of a friend."

"A friend?"

"He was called Sasha. He saved my life . . . By making me laugh, like you do."

"I'll take that as a compliment."

"It is one. Where are we going?"

"The Pardons."

" . . . "

"It's the name of a road in La Bourboule. It's where my father was born. Where some of my family still live . . . They even get married, occasionally."

"They're going to wonder who I am."

"I'll tell them you're my wife."

"You're crazy."

"Not enough."

"What are we going to give the young couple?"

"They're not that young, in fact. They'd both lived a bit before they met. My cousin is sixty-one and her future husband around fifty. There's a gas station about twenty kilometers away, we'll find them some jokey presents. And also, Nathan needs to get changed."

"I'm already changed."

"You're always changed. You live changed . . . You're always dressed for a ceremony, whether it's a wedding or a funeral."

I burst out laughing for the second time.

"And you? Aren't you getting changed?"

"No, me, never. It's jeans and sweater in winter, jeans and T-shirt in summer."

He looks at me and smiles at me.

"You're really going to buy your wedding presents in a gas station?"

"Really."

While Julien is filling up on gas, I go to the shop with Nathan. I hold his hand. An old habit. Those gestures you never forget. That are part of us, without thinking. Like a hair color, a familiar smell, a resemblance. It's been such a long time since I held the hand of a child. I'm so moved, feeling his little fingers gripping mine. He's humming a tune I don't know.

I feel lighthearted wandering around the shop. Nathan is wide-eyed at the galaxy of chocolate bars and sweets beside the registers.

I stop outside the door leading to the men's restroom.

"I'm not allowed in there, I'll wait for you here."

"O.K."

Nathan goes off to lock himself in with his bag of clothes. He's back out five minutes later, proudly sporting a three-piece suit of light-gray linen and a white shirt.

"You look very handsome, Nathan."

"Got any gel?"

"Gel?"

"For my hair."

"I'll go and see if they sell any here."

While we scour the many shelves for gel, Julien buys two novels, a recipe book, a box of cakes, a barometer, table mats in every color, a map of France, three DVDs, a compilation of greatest film scores, a globe, aniseed balls, a man's rain jacket, a lady's straw hat, and a stuffed toy. He asks the cashier to wrap it all up in gift paper. The cashier doesn't have any. And adds, with a smile, that we're not at the Galeries Lafayette here, but on the A89. Julien finally finds a large canvas tote with the WWF logo, and fits everything inside it. Nathan asks him to buy some colorful labels to stick on the bag and brighten up the panda, giving it bamboo and a blue sky. Julien replies, "Brilliant idea, son."

I feel as though I'm another woman, that I've switched lives. That I'm in someone else's. Like Irène, when she swapped her beige for brightly colored clothes and sandals in Cap d'Antibes.

Nathan and I finally unearth the last pot of "steel-strong" hair gel, which had ended up beside two razors, three toothbrushes, and a packet of wet wipes. We let out a triumphant cheer. I burst out laughing for the third time.

Nathan is delighted and goes off to do his hair in the toilets. He emerges with his hair sticking out in all directions, he must have slapped the whole pot on his head. Julien looks dubiously at his son, but says nothing.

"Do I look handsome?"

Julien and I say yes at the same time.

73.

No express train will take me towards bliss,
No old banger reach it, no Concorde have
your wingspan, no ship sail, except you.

SEPTEMBER 1996

Philippe's days had always followed the same pattern. Get up at around 9 A.M. Breakfast made by Violette. White coffee, toast, unsalted butter, cherry jam with no bits. Shower and shave. Ride bike until 1 P.M. Take country roads, dice with death daily by accelerating where he knew there was never a cop or speed trap. Lunch with Violette.

Mortal Kombat, his video game, on the Mega Drive until 4 or 5 P.M. Bike ride until 7 P.M. Supper with Violette. Then he'd set off on foot for the Grand-Rue, saying he needed a walk, to meet up with a mistress, or join some debauched gathering at *L'Adresse*. In that case, he'd go by bike and not return before one or two in the morning. If he didn't feel like doing a thing, due to a rainy forecast or extreme lethargy, he watched the television. Violette remained near him, reading or watching his chosen film.

Since he had caught her with the cemetery keeper, a fortnight ago, Philippe didn't see Violette the same way anymore, he watched her out of the corner of his eye. He wondered whether she was thinking about that old man, whether she phoned him in his absence, whether she wrote to him.

For the past week, when Philippe came home, he pressed the phone's "last call" button, but always fell on the unpleasant voice of his mother, whom he'd phoned the day before, or the day before that, and hung up on it.

He *had* to phone her every other day. It was a ritual. And the words were always the same: "How are you, son? Eating well? Sleeping enough? Health O.K.? Take care on the road. Don't ruin your eyes on your video games. And your wife? Work O.K.? Is the house clean? Does she wash the sheets every week? I'm keeping an eye on your accounts. Don't worry, you're not short. Your father transferred money into your life insurance last week. My pains are troubling me again. Really, we've never had any luck, oh no, we really haven't. People are so disappointing. Watch out. Your father is trying less and less. Thank goodness I'm here to watch over you two. Bye for now, son." Every time he hung up, Philippe felt bad. His mother was a razor blade causing him increasing irritation. Sometimes he wondered if she had any news of her brother, Luc. He missed his uncle. And Françoise's absence killed him. But his mother would reply, with annoyance, or sadness if she wanted to make him feel guilty: "Don't speak to me of those people anymore, please." His mother threw Françoise and Luc into the same trash bag.

Apart from these conversations, which irritated him, Philippe's life was, seemingly, a well-oiled machine. He had remained the boy Françoise had accompanied that last time to the station at Antibes in 1983: a capricious child. An unhappy child.

But two pieces of news arrived, within five minutes of each other, to bring his seamless days to a halt. The first came by mail.

Just as he was tucking into one of his pieces of toast, hot and crusty just as he liked it, Violette announced to him that the barrier was going to be automated in May of 1997. They had eight months to find new jobs. She placed the letter addressed to them both on the table, between the pot of jam and the melted butter, and went off to lower the barrier for the 9:07.

I'm going to lose Violette. That was Philippe's first thought upon reading the letter. There would be nothing left to keep her now. Their roof and their work still linked them, he wasn't even sure why. Linked them by a thread so fine, it was almost invisible. Apart from Léonine's bedroom, with its permanently closed door, they had nothing left in common. Once she lost the barrier, she would leave forever, to be with the old man at the cemetery.

He saw a woman talking to Violette through the kitchen window. He didn't recognize her immediately. His first thought was that it was one of his mistresses, come to grass on him, but it was fleeting: the women he frequented weren't the sort to be jealous. He took no risks. He sullied himself, sullied Violette, but took no risks.

In the meantime, he saw that Violette was growing paler as the woman spoke to her.

He went straight outside and found himself face to face with Léonine's teacher. What was her name again?

"Hello, Mr. Toussaint."

"Hello."

She, too, was pale. She seemed distraught. She turned her back on him and quickly walked away.

The 9:07 went by. Philippe saw a few faces at the carriage windows and thought of when Léonine would wave at them. Silently, as if on automatic pilot, Violette raised the barrier, and then said to Philippe:

"Geneviève Magnan committed suicide."

Philippe recalled the last time he had been outside Magnan's place, a little over two weeks ago. The cops' van, the women in dressing gowns under the streetlights. She must have committed suicide after seeing him. He had wept in front of her. "I'd never have done any harm to kids." Was it the weight of guilt that had pushed her toward death?

Violette added:

"Please see to it that she's not buried in the same cemetery as Léonine."

Philippe promised. Even if it meant digging her up with his own hands, he promised Violette.

Violette repeated several times:

"I don't want her defiling the earth of my cemetery."

Philippe didn't take a shower that morning. After hastily brushing his teeth, he got on his bike and left. Leaving Violette behind him, desolate, standing beside a barrier she wouldn't need to lower for a good two hours.

74

You'll see my pen feathered with sunlight,
snowing on the paper the archangel of awakening.

W*hy does the time that passes*
Look hard at us and then part us
Why don't you stay with me
Why are you leaving
Why do life and boats
That go on water have wings . . . "

The event room is empty. Just two waitresses finish clearing the tables, one pulling off the last paper tablecloths, the other sweeping up white confetti.

Julien and I are dancing alone on a makeshift dance floor. The remaining lights from a disco ball reflect tiny stars on our creased clothes.

Everyone has left, even the newlyweds, even Nathan, who is sleeping over at his cousin's. Only Raphaël's voice rings out from the speakers. It's the last song. After that, the DJ, a rather portly uncle by marriage, will pack up and go.

I want to draw out the day I've just had. Stretch it out. Like when we were in Sormiou, and night had long fallen, and we couldn't bear to retire to the chalet. Our toes couldn't bear to leave the water lapping the shore.

I hadn't laughed like that since then. Since never. I'd never laughed like I did today. I laughed with Léonine, but you don't laugh with your child the way you do with other people. They're laughs that come from somewhere else, elsewhere. Laughter, tears, terror, joy, they're all lodged in different parts of our bodies.

> *"And there goes another day*
> *In this small life, one mustn't die of boredom . . . "*

The song is finished. Through the mike, the DJ wishes us good evening. Julien calls out, "Good night, Dédé!"

I'd never been to a wedding, apart from my own. If they're all as joyful and amusing, I'll gladly change my habits.

While I slip on my jacket, Julien disappears into the kitchen and returns with a bottle of champagne and two plastic flutes.

"You don't think we've drunk enough already?"

"No."

Outside, the air is sweet. We walk side by side, Julien holding my arm.

"Where are we going?"

"It's three in the morning, where do you think we're going? I'd love to take you home with me, but it's about five hundred kilometers from here, so we're going to a hotel."

"But I have no intention of spending the night with you."

"Ah, well, that's a great shame, because I do. And this time, you won't run away."

"You're going to lock me up?"

"Yes, until the end of your days. Don't forget I'm a cop, I have all the powers."

"Julien, you know that I'm unfit for love."

"You're repeating yourself, Violette. You're exhausting me."

And here it is again. It's like bubbles of silliness, bubbles of joy that rise up to my throat, caress my mouth, shake my stomach with elation, and make me explode with laughter. I didn't know that this sound, this particular note existed inside me. I feel like a musical instrument with an extra key. A happy design flaw.

Is that what youth really is? Can one make its acquaintance at almost fifty years old? I, who never had a youth, might I have kept it preciously without realizing? Might it never have left me? Is it making its appearance today, a Saturday? At a wedding in Auvergne? In a family that isn't mine? Beside a man who isn't mine?

We arrive at the hotel, and its door is double locked. Julien looks distraught.

"Violette, you have before you a prize idiot. Yesterday, I had the receptionist on the phone, asking me to come and collect the keys and entry codes on arrival this afternoon . . . And I forgot."

I'm off again. I can't stop myself anymore. I laugh so hard that my peals of laughter all seem to echo each other, as if my sound system were at peak volume. It feels so good, it hurts my stomach. I'm out of breath, and the more I try to catch it, the more I laugh.

Julien watches me, amused. I try to say to him: "You're going to struggle with locking me away until the end of my days," but the words won't come out anymore, my laughter's blocking everything. I can feel tears rolling down, which Julien wipes away with his thumbs, while laughing all the more himself.

We walk over to his car. We make a funny couple, me bent double, and him, clutching his bottle of champagne, trying his best to move me forward, plastic flutes in both trouser pockets.

We settle side by side at the back of the car, and Julien shuts my laughter up by kissing me. A silent joy takes root deep inside me.

I have the feeling that Sasha's not far away. That he's just given Julien directions for planting little shoots of me in my every vital organ.

75

I'm a stroller, I have "other side of the river" syndrome.

Today, Pierre Georges (1934–2017) was buried. His granddaughter had painted the coffin. Images of moving naivety. She had spent three days painting some countryside and a blue sky on the bare wood. No doubt thinking that her grandfather would stroll around it, in the beyond.

Pierre was called Elie Barouh, like the singer, but before the war his parents, both buried in Brancion, had to change his first name and surname. A woman rabbi came from Paris to pay final homage to him. She is France's third woman rabbi. She sang her prayers, it was very beautiful. She recited the Kaddish when the coffin was lowered into the family vault, where Pierre's parents have lain for decades. Then everyone threw a little sand onto the coffin. After the countryside and the blue sky, by throwing white sand, Pierre's family and friends also gave him the seaside.

Since it wasn't his God being invoked, Father Cédric stayed in my kitchen during the ceremony.

It is said that a man has the family he deserves. Seeing Pierre's children and grandchildren around his tomb, all united around the same farewell, I thought what a fine person Pierre must have been.

Afterwards, drinks had been organized in the small event room at the town hall. Pierre's family and friends gathered there to sing songs for him. The doors were open and I could hear the voices and music from my house.

The woman rabbi, whose name is Delphine, came for a coffee

at the house. Cédric was still there. The man of the church and woman of the synagogue were a nice sight, together, in my kitchen. Their faiths, their laughter, and their youth all blended together. I thought how Sasha would have loved it.

Since it was sunny, I went out to work in the garden. Delphine and Cédric sat under my arbor and stayed more than two hours, talking and laughing some more.

Delphine seemed entranced by the beauty of my plants and fruit trees. Cédric took her around as if he were the proud owner. As if it were his God, whose house was nearby, who had produced all these little miracles.

While planting my eggplants, I heard one of the songs the family and friends of Pierre Georges were singing on the town hall square. They must have left the event room to sit under the trees.

Even Delphine and Cédric went quiet to listen to it.

No, I no longer feel like flattering myself
By desperately seeking the echo of my "I love you"
No, I no longer have the heart to break my heart
By parodying games that I know off by heart . . .
You, who today offers me the finest of spectacles
With such beauty, you could have found obstacles . . .
But I no longer see any of its lovely mystery
I'm scared nothing will come of what I fear or hope
Because despite all the dreams locked in my soul
I will never again have the courage to love . . .

Bent over my soil, I wondered whether it was for Pierre or for me that they were singing it.

At around 6:30 P.M., everyone returned to their cars to head back to Paris. Once again, I heard the sound that I hate so much, that of car doors slamming.

My three guys had supper with me, outside. I made them an

improvised salad, along with sautéed potatoes and fried eggs. We thoroughly enjoyed it. The cats joined us, as if to listen to our disjointed, banal, but cheerful chatter. Nono repeated all through supper, "Isn't it good to be here, at our Violette's?" And we responded, in unison, "So good." And Elvis added, "*Donte live mi nao.*"

They left at around 9:30 P.M. The days are longest during the month of June. I stayed in the garden, sitting on a bench, to listen to the silence. To listen to all that noise that Léonine will never make again, apart from a little love song in my heart, whose tune only I know.

I think again of Nathan on the back seat. Of our return on Sunday morning, all three of us, in the car. Our hangovers, Julien's and mine, notched into a twig, green wood, a young shoot, a mere leaf, barely peeping out of the soil, two or three roots, more like threads, so easy to pull out. A sprouting of childish love to uproot. Now you see it, now you don't.

The gel had left white patches in Nathan's hair. A bit like snow. Julien told him that, as soon as they arrived in Marseilles, he must wash his hair several times before returning to his mother's house. Nathan made a face, searching my eyes for support.

They dropped me outside my house, at the road-side door. They were about to set off, but Nathan wanted to see the animals. Florence and My Way came and rubbed themselves against his little legs. Nathan petted them for a long time. He asked me:

"How many cats have you actually got?"

"Right now, eleven."

I recited their names, it sounded like a poem by Prévert.

He chuckled with laughter. We refilled the bowls with dry cat food, throwing the old stuff to the birds. Gave them fresh water. Julien, meanwhile, had gone to Gabriel's tomb to see his mother's urn.

When he returned, Nathan begged him to stay a bit longer. And me, I wanted to beg his father to stay a lot longer. But I said nothing. They had tea in my garden and then set off. I walked with them to the car. Before getting in, Julien tried to kiss me on the mouth, I drew back. I didn't want to be kissed in front of Nathan.

Nathan wanted to sit in the front, his father told him, "No, when you're ten years old." Nathan moaned, and then planted a kiss on my cheek. "Goodbye, Violette."

I had a burning desire to cry. As they slammed shut, their car doors were louder than the others had been. And yet I behaved as if their leaving didn't bother me. As if I were relieved. As if I had a thousand other things to do.

After thinking about all that on my bench, I go into the house and close both doors, road-side and cemetery-side. Eliane follows me up to my bedroom and stretches out at the foot of the bed. I open the windows to let in the sweet evening air. I apply my rose cream, open the drawer of my bedside table, and sink back into Irène's journal.

Before browsing through her pages of writing, it dawns on me that she knew her grandson for a few years. I wonder what kind of grandmother she was. How she had greeted Nathan's birth. I work out that he was born one year after Gabriel's death.

Irène's and Gabriel's love reminds me of the game Hangman, where you have to guess a word. And I haven't yet found the one that defines that love.

When he had entered my house, Julien had brought his mother and Gabriel with him.

How will our encounters end?

76

The family isn't destroyed, it changes.
A part of it merely becomes invisible.

SEPTEMBER 1996

That morning, after promising Violette that Geneviève Magnan wouldn't be buried in the Brancion cemetery, Philippe had first headed for Mâcon, but at the last moment, he'd kept going and descended to Lyons, and then Bron. He'd reached the Pelletier garage by mid-afternoon. He had parked far enough away not to be seen. The garage was just as he remembered it. White and yellow walls. He hadn't set foot in there for thirteen years, and even though he was too far away, he could smell that blend of engine oils. That smell he loved so much.

Only the models and makes of the cars on show, seen through his visor, had changed. He had kept his helmet on his head for hours. He had waited a long time to see *them*.

At around 7 P.M., upon seeing Françoise and Luc, side by side, in their Mercedes, her at the wheel, him beside her, his heart had let rip like a crazed boxer. Its pounding had reached his throat. The car's rear lights had long disappeared when Philippe thought back to the best moments of his life with them. Those moments when he had really felt loved and pro-tected. Those moments when no one expected anything of him. Those moments far away from his parents. He hadn't fol-lowed the Mercedes. He just wanted to see them, be sure that they were still there, alive. Just that, alive.

And then he had headed for La Biche-aux-Chailles. The wretched place where Geneviève Magnan and Alain Fontanel lived. He had driven through the night. He liked riding his bike at night, with the dust and the moths in the headlights.

He had parked outside their house. A light was on in a downstairs room. Despite the circumstances, Philippe hadn't hesitated to knock on the door. Alain Fontanel was alone, and somewhat tipsy. The black eye Philippe had given him two weeks earlier had almost gone.

"Geneviève's did herself in. You won't be getting it off tonight."

That's what Fontanel had said to Philippe on finding him at the door. The words had knocked Philippe for six and made him heave. He had almost thrown up. How could he have sunk so low?

The man standing before him was the lowest of the low, but so was he. He was the one who'd had a thing with Magnan. Who had "lent" her to a pal one night, without a second thought.

Philippe felt queasy thinking about it. He leaned against the door frame. That evening, faced with this drunkard eyeballing him, Philippe grasped how much Magnan had suffered at the hands of the two bastards that had trashed her: him and Fontanel. And that suffering pierced him like an icy wind. As if Geneviève's ghost had stabbed him with the blade of a long knife. Darkness crashed down on him.

Seeing him reeling, Fontanel smiled nastily and turned his back on him, without closing the front door. Philippe followed him down a dark corridor. Inside, there was that musty smell, that smell of staleness, grease, and dust combined that you get in places where the air is never let in. Where no duster or mop has ever been seen. Philippe had thought of Violette, who aired the house even in winter. Violette. As he followed Fontanel, Philippe felt an intense desire to hold her in his arms. To hold her tighter than he ever had. But as the old man at the cemetery doubtless had.

The two men sat at the dining-room table. A dining room with no dining, just dozens of empty beer bottles on a plastic tablecloth. Two or three empties of vodka and other spirits. And, as though the Devil had decided to keep them company between these wretched walls, they started silently drinking.

It was only much later that Fontanel had spoken, when Philippe's eyes had fallen on, and been unable to leave, the portrait of two young boys. Two framed grins on the corner of an ageless, filthy sideboard. A special school photo of siblings together, so their parents had an extra memento.

"The kids are with Geneviève's sister. Much better off with her than with me. Never been a good father . . . And you?"

"   . . . "

"About the girls' deaths, about your kid, Geneviève, she wasn't to blame . . . I mean, she did nothing on purpose. Me, I only know the end of the story, when she came to wake me up. Sound asleep I was, thought I was having a nightmare. She shook me, like some madwoman. She was blubbering and hollering all at once, couldn't understand what she was jabbering on about . . . She spoke about you, told me your daughter was there, about her supply job at the school in Malgrange, about fate, cruel as can be . . . She spoke of her mother, I thought she'd hit the bottle. She pulled me by the arm, screaming, 'Come! Come quickly! It's horrific . . . horrific,' never said such things before, Geneviève hadn't. When I got to that room downstairs, it was too late. . ."

Fontanel downed a bottle of beer in one go, followed by a glass of vodka. He sniffed loudly, and then spat out his words, staring at a tear in the plastic tablecloth, scratching at it with his nails.

"The boss, that Croquevieille, she paid me peanuts for doing maintenance. The electrics, plumbing, painting, the parks . . . parks, my ass. Grass and gravel. Geneviève, she did the shopping and cooking in the summer. The boss, she gave us overtime if we both slept there when the kids arrived . . . For supervising and being an extra presence. That evening, Geneviève wasn't supposed to be working. But when the kids went to bed, Lucie Lindon asked Geneviève to replace her for a couple of hours, supervise the ground-floor rooms. Lindon wanted to go upstairs to smoke a joint in Letellier's room. Geneviève didn't dare refuse . . . That Lindon was always helping her out. But Geneviève didn't stay at the château. She went off. She left the girls on their own to go to her sister's, to see our kids, because our youngest was ill and she was worried sick. In summer, it drove her nuts having to leave them while others swanned off to the beach . . . She blamed me, 'You're just a good-for-nothing, can't even fucking take us to the beach . . .'"

Fontanel had gone for a pee, whistling "*Vie de merde.*" When he was back in the dining room, he had sat on the other side of the table, in a different seat. As if his had been taken by someone in his absence.

"Geneviève must have been gone for an hour, tops. When she got back, and opened the door of Room 1, she came over dizzy, crashed to the floor . . . Already, that afternoon, she'd almost passed out. She thought she must be sick . . . That she'd picked up our kid's virus. She struggled to get up . . . She opened the window to gulp some fresh air . . . That's what saved her. It was five minutes later that she said to herself something wasn't right . . . That the girls were sleeping too soundly. Geneviève didn't get it straight away . . . Carbon monoxide, it's a gas you can't smell . . . In each room, there was an individual water heater, old as time . . . Ancient things that didn't work at all anymore, but that weren't allowed to be touched . . . And yet someone had. Geneviève clocked it straight away because those bloody things were stuck behind a false cupboard, and that one had been opened . . . The door was just hanging open."

Alain Fontanel opened another bottle, using a lighter lying on the table, while still talking.

"We all knew the fixtures in the château were rotten . . . A ticking time bomb. There was nothing I could do. It was too late. Asphyxiated . . . Poisoned by carbon monoxide. The four of them."

Fontanel went silent. His voice had betrayed emotion for the first time. He lit a cigarette, closing his eyes.

"I immediately switched off the water heater. I even found the match used to get it going. Geneviève, she's never been able to lie . . . When you were having it off with her, I knew it. She went all gooey-eyed. Totally daft. Stank like a perfume factory, wore stuff on her face, shoes that crippled her . . . That evening, I saw in her eyes she hadn't done it, she wasn't to blame. I saw her terror. She stank of death . . . And anyway, you have to know what you're doing to start an old thing like that. She wouldn't have been up to it . . . It was strictly forbidden to touch the château's old water heaters. And the staff all knew that. It was drummed into us often enough. It wasn't written in the rules, or the boss would've gone straight to jail, but us, we knew . . . She should've had them removed . . . Croquevieille, when it came time to get parents to cough up, she was right there, but when it came to paying for new gear, she was gone. The only new hot water tanks were the ones in the communal showers."

Someone knocked on the door. Fontanel didn't open. He just grumbled, "Bloody neighbors," and refilled his glass. While Fontanel was telling the story, Philippe didn't move. He drank long glasses of vodka, at regular intervals, to burn away the pain, drown the sorrow.

"Geneviève panicked. Said she didn't want to go to prison. That if anyone knew she'd gone off to see her kids, she'd get the blame for everyone. Begged me to help her. At first, I said no. 'And how d'you think I can help you?' I said. 'We'll tell the truth, that it was an accident . . . We'll find the idiot who did that.' She went berserk, face all twisted . . . She swore at me, threatened me. Said she'd tell the whole band of cops that I spied on the supervisors . . . that she'd seen me stealing their panties from the dirty laundry . . . that she had proof. I gave her a big slap to shut her up . . . And then I remembered that, when I was in the army, one night a squaddie had burnt down part of the barracks by forgetting a saucepan of food on a badly switched off gas cooker . . . That's how I had the idea . . . With fire, everything disappears. When everything burns, no one goes to jail . . . Especially if it's little kids making the mistake of forgetting a pan of milk on the stove."

Right then, Philippe would have liked to ask Fontanel to shut up. But he was incapable of opening his mouth, of uttering a single word. He would have liked to get up, leave quickly, run away, cover his ears. But he remained frozen to the spot, paralyzed, powerless. As if two icy hands were pinning him to his chair.

"It's me who set fire to the kitchen . . . Geneviève who put the mugs in the girls' room . . . I waited at the end of the corridor, left their door ajar. Geneviève went up to our room . . . Since that night, she'd never stopped blubbing . . . She was scared, too . . . Said you or your wife, you'd end up coming to skin her alive . . . "

Shudders coursed through Philippe. Like shocks from invisible electrodes.

"When the flames reached the room, I ran upstairs to give a good kicking to Letellier's door . . . I hid away with Geneviève in our room. Lindon woke up, went down to the ground floor, screamed when she saw the fire, I acted like I'd just got out of bed, didn't understand what was going on . . . Letellier wanted to go into the room, but it was too late . . . Flames too high. We got everyone evacuated . . . By the time the fire brigade arrived, there were nothing left . . . Looked like Hell, but much worse . . . Lindon never dared ask Geneviève where she was that evening, why and how the girls had got up to go into the kitchen without anyone realizing, because all that was basically her fault. Never found out who'd lit that water heater . . . Or why . . . Or at what point . . . You can imagine, I checked in the other rooms, no one had touched 'em . . . And I never said a word."

Philippe had passed out. He reopened his eyes, his head heavy, his tongue thick, embers in his stomach.

Alain Fontanel was still sitting in the same place, staring into space, eyes bloodshot, glass in hand. He hadn't smoked the cigarette he still held between his fingers; the ash had dropped onto the plastic tablecloth.

"Don't look at me like that, I know for sure it wasn't Geneviève who did that. Don't look at me like that, I tell you, I'm a nasty piece of work . . . people avoid me, see me coming and they cross the street, but never have I touched a hair on a kid's head."

* * *

Geneviève Magnan was buried on September 3rd, 1996. Irony of fate or unhappy coincidence, it was the day Léonine would have celebrated her tenth birthday.

When she was lowered into the family vault in the small cemetery at La Biche-aux-Chailles, three-hundred-odd meters from her house, Philippe had already gone back east, to the trains.

During the winter of 1996–97, he didn't go to *L'Adresse,* and he left his motorbike sleeping in the garage.

His parents came to pick him up once, in January, to go to the Brancion cemetery and pay their respects to Léonine, but he refused to get in the car. Like an obstinate child. Like when he went on holiday with Luc and Françoise, despite his mother's disapproval.

He spent six months playing Nintendo, mindlessly playing games that required him to save a princess. He saved her hundreds of times, having failed to save his own, the real one.

One morning, between the toast ritual and lunch, Violette told Philippe that the cemetery keeper's job at Brancion-sur-Chalon was becoming vacant, and that she wanted that job more than anything in the world. She conjured up a kind of happiness to him. She described the position to him as if it were a place in the sun, a five-star vacation.

He looked at her as if she'd lost her mind. Not because of what she was proposing, but because he realized that she was proposing that they continue to live together. At first, instinctively, he said no, because he thought she just wanted to be closer to the old cemetery keeper, but that didn't make sense. If she'd wanted to be closer to him, she would have left Philippe and gone and moved in with him. He realized that she wanted to carry on, that he was part of her plans, of her future.

The thought of becoming a cemetery keeper horrified him. But he wouldn't have to do any more than at Malgrange. Violette would take care of everything. And anyhow, what else could he have done? He'd had an appointment at the employment agency the previous day, had been told to update his CV. Update it to what? Apart from tinkering on motorbikes and seducing loose women, he had no skills. They had suggested training to become a mechanic, to work in a garage or at a dealer's; he presented well, he could also move into sales. The vision of himself as a salesman, getting commissions on cars, and the maintenance contracts that followed, disgusted him. The alarm clock going off just for him was never going to happen: office hours to stick to, suit and tie, thirty-nine-hour weeks, he'd rather die. An unthinkable nightmare. He'd never felt like working, apart from at eighteen, in Luc's and Françoise's garage.

By accepting this undertaker's job, a salary would keep

landing every month, a salary he wouldn't touch. Violette would do the shopping with hers, the cooking, the cleaning. He'd still have his wife warming his bed, his toast, clean sheets and china; he'd just have to take his routine with him, along with his favorite yogurt brand. And continue his life of an eternal adolescent. As Violette had said, she'd drape curtains over the windows of their house, and he wouldn't have to attend funerals. He'd set up his Nintendo in a closed room and save princesses, one after the other, to avoid being disturbed by some gravedigger or some lost visitor looking for a tomb.

And finally, it would be the chance to find out which son of a bitch had relit the water heater, on the night of July 13th–14th, 1993, at the château of Notre-Dame-des-Prés. He'd be on the spot to ask questions, smash a few teeth in, get the silence to talk. He'd do it secretly, so no one would ever come and take back or reclaim the insurance money he'd received, the damages paid for the accidental death of Léonine.

This obsession with putting any money aside, as his mother had taught him, disgusted him, but it was stronger than him. A genetic illness. A virus, a deadly bacterium. This stinginess was like a congenital defect. A cursed legacy he couldn't fight. Money put aside to go where? To do what? He had no idea.

They moved in August of 1997. They did the journey in a van of barely twenty cubic meters; they didn't possess much.

The old man from the cemetery wasn't there anymore. He'd left a note on the table. Philippe pretended not to notice that Violette already knew the house's every nook and cranny. When they had only just arrived, she disappeared into the garden. She called him, told him to come and see, "Come! Come quickly!" Philippe hadn't heard that smile in her voice for years. When he found her, crouching at the back of the vegetable garden, picking plump tomatoes, red as a young girl's cheeks, when he saw her biting into one of them, it reminded him of the sparkle in her eyes at the maternity hospital, on the

77.

It's better to mourn you than not to have known you.

O ctober 22nd, 1996
Most precious Violette,
It's already two months since your husband forbade you to return here. I miss you. 'Say, when are you coming back?' as Barbara sings.

This morning I listened to some Barbara, and it's amazing how perfectly her voice goes with autumn, the smell of wet earth, not the sort roots grow in, but that they gently sleep in to return stronger, preparing to draw on that strength in winter. Autumn is a lullaby for the life that will return. All those leaves changing color, it's like some haute couture fashion show, just like the notes in Barbara's voice are. Personally, Barbara amuses me. When you really listen to her, you can hear that, for her, nothing is that serious, despite its seriousness. I could have fallen madly in love with her, especially if she'd been a man. What can I say, like her, 'I don't have the virtue of sailors' wives.'

Thanks to this late season being mild, and no frost yet, I've actually just picked the last tomatoes, peppers, and zucchini. All Saints' Day approaches, it's like an invisible line: once it's over, no more summer vegetables. My lettuces are still as fine, in a month's time, there'll only be my sugarloaf chicory left. The cabbages are emerging from the soil. While awaiting the first frosts, I've already turned over some beds, which I've covered in manure—where we picked the potatoes and onions together last August. My farming friend brought me five hundred kilos of shit, which I stored under the tarpaulin beside the shed. I cover *it because, if it rains, the best of the manure gets washed away, leaving just the straw. It stinks a bit, but not too badly (it's always better than those ghastly chemical fertilizers). I don't think I'm bothering my closest neighbors. Speaking of whom, Edouard Chazel (1910–1996) was buried three days ago—died in his sleep. Sometimes I wonder what one can see at night to want to die of it.*

I heard about Geneviève Magnan, a very sad end. I think it's best to forget, Violette. I think you need to keep going and stop trying to find out how, why, who. The past isn't as fertile as the shit I spread on the ground. It's more like quicklime. That poison that burns stumps. Yes, Violette, the past poisons the now. Forever turning things over means dying a little.

Last month, I started pruning the old rosebushes. The weather has been too nice for mushrooms. Usually, at the end of summer, if there have been two or three storms with lots of rain, the chanterelles appear seven days later. Yesterday, I went into the woods, that secret spot where I usually find plenty of them, and I returned home like a Parisian, almost empty-handed. Just three chanterelles taunting me at the bottom of the basket. Like a litter of maggots, they were. I still ate them in an omelette. Serves them right! Last week, I saw the mayor, and spoke to him about you, highly recommended you. He wants to meet you and isn't against the idea of you replacing me. I warned him that you wouldn't be alone, that you had a husband. At first, he grimaced, because it means an extra salary, but since there used to be four gravediggers, and now there are only three, as a couple you should come within budget. So, if I were you, I wouldn't hang around. Before some person comes begging to him—there's always a nephew, cousin, neighbor after a municipal position. Admittedly, people aren't exactly lining up to become cemetery keepers, but all the same, let's not be complacent! It's out of the question that I leave my cats and my garden to anyone other than you!

Come back here so I can organize for you to meet the

mayor. Generally, one has to be wary of elected officials, but him, he's a pretty decent sort. If he gives you his word, you won't have to sign an offer of employment. So, you urgently need to think of some lie to get here as soon as possible. Have I already told you about the virtue of lying? If I forgot to, tie a knot in your hankie.

With fondest love, precious Violette,

Sasha

"Philippe, I have to go to Marseilles!"

"But it's not August."

"I'm not going to the chalet. Célia needs me for a few days, at her house. Three or four at the very most . . . If there are no complications. Without counting the journey."

"Why?"

"She's going to the hospital and has no one to look after Emmy."

"When?

"Straight away, it's an emergency."

"Straight away?!"

"Yes, it's an emergency, I tell you!"

"What's wrong with her?"

"Appendicitis."

"At her age?"

"There's no age for having appendicitis . . . Stéphanie will take me to Nancy and then I'll get a train. Until I arrive, Emmy will stay with a neighbor . . . Célia begged me, she's only got me, I have to go, and go fast. I've left you all the train timetables on a sheet of paper beside the phone. I've done the shopping, you'll only have to heat up your blanquette or gratin in the microwave, there are two of those pizzas you like in the freezer, I've filled the fridge with yogurts and ready-made salads. At lunchtime, Stephanie will drop off a fresh baguette for you. I've put the packets of cookies in the drawer, under the cutlery, for you as usual. I'm off, see you in a few days' time. I'll call you when I get to Célia's."

* * *

During the car journey, which took around twenty-five minutes, and in what little I said to her, I lied to Stéphanie. I served up the same story to her as to Philippe Toussaint: Célia had appendicitis, I had to hurry to collect her granddaughter Emmy. Stéphanie didn't know how to lie. If I'd told her the truth, she would have spilled the beans without meaning to. She would have blushed and stammered in front of Philippe Toussaint on meeting him.

Stéphanie had got herself replaced at her register for an hour to take me to Nancy. We didn't say much to each other in the car. I think she told me about a new brand of organic biscottes. For a few months, organic products had been appearing on the Casino shelves, and Stéphanie spoke to me about them as if they were the Holy Grail. I wasn't listening to her. I was rereading Sasha's letter in my mind. I was already in his garden, in his house, in his kitchen. I couldn't wait. Looking at the white tiger dangling from the Panda's rearview mirror, I was already searching for the right words, the right arguments to get Philippe Toussaint to accept moving, accept the cemetery keeper job.

I took a train to Lyons, another to Mâcon, and then the coach that passed outside the château. I closed my eyes as we drew level with it.

It was late afternoon when I pushed open the door of my future house. The daylight had almost gone, and it was bitterly cold. My lips were chapped. Inside, the air was sweet. Sasha had been burning candles and there was still that delicious smell, those handkerchiefs he soaked with *"Rêve d'Ossian."* When he saw me, he just said, smiling:

"I give thanks to the virtue of lying!"

He was in the middle of peeling vegetables. His hands, which shook a little, held the peeler like some precious stone.

We shared some truly delicious minestrone. We spoke of the garden, of mushrooms, of songs and books. I asked him where he would be going, if we moved in here. He told me that he already had everything planned. That he would travel and stop where he pleased. That his pension would be as meager as he was, but for the little he ate, it would suffice. That he would travel on foot, in second class, and by hitchhiking. Those were the only walks he felt like experiencing. He wanted to offer himself the unknown. With his friends as stop-offs. He only had a few, but they were true friends. Visiting them was part of his plan, too. Looking after their gardens. And if they didn't have one, making them one.

India was Sasha's focal point. His best friend, Sany, was Indian, and Sasha had met him as a child. The son of an ambassador, Sany had lived in Kerala since the 70s. Sasha had visited him there countless times, once with Verena, his wife. Sany was the civil godfather of Emile and Ninon, their children. Sasha wanted to end his life over there. Sasha never said "end my life," but rather "keep going until my death."

For dessert, he produced some rice pudding he had prepared the previous day, in assorted glass yogurt pots. I dug deep with my spoon to reach the caramel right at the bottom. As he watched me doing this, Sasha's voice changed:

"In losing my loved ones, I also lost an enormous weight. The worry of leaving them alone after my death, of abandoning them. The fear of imagining that they might be cold, in pain, hungry, and that I'd no longer be there to take them in my arms, protect them, support them. When I die, no one will mourn me. There'll be no grief after me. And I'll leave lightly, relieved of the weight of their lives. It's only egoists who tremble over their own death. Everyone else trembles for those they leave behind."

"But I will mourn you, Sasha."

"You won't mourn me the way my wife and two children would have mourned me. You'll mourn me the way one does when losing a friend. You'll never mourn anyone as you mourned Léonine. That you well know."

He boiled some water for the tea. He said he was happy I was there. That I would be among the real friends he would visit during his retirement. He specified, "During your husband's absences."

He put some music on, Chopin sonatas. And he spoke to me of the living and the dead. Of the regulars. Of widows. The toughest thing would be children's funerals. But no one was obliged to do anything. There was a real solidarity between the cemetery staff and the funeral directors. One could be replaced. A gravedigger could replace a pallbearer, who could replace a monumental mason, who could replace the funeral director, who could replace the cemetery keeper, when one of them felt unable to face a difficult funeral. The only person who couldn't be replaced was the priest.

I would see it all, hear it all. Violence and hatred, relief and misery, resentment and remorse, grief and joy, regrets. All of society, all origins, all religions on a few hectares of land.

On a daily basis, there were two things to pay attention to: not locking visitors in—after a recent death, some mourners lost all notion of time—and watching out for theft—it wasn't uncommon for occasional visitors to help themselves, from neighboring tombs, to fresh flowers and even funerary plaques. ("To my grandmother," "To my uncle," or "To my friend" could apply in most families.)

I would see more elderly people than young. The young went far away for their studies, or work. The young didn't visit tombs much anymore. And if they did come, it was a bad sign, it was to visit a friend.

The next day would be November 1st, the biggest day of

the year. As I would see, directions would have to be given to all those who weren't used to visiting. Sasha showed me where all the different plans of the cemetery were kept, and the index cards of the names of people who had died in the previous six months, in a hut-turned-office outside the house, cemetery-side. He specified that the rest, those who had died before that, were filed away at the town hall.

I reflected that Léonine was already filed away. So young and already filed away.

Written on these index cards, for each tomb, was the name and date of death, and the location.

On exhumation days, which remained rare, I would have to watch out that surrounding tombs didn't get damaged. One of the three gravediggers was particularly clumsy.

Certain visitors had special permission to drive into the cemetery. I would soon recognize them, just from the sound of the engine, particularly since most of them were little old men who made the clutches of their Citroëns screech.

Everything else I would pick up gradually. No day would be the same. I could turn it into a novel, or write the memoir of the living and the dead, one day, when I had finished reading, for the hundredth time, *L'Oeuvre de Dieu, la part du Diable*.

Sasha wrote an initial list in a brand-new notebook, a school exercise book. He wrote down the names of the cats that lived in the cemetery, their characteristics, what they ate, their habits. He had cobbled together a kind of cat home, with sweaters and blankets, in the Spindles section, at the back, to the left. Where no one came to pay their respects anymore, ten square meters with no passersby, where, with the gravediggers' help, he had put up a shelter. A dry, warm place for winter. He wrote down the details for the vets in Tournus, father and son, who made the journey there for vaccinations, sterilizations, and treatments, for only half the fee. Dogs could turn up there, to sleep on their owners' tombs; I would have to look after them.

On another page, he noted down the names of the gravediggers, their nicknames, their habits, their duties. And those of the Lucchini brothers, their addresses and their roles. And finally, the name of the person in charge of death certificates at the town hall. He concluded with these words, "For two hundred and fifty years, now, people have been buried here, and that's not about to stop."

As for the rest of the exercise book, he took two days to fill it. With everything concerning the garden, the vegetables, the flowers, the fruit trees, the seasons, the planting.

The following day, All Saints' Day, a light layer of frost had appeared on the earth in the garden. Before the cemetery gates were opened, I helped Sasha pick the last summer vegetables in the dark. We were both on the frozen paths, flashlight in hand, wrapped in our coats, when Sasha brought up Geneviève Magnan. He asked me how I had felt on learning of her suicide.

"I always thought that the children hadn't set fire to the kitchen. That someone hadn't stubbed out a cigarette properly, or something like that. I think Geneviève Magnan knew the truth and she couldn't bear it."

"Would you want to know?"

"After Léonine's death, knowing is what kept me going. Today, what matters for her, for me, is making flowers grow."

We heard the first visitors parking outside the cemetery. Sasha went to open the gates to them. I accompanied him. Sasha said to me, "You'll see, you'll adapt to the opening and closing times. In fact, you'll adapt to the grief of others. You won't have the heart to make visitors who arrive early wait, and it will be the same in the evening. Sometimes, you won't have the heart to ask them to leave."

I spent the day observing the visitors, arms laden with

chrysanthemums, and wandering the avenues. I went to visit the cats, who rubbed up against me. I pet them. They did me good. The previous day, Sasha had explained to me that numerous visitors transferred their emotions onto the animals in the cemetery. They imagined that their deceased loved ones were channeled through them.

At around 5 P.M., I went over to see Léonine, not her, but her name written on a tombstone. My blood froze when I caught sight of Father and Mother Toussaint, placing yellow chrysanthemums on her grave. I hadn't seen them since the tragedy. When they came to collect their son twice a year, and parked outside the house, I didn't look at them through the window. I just heard the sound of their car's engine and Philippe shouting to me, "I'm off!" They had aged. He had become stooped. She still held herself rigidly upright, but she'd shrunk. Time had diminished them.

They mustn't see me, they would have immediately told Philippe Toussaint, who thought I was in Marseilles. I watched them, hidden like a thief. As if I had done something wrong.

Sasha came up behind me, I jumped. He took me by the arm, without asking me any questions, and said to me, "Come, we're going home."

In the evening, I told him about Father and Mother Toussaint at Léonine's tomb. I told him about the mother's nastiness. The disdain she directed at me as soon as she looked at me without seeing me. It was they who were the killers, they who had sent my daughter to that wretched château. They who had organized her death. I told Sasha that maybe coming to live in Brancion, working in this cemetery, wasn't a good idea. Bumping into my in-laws twice a year, along the cemetery's avenues, seeing them placing pots of flowers to assuage their guilt, was too much for me. Today, they had returned me to my grief. There wasn't a minute, not a second of my life when I didn't think of

Léonine, but now it was different. I had transformed her absence: she was elsewhere, but closer and closer to me. And today, upon seeing the Toussaints, I had felt her moving away.

Sasha replied that the day they knew that my husband and I lived here, they would avoid me and no longer come. That being here would be the best way never to see them again. To get rid of them forever.

The following morning, I met with the mayor. I had barely set foot in his office before he told me that Philippe Toussaint and I would be employed starting in August of 1997 as cemetery keepers. That we would each receive the minimum wage, a house that went with the job, and that any water and electricity we used, as well as our household taxes, would be paid for by the council. Did I have any other questions?

"No."

I saw Sasha smile.

Before letting us go, the mayor served us vanilla-flavored tea, made with a teabag, and stale biscuits, which he dunked in his cup like a child. Sasha didn't dare refuse, even though he loathes tea made with a teabag. "Porous plastic attached to vulgar string, the shame of our civilization, Violette, and they dare to call that 'progress.'" Between biscuits, the mayor spoke to me while consulting his calendar:

"Sasha must have warned you, you're going to see all sorts. Around twenty years ago, we had rats in our cemetery, lots of rats. We called the pest controller, and he scattered powdered arsenic liberally between the tombs, but the rats continued to wreak havoc, and no one dared set foot in the cemetery. It was like something out of Camus's *La Peste*. The pest controller increased the amount of poison, but still no success. The third time, he laid the same traps, but instead of leaving, he hid to try to understand, to see how the rats reacted. Well, you won't believe me, but a little old lady turned up with a dustpan and brush, and she swept up all the powdered arsenic! She'd been selling it on the side for months! The following day, we made the newspaper headlines: 'Arsenic trafficking at Brancion-en-Chalon cemetery'!"

78.

There are so many fine things you don't know about, the faith that brings down mountains, the white spring in your soul, think of it as you fall asleep, love is stronger than death.

Every tomb is a garbage can. It's the leftovers that are buried here, the souls are elsewhere."

After murmuring these words, Countess de Darrieux downs her brandy in one go. Odette Marois (1941–2017) has just been buried, the wife of the countess's great love. She is recovering from her emotions, sitting at my kitchen table.

The countess attended the ceremony from a distance. Odette's children know that she was their father's mistress, their mother's rival; they cold-shoulder her.

From now on, the countess can place her sunflowers on her lover's tomb, without me finding them later, petals torn off, at the bottom of a garbage can.

"It's as if I've lost an old friend . . . And yet we detested one another. But then, deep down, old friends always detest one another a little. And I'm jealous; she's the one who's joining my lover first. She really will have had first dibs all her life, the bitch."

"Are you still going to put flowers on their tomb?"

"No. Not anymore, now that she's under there with him. It would be too indelicate of me."

"How did you meet your great love?"

"He worked for my husband. Looked after his stables. He was a handsome man . . . if you'd just seen his ass! His muscles, his body, his mouth, his eyes! They still send me aquiver today. We remained lovers for twenty-five years."

"Why didn't you leave your respective husbands?"

"Odette threatened him with suicide: 'If you leave me, I'll kill myself.' And anyhow, Violette, between you and me, it suited me fine. What would I have done with a great love twenty-four hours a day? Because it's hard work! I've never been able to do a thing with my hands, apart from read and play the piano, he would have soon got tired of me. Whereas that way, we frolicked when we felt like it, I was pampered, pomaded, perfumed, well put together. My fingers never stank of cooking or sour milk, and that, believe me, men really appreciate. You must admit, it was cushy. Trips around the world on my husband's arm, palaces, swimming pools, and dips in the South Seas. I would return tanned, available, rested, I would meet up with my great love, and we would love each other even more passionately. I felt as if I were Lady Chatterley. Of course, I always led him to believe that the count, twenty years my senior, no longer touched me, that we slept in separate rooms. And he told me that Odette wasn't remotely interested in sex. We lied to each other out of love, so as not to spoil us. Every time I listen to Brel's 'The Old Lovers' Song,' I shed a little tear . . . Speaking of teardrops, I wouldn't mind a final little drop of your brandy, Violette. I sorely need it, today . . . Every time I came across Odette, she gave me a dirty look, I loved that . . . I smiled at her, on purpose. My husband and my lover died within a month of each other. Both from a heart attack. It was terrible. I lost everything, from one day to the next. Earth and water. Fire and ice. It's as if God and Odette had combined forces to annihilate me. But anyway, I had some wonderful years, I never complain . . . Now, my final wish is to be cremated and have my ashes thrown into the sea."

"You don't want to be buried beside the count?"

"Beside my husband for eternity?! Never! I'd be too scared of dying of boredom!"

"But you've just told me it's the leftovers that are buried here."

"Even my leftovers could be bored beside the count. He was a real downer."

Nono and Gaston come in to make themselves a coffee. They look surprised to see me roaring with laughter. Nono blushes. He has a crush on the countess. Every time he sees her, he blushes like a schoolboy.

Father Cédric arrives a few minutes later, and kisses her hand.

"So, Father, how was it?"

"It was a funeral, Countess."

"Did her children play some music for her?"

"No."

"Oh, what idiots, Odette adored Julio Iglesias."

"How do you know?"

"A woman knows everything about her rival. Her habits, her perfume, her tastes. When a lover turns up at his mistress's, he should feel like he's on holiday, not back home."

"None of that sounds very Catholic, Countess."

"Father, people need to sin, or your confessional would be empty. Sin is your stock-in-trade. If people had nothing more to be ashamed of, there would be no one in the pews of your church."

The countess looked around for Nono.

"Norbert, would you be so kind as to accompany me back, please?"

"Nono becomes flustered and blushes even more.

"Of course, Countess."

Nono and the countess had barely passed through my door before Gaston broke his cup. As I bend over to sweep up the shards of china with my dustpan and brush, Gaston whispers in my ear, "I'm wondering if Nono's going to get it on with the countess."

79.

In the time linking heaven and earth,
the finest of mysteries is hidden.

IRÈNE FAYOLLE'S JOURNAL

May 29th, 1993
Paul is ill. According to our family doctor, he's show-
ing symptoms of a complication of the liver, stomach,
or pancreas. Paul suffers and doesn't get treatment. Strangely,
instead of getting tests done, seeking medical opinions from spe-
cialists, in one week he's consulted three clairvoyants, who pre-
dicted that he would have a long and happy life. Paul has never
shown the slightest interest in mediums or anything like that.
He reminds me of those atheists who start talking to God when
their boat is sinking, and I have the feeling that he became ill
because of me. That my lies to go and join Gabriel in a hotel
room finally got to him.

Lyons, Avignon, Châteauroux, Amiens, Epinal. For a year
now, Gabriel and I have been bed-hopping like others go island-
hopping.

I made two appointments for Paul to have a scan at the Paoli-
Calmettes Institute; he didn't go to them. Every evening, when
I tell him that he urgently needs to seek treatment, he smiles at
me and replies, "Don't worry, everything will be fine."

I can see that he's suffering, that he's lost weight. At night, in
his sleep, the pain makes him moan.

I'm in despair. What is he after? Has he gone mad or become
suicidal?

I can't force him into my car so I can take him to the hospi-
tal. I've tried everything—smiles, tears, anger—nothing seems
to affect him. He's letting himself die, he's drifting away.

I begged him to speak to me, to explain why he was doing this. Why this giving up. He went off to bed.

I'm lost.

June 7th, 1993

This morning, Gabriel called me at the rose nursery. He sounded happy, he's in court in Aix all week, he wants to see me, spend all his nights with me. He tells me that he thinks only of me.

I told him that it was impossible. That I couldn't leave Paul on his own.

Gabriel hung up on me.

I took up the snow globe placed on the counter, and I smashed it with all my might against a wall, screaming.

Not even real snow, just polystyrene. Not even real love, just nights in hotels.

We've gone mad.

September 3rd, 1993

I poisoned Paul's herbal tea. I put strong sedatives in it so he'd be knocked out and I could call for an ambulance.

They found Paul flat out in the middle of the sitting room and took him to the ER, where he was examined.

Paul has cancer.

He is so weak due to the illness and the drugs I made him swallow that the doctors have decided to hospitalize him for an unspecified amount of time.

Paul's toxicology tests showed that he had absorbed a massive dose of sedatives. He made out to the doctors that he had taken them, that he just wanted the pain to go away. He said that so that I wouldn't be questioned about it.

I explained to Paul why I had done it; I didn't have any choice, it was the only way I had found to make him finally go to the hospital. He told me that he was deeply moved that I loved him that much. He thought I didn't love him anymore.

Sometime, I would like to disappear with Gabriel. But only sometimes.

December 6th, 1993

I phoned Gabriel to tell him about the operation, the chemotherapy. To tell him we wouldn't be seeing each other anymore for now.

He replied, "I understand," and then hung up.

April 20th, 1994

This morning, a pretty pregnant woman came into the rose nursery. She wanted to buy some old roses and peonies to plant on the day her baby arrived. We talked about this and that. Particularly about her garden and her house, with its southwest aspect, ideal for planting roses and peonies. She told me she was expecting a girl, which was wonderful, and I replied that I had had a son and that was just as wonderful. That made her laugh.

It's so rare that I make others laugh. Apart from Gabriel. And my son, when he was small.

When it came to paying, the client wrote a check and gave me an identity card, saying:

"Forgive me, it's my husband's. But the surname and address are the same."

On the check I saw that she was called Karine Prudent, and lived at 19 Chemin des Contamines, Mâcon. Then I saw that the ID was Gabriel's. His photo, his date of birth, his place of birth, the same address, 19 Chemin des Contamines, Mâcon, his fingerprint. It took me a few seconds to understand. To make the connection. I felt myself going red, my cheeks burning. Gabriel's wife looked at me steadily, without lowering her eyes, and then took the ID back from me to slip it into the inside pocket of her jacket, against her heart, above the future baby.

She left carrying her plants in a cardboard box.

October 22nd, 1995
Paul is in remission. We went to celebrate that with Julien. My son lives in an apartment close to his school. I am living alone right now. I feel alone, like before his birth. Children fill our lives and then leave a great void, a massive one.

April 27th, 1996
Three years, now, that I've not heard from Gabriel. On each of my birthdays, I think he'll get in touch. I think, I believe, or I hope?
I miss him.
I imagine him in his garden with his wife, his daughter, his peonies, and his roses. I imagine him being bored stiff, he who only loves smoky brasseries, courts, lost causes. Me.

80

Speak to me in the easy way which you always used,
Put no difference in your tone,
Wear no forced air of solemnity or sorrow.
Laugh as we always laughed at the little jokes we shared
together.

SEPTEMBER 1997

Four weeks, now, that Philippe had been living in Brancion-en-Chalon. Every morning, the moment he opened his eyes, the silence got him down. In Malgrange, there was the traffic, the cars and trucks that passed their house, that stopped when Violette lowered the barrier, and the bell ringing out, the sound of the trains whizzing by. Here, in this dreary countryside, the silence of the dead terrified him. Even the visitors prowled around. Only the church bell ringing every hour reminded him, with its lugubrious sound, that time was passing and nothing happening.

Four weeks that he'd been here, and he already hated the place. The tombs, the house, the garden, the whole area. Even the gravediggers. When their van came through the gates, Philippe avoided them. He waved at them from a distance. He didn't want to get friendly with those three morons. A half-wit who called himself Elvis Presley; another one who was always having a laugh and picking up dubious cats, and all sorts of other creatures, to take care of them; and the third, who went flying the moment he missed a step, and looked as if he was straight out of a lunatic asylum.

Philippe had always been wary of men who were interested in animals. It was a girly thing, melting in front of a ball of fluff. He knew that Violette dreamt of having cats and dogs, but he refused. He pretended he was allergic to them. The truth was, he was scared of them and found them gross. Animals disgusted him. The trouble was, the cemetery was teeming with cats because Violette, and two of the three morons, fed them.

For the first time since they'd moved there, a funeral was scheduled for 3 P.M. that day. He'd set off early in the morning for a ride. Usually, he came back at midday, but he was afraid of coming across the bereaved family and the hearse. He'd driven aimlessly around the countryside and had arrived at Mâcon at lunchtime.

While waiting at a red light, he'd seen some children coming out of a primary school. In a group of little girls, he'd thought he recognized Léonine. Same hair, same hairstyle, same look, same walk, and, in particular, same dress. The pink-and-red one with white spots. At that moment, he'd thought: *What if Léonine wasn't in the room when everything burned down? What if Léonine was still alive somewhere? If she'd been stolen from us?* People of Magnan's and Fontanel's breed were capable of anything.

He'd switched off his bike's engine and walked towards the child. Then, as he approached her, he remembered that the last time he had seen Léonine, she'd been seven. And that today, she'd no longer be in a group of children shouting and skipping, but with middle-schoolers. That she wouldn't fit into her pink-and-red dress with white spots anymore.

As he got back on his bike, the hatred had returned. Hatred of his daughter's death. He lived here, in this wretched place, because of *them*.

He'd stopped at a roadside café, wolfed down a steak and fries, and, once again, on a paper napkin, had written:

Edith Croquevieille
Swan Letellier

Lucie Lindon
~~Geneviève Magnan~~
Eloïse Petit
~~Alain Fontanel~~

What was he going to do with these names? The names of those guilty of being there, guilty of negligence. Who had lit that damned water heater? And why? Had Fontanel just spun him a yarn? But to what end? Now that Geneviève Magnan was dead, he could have just said that she was to blame. He could have told him that the fire was accidental. Stuck to the domestic-accident theory. He could have said nothing at all, too. For the first time, Alain Fontanel had seemed sincere when he'd spoken all in one breath, without stopping, without thinking. But his words were steeped in alcohol. As was Philippe's perception of them. They were both drunk in that dining room of the devil.

Philippe reread the list of names that he was writing too often. He must follow through. Meet the other protagonists, one on one. It was too late not to know.

* * *

NOVEMBER 18TH, 1997

While showing a woman patient into the waiting room, Lucie Lindon had recognized him immediately. She could remember perfectly the face of each parent she had seen in court, those called "the claimants." And him, Léonine Toussaint's father, she had noticed him especially because he was on his own and particularly handsome. On his own, without his wife, alongside the couples who were the parents of Anaïs, Nadège, and Océane.

She had testified right in front of them. Explained that there hadn't been anything she could do that night except evacuate the other rooms and alert the rest of the staff. That she hadn't heard the children getting up to go to the kitchen.

Since the death of the little girls, Lucie Lindon was forever cold. As though she were living permanently in a draft. She could cover herself up, but she still shivered all over. The tragedy had plunged her into a freezing desert that consumed her, just as the fire had consumed the children. A fine layer of frost had slipped beneath her skin. Upon seeing Léonine's father, she crossed her arms and rubbed her hands up and down them, as if to warm herself up.

What was he doing there? None of the families lived in the area. Did he know who she was? Was he there by chance, or specifically to see her? Did he have an appointment, or did he want to speak to her?

Sitting facing a window, with his motorbike helmet at his feet, he seemed to be waiting his turn. Toussaint. Lucie Lindon looked for the name in the schedule of the three doctors in that morning, at the office where she was a medical secretary, but saw no sign of it. For more than two hours, the doctors went to open the waiting-room door, but they never called for Mr. Toussaint. At midday, he was still there, sitting facing the window. Along with two other patients waiting their turn. Half an hour later, when the waiting room was empty, Lucie Lindon went in and closed the door behind her. He turned his head in her direction and stared at her. Blonde, fine features, quite pretty. In other circumstances, he would have chatted her up. Although he'd never chatted anyone up, merely summoned them before helping himself.

"Hello, sir, do you have an appointment?"

"I want to speak to you."

"To me?"

"Yes."

It was the first time she was hearing the sound of his voice. She was disappointed. It revealed a somewhat drawling, rural accent. The birdsong didn't live up to the plumage. She was thinking that for a few seconds, and then began to panic. And her hands to shake. She again rubbed them nervously, up and down her arms.

"Why me?"

"Fontanel told me that you asked Geneviève Magnan to supervise the children in your place that evening . . . Is that true?"

He had said it without the slightest tone. Neither anger, nor hatred, nor passion. He had said it without introducing himself, he knew that Lucie Lindon recognized him, had placed him. That she would understand the significance of the words "that evening."

Lying would be pointless. Lucie sensed that she had no choice. Fontanel—just the name horrified her. A lecherous old dog with shifty eyes. She had never understood why he had been employed to work in the château, around children.

"Yes. I asked Geneviève to stand in for me. I was with Swan Letellier upstairs. I fell asleep. Someone knocked on the door, I went down and I saw . . . the flames . . . There was nothing I could do, I'm so sorry, nothing . . . "

Philippe got up and left without saying goodbye to her. So far, Fontanel hadn't lied.

* * *

DECEMBER 12TH, 1997

"Did someone hate you?"

"Hate me?"

"Before the fire, could someone have had a grudge against you?"

"A grudge against me?"

"A grudge against you to the extent of sabotaging equipment?"

"I don't understand, Mr. Toussaint."

"Were the water heaters installed in the ground-floor rooms defective?"

"Defective?"

Philippe grabbed Edith Croquevieille by the collar. He had waited for her in the underground car park of the Cora supermarket, in Epinal. She had moved to Epinal, with her husband, after being released from prison. Philippe had waited patiently there for her to return with her shopping cart, open the trunk of her car, and fill it with her groceries. She had to be on her own.

When he had approached her, menacingly, it had taken her a few seconds to place him. Then she had thought to herself that he was there to kill her, not question her. She had thought: *That's it, it's over, I'm living my final moments.* She lived with the idea that, one of these days, one of the parents would kill her.

Since knowing where she lived, Philippe had watched her for two whole days. She never went anywhere without her husband. He accompanied her everywhere, the shadow of her shadow. This morning, for the first time, she had left her home on her own, at the wheel of her car. Philippe had, in turn, followed her closely.

"I've never hit a woman, but if you carry on answering my questions with a question, I'm going to smash your face in . . . And believe me, I've got nothing to lose. That's already happened."

He loosened his grip. Edith Croquevieille saw that Philippe's blue eyes had darkened. As though anger had dilated his pupils.

"To be clear, is it true that the children washed their hands with cold water in their room because the water heaters were past it?"

She thought for two seconds and then whispered a barely audible "Yes."

"Did all the staff know not to touch those water heaters?"

"Yes . . . They hadn't been used for years."

"Could a child have got one working?"

She turned her head nervously from left to right before replying:

"No."

"Why not?"

"They were more than two meters above the ground and hidden behind a security hatch. There was no risk."

"Who could have done so, despite that?"

"Done what?"

"Got one of the water heaters working?"

"Absolutely no one. No one."

"Magnan?"

"Geneviève? Why would she have done that? Poor Geneviève. Why are you talking to me about the water heaters?"

"Fontanel, did you get on well with him?"

"Yes. I never had a problem with my staff. Ever."

"And with a neighbor? A lover?"

Edith Croquevieille's face kept falling as Philippe bombarded her with questions. She couldn't understand what he was getting at.

"Mr. Toussaint, until July 13th, 1993, my life was like clockwork."

Philippe loathed that expression. His mother often used it. Philippe felt like killing Croquevieille. But what would have been the point? This woman was already dead. She was quite a sight, all buttoned up in a sad coat. Sad expression, sad eyes. Even the features of her face had hanged themselves. He turned his back on her and left without saying a word. Edith Croquevieille called out:

"Mr. Toussaint?"

He turned back to her, half-heartedly. Didn't want to see her anymore.

"What are you after?"

He didn't reply to her, got back on his bike, and headed, reluctantly, for Brancion-en-Chalon. He was cold, he was tired. He'd been gone for three days without contacting Violette. He felt like getting back to clean sheets. He felt like playing with his controllers, and not thinking anymore, returning to his old habits, not thinking anymore . . .

81

*I'm not sure you're inside of me, or that I am inside of you,
or that I own you. I think we're both inside of another
being we have created called "us."*

G abriel Prudent didn't like what his wife picked. He
automatically fell asleep in front of the films she
rented from Vidéo Futur, the VHS temple on the corner of their street. She always rented romantic comedies.
Gabriel preferred Claude Lelouch's *L'aventure c'est l'aventure*,
the dialogues of which he knew by heart, or Belmondo and
Gabin in *Un singe en hiver*.

With the exception of Robert De Niro, Yanks didn't do
much for him, on the whole. But he never did anything to
annoy Karine. And also, he liked that Sunday-evening ritual,
sitting on the sofa, snuggled up to his wife, eyes closed in her
warmth, in her spicy perfume. The dialogues in English gradually faded away. As he fell asleep, he imagined beautiful actors
with impeccably blow-dried hair meeting, tearing each other
apart, separating, bumping into each other on a street corner,
and finally kissing, wrapped in each other's arms. Karine, red-
eyed after the soppy film, would gently wake him up during
the closing credits, and say, at once amused and annoyed,
"Darling, you fell asleep again." They would get up, stop at the
room of their child, who was growing too fast, look at her with
wonderment, and then make love, before he left once again, on
Monday morning, for the courts, where the accused, protest-
ing innocence, awaited him.

On that evening in 1997, Gabriel didn't fall asleep. As soon
as Karine slotted the video into the recorder, and the first
images appeared, he was gripped by the story. As though

consumed by it. He didn't see an extraordinary man and woman acting, but actually living their passion before his very eyes. As though he, Gabriel, were the privileged witness of it. As he was of all those strangers who filed onto the witness stand, whom he questioned for the prosecution or the defense. He sensed Karine silently looking at him, repeatedly, concerned that he hadn't fallen sound asleep.

And when, in the final minutes of the film, the heroine, seated beside her husband, didn't open the door of his car to go to the other car, in which her lover awaited her, and when the latter switched on his turn signal to leave forever, Gabriel felt the emotional dam he'd put up over the past four years to forget Irène gradually give way to the pressure of a storm, a hurricane, a natural disaster. He felt the rain of the film's final images running over him. He saw himself again, on the way back from Cap d'Antibes, waiting for Irène in his car. "I'll be back in five minutes, when I've dropped off the car keys." He had waited for her for hours, clutching the steering wheel. For the first few minutes, behind his windshield, he had imagined life at Irène's side. He had dreamt of a future in which he would be two. And then the wait had gone on forever.

He had finally let go of the steering wheel. He had got out of his car to go into the rose nursery. He had fallen on a shop assistant who hadn't seen Irène for several days. He had searched for her in the streets, randomly, desperately, refusing to understand that she wouldn't return, that she'd made the choice to remain in her life, that she wouldn't change anything for him. Doubtless out of love for her husband and her son. Against her will—there was an expression he'd heard many a time in trials.

He had got back in his car, and through his windshield, in the headlights, he had seen darkness, and nothing else.

And then one morning, at the office, he had been told that Irène Fayolle had requested an appointment. At first, foolishly, he had thought it was just a similar sounding name. But when he had seen that phone number he knew off by heart, the number for the rose nursery he had never dared to call, he had known it was her.

There had been Sedan, other hotels, other towns for a year, and then Paul's illness and Cloé's birth. On one side illness, on the other, hope.

No news from Irène for more than four years. What had become of her? How was she? Had Paul pulled through? Did she still live in Marseilles? Did she still have her rose nursery? He remembered her smile, her look, her smell, her skin, her freckles, her body. Her hair that he had so loved to mess up. With her, it had never been like with the others, with her it had been better.

As he watched the closing scene of the film, when the children scatter their mother's ashes from a bridge, Gabriel cried. In Gabriel's world, men didn't cry. Even when hit with the craziest verdicts, the most unexpected, the most unlikely, the happiest, the saddest. The last time he had cried, he must have been eight years old. He'd had a gash in his head stitched up without anesthetic after falling off his bike.

As for Karine, she didn't cry. Normally, while watching such a melodrama, she would have been wringing out her handkerchief, but the attention Gabriel had paid to the film stopped her from feeling anything but fear.

She remembered Irène in the rose nursery. The fineness of her hands, the color of her hair, her clear skin, her perfume. She remembered the morning when she had handed her Gabriel's identity card, to convey to her that she existed, and was pregnant.

Karine had discovered Irène's existence when Gabriel's office had left him a message: the concierge of the Hôtel des Loges, in Lyons, wished to return some belongings Gabriel had left behind during his recent stay. The previous week, her lawyer husband had been working in Lyons's criminal court. Karine had called the hotel, spoken to the concierge, given their home address, and, two days later, had received a parcel containing two white silk blouses, an Hermès scarf, and a brush on which a few long, blond hairs were caught. At first, Karine had thought it must be a mistake, and then she had remembered Gabriel. His gloomy demeanor when he had returned from Lyons, even though he had won his case on appeal. She had thought he was ill, he had looked rough. She had mentioned it to him, he had brushed it aside with a flick of the hand, and said, with a weary smile, that he was just very tired.

The following night, Gabriel had called out to someone in his sleep several times: Reine. The following morning, Karine had mentioned it to him. "Who is Reine?" Gabriel, his nose in his cup of coffee, had reddened.

"Reine?"

"You were saying that name all night."

Gabriel had laughed with that laugh she loved so much, a booming laugh, and had replied: "That's the wife of the accused. When she realized that her husband had been acquitted, she fainted." Bad choice. Karine knew about the case of Cédric Piolet, whose wife was called Jeanne. But she hadn't batted an eyelid—one can change one's name, or have two names.

For several nights, Gabriel had continued to call out Reine in his sleep. Karine had put it down to work, pressure. Her husband took on too many cases.

When Karine had met Gabriel, he was a widower and separated from his last partner. When she had asked him if there was someone in his life, he had replied, "From time to time."

As she held the two silk blouses that smelled of "*L'Heure bleue*," she had remembered that. Karine had thrown the Guerlain-scented garments and scarf, along with the hairbrush, into the bin. These things didn't belong to some transient tart, it was far more serious than that. In recent months, Gabriel had changed. When he came home, his mind seemed to be elsewhere. He was preoccupied with something, as though tormented. Karine had noticed that he drank more wine at the table. When she had pointed it out to him, Gabriel had quoted the screenwriter Michel Audiard, "If I were to miss anything, it wouldn't be the wine, it would be the intoxication." There was another woman in Gabriel's lies.

It hadn't been hard to find the number that appeared regularly on the last itemized phone bills. The same number cropping up during the weeks when Gabriel was around, either at his office or working from home. Always at about 9 A.M. Conversations that rarely exceeded two minutes. Enough to wish each other a lovely day and then hang up. Karine had called that number herself. A young girl had answered:

"The rose nursery, hello."

Karine had hung up. She had called the following week, and fallen on the same person:

"The rose nursery, hello."

"Yes, hello, my rosebushes are diseased, they have strange yellowish marks on the edge of their petals."

"Which varieties?"

"I don't know."

"Could you come to the nursery with one or two cuttings?"

Karine had called a third time. Still the same voice:

"The rose nursery, hello."

"Reine?"

"Hold on, please, I'll pass her to you. Who's speaking?"

"It's personal."

"Irène, you're wanted on the phone!"

Karine had got it wrong: it wasn't Reine that Gabriel was calling out in his sleep, but Irène. Someone had come to pick up the receiver, and this time, Karine had heard a feminine voice that was deeper, more sensual:

"Hello?"

"Irène?"

"Yes."

Karine had hung up. That day she had cried a good deal. Gabriel's "from time to time," that was *her*.

Finally, she had called a fourth and last time.

"The rose nursery, hello."

"Hello, could I have your address, please?"

"69 Chemin du Mauvais-Pas, in the Rose district, Marseilles 7."

Karine ejected the video and put it back in its cover. Gabriel was still sitting on the sofa, ashamed of having cried. It was his turn to have that guilty look he spent his life defending.

As she put the film into her handbag, so as not to forget it on her way to work the following morning, she said to Gabriel:

"Four and a half years ago, when I was pregnant with Cloé, I saw Irène."

Gabriel, although used to being confronted in court with the most complex and sordid cases, with every level of humanity, didn't know what to say to his wife. He was flabbergasted.

"I went to Marseilles. I bought roses and white peonies from her. When paying, I introduced myself. Those flowers, I didn't plant them in our garden, I threw them into the sea . . . Like when someone dies."

That evening, they didn't stop at the child's bedroom before going to their own, and didn't make love. In bed, they turned their backs on each other. She didn't sleep at all. She imagined Gabriel, eyes wide open, not able to sleep, remembering scenes from the film he'd just seen, and those he had lived with Irène. They never broached the subject of Irène ever again. They separated a few months after that Sunday. Karine regretted for a long time having rented *The Bridges of Madison*

County. And, unlike Gabriel, she never watched it again, despite its numerous showings on television.

* * *

IRÈNE FAYOLLE'S JOURNAL

April 20th, 1997

One year, now, that I haven't touched this journal. But I can't bring myself to part with it. I hide it at the bottom of a drawer, under my lingerie, like a young girl. Sometimes I open it and I'm off for a few hours. Basically, memories are summer holidays, private beaches. One doesn't keep a journal when one has passed a certain age, and I've long passed it, my certain age. I suppose Gabriel will always take me back to being fifteen.

He has lost a lot of hair. He has filled out a little. His eyes are still just as serious, beautiful, dark, deep. His voice cavernous, unique. A symphony. My favorite one.

I met Gabriel again in a café near the rose nursery. He let me order tea without one of his "that's a sad drink" kind of comments, and he didn't pour calvados into it. I found him calmer, he seemed less tormented, less angry. Even though he has always been charming, Gabriel is an angry man. No doubt due to the accusations of others that he spends his life shouldering, disproving on their behalf. One evening, when we were in Cap d'Antibes, he told me that the injustice of certain verdicts would be the death of him. That certain convictions gnawed him to the bone. Before ordering coffee after coffee to tell me about the last few years of his life, his little girl, his big girl, the one who is married, his last wife, his divorce, his work, he asked me for news of Paul and Julien. Paul especially, his cancer, the remission. The days following the illness, once he knew that he had come through.

Gabriel told me that he understood me, that he had stopped smoking, that he had seen a film that had shattered him, that he didn't have much time, was expected in court in Lille the following day, had to take a plane, had a late-afternoon meeting with his colleagues. It's the first time he didn't ask me to go with him, to accompany him. We stayed together for an hour. For the last ten minutes, he held my hands in his, and before leaving, closed his eyes and kissed them.

"I would like us to lie together in the cemetery. After this failed life, I would like us at least to make a success of our death. Do you agree to spend eternity beside me?"

I answered yes, without thinking.

"You won't slip away this time?"

"No. But you'll only have my ashes."

"Even as ashes, I want you close to me for eternity. Our two names together, Gabriel Prudent and Irène Fayolle—they're as lovely as Jacques Prévert and Alexandre Trauner. Did you know that the poet and his set designer were buried side by side? I think it's wonderful to be buried with your set designer. You, basically, you were my set designer. You gave me the most beautiful landscapes."

"Are you going to die, Gabriel? Are you ill?"

"That's the first time you've said 'tu' to me. No, I'm not going to die, well, I don't think so, it's not in the cards. It's because of the film I told you about earlier. It shook me. I have to go. Thank you, see you soon, Irène, I love you."

"I love you, too, Gabriel."

"At least that's one thing we have in common."

82

Here lies my love.

It happened one morning in January of 1998. I could only just make out their names. Their wretched names. Magnan, Fontanel, Letellier, Lindon, Croquevieille, Petit. They were slipped into the back pocket of a pair of Philippe Toussaint's jeans, and were almost illegible. The list had gone through the wash, the ink had run, as if someone had cried for a long time onto the soggy paper. I had hung his trousers to dry on the bathroom radiator, and when I went to get them, had noticed something sticking out. It was a piece of paper tablecloth, folded in four, on which, once again, Philippe Toussaint had written their names.

"Why?"

I had sat on the edge of the bath saying this word, several times: "Why?"

We had been living in Brancion-en-Chalon for five months. Philippe Toussaint escaped every day in two ways: on rainy days, with his video games; on fine days, on his bike. He had continued with the habits he had in Malgrange, but his absences were lengthier.

He avoided the cemetery visitors, the funerals, the opening and closing of the gates. He was far more afraid of the dead than of the trains. Of the bereaved visitors than of the SNCF passengers. He would meet up with fellow motorbike enthusiasts to go on rallies in the countryside. Long tours that culminated, I believe, in extramarital diversions. At the end of 1997, he had gone away for four days in a row. He had returned exhausted from his trip and, curiously, I had immediately seen, understood, sensed that he hadn't met up with one of his mistresses like he usually did.

On arrival, he had said to me, "Sorry, I should have called you, we went further than planned with the others, and there weren't any phone booths on our route, it was in the sticks." It was the first time Philippe Toussaint was explaining himself. The first time he was apologizing for not having given a sign of life.

He had returned on the day of the exhumation of Henri Ange, killed in action aged twenty-two in 1918, at Sancy, in Aisne. On the white headstone one could still make out the words: "Eternally missed." Henri Ange's eternity had come to an end in January 1998, his remains thrown into the ossuary. My first exhumation. The gravediggers and I hadn't been able to do a thing to spare his rest. His tomb was too dilapidated and eroded by decades of moss.

As the gravediggers were opening the coffin, ravaged by the weather, the damp, and vermin, I had heard Philippe Toussaint's motorbike. I had left them to finish their work without me. I had headed to the house out of habit. When Philippe Toussaint came home, I received him . . . Like servants when the master returns.

He had removed his helmet slowly, he looked ill, his eyes tired. He had taken a long shower and eaten lunch in silence. Then he had gone upstairs to have a nap, and had slept until the following morning. At around 11 P.M., I had joined him in our bed. He had shifted himself right behind me.

The following morning, after having his breakfast, he had set off again on his bike, but only for a few hours. Later, he had admitted to me that, during those four days away, he had gone to Epinal to speak to Edith Croquevieille.

We had been living here for five months, and I hadn't returned to Geneviève Magnan's to question Fontanel, or to the restaurant where Swan Letellier worked. I hadn't tried to find out where the two supervisors lived so as to speak to them. The director must have come out of prison—she had only got a year without remission. I had never passed in front of the château again. I no longer heard Léonine's voice asking me why everything had burned down that night. Sasha hadn't been wrong: this place was restoring me.

I had immediately found my bearings in this cemetery, in the house, in the garden. I liked the company of the gravediggers, the Lucchini brothers, and the cats, who came increasingly often for a coffee on the one hand, a saucer of milk on the other, in my kitchen, when my husband wasn't there. When Philippe Toussaint's motorbike was parked outside the roadside door, they never came in. There was no friendliness between them, just hello and goodbye. The men from the cemetery and Philippe Toussaint had no interest in each other. As for the cats, they avoided him like the plague.

Only the mayor, who visited us once a month, didn't care whether Philippe Toussaint was there or not; it was always me that he addressed. He seemed to be satisfied with "our" work. On November 1st, 1997, having seen the pine trees I had planted, when he was paying his respects at his family tomb, he had asked me to grow and sell a few potted plants in the cemetery, as a sideline, and I had accepted.

The first funeral I had attended as cemetery keeper had been in September of 1997. From that day on, I started recording what was said, describing those present, the flowers, the color of the coffin, the tributes inscribed on the funerary plaques, the weather, the poems or songs chosen, whether a cat or a bird had approached the tomb. I had immediately felt the necessity to leave some trace of those last moments, so that nothing got forgotten. For all those who weren't able to attend the ceremony due to pain, grief, distance, rejection, or exclusion, someone would be there to say, to testify, to tell, to report.

As I wished had been done for the funeral of my daughter. My daughter. My great love. Had I abandoned you?

Sitting on the edge of the bath, with the scrap of paper tablecloth in my hands, their names fading before my eyes, I felt an irrepressible urge to do like Philippe Toussaint, to leave for a few hours. Get out of here. Walk somewhere else. See other streets, other faces, window displays of clothes and books. Return to life, to a river. Apart from the shopping I did in the small town center, I hadn't left the cemetery for five months.

I went out and along the avenues of the cemetery, looking for Nono so that he could drop me off in Mâcon and pick me up in the late afternoon. He asked me if I had a driving license.

"Yes."

He handed me the keys of the council's utility vehicle.

"I'm allowed to drive it?"

"You're a council employee. I filled her up this morning. Have a good day."

I drove toward Mâcon. Since Stéphanie's Fiat, I hadn't touched a steering wheel, felt that kind of freedom. I sang as I drove: "*Douce France, cher pays de mon enfance, bercée de tant d'insouciance, je t'ai gardée dans mon coeur.*" Why did I sing that? The songs of Charles Trenet, my imaginary uncle, have always been a part of me, like nonexistent memories.

I parked in the center of town. It must have been around 10 A.M., the shops were open. First, I had a coffee in a bistro, watched the living arriving and leaving, walking on the sidewalks, their cars stopping at the red lights. Living people who weren't bereaved.

I crossed the Saint-Laurent bridge, walked along the Saône, and then wandered through the streets. It's on that day that my winter wardrobe and summer wardrobe first started. I bought myself a gray dress and a pink polo-neck on sale.

At lunchtime, I wanted to get closer to the restaurant quarter to buy a sandwich. It was cold, but the sky was blue. I felt like having lunch beside the water, throwing my crusts to the ducks. As I thought back to the Siamese cat that had saved my life the evening I'd waited for Swan Letellier, I got lost. I found myself in streets I didn't recognize. At a crossroads, I thought I knew where I was, but instead of going in the right direction, I moved further away from the town center. The streets were lined with houses and apartment buildings. I looked at the fences, the empty swings, the garden furniture shrouded in plastic because it was January.

It's at that moment that I saw it, propped on its stand, one of its wheels attached to a lock. Philippe Toussaint's motorbike was parked about a hundred meters away from me. My heart started beating as if I were a little girl who didn't have her parents' permission to be out of the house. I felt like turning around and running, but something held me back: I wanted to know what he was doing there. When he would leave at about 11 A.M. and return at about 4 P.M., I imagined that he went very far. Sometimes, when he got back, he told me what he had seen. It wasn't unusual for him to cover more than four hundred kilometers in a day. Looking at his Honda, it struck me that I had only ever seen it parked outside our house. Philippe Toussaint had never suggested taking me somewhere. There had never been two helmets at the house, just his one. And when he changed it, he sold the old one.

A dog barked behind a fence, I jumped. At the same moment, I glimpsed him through the window of a building fronted by a yellowing lawn, on the other side of the road. He crossed a room on the ground floor and I recognized his silhouette, his bearing, the bomber jacket he was hurriedly putting on, his weasel face, his scrawniness: Swan Letellier. I had pins and needles in my hands, as if I'd held the same position too long. He was inside a small, concrete apartment building with three floors, painted in faded pastels. The old balconies with worn railings were showing their age, and the few empty window boxes still hanging from them appeared to have seen many springs, but few flowers.

Swan Letellier arrived in the hall, pushed open an aluminum door, and walked along the opposite sidewalk. I followed him until he went into the local bar. He went straight to the back of it. Where Philippe Toussaint was waiting for him. He sat at his table, opposite him. They spoke calmly, like two old acquaintances.

Philippe Toussaint was piecing together the story, but which one? He was looking for something, someone. Hence that list, always the same one, that he wrote on the back of a bill or a tablecloth, as though to solve a puzzle.

Through the glass, I could only see his hair. Like that first evening at the Tibourin, when he had his back to me. When, from behind the bar, I had contemplated his blond curls turning from green to red to blue under the revolving lights. The curls had gone a bit white, and the rainbow of his youth had gone out. As had the prism of light through which I admired him. I thought of how, for years now, whenever I looked at him, the weather was always overcast. The pretty girls who were whispering sweet nothings in his ear, as I studied his perfect profile, had disappeared. Must have only been flabby women now in his makeshift beds. The perfume they left on his skin had changed, the refined fragrances had become cheap scents.

They were alone at the back of the gloomy bistro. They spoke for fifteen minutes, and then Philippe Toussaint suddenly got up to go. I only just had time to dodge into an alley at the side of the bar. He started up his bike and was off.

Swan Letellier was still inside. He was just finishing his coffee when I approached him. I could see that he didn't recognize me.

"What did he want?"

"Sorry?"

"Why were you talking to Philippe Toussaint?"

As soon as he placed me, Letellier's features hardened. He replied, curtly:

"He says the kids were asphyxiated by carbon monoxide. That someone would've lit a water heater, or some such thing. Your husband's looking for a culprit who doesn't exist. If you want my advice, you'd both be better just moving on."

"You can take your advice and shove it."

Letellier's eyes widened. He didn't dare utter another word. I went out into the street and spewed bile onto the sidewalk, like a drunkard.

83

People have stars that aren't the same.
For those who travel, stars are guides, for
others, they are nothing but little lights.

S ometimes, I regret having scolded Léonine when she had
disobeyed me or thrown a tantrum. I regret having
dragged her out of bed to go to school when she would
have liked to sleep a little longer. I regret not having known
that she would only be passing through . . . I never regret for
long. I prefer to conjure up the lovely memories, carry on living with what happiness she left me."

"Why didn't you have other children?"

"Because I wasn't a mother anymore, just an orphan.
Because I didn't have the father that went with my other children . . . And also, it's tough for children to be 'the others,'
'those that came after.'"

"And now?"

"Now I'm old."

Julien bursts out laughing.

"Shush!"

I place my hand over his mouth. He grabs my fingers and
kisses them. I'm afraid. Afraid of the mess in my house.
Afraid of the car doors that will slam in a few hours' time.
Afraid of heading straight for disaster with this affair that
isn't one.

Nathan and his cousin, Valentin, are sleeping on the sofa
close to us. You can make out their little bodies, top to tail,
under the tangled sheets and blankets. Their dark hair on the
two white pillows, like a piece of the countryside sticking out,
a little path smelling of hazelnut. Running your fingers through

a child's hair is like walking on the dead leaves in a forest at the start of spring.

Julien, Nathan, and Valentin arrived from Auvergne yesterday evening. During his stay at the Pardons, Nathan had apparently pestered his father, "We're not going back to Marseilles, we're going to Violette's, we're not going back to Marseilles, we're going to Violette's . . . " Until Julien gave in and drove to the cemetery. They arrived at around 8 P.M., after the gates had been closed. They knocked on the road-side door, but I didn't hear them. I was in my garden, busy pricking out my last lettuce seedlings. The two boys crept up behind me, "We're zombies!" Eliane barked and the cats came closer, as if they remembered Nathan.

Yesterday evening, I wanted to be alone, I felt tired, I wanted to retire early, watch a TV series from my bed. Not speak. Above all, not speak anymore. I did my best not to show them that I didn't feel like seeing them. I would have liked to be happy about this surprise. But I wasn't. I thought Nathan was talking too loudly, I thought Julien was too young.

Julien was waiting for us in the kitchen. Embarrassed, he said to me, "Sorry for turning up on a whim, but my son is in love with you . . . Can we take you out for dinner? . . . I've booked my room at Madame Bréant's."

As soon as he opened his mouth, I felt solitude falling off me like a dead skin. His voice seemed to shine on me, as if he had switched on a lamp above my head. Like when a day seems gloomy, and then a leaden sky cracks and the sun appears from nowhere to light up certain parts of the landscape. I wanted them to stay, all three of them.

No question of going to a restaurant, they would eat at my house. No question of sleeping at Madame Bréant's, they would sleep here. I made them croque-monsieurs with extra cheese, pasta shells, fried eggs, and a tomato salad. Julien helped me set the table. For dessert, I had some strawberry sorbets in the freezer. Stashing sweets, ice cream, chocolate cakes in my drawers, yogurts in the fridge. The same old habit as taking Nathan's hand in mine.

I made Julien drink a lot of white wine so he couldn't change his mind, so he wouldn't go to sleep at Madame Bréant's, but stay here, with me.

Once I had cleared away the dirty dishes, I made up a bed for the two children on the big sofa, the one I slept on when I visited Sasha. The boys cheered and started jumping on the poor old springs, which squeaked with joy.

Before going to bed, they begged me to take them around the avenues of the cemetery "to see the ghosts." They asked me many questions as they read the names on the headstones. They asked me why some tombs had lots of flowers and others didn't. They read out the dates, told me that most of the dead were really, really old.

Frightfully disappointed not to have seen a single ghost, they asked me to tell them some "scary stories." I told them about Diane de Vigneron and Reine Ducha, supposedly glimpsed in the vicinity of the cemetery, at the edge of the road, or in the streets of Brancion-en-Chalon. The children started to blanch, so, to reassure them, I told them that these were just legends, and that, personally, I'd never seen them.

Julien was waiting for us on a bench in the garden. He was smoking a cigarette beside Eliane, and stroking her, lost in thought. He smiled when the children told him that we hadn't seen a single ghost, but that some people had already encountered some inside and beside the cemetery. They urged me to show them the images of Diane as a ghost on the old postcards. I convinced them that I had lost them.

All four of us went inside. The boys checked three times that the doors were double-locked. I left the light on for them in the corridor leading to my room. But one look at Madame Pinto's dolls, and they requested a night-light each.

Julien and I went upstairs, avoiding knocking over the dolls. He followed me. At one moment, I stopped. I felt his breath in the nape of my neck, he stroked the small of my back, and whispered, "Hurry up."

Barely had we closed the door before the two boys were opening it to come and sleep in my bed. We lay on either side of them until they fell asleep, stroking their heads, and sometimes our hands met, found each other, linked in Nathan's hair.

And then we went downstairs to the sofa, to make love. At around 4 A.M., the boys lifted our sheets to curl up with us. We were packed together like sardines. I didn't sleep a wink as I listened to their breathing, with the rapt attention I gave the Chopin sonatas that Sasha always played.

At 6 A.M., Julien took me by the hand and we went back up to my room to make love. I never thought I would make love several times with the same man. Only with someone passing through. A stranger. A visitor. A widower. Someone desperate. Just once, to kill time.

Now we're whispering, noses in our mugs of coffee. My hands smell of cinnamon and tobacco. My body smells of love, roses, and perspiration. My hair is tangled, my lips chapped. I'm afraid. Later, when Julien leaves, because he will leave, solitude will be back to keep me company, faithful and undying.

"And you, why didn't you have other children, after Nathan?"

"Same thing. Didn't meet the mother that went with them."

"What's Nathan's mother like?"

"In love with another man. She left me for him."

"That's tough."

"Oh yes, really tough."

"You still love her?"

"I don't think so."

He gets up and kisses me. I hold my breath. It's so lovely to be kissed in summertime. I feel clumsy, all fingers and thumbs. I've forgotten the moves. One learns how to save lives, but never how to bring one's own skin, and that of another, back to life.

"As soon as the children are awake, we'll be off."

" . . . "

"If you'd seen your face, yesterday evening, when we turned up . . . God, I felt bad . . . If Nathan hadn't been there, I'd have bolted."

"It's because I'm not used to it anymore . . . "

"I won't be back, Violette."

" . . . "

"I don't want to come to have it off with you, once a month, at your cemetery."

" . . . "

"You live with dead people, novels, candles, and a few drops of port. You're right, there's no place for a man in all that. Let alone a man with a kid."

" . . . "

"And also, I can see in your eyes that you don't believe in our story."

" . . . "

"Speak, please. Say something."

"You know the two of us can't last."

"Of course, I know it. Well, no, I know nothing. It's you who knows. Get in touch from time to time. But not too often, or I'll keep waiting."

84

Here we are today, at the edge of the void,
Because we're searching everywhere
for the face we have lost.

IRÈNE FAYOLLE'S JOURNAL

February 13th, 1999
I don't know how Gabriel knew about Paul's death. I caught sight of him this morning at the St-Pierre cemetery. Standing back, hiding behind another tomb, like a thief.

My husband was being buried, and me, I only had eyes for Gabriel. Who am I? What kind of monster am I?

I lowered my eyes to say a silent prayer to Paul, and when I raised them, Gabriel had gone. My eyes searched desperately for him, scoured every corner of the cemetery, in vain.

I started crying like a "widow."

When a woman loses her husband, she's called a widow. But when a woman loses her lover, what's she called? A song?

November 8th, 2000
I'm selling the rose nursery.

March 30th, 2001
This morning, Gabriel phoned me. He calls me about once a month. Every time I answer, he seems surprised to hear my voice. He asks me a few questions: "How are you? What are you doing? What are you wearing? Is your hair tied back? What are you reading at the moment? Been to the movies lately?" He seems to be reassuring himself that I really exist. Or that I still exist.

April 27th, 2001
Gabriel came to my place for lunch. He liked my new apartment, told me it was just like me.

"The rooms are luminous and fragrant, like you."

It amused him that I was living on rue Paradis.

"Why?"

"Because you're mine."

"I'm your paradise intermittently."

"You know the curves heartbeats produce on an electrocardiogram?"

"Yes."

"The curves of my heart, that's you."

"You're a smooth talker."

"I should hope so. I'm paid a fortune for it."

He told me that I didn't know how to cook, that my gift was getting flowers to grow, not cooking some creature in a casserole.

He asked me whether I missed my work.

"No. Not really. The flowers maybe, a little."

He asked me if he could smoke in the kitchen.

"Yes. You've gone back to cigarettes?"

"Yes. It's like with you, I can't stop myself."

As usual, he spoke to me of his ongoing cases, of his big daughter he hardly heard from, and of his little one, Cloé. He told me that he missed her too much, that he would probably go back to living with her mother.

"Yes, to live with my daughter again, I'll have to go back to square Karine. And going back isn't really my thing."

He asked me for news of Julien, too.

Before leaving, he kissed my lips. As if we were two adolescents. "Amour"—is the word masculine or feminine?

October 22nd, 2002

It's Gabriel day.

Now, whenever he's passing through Marseilles, he comes to have lunch here. He gets two daily specials at the delicatessen down below (because what I cook is disgusting: "Not enough

*butter, not enough cream, not enough sauce, you boil everything,
I prefer my vegetables simmered in wine.")*

He rings at my door with our lunch in foil containers. He
always finishes what's left on my plate. Generally, I eat little.
And when Gabriel is in my kitchen, I eat less than little.

He's living with Karine again to be close to Cloé. Or so he
says. Indeed, I make that point to him, "Or so you say." He
replies, "Don't be jealous, you have no reason to be jealous. Of
anyone."

"I'm not jealous."

"A little, maybe. I certainly am. Are you seeing someone?"

"Who on earth would I be seeing?"

"I don't know, a lover, a man, men—you're beautiful. I know
you turn heads whenever you arrive somewhere. I know you're
desired wherever you go."

"You, I'm seeing you."

"But we don't sleep together."

"Want to finish what's on my plate?"

"Yes."

April 5th, 2003

It's a Gabriel day. He called me yesterday evening, he'll come
to my place in the late afternoon, after court. I must get some
Suze, Gabriel loves that aperitif.

There are the days without. And the Gabriel days.

November 25th, 2003

Yesterday evening, Gabriel arrived late. He ate some leftover
soup, a yogurt, and an apple. He drank a glass of Suze, too. I
could tell that it was to please me.

"If I fall asleep, tomorrow morning, wake me at 7 A.M., please."

He said that as if he was used to sleeping over, when it had
actually never happened. Twenty minutes later, he dozed off on
my sofa. I put a blanket over him. I couldn't sleep a wink because

*he was in the room next door. The man next door. All night, I
thought:* Gabriel is my man next door. *I remembered a scene
from Truffaut's film,* The Woman Next Door, *when Fanny
Ardant leaves the hospital and says to her husband, while thinking of her lover whom she's about to kill, "That's good, you
thought of bringing me my white blouse, I love it [she inhales it]
because it is white."*

*This morning, I found Gabriel lying on his front; he had
kicked off his shoes. There was the smell of stale smoke in the
sitting room; he'd got up during the night to smoke. A window
was half-open.*

*I was sorry he hadn't come to join me in my bed. He took a
shower, had a quick coffee. Between each gulp, he said to me,
"You're beautiful, Irène." As usual, before leaving, he kissed my
lips. When he arrives, Gabriel inhales deeply at my neck. When
he leaves, Gabriel kisses my lips.*

July 22nd, 2004
*I've decided to sleep with Gabriel. At our age, there's a
statute of limitations. And anyhow, we're hardly going to have it
off when we're in eternity. As soon as I opened the door to my
apartment, Gabriel knew, saw, read, sensed that I wanted him.
He said:*

"Oh no, this is where the shit starts."

"It won't be the first time."

"No, it won't be the first . . ."

I didn't allow him time to finish his sentence.

85.

Do not stand at my grave and weep,
I am not there, I do not sleep.
I am a thousand winds that blow.

My list for Nono is done. This year, like every year, he's the one who's going to stand in for me, who's going to take over watering the flowers on the tombs of families who are on holiday. As for Elvis, he will take care of Eliane and the cats. And Father Cédric will look after the vegetable garden, and the flowers in the garden. I've given him the index card handwritten by Sasha—he did one for every month.

AUGUST
Priority of the month: watering.

Watering must be done in the evening because then you get the coolness all night, but, importantly, not too early; otherwise, the earth is still hot and the water evaporates immediately, so watering too early is like pissing in the wind.

Watering must be done at nightfall with a watering can—use water from the well or collected rainwater. The can is gentler than the hose; use the hose and you flatten the soil and it can't breathe anymore. The soil must breathe. That's why, occasionally, you should scratch carefully with a hook around the base of plants, to aerate it.

Pick ripe vegetables.

Tomatoes can wait a few days.

Eggplants every three days, otherwise they fatten and harden.

Beans every day. And to be eaten at once. Either preserve them, or freeze them after removing stalks, or distribute them to people around you.

Ditto for everything else: never forget that one grows to share, otherwise it's pointless.

Father Cédric won't be alone in tending the vegetable garden. Since the dismantling of the "Jungle" in Calais, some Sudanese families have been lodged at the château in Chardonnay. He goes there three times a week to help the volunteers. A young couple, Kamal and Anita, both nineteen, are due to have a baby. Father Cédric got permission from the authorities to have them stay with him. He will try to protect them for as long as possible, once the child is born. Long enough for them to return to studying, get a diploma, and, crucially, a permanent right to remain. It's a precarious situation—Father Cédric says he's living on a powder keg, but it's a vulnerability he welcomes. And as long as it lasts, he will embrace the joy of sharing his daily life with an adopted family. Whether it lasts a month or ten years, he will have lived it.

"Everything is ephemeral, Violette, we're merely passing through. Only God's love remains steadfast in all things."

Since they have been living at the presbytery, Kamal and Anita come to my kitchen every day, and unlike the others, stay longer. Anita is madly in love with Eliane, and Kamal with my vegetable garden. He spends hours deciphering Sasha's index cards and my Willem & Jardins catalogues, when he isn't giving me a hand. He's really good at it. The first time I told him he had a green thumb, he didn't understand and responded, with bafflement, "But Violette, I'm black."

I gave my Boscher reading-method book, *The Little Ones' Day Out*, to Anita. She reads it aloud to me, and when she makes a mistake, stumbles over a word, I correct her without even looking at the pages, since I know it by heart.

When Anita opened the book for the first time, she asked me if it belonged to my child; I replied with a question, "May I touch your tummy?" She replied: "Yes, do." I laid my hands flat on the cotton of her dress. Anita started laughing because I was tickling her. The baby gave me a few kicks. Anita told me that he was also laughing. And so, we laughed, all three of us, in my kitchen.

If someone dies and there's a funeral to organize, it's Jacques Lucchini who will stand in for me. Since I had to give Gaston something to do during my absence, I asked him to collect my mail and put it on the shelf beside the phone. I'm almost certain that he won't be able to break one of my letters.

From my bed, I contemplate my still-open suitcase, sitting on top of my chest of drawers. I'll finish packing it tomorrow. I always take too much stuff to Marseilles. I wear almost nothing at the chalet. There's too much "just in case" in my luggage.

The first time I saw that suitcase was in 1998. Philippe Toussaint had gone for good, but I still didn't realize it. Four days earlier, he had kissed me goodbye, mumbling, "See you later." He was due to question Eloïse Petit, the second supervisor. The only one left he hadn't spoken to. He had said to me, "After that, I'm done. After that, we change our life. I can't stand any more of all this, these tombs. We'll go and live in the Midi."

He changed life on his own.

On Eloïse Petit day, he changed direction. Instead of going to see her, he headed to Bron, to see Françoise Pelletier again.

For four days, I was on my own. I was kneeling at the back of the vegetable garden, my nose in the leaves of the nasturtiums I'd attached to bamboo stakes. Like every time Philippe Toussaint was away, the cats had gravitated to the house, and were playing hide-and-seek around me, all darting about, and one of them ended up knocking over a basin of water, they all jumped, and, in their panic, landed in the water. I couldn't stop laughing. I heard a familiar voice, coming from the door of the house, saying, "It's good to hear you laughing all on your own."

I thought I was hallucinating. That the wind in the trees was playing a mean trick on me. I looked up and saw the suitcase on the table under the arbor. It was as blue as the Mediterranean on really sunny days. Sasha was standing in front of the door. I went over to him and stroked his face because I couldn't believe it was really him. I thought he had forgotten me. I said to him, "I thought you had abandoned me."

"Never, do you hear me, Violette? Never will I abandon you."

He gave me a rough outline of his first months of retirement. He had visited Sany, his almost-brother, in the south of India. In Chartres, Besançon, Sicily, and Toulouse, he had visited palaces, churches, monasteries, streets, other cemeteries. He had swum in lakes, rivers, and seas. Had soothed aching backs, sore ankles, and superficial burns. He had just come from Marseilles, where he had done some window boxes of aromatic plants for Célia. He wanted to give me a hug before going to Valence to pay his respects at the tombs of Verena, Emile, and Ninon, his wife and children who were buried there. Then he would return to India to be with Sany.

He had just dropped his things off at Madame Bréant's. He was going to stay two or three nights there, long enough to see the mayor, Nono, Elvis, the cats, and the others.

That blue suitcase was for me. It was full of presents. Teas, incense, scarves, fabrics, jewelry, honeys, olive oils, Marseilles soap, candles, amulets, books, Bach LPs, sunflower seeds. Everywhere Sasha had been, he'd bought me a souvenir.

"I've brought you back an impression for each trip."

"The suitcase, too?"

"Of course, one day you, too, will set off."

He walked around the garden with tears in his eyes. He said, "The pupil has surpassed the teacher . . . I knew you'd do it."

We had lunch together. Every time I heard an engine in the

distance, I thought it might be Philippe Toussaint returning. But no.

* * *

Nineteen years later, it's a different man I find myself waiting for. In the morning, when I open the gates, I look for his car in the car park. Sometimes, along the avenues, when I hear steps behind me, I turn around, thinking: *He's here, he's come back.*

Yesterday evening, I thought someone was knocking on my road-side door. I went down but there was no one there.

And yet, the last time Julien slammed his car door and said to me, "Be seeing you," just as if bidding me farewell, I did nothing to keep him. I smiled and replied, confidently, "Yes, safe journey," just as if I were saying to him, "It's for the best." When Nathan and Valentin waved at me from the back of the car, I knew I wouldn't be seeing them again.

Since that morning, Julien has given me just one sign of life. A postcard from Barcelona to tell me that Nathan and he would be spending the two months of summer over there. And that Nathan's mother would be joining them from time to time.

The meeting of Irène and Gabriel will have helped Julien and Nathan's mother. I was a bridge, a crossing between them. Julien had needed to know me to realize that he couldn't lose the mother of his child. And thanks to Julien, I know that I can still make love. That I can be desired. Which is at least something.

86

We have come here in search, in search of something or someone. In search of that love that is stronger than death.

January 1998

On the day Violette had seen him talking with Swan Letellier in Mâcon, Philippe had felt someone's eyes on the back of his neck. A familiar presence behind him. He had paid it no attention. Not really. Not enough to turn around. Swan Letellier was now facing him. *The face of a rat.* This thought had already crossed his mind at the trial. Small, deep-set eyes, craggy cheeks, thin mouth.

On the phone, Letellier had said to him, "Meet me at the local bar, around midday, it's quiet then."

Like the others, Philippe had coldly asked him the same questions, his tone and look menacing, "Don't lie, I have nothing to lose." He always stressed the final one: who could have turned on a rickety old water heater?

Letellier didn't seem to know what had gone on that night. He had turned white as a sheet when Philippe had told him, in one breath, what Alain Fontanel had admitted: Geneviève Magnan going off to hug their sick son, then returning to the château and panicking at finding the four bodies, asphyxiated by carbon monoxide, the idea of starting the fire to make it look like a domestic accident, Fontanel kicking Letellier's door to wake him up, wake all the staff up.

But Letellier hadn't believed this story. Fontanel was an alky, he must have said any old thing to a father searching for an explanation for the inexplicable.

He did remember the muffled banging on the door. Their

difficulty waking up because they had been smoking joints with the supervisor. The smell, the smoke, the fire. How inaccessible Room 1 was, the flames already too high, that impenetrable barrier. That sudden hell. That moment you tell yourself that it's a nightmare, that none of it's real. He could still see the girls outside in their nighties, barefoot in their slippers or badly laced shoes, and all the staff going crazy. Mother Croquevieille choking. And the others, shocked, shaking, and praying. The wait for the fire brigade. Counting, and counting again, how many children were safe and sound. Their sleepy eyes, when they, the adults, would never sleep soundly again. The little girls, terrified by the flames and the grown-ups' wan faces, asking for their parents. Whom they had had to call, inform, one after the other. Whom they had had to lie to, also, not admitting that inside, four of the girls had perished.

Swan Letellier had added that he still felt guilty to that day. None of it might have happened had the supervisor remained on the ground floor.

Lucie Lindon and he had said nothing to the authorities about Geneviève Magnan because they had felt at fault. Lucie Lindon shouldn't have asked Geneviève Magnan to stand in for her. But Swan had really insisted on it. They had all failed in their duty.

Croquevieille, who would do anything not to spend a centime—the ill-fitting lino in the rooms, the asbestos under the eaves, the fiberglass that no longer insulated anything, the peeling paintwork, the lead pipes, the fire that had spread too fast, the toxic fumes given off by ancient kitchen units. No, no one was in the clear, not Magnan, or Lindon, or Fonatanel, or himself. They were all up to their necks in it, and it was too much to bear . . . The only thing he was sure about was that no one would have intentionally turned on one of the water heaters on the ground floor. All the staff knew that they mustn't be touched. Indeed, those old things were hidden behind plasterboard units, out of the children's reach. He well remembered Edith Croquevieille's words the day before the first guests, of those due in the next two months, arrived: "It's the middle of summer, our guests can wash their faces with cold water, and the rest with hot water in the brand-new communal showers." Swan Letellier remembered because he did the cooking and serving of the food. The fryers and refectory were his domain. He couldn't care less about the château's washing facilities.

Then he had gone quiet. He had had a few gulps of coffee, looking troubled, silently going over what Philippe had just told him. Was this extraordinary version of events to be believed? Fontanel supposedly setting fire to the kitchen? The children inhaling a toxic gas? Letellier had ordered an espresso from the bistro's waiter with just a flick of his hand. He was clearly a regular there. Everyone said "*tu*" to him.

When Letellier had learned of Geneviève Magnan's suicide, he hadn't been surprised. Since that night, she had been just a shadow of her former self. You only had to see the state she was in at the trial. The last time he had spoken to her was the day the wife had come to wait for him outside the restaurant where he worked. He had called Geneviève in a panic to tell her that she had come asking him questions. Philippe heard himself asking, aggressively:

"What wife?"

"Yours."

"You must be confusing her with someone else."

"Don't think so. She said to me, 'I'm the mother of Léonine Toussaint.'"

"What did she look like?"

"It was dark, I don't really remember anymore. She was waiting for me outside the restaurant, on a bench. You didn't know?"

"When was this?"

"About two years ago."

Philippe had heard enough. Or said enough. He was there to ask questions, not be asked any. He had got up, grunting goodbye, and Letellier had watched him leave without understanding. As he had turned, Philippe had thought he had seen Violette on the sidewalk, behind the window. *I'm going nuts.* He had driven straight home to Brancion.

For the first time, he had found the cemetery house empty. For the first time, he had gone all round the avenues to find her, but in vain.

Who was Violette, really? What did she do when he went off for entire days? Whom did she see? What was she after?

Violette had come home two hours after him. She was very pale as she came through the door. She had stared at him for a few seconds, as though surprised to discover a stranger in her kitchen. And then she had handed him a piece of paper: "Léonine was asphyxiated?"

On the washed-out paper he had recognized his handwriting, the names scribbled on the back of a tablecloth had almost disappeared. The ink had run so much, they were virtually illegible.

Violette's question had hit him like an electric shock. He had tried to think of a lie but couldn't, had spluttered, as if Violette had just caught him in the arms of one of his mistresses:

"I don't know, perhaps, I'm looking . . . I'm not sure I know . . . I want . . . I'm a bit lost."

She had gone up to him and stroked his face with infinite tenderness. And then she had gone up to bed without a word. Hadn't laid the table or prepared supper. When he had stretched out beside her, she had taken his hand and asked the same question, "Léonine was asphyxiated?" If he said nothing, she would just keep asking the same question.

So, Philippe had told her everything. Everything, apart from his relationship with Geneviève Magnan. He had told her of his conversations with Alain Fontanel, that first time when he had beaten him up in the cafeteria of the hospital he worked at; with Lucie Lindon in the doctors' waiting room; with Edith Croquevieille in Epinal, in the underground of a supermarket; and with Swan Letellier that very day, in a bistro in Mâcon.

Violette had listened to him in silence, his hand in hers. He had spoken for hours in the darkness of their room, without seeing her face. He had sensed her attentiveness, her hanging on his every word. She hadn't moved. Hadn't asked any other question. Philippe had finally asked her the one he was dying to ask:

"Is it true that you went to see Letellier?"

She had replied without thinking:

"Yes. Before, I needed to know."

"And now?"

"Now I have my garden."

"Who else did you see?"

"Geneviève Magnan, once. But you already know that."

"Who else?"

"No one. Just Geneviève Magnan and Swan Letellier."

"Do you swear to me?"

"Yes."

87

No remorse. No regrets.
A life fully lived.

Even today, when I watch *Fanny*, *Marius*, or *César* on the television, I get tears in my eyes as soon as I hear the first lines, even though I know them by heart. They are tears of childhood, joy, and admiration combined. I love the faces of the actors, Raimu, Pierre Fresnay, and Orane Demazis, in black-and-white. I love their every gesture, their looks. The father, the son, the young woman, and the love. I would have liked to have a father who looked at me how César looks at his son, Marius. I would have liked a youthful romance like that of Fanny and Marius.

The first time I watched *Marius*, the first part of the trilogy, I must have been about ten years old. I was alone at my foster family's. If memory serves, the other children had gone off on holiday, or to visit relatives. It was summer, there was no school the following day. My family had friends around, they had set up a barbecue in the garden. They gave me permission to leave the table. When I went into the dining room, I was confronted by the big television, which was on. And that's when I discovered this story with no colors. The film had started about half an hour before. Fanny was weeping over the checked tablecloth in the kitchen, opposite her mother, who was slicing the bread. The first line I heard was: "Come, now, you ninny, have your soup, and don't go crying into it, it's already too salty."

I was immediately fascinated by the faces and the dialogues, the humor and the tenderness. Impossible to switch it off. That evening, I went to bed very late because I watched the whole trilogy.

I still love the simplicity, universal and complex, of their feelings. I love the words they say, so poetic, so apt. That music in their voices.

I think I loved Marseilles and the Marseillais before even encountering them, like an intuition, an anticipatory dream. That raw beauty, it gets to me every time I return to Sormiou, as I descend the steep little road that leads to the big blue sea. I understand Marcel Pagnol, I understand how the characters in his trilogy would come from there. From those sheer rocks, bleached by the sun, that searing heat, that clear, turquoise water playing hide-and-seek with a spotless sky, those umbrella pines just where nature intended, no fuss. This landscape puts on no airs, it is simple and majestic. It just makes sense. It's Marius's yearning to be a sailor. It's Monsieur Panisse, who "makes sails so the wind carries off other people's children," as César says.

When I open up the red shutters of the chalet with Célia, and I find once again the old cupboard in the kitchen, the bare-wood table with its yellow chairs and the draining board above the sink, the little bunches of dried lavender, the patch-work of tiles, and the sky-blue paneling, I think of César, who stops Marius and Fanny from kissing because she is married to another man: "Children, no, don't do that, Panisse is a decent man, don't seek to make him look ridiculous in front of his family's furniture."

It was Célia's maternal grandfather who built this chalet in 1919. Before he died, he made her promise never to part with it. Because that roof, it was worth all the palaces in the world.

It's been twenty-four years now that I've been coming here. And every summer, Célia spends the day before my arrival filling up the fridge and putting clean sheets on the beds. She buys coffee and filters, lemons, tomatoes and peaches, ewe's milk cheese, washing powder, and Cassis wine. I can implore her all I like, assure her that I can do the shopping myself, at least reimburse her, but she won't hear of it, and repeats to me every time: "You welcomed me into your home when you didn't even know me." I tried leaving an envelope of money in a drawer. A week later, Célia returned it to me in the mail.

Once the shutters are open and my clothes put away, I go to visit the few native fishermen, who live down below, in the Calanque, all year round. They speak to me of the sea, which is increasingly losing fish, just as the locals are their accent. They give me sea urchins, small squid, and sugary desserts made by their wives or mothers.

Earlier on, Célia had been waiting at the end of the platform. The train arrived an hour late, she smelled of the coffee she had drunk while waiting for me. A year since I'd last seen her. We hugged each other tight.

She said to me:

"So, my dear Violette, what's new?"

"Philippe Toussaint is dead. And after that, Françoise Pelletier came to see me."

"Who?"

88

From where I am, I smile, because my life
was good and, above all, I loved.

Philippe Toussaint never returned, and Sasha remained
at Madame Bréant's.

Before I knew, on the day I opened the blue suitcase full
of presents, I told Sasha that the man I shared my life with,
without ever having really shared it, was probably better than
he'd given the impression of being.

Before I knew, I told Sasha that the man I thought was just
selfish, whom I no longer listened to or looked at, the man
who'd given up on me, drowning in the depths of solitude, had
appeared to me in a new light when I'd seen him in a Mâcon
bistro with Swan Letellier.

Before I knew, I told Sasha that, on the evening Philippe
Toussaint had returned from Mâcon, he'd told me that he was
searching for the truth about the sequence of events. That he'd
questioned, sometimes persecuted, the château staff. At the
trial he'd believed no one. Apart from Eloïse Petit—he hadn't
yet tracked her down.

My husband had told me all about Alain Fontanel and the
others. I had taken hold of his hand for fear of falling, when we
were lying side by side in our bed. I had imagined the words
and the faces of those who had seen my daughter alive for the
last time. Those who hadn't managed to take care of her, of her
smile. Those who had proved to be negligent.

The little girls left on their own while the supervisor and the
cook were upstairs, fornicating and smoking joints. Geneviève
Magnan gone, leaving the children unsupervised. The director,

the sort that sweeps things under the carpet, fit only for collecting the parents' checks.

So as not to be overcome when he'd told me what Fontanel had said, the story about the defective water heater, the asphyxiation, I'd focused on the fragrance of the new washing powder I'd used to wash our sheets the previous day, "tropical breeze." So as not to howl in our bed, I'd kept thinking of the illustrations on that drum of washing powder, pink and white Tahitian flowers. Those flowers had led me to think of the patterns on Léonine's dresses. Her dresses were like imaginary flying carpets that I rode when the present became too unbearable. All night, I breathed in the smell of my clean sheets while listening to Philippe Toussaint talking to me for almost the first time.

Before I knew, I'd stroked his face once again, and we'd made love like when we were young, when his parents would fall on us without warning. Before I knew. Before I knew that he'd slept with Geneviève Magnan when we lived in Malgrange-sur-Nancy, I'd believed him for almost the first time.

* * *

Philippe Toussaint never returned and Sasha remained at Madame Bréant's.

After he'd been absent for a month, in 1998, I went to the police station to report the disappearance of my husband. I did so on the advice of the mayor. Otherwise, I wouldn't have bothered. The sergeant who received me made a strange face. Why had I waited so long to report someone missing?

"Because he often went off."

He took me into an office next to the reception to fill in a form and offered me a coffee that I didn't dare refuse.

I gave his particulars. The police officer asked me to come back with a photo. We hadn't taken any since arriving at the cemetery. The most recent was the one taken in Malgrange-sur-Nancy, when he had put his arm around my waist while giving the journalist a nice smile.

The sergeant asked me to specify the make of his motorbike, the clothes he was wearing the last time I had seen him.

"Jeans, black leather biker boots, black biker jacket, and a red polo-neck sweater."

"Any distinguishing features? Tattoo? Birthmark? Visible moles?"

"No."

"Did he take anything with him, important papers that might suggest a prolonged absence?"

"His video games and the photos of our daughter are still in the house."

"Had his behavior or habits changed in recent weeks?"

"No."

I didn't tell the police officer that the last time I had seen Philippe Toussaint, he was about to go to Eloïse Petit's workplace in Valence. He had tracked her down, she was an usher at a movie theater over there. He had phoned her from the house, she had said she would meet him on Thursday the following week, at 2 P.M., outside the theater.

On that day, Eloïse Petit had called in the afternoon. She must have traced the number Philippe Toussaint had called her from. When I answered, I thought it was the town hall, the death-notice department. It was the time they regularly phoned me to inform me of something, or to ask me details about a funeral past or future, a surname, a first name, a date of birth, a vault, a cemetery location. When Eloïse Petit had introduced herself, her voice was shaky. I hadn't immediately understood what she was saying. When I had finally grasped who she was, what her call was about, my hands had gone clammy, my throat dry.

"Was there a problem?"

"A problem? Mr. Toussaint isn't here, we had an appointment at 2 P.M., I've been waiting for him outside the movie theater for two hours."

Anyone else would have imagined there had been an accident, would have called all the hospitals between Mâcon and Valence; anyone else would have said to Eloïse Petit: "Where were you the night Room 1 burnt down? Were you sleeping easy next door?" But I had replied to her that there was nothing to understand, Philippe Toussaint was, and always would be, unpredictable.

There had been a long silence at the other end of the line, and then Eloïse Petit had hung up.

I didn't tell the sergeant that, seven days after Philippe Toussaint's "flight," seven days after the appointment with Eloïse Petit he had missed, a young woman had come to pay her respects at the tomb of the children, of my child. And that, distraught, she had found herself, like many other visitors, buying flowers and having a hot drink at my place. When I had seen that young woman behind my door, I had recognized her instantly: Lucie Lindon. In the photo I had kept, she was younger, in color, and smiling. In my kitchen, she was white and had shadows under her eyes.

I had made her some tea and added more than a drop of eau-de-vie—paradoxical, when I would have liked to pour in rat poison. I made her drink a cup and a little glass of spirits, two little glasses of spirits, then three. And as I was hoping, she had finally poured her heart out.

I still have the marks from my nails on the palm of my left hand. The marks I made as Lucie Lindon spoke. My lifeline is covered in scars since that day. I remember the dried blood in my palm, my clenched fist so she wouldn't see, so she would never know.

Lucie Lindon told me that she was on the staff at the château of Notre-Dame-des-Prés.

"You know, that holiday camp where everything burned down five years ago, the four children are buried here. Since the tragedy, I can't sleep anymore, I can still see the flames; since the tragedy, I'm forever cold."

She continued to talk. And me, I continued to serve her. With my left fist clenched, my nails digging into my flesh; I was already suffering too much to feel physical pain. After soliloquizing, she finally let out that "poor Geneviève Magnan" had had a relationship with the father of little Léonine Toussaint.

"A relationship?"

I had a kind of iron taste in my mouth. A taste of blood. As if I had just drunk steel. But I managed to repeat, "A relationship?"

Those are the last words I uttered in front of Lucie Lindon. After that I kept quiet. After that she got up to go. She stared at me. With the back of her arm, she wiped away the tears streaming from her eyes, nose, and mouth. She sniffed noisily and I felt like hitting her.

"Yes, with the father of little Léonine Toussaint. It went on one or two years before the tragedy. When Geneviève worked at a school . . . Near Nancy, I think."

I didn't tell the sergeant that I had screamed my hatred and my pain in Sasha's arms when I had realized that it was Magnan who had killed four children to get her revenge on him, on us, on our daughter. I didn't tell him that Philippe Toussaint had questioned the staff from the château where our child had met her death. And that was after the trial, because he no longer believed anyone. And for good reason. He must have been seeking, by whatever means, to put himself in the clear. It wasn't a culprit he was looking for, it was proof of his own innocence.

Finally, the sergeant asked me if Philippe Toussaint might have had a mistress.

"Many."

"What do you mean, many?"

"My husband always had many mistresses."

There was an awkward moment. The sergeant hesitated before writing on his form that Philippe Toussaint screwed everything that moved. He blushed a little, and poured me another cup of coffee. He would call me if there was any news. Would issue a missing-person's description. I never saw that man again until the day he buried his mother, Josette Leduc, née Berthomier (1935–2007). He smiled sadly at me when he saw me.

* * *

Once I did know that Philippe Toussaint had had a relationship with Geneviève Magnan, I lost Léonine a second time. His parents had taken her from me by accident; their son had snatched her from me intentionally. The accident became murder.

I ransacked my memory, searched a thousand times through those mornings I took my daughter to school, the late afternoons I went to fetch her, I tried everything to remember that nursery assistant at the back of the classroom, in a corridor, in front of the coatracks, in the playground, under the shelter, one word, one sentence she might have said to me. Even just a "Hello," or a "Goodbye, see you tomorrow," "Lovely weather," "Wrap her up warm so she doesn't get cold," "She seems tired today," "She forgot her activities book, the one with the blue cover." At the school party, between the songs and the streamers, the exchanges Geneviève Magnan might have had with my husband. Looks, a smile, a gesture. The silent complicity of lovers.

I searched for when they saw each other, how many times, why she had taken revenge on children, how on earth Philippe Toussaint must have treated her for her to end up doing such a thing. I searched until I was banging my head against a brick wall. But I found nothing. Like an absence of myself.

I had only caught sight of her, not looked properly; she was part of the school furniture, and those drawers were double-locked to me. *Can't even remember, Violette.* After I had discovered it, that unacceptable fact, Sasha replaced me for the daily running of the cemetery, because I went back to being good for nothing. Good for just staying like that, sitting or lying down, dazed, and searching.

If Sasha hadn't come back at that very moment in my life, with the blue suitcase and presents, Philippe Toussaint would have finally finished me off. Once again, Sasha looked after me. Not to teach me how to plant, but how to weather this new winter that had hit me. He massaged my feet and back, made me tea, lemon juice with water, and soups. He cooked me pasta and made me drink wine. He read to me and kept the garden going, from the stage it was at. He sold my flowers, watered them, and accompanied bereaved families. He told Madame Bréant that he would be staying for an indefinite period of time.

Every day, he forced me to get up, wash, get dressed. And then he let me lie down again. He brought meals up to me on a tray, which he made me eat, grumbling, "Some retirement you're giving me here." He put music on in the kitchen, leaving the corridor door open so I could hear it from my bed.

And then, just like the cemetery cats, the sun reached as far as my room, reached under my sheets. I opened the curtains, and then the windows. I went back downstairs to the kitchen, boiled the water for the tea, and aired the room. I finally returned to the garden. Finally gave fresh water to the flowers. I welcomed the families once again, served them something hot or strong to drink. I went on a lot: "Can you imagine, Sasha? Philippe Toussaint slept with Geneviève Magnan!" All day long, I kept on at him about the same things, "I can't even turn her in, she's dead, can you imagine, Sasha? She's dead!"

"Violette, you must stop looking for reasons, otherwise it's yourself you will lose."

Sasha reasoned with me:

"It's not because they knew each other that she took it out on some children. It is, without any doubt, an appalling coincidence, a pure accident. Really. Only an accident."

While I harped on, Sasha convinced me. While Philippe Toussaint sowed evil, Sasha sowed only goodness.

"Violette, the ivy is stifling the trees, never forget to cut it back. Never. As soon as your thoughts are turning dark, take your pruning shears and cut back those troubles."

Philippe Toussaint disappeared in June of 1998.

Sasha left Brançion-en-Chalon on March 19th, 1999. He left once he was sure that I had fully accepted that the tragedy was accidental, not intentional.

"Violette, with that under your belt, that certainty, you'll be able to move forward."

I presume he left at the beginning of spring to be sure I would have all summer to get over his absence. The flowers would grow again.

He spoke often of his last trip. But as soon as he mentioned it, he sensed I wasn't yet ready to let him go. He wanted to get another flight to Mumbai and go down to the south of India, to Amritapuri in Kerala. He wanted to settle there, just like at Madame Bréant's, for an indefinite period of time. Sasha often said:

"Being in Kerala, close to Sany, until I die is an old dream. In any case, at my age, no dream is young. They're all long in the tooth."

Sasha didn't want to be buried beside Verena and his children. He wanted his body to be burned on a pyre, over there, on the Ganges.

"I'm seventy years old. I still have a few years ahead of me. I'm going to see what I can do with their soil. How I can pass on the little I know about plants. And also, I can carry on soothing pain. These plans delight me."

"You're going to give your green fingers to the Indians?"

"To anyone who'll have them, yes."

One evening, we were having supper together and talking about John Irving, and *L'Oeuvre de Dieu, la part du Diable*. I told Sasha that he had been my personal Dr. Larch, my surrogate father. And he replied that one day soon, he was going to let go of my hand, that he sensed I was ready. That even surrogate fathers had to let their children go. That one morning, he wouldn't come to the house bringing me fresh bread and the *Journal de Saône-et-Loire*.

"But surely you wouldn't leave without saying goodbye to me?!"

"If I said goodbye to you, Violette, I would never leave. Can you imagine us hugging each other on a station platform? Why put ourselves through the unbearable? Don't you think we've given enough to sorrow already? My place is no longer here. You are young and the sun is shining, I want you to make a new life for yourself. Starting tomorrow, I'll be saying goodbye to you every day."

He kept his promise. From the next day forward, every evening before leaving for Madame Bréant's, he would hug me, saying, "Goodbye, Violette, look after yourself, I love you," as if it were the last time. And the following day he would be back. He would put the baguette and newspaper down on my table, between the tea caddies and the flower, tree, and garden magazines. Then he would chat with the Lucchini brothers, Nono, and the others. He would go around the avenues with Elvis to see the cats. Help the visitors who were looking for a particular avenue or name. Give a hand to Gaston with the weeding. And in the evening, after the supper we shared, he would hug me again, saying, "Goodbye, Violette, look after yourself, I love you," as if it were the last time.

His goodbyes lasted all winter. And on the morning of March 19th, 1999, he didn't come. I went knocking on Madame Bréant's door, Sasha had left. He had packed his suitcase several days before, and, when he had returned the previous evening, he had finally decided to fulfill his old dream, the one that was longest in the tooth.

89

We lived together in bliss.
We rest together in peace.

IRÈNE FAYOLLE'S JOURNAL

February 13th, 2009
My old sales assistant just phoned me, "Madame Fayolle, on the TV, they've just said that your lawyer friend had a heart attack, in court, this morning . . . He died on the spot."

On the spot. Gabriel died on the spot.

I often told him that I would die before him. What I didn't know was that I would die at the same time as him. If Gabriel dies, I die.

February 14th, 2009
Today is Saint Valentine's Day. Gabriel hated Saint Valentine's Day.

When I write his name, Gabriel, Gabriel, Gabriel, in this journal, I feel that he's close to me. Maybe it's because he hasn't been buried. Until the dead have been buried, they remain close by. That distance they put between us and heaven isn't yet there.

The last time we saw each other, we argued. I asked him to leave my apartment. Furious, Gabriel went down the stairs without a backward glance. I waited for the sound of his steps, I waited for him to come back up, but he never did. He usually called me every evening, but since our argument, my telephone has remained silent. I'll never be able to change those things now.

February 15th, 2009
What I still have of Gabriel is the freedom I relish every day, thanks to him. It's the clothes bought in Cap d'Antibes at the

bottom of a drawer; an open bottle of Suze in the bar; a few train tickets, round-trip; three novels, L'Oeuvre de Dieu, la part du Diable and Jack London's Martin Eden. And Une femme, by Anne Delbée, which he gave me in a very rare edition. Gabriel was fascinated by Camille Claudel.

A few years ago, I joined him to spend three days in Paris. As soon as I arrived, he took me to the Musée Rodin. He wanted to see Camille Claudel's works with me. In the garden, he kissed me in front of Les Bourgeois de Calais.

"It's Camille Claudel who sculpted their hands and feet. Look how beautiful they are."

"You also have beautiful hands. The first time I saw you pleading in court, in Aix-en-Provence, I looked only at them."

That's what Gabriel was like: where you didn't expect him to be. Gabriel was a rock, he was solid and powerful. A macho man, who would never have accepted a woman paying a bill, or pouring herself a glass of wine in front of him. Gabriel was masculinity incarnate. When I presumed he would worship Rodin rather than Claudel, that he would prostrate himself before his Balzac, or his Penseur, I saw him bowing down to La Valse, by Camille Claudel.

Inside the museum, he didn't let go of my hand. Like a child. He had all of Rodin's most majestic sculptures in front of him, but he wasn't interested.

When he spotted Les Causeuses, the little sculpture by Camille Claudel, on its pedestal, he squeezed my fingers very hard. Gabriel leaned toward them, stayed like that for a long while, as time stood still. He seemed to be breathing them in. His eyes shone in front of these four little women, in green onyx, born more than a century ago. I heard him murmur, "Their hair's messy."

As we left, he lit a cigarette and admitted to me that he had waited for me to be with him before visiting this museum, that he knew, before even entering, that he would need my hand to hold to avoid stealing Les Causeuses. *As a student, he had fallen in love with them from a photograph. He had always desired them, so much so that he wanted to possess them. He knew that when he first saw them in the flesh, he would need restraining.*

"Just because I defend louts doesn't mean I'm not one myself. These chattering girls, they're so delicate, so small, I knew very well I could slip them under my coat and run off with them. Can you imagine owning them at home? Looking at them every evening before going to bed, finding them there every morning while drinking your coffee?"

"You spend your life in hotels, it would have been slightly tricky, all the same."

He burst out laughing.

"Your hand stopped me from committing a crime. I should have lent it out to all the idiots I defend, it would have prevented them from making all sorts of stupid mistakes."

That evening, we dined at the Jules Verne restaurant, at the top of the Eiffel Tower. Gabriel said to me, "During these three days, we're going to pile on the clichés, nothing in the world beats clichés." As he was finishing his sentence, he fastened a diamond bracelet around my wrist. A thing that shone like a thousand suns against my pale skin. It sparkled so much, you would have thought it a fake. Like the imitation stuff the actresses wear in American soaps.

The following day, at the Sacré-Coeur, I was just placing a candle at the feet of the golden Virgin when he fastened a diamond necklace around my neck, while kissing my nape. He took me by the shoulder and pulled me toward him, whispering in my ear, "My darling, you look like a Christmas tree."

On the last day, at the Gare de Lyons, just before I got on my train, he took my hand and slipped a ring onto my middle finger.

"Don't get me wrong. I know you don't like jewelry. I haven't given it all to you to wear. I want you to sell these trinkets and treat yourself to holidays, somewhere to live, whatever you like.

And never thank me. That would kill me. I don't give you presents so you can thank me. It's just to protect you, should anything happen to me. I'll come and see you next week. Call me when you get to Marseilles. I'm missing you already, these separations are too hard. But I love that I miss you. I love you."

I sold the necklace to buy my apartment. The bracelet and ring are in a safe at the bank, my son will inherit them. My son will inherit from my great love. Poetic justice. Gabriel sought justice.

Gabriel was a man of forthright character. Woe betide anyone who annoyed him. Including me. And yet, the last time I saw him, I did just that. He had openly criticized a female colleague of his, the newspapers were all commenting on it. This colleague had defended a woman who, having suffered her husband's sadism for years, had finally killed him. I dared to reproach Gabriel for criticizing his colleague.

We were both in my kitchen, after making love, he was smiling, seemed lighthearted, simply happy. As soon as Gabriel came through my door, he relaxed, as if jettisoning suitcases that were too heavy. While drinking my tea, I questioned him, reproachfully: how could he have criticized a lawyer who was defending a persecuted woman? How could he be so Manichean? What sort of a man had he become? Who did he think he was? Where were his ideals?

Wounded, Gabriel flew into a mad rage. He started yelling. That I knew nothing about it, that this case was far more complex than it seemed. What business was it of mine? I should just drink my tea and shut up; all I'd ever managed to do was create wretched roses that I just ended up cutting; in fact, I spoiled everything.

"You haven't got a clue, Irène! You've never bothered to make one fucking decision in your whole damn life!"

I finally put my hands over my ears, not to hear him anymore. I asked him to leave my apartment immediately. When I saw him getting dressed, looking solemn, I already regretted it. But it was too late. We were both too proud to apologize. We deserved better than that. Parting in the middle of a fight.

If I could just go back . . .

I feel like opening my windows and shouting out to any passersby, "Make it up to each other! Apologize! Make peace with those you love! Before it's too late."

February 16th, 2009

A solicitor has just called me: Gabriel had arranged things so I would be buried with him in the cemetery in Brancion-en-Chalon, the village he was born in. The solicitor asked me to come by his office, where Gabriel had left an envelope for me.

"'My darling, my sweet, my dearest, my wonderful love, from dawn to dusk, I still love you, you know. I love you.'

I who plead, object, improvise, defends murderer, the innocent, victims, I steal Jacques Brel's words to tell you my deepest thoughts.

If you're reading this letter, it means I've passed on. I've beaten you to it, definitely a first. I have nothing else to write to you that you don't already know, except that I've always hated your name.

Irène, how ghastly is that, Irène. Everything suits you, you can wear anything. But a name like that, it's like bottle green or mustard yellow, it suits no one.

That day I waited for you in my car, I knew you wouldn't come back, that I was waiting for you for nothing. It's that nothing that kept me from immediately driving off.

She won't come back, I have nothing left.

I've missed you so much. And it's only just beginning.

Our hotels, love in the afternoon, you under the sheets . . . You will remain all of my loves. The first, the second, the tenth, and the last. You will remain my loveliest memories. My great expectations.

Those provincial towns that became capital cities as soon as you hit their sidewalks, that I'll never forget. Your hands in your pockets, your perfume, your skin, your scarves, my native land.

My love.

You see, I didn't lie, I've left you a place beside me for eternity. I wonder whether, up there, you'll carry on saying 'vous' to me.

Don't rush, I have plenty of time. Make the most of the sky seen from below for a little longer. Make the most, in particular, of the last snows.

See you later,

Gabriel"

March 19th, 2009

I visited Gabriel's tomb for the first time. After all the crying, after wanting to dig him up, to shake him, to say to him: "Tell me it's not true, tell me you're not dead," I placed a new snow globe on the black marble covering him. I promised Gabriel I'd be back to give it a shake from time to time. I gazed at this tomb that I will be in later.

I replied to his letter out loud:

"My love, you, too, will remain my loveliest memories . . . I've had fewer women than you, well, I mean fewer men than you, I've known so few. You only had to make a move to seduce. And even then, maybe not. You didn't have to do a thing, just be you. You are my first love, my second love, my tenth love, my last love. You have taken my whole life. I will come and join you in eternity, I will keep my promise. Keep my place warm, like in the hotel rooms I'd meet you in, when you were early, you'd keep my place warm in those beds we passed through . . . You must send me the address to eternity, such a voyage needs preparation. I'll see whether I find you in a train, a plane, or a boat. I love you."

I stayed with him for a long while. I arranged the flowers on his tomb, threw away the ones in cellophane that had wilted, read the funerary plaques. I think that's what they are called.

It's a lady who looks after the cemetery where Gabriel is buried. Which is wonderful. He who so loved women. She went past me, greeted me. We exchanged a few words. I didn't know such a job existed. That people were paid to look after cemeteries, watch over them. She even sells flowers at the entrance, near the gates.

Continuing to write this journal is continuing to keep Gabriel alive. But my God, how long life is going to seem to me.

90

*November is eternal, life is almost
beautiful, memories are dead ends
that we just keep turning over.*

JUNE 1998

Although there were barely two hundred kilometers of
highway between Mâcon and Valence, the journey had
seemed interminable to him. When Philippe drove
aimlessly, no journey seemed long to him. But when he had to
get from point A to point B, he balked. Constraint was something he would never be able to handle.

Since Violette had discovered that he was trying to get to
the truth, he'd lost the desire. As though it being his secret was
all that kept him going on this wild goose chase. And having
spoken about it had made him lose impetus. Totally. Talking
hadn't freed him, it had drained him.

Even Violette seemed to have turned her back on the past.

He'd speak to Eloïse Petit, and then move on to something
else. This meeting with the former supervisor was like a final
appointment with the past.

Eloïse Petit was waiting for him, as arranged, outside the
movie theater where she worked. She was standing under the
screening times. Above her hung a huge poster for *The English
Patient*. Philippe had immediately spotted her, despite all the
hustle and bustle around the ticket desk. The people streaming into or out of the various screenings. They had seen each
other two years before, at the trial, and had recognized each
other instantly.

As though afraid of gossip, Eloïse had taken Philippe to a
Relais H café, two streets away, not far from the Valence railway station. They had walked side by side in silence. Philippe

still felt that great emptiness, that despondency. He had wondered what on earth he was doing there, on that sidewalk. He didn't even have any questions left to ask Eloïse. What the hell did she care about a water heater? What did she know about water heaters?

They ordered two croque-monsieurs, a small bottle of Vittel water, and a Coke. Eloïse exuded great gentleness. Philippe felt he could trust her, unlike all the others. She wouldn't try to lie. She seemed sincere before she even opened her mouth.

Eloïse described the children's arrival on July 13th, 1993. The allocating of rooms, according to friendships. The children who already knew each other didn't want to be separated. She and Lucie Lindon had tried to make everyone happy, and seemed to have succeeded. With the supervisors' help, the girls had put away their clothes and belongings in the lockers in their rooms, beside their beds.

Then there had been tea, and a walk in the grounds of the château, and out to the fields to see the ponies, and bring them back to the stables for the night. The children had loved hosing down the animals while splashing each other, then grooming them, leading them into their stalls, and feeding them with the adults' help. They were happy as larks when they sat down for supper. The noisy refectory—twenty-four excited little girls, all chatting loudly. They had returned to their respective rooms at around 9:30 P.M., once they had visited the communal showers.

"Why didn't they wash in the bathroom in their rooms?"

This question surprised Eloïse.

"I don't know now . . . The shower room was new. I remember washing there, too."

Eloïse thought about it while chewing her lip.

"I remember, there was no hot water in the bathroom in my room."

"Why?"

She puffed out her cheeks as though blowing up a balloon, and replied, apologetically:

"I don't know . . . The pipes were old. The château was falling apart, somewhat. It smelled pretty musty inside. And also, if you had to ask Fontanel to change even just a lightbulb, you'd be lucky if it got done."

The children came from the north and the east of France, Eloïse continued. The journey, the heat, the afternoon's activities had exhausted them. They had gone to bed with no fuss. She and Lucie Lindon had checked on the rooms at around 9:45 P.M. to make sure all was well. Six rooms altogether, three on the ground floor, three upstairs. Four children to a room. The little girls were all in bed. Some were reading, others chatting, swapping photographs or drawings from bed to bed. Children's conversations: "Your pajamas are nice," "Will you lend me your dress?" "Wish I had shoes like yours." Their cats, their homes, their parents, their brothers and sisters, school, teachers, friends. And most of all, ponies. That's all they could think about: the following day, they were going to ride the ponies.

Eloïse Petit hesitated before talking about Room 1 with Philippe. She didn't named Léonine, Anaïs, Océane, and Nadège. Merely said "the children in Room 1," briefly lowering her eyes before continuing.

It was the last room the supervisors had been to. The girls were already half-asleep when she and Lucie Lindon had gone in to ask them if everything was O.K., give them each a little flashlight in case they needed to get up during the night, and tell them that Lucie was in the room next door, if one of them had a nightmare or a tummyache. A night-light would remain on in the corridor all night.

Then, Eloïse had gone up to her room, and Lucie to see Swan Letellier. Geneviève Magnan was supposed to stay around the ground-floor rooms in the meantime. Before the two supervisors had gone upstairs, they had seen Geneviève sitting in the kitchen. She was cleaning copper pans, all spread out on the large table. She had said good night to them, looking sad, or maybe weary. Eloïse couldn't have said which.

"I went up to my room, I dozed off. At one point, I got up to close my window, because it was banging against the casing."

A strange light crossed Eloïse's blue eyes. As if she were reliving that moment, looking through the window at something going by in the distance. The way one peers over the shoulder of a person one's speaking to at the sight of a familiar silhouette or some curious, unexpected movement.

"Did you see something?"

"When?"

"When you closed your window."

"Yes."

"What?"

"Them."

"Who's them?"

"You know who."

"Geneviève Magnan and Alain Fontanel?"

Eloïse Petit shrugged her shoulders. Philippe didn't know what to make of this gesture.

"Is it true you had a relationship with Geneviève?"

"Who told you that?"

"Lucie. She told me that Geneviève loved you."

Philippe closed his eyes for a few seconds, and then, with a heavy heart, replied to her:

"I've come to talk to you about my daughter."

"What do you want to know?"

"I want to know who switched on the water heater in the bathroom of Room 1. The children were asphyxiated by carbon monoxide. And yet everyone knew that those damn water heaters weren't to be touched!"

Philippe had shouted too loud. The customers, buried in their newspapers, and in the line at the registers turned around to stare at the two of them.

Eloïse blushed as if it were a lovers' quarrel. She spoke to Philippe as if he were not in his right mind. The way one speaks gently to the mad so as not to antagonize them:

"I don't understand what you're saying."

"Someone switched on the water heater in the bathroom."

"What bathroom?"

"The one in the room that burned down."

Philippe could see that Eloïse didn't understand a wretched word of what he was saying. At that moment, he started to have doubts. This water heater story didn't stack up, it was nonsense. He had to face facts: either Geneviève Magnan or Alain Fontanel had set fire to Room 1 to take revenge on him.

"Is that what would have started the fire? The old water heater?"

Eloïse's question drew him away from his grim thoughts.

"No, the fire, that would have been Fontanel . . . to make it look like a domestic accident. He would have been covering up for Magnan."

"But why?"

"Because, apparently, she went off that evening. She didn't stay close to the girls, and when she returned, she would have . . . It was too late . . . The children were asphyxiated."

Eloïse covered her mouth with both hands. Her big, blue eyes started to shine. Philippe remembered the day he had swum in the Mediterranean to fetch Françoise and she had struggled. Eloïse had the same panicked look as her, on the verge of drowning.

Philippe and Eloïse said nothing more to each other for at least ten minutes. They hadn't touched their plates. Philippe finally ordered an espresso.

"Would you like anything else?"

"Maybe it's them."

"Fontanel and Magnan, yes."

"No, those people."

"What people?"

"The couple you know, that I saw leaving the courtyard when I closed my window."

"What couple?"

"The people you came with the day after the fire. Your parents, well, I believe they're your parents."

"I don't understand a word you're saying to me."

"But come on, you must have known that they came to the château that evening, surely?"

"What parents?"

Philippe felt himself losing his footing, as though falling from the top floor of a skyscraper.

"On July 14th, you all arrived together. I thought you knew that they had been to the château the previous day. It happens all the time, families coming to visit their children, but never in the evening. That's why it surprised me."

"You're crazy. My parents live in Charleville-Mézières. They couldn't have been in Burgundy on the night of the fire."

"They were there, I saw them. I swear to you. When I closed my window, I saw them leaving the château."

"You must be mistaken . . ."

"No. Your mother, her chignon, her appearance . . . I'm not mistaken. I saw them again on the last day of the trial in Mâcon. They were waiting for you outside the court."

Then Philippe remembered. It was like lightning, a shock, as if a tiny detail buried in his subconscious for years was appearing to him in the full light of day. Something abnormal, incoherent, which, owing to the circumstances, he hadn't really registered, just sensed, on that July 14th, 1993.

He had phoned his parents and said to them, "Léonine is dead." They had come to pick him up a few hours later, and, for the first time, Philippe had sat in front, beside his father; his mother was lying on the back seat. Shattered, and dazed with grief, Philippe hadn't opened his mouth for the entire journey. From time to time, he heard his mother moaning in the back. He knew that his father was silently reciting Hail Marys.

When Philippe thought of his father, he thought of someone holier-than-thou who toed the line in front of his wife. Philippe had dreamt of being the son of Luc, his uncle. Mother Nature had got it wrong: he was born to the sister, when he would have liked to be born to the brother.

Just as Eloïse had mentioned his parents, he remembered that his father hadn't needed directions, hadn't asked him for the address. He had gone there as if he knew the way. When you left the highway, the village of La Clayette was signposted, but nothing indicated which way to turn to reach the château. But when Philippe was a child, his parents were always arguing because his father had no sense of direction and his mother got annoyed. If he hadn't got lost that day, maybe it was because he had already been there before.

Eloïse was staring at him while he was replaying this grim journey in his mind. Despite the horror written all over his face, she thought him handsome. She tried to remember Léonine's features, but couldn't. The four children had disappeared from her memory. She was forever searching for them, but no longer found them. All that remained to her were their voices, when they had asked questions about the ponies. She hadn't told Philippe that Léonine had lost her *doudou*, and that, together, they had hunted everywhere for it. Léonine had said to her, "It's a rabbit that's the same age as me." Until she could find it, Eloïse had found a little forgotten bear in the storeroom for her. And she had promised Léonine that the following morning, she would search the whole castle for it, and would find it.

Philippe brought her back down to earth:

"I want you to swear, on Léonine's life, that you will never speak of this to anyone."

Eloïse wondered whether Philippe had just heard her thoughts. She was incapable of uttering a word. He insisted:

"The two of us, we never saw each other, never spoke . . . Swear!"

As though in court, Eloïse raised her right hand and said, "I swear."

"On Léonine's life?"

"On Léonine's life."

Philippe wrote down the landline number for the house at Brancion cemetery and handed it to her.

"In two hours' time, you call this number, my wife will answer. You introduce yourself and tell her that I didn't come to the appointment, that you waited all afternoon for me."

"But . . . "

"Please."

Eloïse felt sorry for him, so she agreed.

"And if she asks me questions?"

"She won't ask you any questions. I've let her down too often for her to ask any."

Philippe got up to pay the bill. He said a brief goodbye to Eloïse as he picked up his helmet, and then returned to his motorbike, parked outside the movie theater.

Glancing at the people coming in and out of the various screenings, he remembered his mother's words, "Trust no one, do you hear me? No one."

Almost seven hundred kilometers. It would be dark when he arrived at Charleville-Mézières.

* * *

Philippe watched his parents for a while through the sitting-room window. They were sitting side by side, on their ancient sofa covered in faded flowers. Like those on abandoned tombs. Those that Violette couldn't bear, and would remove.

The father was asleep, the mother gripped by a TV show, a rerun. Violette had already seen it. A love story between a priest and a young girl, set in Australia, or some other faraway land. Violette had secretly cried at some parts. He had sensed her wiping away her tears on her sleeve. His mother was staring at the actors, her lips pursed, as if she thought they were making wrong choices and she wanted to stick her oar in. Why had she picked this soppy program? If the circumstances hadn't been so serious, Philippe would have laughed.

Philippe had grown up in this house that, right now, seemed like a stage set. Over the years, the shrubs had grown, the hedges filled out. His parents had had the chain-link fence changed to a white picket fence, like in American TV shows; the façade's roughcast resurfaced; and two lion statues installed on either side of the front door. The granite wildcats seemed bored stiff at this house stuck in the 70s. But his parents had to show the neighbors that they were public-sector management. Both retired from the PTT, the postal and telecoms service, he having started as a postman, she as an admin assistant, they had both climbed the ladder and become low-grade managers. And when there had finally been some money, they had put it aside.

Philippe still had the house keys on him. He'd been carrying the same key ring around since childhood, a miniature rugby ball that had lost both its shape and its colors. His parents had never changed the locks. What for? Who on earth would want to go in there, to find the father lost in his prayers, the mother in resentment? Two gherkins in a jar of vinegar.

He hadn't set foot in this house for years. Since he had met Violette. Violette. Not once had they invited her. They had always looked down on her.

Chantal Toussaint screamed when she saw her son standing at the door of the sitting room. Her cry woke up her husband, who jumped.

As he was about to open his mouth, Philippe saw portraits of Léonine hanging on the walls, two taken at school. That reminded him of Geneviève Magnan, her smile in those corridors reeking of ammonia. He suddenly felt dizzy and gripped the sideboard.

Violette had taken down the portraits of their daughter. She had put them away in a drawer, beside her bed, in her wallet, and between the pages of that big book she was forever rereading.

His mother approached him, muttering, "Everything alright, son?" With one gesture, Philippe commanded her not to come any closer, to keep her distance. The father and mother exchanged glances. Was their son sick? Mad? He was scarily pale. He had the same look as on the morning of July 14th, 1993, when they had taken him to the scene of the tragedy. He'd aged by twenty years.

"What the hell were you doing at the château on the evening of the fire?"

The father glanced at the mother, waiting for permission to reply. But as usual, she was the one who spoke. With the voice of a victim, of the nice little girl she had never been.

"Armelle and Jean-Louis Caussin met us in the village of La Clayette before dropping off Catherine . . . that is, Léonine, and Anaïs at the château. We said we'd meet them in a café, we did nothing wrong."

"But what the hell were you doing over there?"

"We were at a wedding in the Midi, you know, your cousin Laurence . . . we made the most of the drive back to Charleville by visiting Burgundy."

"You have never made the most of anything, NEVER. I want the truth."

The mother hesitated before replying, setting her lips and breathing in deeply. Philippe stopped her immediately:

"Do me a favor, don't start sniveling."

Never had her son spoken to her like this. The polite, well brought up boy, who said: "Yes, Mommy," "No, Mommy," "O.K., Mommy," was well and truly dead. He had started to disappear when he had lost his daughter. He had completely disappeared once he had buried himself with Violette. Philippe had warned them, "I forbid you from setting foot in the cemetery, I don't want you bumping into Violette."

Before the tragedy, the only times he had disobeyed his mother were when he went on holiday with her brother Luc and his young wife, whose skirts were far too short. Philippe had always been drawn to lower-class women. Girls, bottom-of-the-range, the gutter.

Chantal Toussaint's voice regained its hard, unforgiving tone. That of a prosecutor.

"I had arranged to meet the Caussins because I wished to see what *your wife* had put into the suitcase of our grand-daughter. To ensure that nothing was missing. I didn't want her to feel ashamed in front of her friends. Your wife was young and Catherine was too often neglected . . . Her long nails, dirty ears, stained or shrunken clothes . . . it made me sick."

"You're talking rubbish! Violette looked after our daughter very well! Her name was Léonine! Do you hear me?! Léonine!"

Awkwardly and roughly, she refastened her dressing gown.

"Armelle Caussin opened the trunk of her car, I checked the contents of the suitcase, while the girls played in the shade, near your father and Jean-Louis. There were plenty of things missing, and I had to throw away her cheap or worn clothes, replace them with new ones."

Philippe imagined his mother calling Armelle Caussin on a

false pretext and rifling through his daughter's little dresses. This right to interfere that she'd always claimed disgusted him. He felt like strangling this woman who had made him despise others. She lowered her eyes to avoid seeing the look of hatred he was directing at her.

"At around 4 P.M., the Caussins left for the château with the children. Your father and I didn't want to start driving back to Charleville before nightfall, because of the heat. We decided to stay in the village. We returned to the café for a bite to eat. When I went to the restroom, I saw Léonine's *doudou* next to the sink. I knew she couldn't fall asleep without it."

Chantal Toussaint grimaced.

"It was filthy . . . I washed it with soap and water—in the heat it would dry fast."

She went to sit down on the sofa, as if the words were too heavy a burden. Her husband followed her, like a faithful mutt expecting a reward, a look, a sign of affection, which would never come.

"We entered the castle without any difficulty: no one around, no supervision, doors wide open. Léonine happened to be behind the first door we opened. She was already in bed. She was surprised to see us. When she saw her rabbit sticking out of my handbag, she smiled and discreetly grabbed it so the other girls wouldn't see her. She must have looked everywhere for it, unable to say anything for fear of being made fun of."

The mother started sobbing. Her husband slipped an arm around her shoulders, she slowly pushed it away; used to this, he withdrew it.

"I asked the girls if they would like me to tell them a story. They said yes. I read them a Grimm fairy tale, *Tom Thumb*. They all fell asleep straight away. Before leaving, I kissed my granddaughter one last time."

"And the water heater?!" Philippe screamed.

His parents, in tears, cowered pitifully before their son's rage.

"What do you mean, water heater, what water heater?" his mother finally muttered between sobs.

"The one in the bathroom! In the room, there was a bathroom! And a fucking water heater! Was it you who touched it?!"

The father opened his mouth for the first time and let out, with a sigh:

"Oh, that . . . "

At that moment, Philippe would have given anything for him to say nothing, as usual. Or say a prayer, any one. But for one hour, just one hour, the man had felt useful in his wife's life, instead of just hanging around, waiting for her to finish reading the story of *Tom Thumb*.

"Your mother asked Léonine whether she was sure she'd brushed her teeth before going to bed, she said yes, but another girl told us that no hot water came out of the tap, that the cold water had hurt her teeth. Your mother asked me to have a quick look, and indeed, I saw that the water heater was switched off, so I . . . "

Philippe fell to his knees in front of his parents, grabbed his father by the collar of his dressing gown, with both hands, and implored him:

"Shut up, shut up, shut up, shut up, shut up, shut up, shut up, shut up, shut up, shut up, shut up . . . "

His parents froze. Philippe stammered a few more inaudible words, and then left the house as he had entered it, in silence.

When he got back on his bike, he knew he wouldn't be taking the road back to the Brancion cemetery. He knew that he no longer had a home. Not tonight, not tomorrow. He had known it ever since he had asked Eloïse Petit to phone Violette and tell her that he hadn't come to their meeting. Violette, who had stopped waiting for him long ago.

That morning, when he had announced to her that he

wanted to start afresh, settle in the Midi, he had seen in her eyes that she was pretending to believe him. Today, he could no longer face her. He never wanted to look her in the eye again.

Chantal Toussaint ran out after him, in just her dressing gown, to reason with him. It was dangerous to be on the road in that state. He was too tired, done in, he must rest, she would get his bed ready, she hadn't touched a thing in his room, not even his posters, she would cook him a beef stroganoff and the crème caramel he loved, tomorrow he'd be able to think more clearly and . . .

"I wish you had died at my birth, Mom. It would have been the luckiest thing in my life."

He started his bike and, without thinking, went in the direction of Bron. In his rearview mirror, he saw his mother collapsing onto the pavement. He knew that his words had signed her death warrant. Today or tomorrow. And his father would follow. He always followed.

He felt nothing but the desire to be with Luc and Françoise and tell them everything. They would know what to do, they would find the right words, they would be able to keep him close, so he no longer had to explain himself to anyone. Return to being the child he had wanted to be: Luc's. This life was done with.

91

And when, taking my burial mound for a pillow,
A water nymph comes gently to doze,
clad in the skimpiest of costumes,
I apologize in advance to Jesus
if my cross's shadow falls over her a touch
for a little posthumous happiness.

IRÈNE FAYOLLE'S JOURNAL

2013

I went into the cemetery lady's house. She looked at me as one does a person one knows by sight but can't place. She was alone, sitting at her table. She was leafing through a gardening catalogue.

"I'm just selecting my spring bulbs. Do you prefer narcissi, or croci? I love these yellow tulips."

Her fingers fell on photos of clusters of flowers. So many varieties.

"Narcissi, I think I prefer narcissi. I also love flowers, I had a rose nursery, before."

"Where was that?"

"In Marseilles."

"Oh . . . I go to Marseilles every year, to the Calanque de Sormiou."

"I used to go there with my son, Julien, when he was little. A long time ago."

The cemetery lady smiled at me as though we shared a secret.

"Would you like something to drink?"

"I'd love a green tea."

She got up to make my tea. I thought she must be around Julien's age. She could have been my daughter. I don't think I would have liked having a daughter. I don't know what I could *have told her, how I would have advised her, directed her. A boy's a bit like a wild flower, a hawthorn, he grows on his own, as long as he has enough to eat, to drink, to wear. As long as you tell him he's handsome, strong. A boy grows well when he has a father. A girl is more complicated.*

The cemetery lady is beautiful. She was wearing a straight black skirt and a fine, gray polo-neck sweater. I thought her elegant. Delicate. She almost made me regret not having had a daughter. She put loose tea into a teapot and strained it. Then she put some honey on the table. It felt good in her home. It smelled good. She told me that she loved roses. Their scent.

"You live alone?"

"Yes."

"At this cemetery, I come to visit Gabriel Prudent."

"He's buried in avenue 19, in the Cedars section. Is that right?"

"Yes. Do you know all the locations of the deceased?"

"Most of them. And he was a great lawyer, there was a crowd at his funeral. Which year was it, again?"

"2009."

The cemetery lady got up to fetch a register, the one for 2009, and she looked up Gabriel's name. So it's true, she does write everything down in books. She read it out loud to me: "February 18th, 2009, funeral of Gabriel Prudent, torrential rain. There were a hundred and twenty-eight people at the burial. His ex-wife was present, as were his two daughters, Marthe Dubreuil and Cloé Prudent. No flowers or wreaths, at the request of the deceased. The family had a plaque engraved, saying: 'In homage to Gabriel Prudent, a courageous lawyer.' "Courage, for a lawyer, is essential, without which the rest counts for nothing; talent, culture, knowledge of the law, all is of use to the lawyer. But without courage, at the decisive moment, there remain merely words, a succession of sentences that shine brightly and then die." (Robert Badinter)' No priest. No cross. The cortege only *stayed for half an hour. When the two funeral directors had finished lowering the coffin into the vault, everyone left. Still raining very heavily."*

The cemetery lady poured me another cup of tea. I asked her to read her notes on Gabriel's funeral again. She did so, willingly.

I imagined the people surrounding Gabriel's coffin. I imagined the umbrellas, the warm, dark clothes. The scarves and the tears.

I told the cemetery lady that Gabriel got angry when people said he was courageous. That there was no courage involved in telling a magistrate that he was an idiot in a roundabout way. That courage was going every day, after work, to Porte de la Chapelle, to distribute meals to the needy, or hiding Jews in one's home in 1942. Gabriel was always repeating to me that he had no courage, that he took no risks.

She asked me whether we had spoken a lot, Gabriel and me. I said yes. And that this thing about Gabriel hating courage should remain between her and me. I didn't want the people who thought they had done well putting those words on his memorial plaque to know that they had got it wrong.

The cemetery lady smiled at me.

"No problem. Everything said between these walls remains secret."

I felt I could trust her, and I spoke to her as if she had added a truth serum to my tea.

"I visit Gabriel's tomb two or three times a year, to shake a snow globe that I left close to his name. I cut out newspaper articles for him, legal columns that interested him, and I read them to him. I give him news of the world, of his world, at any rate. Cases that are criminal, passionate, eternal. I visit the tomb of my husband, Paul, more frequently, at the Saint-Pierre cemetery in Marseilles. Each time, I ask him to forgive me. Because I will be buried beside Gabriel. My ashes will be placed beside him. Gabriel made all the arrangements with his solicitor, as have I. No one will be able to object to it. We weren't married. You know, I wanted to come here to tell you that the day my son, Julien, finds out about it, it's you he will come to question."

"Why me?"

"When he discovers that my final wish was to rest beside Gabriel, and not his father, he will want to understand. He will want to know who Gabriel Prudent was, and the first person he will ask will be you. Because the first person he will come across when he walks through the gates of this cemetery will be you. As I did, the first time I came."

"Is there something in particular you would like me to tell him?"

"No. No, I'm sure you will find the right words. Or that, for once, Julien will find his own to speak to you. I'm sure you will know how to help him, support him."

I was sorry to leave the cemetery lady. I knew it was the last time I would come to Brancion-en-Chalon. I got back on the road. I returned to Marseilles.

2016

I have finished my journal. I will soon be rejoining Gabriel. I know it. I can already detect the smell of his cigarettes. I can't wait. When I think that, the last time we saw each other, we argued. It's time to patch things up.

I remember her perfume. I no longer remember her face. Just her white hair, her skin, her fine hands, her raincoat. And especially her perfume. I remember the gentleness of that moment. And the words she applied to Gabriel. Her voice has remained with me, too, its echo, when she told me that, one day, her son would be coming to see me.

When Julien knocked on my door that first time, he made me forget Irène. I found him handsome, in his crumpled clothes. He didn't look like his mother. She had the complexion of a blonde, smooth, fair, and delicate, whereas her son was typically dark, with messy hair and skin that had soaked up plenty of sun. I loved his tobacco hands touching me. But I was also too scared of them.

Before leaving for Marseilles, I phoned him several times, but his number just rang and rang. It was as if he no longer existed. I even rang his police station, I was told that he had left. But he could be written to, his mail was being forwarded.

What could I write to him?

Julien,
I'm crazy, I'm alone, I'm impossible. You believed me, and I did everything I could so you would.

Julien,
I was so happy in your car.

Julien,
I was so happy with you on my sofa.

Julien,
I was so happy with you in my bed.

Julien,
You are young. But I don't think we care.

Julien,
You are too curious. I hate it when you act like a cop.

Julien,
Your son, I'd be up for him being my stepson.

Julien,
You really are my type of man. But, in fact, I've no idea. I imagine that you're really my type of man.

Julien,
I miss you.

Julien,
I'm going to die if you don't come back.

Julien,
I'm waiting for you. I'm hoping for you. I'm happy to change my habits if you'll change yours.

Julien,
O.K.

Julien,
It was good, it was lovely.

Julien,
Yes.

Julien,
No.

Life has ripped out my roots. My spring is dead.

I close Irène's journal with a heavy heart. The way one closes a novel one has fallen in love with. A novel that's a friend from whom it's hard to part, because one wants it close by, in arm's reach. Deep down, I'm happy that Julien left me his mother's journal in memory of them. When I'm back home, I'll place it among the books I keep preciously on the shelves in my bedroom. In the meantime, I slip it into my beach bag.

It's 10 A.M., I'm leaning against a rock, sitting on the white sand in the shade of an Aleppo pine. Here, the trees grow through the cracks in the rock. The cicadas began to sing when

I closed Irène's journal. The sun is already beating down. I can feel it prickling my toes. In summer, the sun here burns your skin in just a few minutes.

The holidaymakers with backpacks are starting to arrive, down the steep path. By midday, the little beach will be covered in towels, coolers, parasols. There aren't many children at Sormiou. In high season, you can only access the creek on foot. You have to walk for a good hour, down from the Baumettes car park. It's not easy for families. Often, the children who end up here have done the journey on their fathers' shoulders, or they live in the chalets, or *cabanons*, during the holidays. They're known as the "*cabanoniers*." The word only exists in Marseilles, you won't find it in any dictionaries.

Here, people are still allowed to smoke in the bars. The postmen sign for registered letters themselves when residents are out, so they won't have to go and collect them. In Marseilles, nothing is done as it is elsewhere.

Yesterday evening, Célia remained with me for supper. She had prepared a seafood paella, which she warmed up in a large pan. In the meantime, I unpacked my blue suitcase, put my dresses on hangers. We took out the little wrought-iron garden table, put a cloth over it, filled two red carafes with water and rosé. We put lots of ice cubes in a yellow bowl, and added a farmhouse loaf and mismatched plates. Everything is mismatched at the chalet. Objects never seem to have reached here together. Célia and I relished the catching up, the swapping of silly stories, the golden rice and the well chilled rosé.

We talked so late that Célia stayed the night. She slept with me like she did that first time in Malgrange-sur-Nancy during the train strike. It was the first time she'd stayed over.

We carried on drinking rosé as we lay in bed. Célia lit two candles. Her grandfather's furniture danced in the light. We left two windows open to create a draft. It felt lovely. It still smelled of paella. The walls had soaked up its aroma. It made me feel hungry again, I warmed myself up a little more. Célia didn't want any. When I placed the empty plate on the floor, I saw Célia's profile. Then her beautiful blue eyes, like two stars in the night. I blew out the candles.

"Célia, I have something to tell you. It's going to keep you from sleeping, but since we're on holiday, it doesn't matter. And I really can't not tell you about 'this.'"

" . . . "

"Françoise Pelletier was the love of Philippe Toussaint's life. It's with her that he lived his last years. He met up with her the day he disappeared, in 1998. But that's not all. I know why he disappeared. Why he never came back home. That night, it's not the fire that killed the children . . . it's Father Toussaint."

Célia gripped my arm, and just whispered, "What?"

"He tinkered with an old water heater in the children's room and switched it on. He didn't know that it was strictly not to be touched. The appliance hadn't been maintained for years. Carbon monoxide kills, it's insidious, odorless . . . the girls died in their sleep."

"Who told you that?"

"Françoise Pelletier. It's Philippe Toussaint who told her everything. That's why he never came home on the day he found out. He couldn't look me in the eye anymore . . . Do you know that song by Michel Jonasz? 'Tell me, tell me even that she left for someone other than me, but not because of me, tell me that, tell me that . . . '"

"Yes."

"It made me feel better knowing that Philippe Toussaint hadn't left because of me. But because of his parents."

Célia gripped my arm even tighter.

I didn't manage to sleep a wink. I thought again of the old Toussaints. They had been dead a long time. A solicitor from

Charleville-Mézières had contacted me in 2000. He was looking for their son.

When daylight came through the windows and the draft
became gentler, Célia opened her eyes.

"We're going to make ourselves a good coffee."

"Célia, I've met someone."

"Well, it's about time."

"But it's over."

"Why?"

"I have my life, my habits . . . For such a long time. And he's
younger than me. And he doesn't live in Burgundy. And he has
a seven-year-old child."

"That's a lot of 'ands.' But a life and habits can be changed."

"You think?"

"Yes."

"You would change your own habits?"

"Why not."

92

Life is but an endless losing of all that one loves.

MAY 2017

Nineteen years, now, that Philippe had been living in Bron. Since he'd done that journey between Charleville-Mézières and Françoise. Nineteen years since he'd turned up one morning at the garage, in a pitiful state. He had decided to be born on that day. To kill the day preceding his arrival. The day before, when he'd spoken to his parents for the very last time. He had drawn a big, black marker line through a past he wanted to leave behind. Put a lid on the Violette years, and double-locked his parents in the dark chamber of his memory.

It had been so easy to be called Philippe Pelletier, to become the son of his uncle. Nephew or son, in people's minds, it amounted to the same thing. Philippe was "part of the family," so a Pelletier.

It had been so easy to put his identity papers away in a drawer. To empty his bank account so his mother was out of the picture. To change this money into bonds. Not to vote. Not to use his social-security card.

Françoise had told him that Luc had died in October of 1996. Luc, dead and buried. Philippe had found the blow hard to take. But he had refused to pay his respects at Luc's tomb. He never wanted to set foot in a cemetery ever again.

Françoise had sold the house a year back, and was living in Bron, two hundred meters from the garage. She'd been very ill, lost a lot of weight, aged a lot, too. Yet Philippe had found her even more desirable than in his memories, but had said nothing. He'd done enough harm around him. Used up his quota of misfortune on others.

He had settled in the guest room. The son's room. The room of a child who had never existed. Just been hoped for. He had bought himself new clothes with the first wage Françoise had paid him in cash. When, a few months after settling in Bron, he'd mentioned moving into a small studio apartment not far from the garage, Françoise had carried on as if she hadn't heard him. So, he had stayed there. In that bizarre cohabitation. Shared bathroom, shared kitchen, shared lounge, shared meals, separate bedrooms.

He had told Françoise everything. Léonine, Geneviève Magnan, the water heater, *L'Adresse*, the orgies, the cemetery, his parents' confession on the sofa in Charleville. Everything, except Violette. He had kept her to himself. On Violette, he'd just said to Françoise, "She's not to blame."

As the years passed, he'd forgotten that he'd been called Philippe Toussaint in another life.

Through living with Françoise, he'd got his spirits back. He'd learned to work well in the garage, to enjoy his days of oil, grease, breakdowns, dented bodywork. Through repairing engines, he'd become reconciled with desire.

In December of 1999, Françoise had been ill; a high fever, too high a fever, a bad cough. Anxious, Philippe had called a duty doctor. While writing his bedside prescription, the doctor had asked Philippe whether Françoise was his wife, and he'd said yes without thinking. Just yes. Françoise had smiled at him from under the sheets without a word. A faint, tired smile. Resigned.

On the doctor's advice, Philippe had run a bath to a temperature of thirty-seven degrees, had guided Françoise to the bathroom, undressed her, and helped her step into the bath, while she clung on to him. It was the first time he was seeing her naked. Her body shivering under the clear water. He had wiped a washcloth across her skin, her stomach, her back, her face, her nape. He had poured water on her forehead. Françoise had said to him, "Watch out, I'm contagious." Philippe had replied, "That I've known for the past twenty-eight years." On the night of December 31st, 1999, to January 1st, 2000, they'd made love for the first time. They'd changed centuries in the same bed.

Nineteen years, now, that Philippe had been living in Bron. That morning, with Françoise, they'd brought up the idea of selling the garage. It wasn't the first time, but this time, it was serious. They wanted some sun. To go and settle around Saint-Tropez. They had enough money to take it easy. And Françoise was going to be sixty-six, with years of work behind her. It was time to reap the rewards.

At lunchtime, Françoise had gone to an estate agent that specialized in the sale of commercial properties and businesses. Philippe had gone back to their apartment to change clothes. He had dressed too warmly that morning, had sweated under his blue overalls. He'd taken a quick shower, pulled on a clean T-shirt. In the kitchen he'd made himself two fried eggs, along with cheese spread on yesterday's bread. While his coffee was brewing, he'd heard the mail falling on the tiled floor. The postman had just slipped it through the gap in the front door. Philippe had automatically picked it up and thrown it on the kitchen table. Apart from *Auto-moto* magazine, to which Françoise had subscribed to please him, he never read the mail. It was Françoise who did all the paperwork.

He was just turning his spoon in his cup when he read, without really reading: "Mr. Philippe Toussaint, c/o Mme. Françoise Pelletier, 13 Avenue Franklin-Roosevelt, 69500 Bron."

He read it again, incredulous at the name, Philippe Toussaint. He hesitated, finally picking up the envelope as if it were a parcel bomb. The envelope was white and bore the stamp of a Mâcon solicitors' office. Mâcon. He remembered the day he'd watched little girls coming out of a primary school. The one that was wearing the same dress as Léonine. The day he'd thought she was alive.

Everything came back to him. It hit him hard and fast, like an uppercut to the stomach. The death of his child, the funeral, the trial, the move, his unease, his parents, his mother, his games consoles, the hot bodies of thin women, the puckered breasts, the fat bellies, the faces of Lucie Lindon and Eloïse Petit, Fontanel, the trains, the tombs, the cats.

Mr. Philippe Toussaint.

He opened the envelope, shaking. He remembered Geneviève Magnan's hands the last time he'd seen her, when she'd said, "I'd never have done any harm to kids." She had said "*vous*" to him, while shaking.

Violette Trenet, married name Toussaint, had instructed a solicitor to settle their divorce amicably. The solicitor was asking Mr. Philippe Toussaint to call the office without delay to make an appointment.

He read snatches of sentences: "bring some identification . . . name of the solicitor's office . . . marriage contract was drawn up . . . profession . . . nationality . . . birthplace . . . same information for each child . . . spouses' agreement to the separation . . . no alimony . . . Mâcon high court . . . desertion of the conjugal home . . . no further action."

Impossible. This had to be stopped, immediately. The time-machine jammed. He stopped reading, slipped the envelope into the inside pocket of his biker jacket, fastened the strap of his helmet, and set off for *that place*. Even if he had sworn never to set foot there ever again.

How had Violette discovered his address? How did she know about Françoise? How did she know her name? His parents couldn't have said anything, they were long dead. And even before dying, they hadn't known where Philippe was living. They had never known that their son was living in Bron with Françoise. Impossible. Philippe would not go to that solicitor's. Ever.

She must leave him in peace. He must leave, move with Françoise, be called Philippe Pelletier. The other surname would always bring him bad luck. Toussaint. A name associated with cemeteries, death, chrysanthemums. A name that stank of the cold and the memory of cats.

Two lives, some hundred kilometers apart. He'd never realized that Bron was so close to Brancion-en-Chalon.

He parked outside the house, on the road-side. A stranger outside a house he'd always hated. That old cemetery keeper's house. The trees Violette had planted in 1997 had grown tall. The gates had been repainted a dark green. He went in without knocking. Nineteen years, now, that he hadn't set foot here.

Did she still live here? Had she made a new life for herself? Of course, that's why she wanted a divorce. To get remarried.

A strange taste in his mouth. Like the barrel of a gun stuck down his throat. An itching to punch something. Hatred was bubbling up. Such a long time since he'd felt this bitterness. He thought back to the gentle, carefree life of the past nineteen years. And now evil was back again. He was returning to being the man he didn't like, the man who didn't like himself. Philippe Toussaint.

He must go back to how he was, that very morning. Clear away this sordid past, once and for all. Not feel pity. No, he would not go to that solicitor's. No. He had torn up his identity papers. Torn up his past.

On the kitchen table, empty coffee cups sitting on gardening magazines. Three scarves and a white cardigan hanging on the coatrack. Her perfume hanging on them. A rose pefume. She was still living there.

He went up to the bedroom. Kicked some plastic boxes containing ghastly dolls. Couldn't stop himself. If he could have punched the walls, he would have. He found the bed-room repainted, a sky-blue carpet, a pale-pink bedcover, almond-green window coverings and curtains. Hand cream on the white bedside table, books, a blown-out candle. He opened the top drawer of the chest of drawers, underwear the same pink as the walls. He lay down on the bed. Imagined her sleeping here.

Did she still think of him? Had she waited for him? Looked for him?

He had put a lid on the Violette years, but for a very long time, he had dreamt of her. He would hear her voice, she was calling him and he didn't reply, he was hiding in a dark corner so she wouldn't notice him, and he would end up covering his ears to stop hearing her pleading voice. For a long time, he had woken up bathed in sweat, between sheets drenched in his guilt.

In the bathroom, perfumes, soaps, creams, bath salts, more candles, more novels. In the laundry basket, lingerie, a short white-silk nightie, a black dress, a gray cardigan.

There was no man in this house. No communal living. So why fucking bother him? Why rake over the shit? To get money? A pension? That's not what the solicitor's letter had said. "Amicably . . . no further action." He could hear his mother: "Watch out."

He went back downstairs. Knocked over the last dolls still standing. He felt like going into the cemetery to visit Léonine's tomb, but decided against it.

A shadow moved behind him, he jumped. An old mutt was sniffing him from a distance. Before he had time to give it a kick, the creature had curled up in its cozy basket. In a corner of the kitchen, he saw bowls of pet food on the floor. He gagged at the thought of living with hairs on his clothes. He went out the back of the house, through the door that led to the private garden.

He didn't spot her straight away. Here, too, all the greenery had climbed upwards, like in Léonine's storybooks. Ivy and creeper on the walls, yellow, red, and pink trees, beds of multicolored flowers. It was as if, just like the bedroom, the garden had been redecorated.

There she was. Crouching in her vegetable garden. Nineteen years, now, that he hadn't seen her. How old was she now?

Don't feel pity.

She had her back to him. She was wearing a black dress with white spots. She had tied an old gardening apron around her waist. Pulled on rubber boots. Her shoulder-length hair was gathered in a black elastic band. A few tendrils were tickling the nape of her neck. She was wearing thick gloves. She raised her right wrist to her forehead as if to wipe away something bothering her.

He felt like wringing her neck and hugging her. Loving her and strangling her. Making her shut up, so she didn't exist anymore, so she disappeared.

Stop feeling guilty.

When she got up and turned toward him, Philippe saw only terror in her eyes. Not surprise, or anger, or love, or resentment, or regret. Just terror.

Don't feel pity.

She hadn't changed. He saw her once more behind the Tibourin bar, her small, delicate form, serving him as many drinks as he wanted. Her smile. Now, wrinkles and strands of hair were mingled on her face. The features were still fine, the mouth still well defined, and the eyes still radiated great gentleness. Time had deepened the furrows on either side of her mouth.

Keep your distance.

Don't say her name.

Don't feel pity.

She had always been more beautiful than Françoise, and yet it was Françoise he had chosen over her. No accounting for taste . . . That's what his mother used to say.

He saw a cat sitting beside her, he got goose bumps, remembered why he was there, back in this wretched cemetery. He remembered that he didn't want to remember anymore. Not her, or Léonine, or the others. His present was Françoise, his future would be Françoise.

Suddenly, he grabbed Violette, gripped her arms hard, too hard, as though to crush her. Like when a man becomes a torturer to stop feeling anything. He must summon hatred. Think of his parents on the flowery sofa. Léonine's suitcase in the Caussins' trunk, the château, the water heater, his mother in her dressing gown, his father stupefied. He gripped Violette's arms without looking her in the eye, he stared at a fixed point, between the eyebrows, a slight dip where the nose began.

She smelled good. Don't feel pity.

"I received a solicitor's letter, I'm returning it to you . . . Listen to me carefully, very carefully, NEVER write to me again at that address, do you hear? Not you, not your solicitor, NEVER. I don't want to read your name anywhere anymore, otherwise I will . . . I will . . . "

He let go of her as suddenly as he had grabbed her, her body slumped like a puppet, he shoved the envelope in her apron pocket, and in doing so, felt her stomach under the fabric. Her stomach. Léonine. He turned his back on her and returned to the kitchen.

As he banged into the table, he made *L'Oeuvre de Dieu, la part du Diable* fall. He recognized the red apple on the cover, it was the book Violette had owned since Charleville, the one she was forever rereading. Seven photos of Léonine escaped from between its pages and scattered over the carpet. He hesitated, and then bent down to pick them up. One year, two years, three years, four years, five years, six years, seven years.

It's true that she looked like him. He slipped them back inside the book, which he put back on the table.

The lid he had put on the Violette years, for the past nineteen years, blew up in his face right then. His child came back to him, first in ripples, then in breaker waves. At the maternity hospital when he'd seen her for the first time, between him and Violette in their bed, snuggled in a blanket, having her bath, in the garden, in front of doors, crossing a room, doing drawings, modeling clay, at the table, in the inflatable swimming pool, in the school corridors, in winter, in summer, her red, slightly shimmery dress, her little hands, her magic tricks. And him, always distant. Him, as though just a visitor in the life of his daughter, whom he'd wanted to be a son. All the stories that he hadn't read to her, all the journeys that he hadn't taken her on.

When he got back on his motorbike, he felt tears dripping from his nose. His Uncle Luc had told him that when you cry from the nose, it's taking over because the eyes' gauge is overflowing. "It's like with engines, son." Luc. He was such a shit, he'd even stolen Luc's wife.

He sped off, telling himself that he'd stop a bit further on to get his breath back, and his senses. Glimpsing the crosses through the gates, he thought about how he'd never believed in God. Doubtless because of his father. The prayers he loathed. He remembered the day of his First Communion, the Mass wine, Françoise on Luc's arm.

Our Father who farts forever
Hallowed be thy bum
Thy condom come
Thy willy be done
On turds as it is in heaven
Give us this day our daily beer
And forgive us our burps
As we forgive those who burp against us

And lead us not into penetration
But deliver us from perverts. Omen.

Over the three hundred and fifty meters he skimmed the wall of the cemetery, faster and faster, three thoughts came crashing into his skull, like some violent pileup. Turning back and saying sorry to Violette, sorry, sorry, sorry. Going home as fast as possible to Françoise and leaving for the South, leaving, leaving, leaving. Being back with Léonine, back, back, back with her.

Violette, Françoise, Léonine.

Seeing his daughter again, feeling her, hearing her, touching her, breathing her in.

It was the first time he truly wanted Léonine. He had wanted her in order to keep Violette close to him. Today, he wanted her like one wants a child. This desire was stronger than the South, Françoise, and Violette. This desire took over everything. Léonine must be waiting for him somewhere. Yes, she was waiting for him. He had understood nothing because he had been a bad father, he would become a daddy for the first time, there, where he would be back with her.

Philippe unfastened the strap of his helmet. Just before accelerating around the first bend, accelerating to plow into the trees of the estate forest down below, he didn't see his life flash past him, he didn't see the images like in a book when the pages are flicked through, he didn't want to. Just before the trees, he glimpsed a young woman on the edge of the road. Impossible. She was staring at him while he was moving at nearly two hundred kilometers an hour, and all around him nothing else was still anymore, except her eyes on him. He just had time to think that he'd seen her before, on an old print. A postcard, perhaps. And then he entered the light.

93

We're at the end of summer, the warmth
of those evening return journeys, back in
our apartments, life continuing as usual.

I've not yet been into the water. Every August, I dread the moment of that first dip. I'm afraid of not finding Léonine. Afraid of not sensing her presence. Afraid that she won't turn up because of me. That she won't hear me calling her, luring her, that my voice won't reach her. That she no longer feels my love enough to come back to me. I'm afraid of no longer loving her, of losing her forever. This fear is unfounded, death will never manage to separate me from my child, and I know it.

I get up, I stretch, I throw my hat onto my towel. I walk toward the vast carpet of emeralds with flashes of pearl. The morning light is harsh, brilliant.

It promises a beautiful day. Marseilles always keeps its promises.

At this hour, if there is any shade, the water is black. The waves are cool, as ever. I advance gently. I plunge my head in. I swim to the depths, closing my eyes. She's already there, she's always there, she hasn't moved from here because she's within me. Her ethereal presence. I breathe in her warm, salty skin, like when she would lie on top of me for a siesta under our parasol. Her hands running across my back, two little marionettes.

My love.

When I resurface, I look the blue of the sky straight in the eye, I know I will carry her forever within me. That's what eternity is.

I swim for a long time, I don't want to get out now, I never do. I observe the pines leaning in the wind, I observe life, I'm very close to it, it's very close to me. Gradually, I near the shore. Sand again under my feet. I turn my back on the beach, I observe the horizon, the still, anchored boats, small white stones suspended in the light. Nothing is more healing than this place in the world where everything is beautiful, where the elements restore the living.

It's hot, the salt stings my face and, even more, my lips. I sink my head under the water, I swim, closing my eyes; I love sensing, listening to the sea beneath me.

I feel a presence, a different presence. Someone brushes against me. Grips my hips and places a hand on my stomach. Clings to my back, mirrors my movements, like a dance, almost a waltz. I can feel his heart knocking on my back, I go along with it, I've understood. Another love, a new heart, someone else's, is being transplanted into mine. I can feel his mouth on my neck, his hair against my back, his hands still walking across me, with steps that are light and delicate. I had so hoped for this without believing in it, without believing it. I rise to the surface, he opens and closes his eyes, his eyelashes against my cheek, butterflies. He breathes me in. I lie on the water, he supports me, I let myself be guided, my body is free, my legs skim the surface of the water, I let myself go, he finds me, I find myself.

We are.

We.

Peals of laughter.

A child.

Three.

Another hand catches my arm and clings to me. Like Léonine's, small, tense, warm.

I hope I'm not dreaming, I hope I'm living. The child jumps into my arms. He plants wet kisses on my forehead, in my hair. He hurls himself backwards and yelps with joy.

"Nathan!"

I call out his name, like some litany.

He makes clumsy, rapid movements. He opens his eyes wide, like a child who hasn't swum for long, a child who is eager and scared all at once. He roars with laughter; his smile has lost two teeth. He pulls goggles over his eyes and ducks his head under the water. He seems more at ease and moves in wide circles. He has slipped a snorkel into his mouth.

He's back out of the water. He spits as he removes his snorkel. He pulls off his goggles, which have left their mark around his big brown eyes, his big, luminous eyes under the Southern light. He looks over my shoulder, he looks at Julien, who whispers in my ear, "Come."

94

Not a day goes by without us thinking of you.

Saturday September 7th, 2017, blue sky, twenty-three degrees, 10:30 A.M. Funeral of Fernand Occo (1935–2017). Oak coffin. Black marble headstone. Vault in which Jeanne Tillet, married name Occo (1937–2009), Simone Louis, married name Occo (1917–1999), Pierre Occo (1913–2001), Léon Occo (1933) are buried.

A wreath of white roses, ribbon: "Our sincere condolences." A wreath of white lilies in the shape of a heart, ribbon: "To our father, our grandfather." On the coffin, red and white roses, ribbon: "The War Veterans."

Three funerary plaques: "To our father, to our grandfather. In memory of this life of loving you and being loved by you"; "To our friend. We won't forget you, you are forever in our thoughts. Your fishing friends"; "You are not far, just on the other side of the path."

Around fifty people are present, including Fernand's three daughters, Catherine, Isabelle, and Nathalie, and his seven grandchildren.

Elvis, Gaston, Pierre Lucchini, and I are standing beside the vault. Nono isn't there. He's getting ready for his marriage to Countess de Darrieux, taking place at 3 P.M. at Brancion town hall.

Father Cédric gives an oration. But it is not only for Fernand Occo that our priest addresses God. Now, every time he speaks to Him, he brings Kamal and Anita with him in his prayers, "Reading from the first Epistle General of John:

Beloved, we know that we have passed from death unto life, because we love the brethren. He that loveth not his brother abideth in death . . . Hereby perceive we the love of God, because he laid down his life for us: and we ought to lay down our lives for the brethren. But whoso hath this world's good, and seeth his brother have need, and shutteth up his bowels of compassion from him, how dwelleth the love of God in him? My little children, let us not love in word, neither in tongue; but in deed and in truth."

The family asked Pierre Lucchini to play Fernand Occo's favorite song during the interment. The one by Serge Reggiani called "My Freedom."

I can't seem to focus on the words, beautiful as they are. I think of Léonine and of her father; I think of Nono slipping on his young groom's suit and Countess de Darrieux knotting his tie; I think of Sasha travelling the waters of the Ganges; I think of Irène and Gabriel saying "*tu*" to each other in eternity; I think of Eliane, who went off to run around the garden of her mistress, Marianne Ferry (1953–2007); I think of Julien and Nathan, who will be here in less than a hour, I think of their arms, their smell, their warmth; I think of Gaston, who will always fall, but whom we will always pick up; I think of Elvis, who will never want to hear any songs except those of Elvis Presley.

For a few months now, I've been like Elvis, forever hearing another song, the same one. It covers all the rest, all the murmurings of my thoughts. It's a song by Vincent Delerm that I listen to constantly, and that's called: "Life ahead of you."

ACKNOWLEDGMENTS

Thanks to Tess, Valentin, and Claude, essential to me and my eternal inspiration.

Thanks to Yannick, my adored brother.

Thanks to my precious Maëlle Guillaud. Thanks to the whole Albin Michel team.

Thanks to Amélie, Arlette, Audrey, Elsa, Emma, Catherine, Charlotte, Gilles, Katia, Manon, Mélusine, Michel, Michèle, Sarah, Salomé, Sylvie, William for your vital support. What luck to have you close by.

Thanks to Norbert Jolivet, who exists in real life, and whose name I didn't change because nothing about that man, Gueugnon's gravedigger for thirty years, should be changed. It's through writing this book that this source of joy and kindness became my friend. I hope to drink coffees and kirs with you for all eternity.

Thanks to Raphaël Fatout, who welcomed me into his unusual, wonderfully humane funeral parlor, "Le Tourneurs du Val," in Trouville-sur-Mer. By speaking to me of his love of the job, of death, and of the here and now, Raphaël trusted me like no other.

Thanks to Papa for his garden and his passionate tutoring.

Thanks to Stéphane Baudin for all his sage advice.

Thanks to Cédric and Carol for the photography and the friendship.

Thanks to Julien Seul, who allowed me to borrow his name.

Thanks to Messrs. Denis Fayolle, Robert Badinter, and Éric Dupond-Moretti.

Thanks to all my friends from Marseilles and Cassis—you're my very own chalet.

Thanks to Eugénie and Simon Lelouch, who suggested this story to me.

Thanks to Johnny Hallyday, Elvis Presley, Charles Trenet, Jacques Brel, Georges Brassens, Jacques Prévert, Barbara, Raphaël Haroche, Vincent Delerm, Claude Nougaro, Jean-Jacques Goldman, Benjamin Biolay, Serge Reggiani, Pierre Barouh, Françoise Hardy, Alain Bashung, Chet Baker, Damien Saez, Daniel Guichard, Gilbert Bécaud, Francis Cabrel, Michel Jonasz, Serge Lama, Hélène Bohy, and Agnès Chaumié.

And finally, THANKS to all those who literally carried my first novel, *Les Oubliés du dimanche*; it's thanks to YOU that I wrote this second novel.